# CHIMERA

---

## FRACTURED ORBIT
### BOOK 2

## HERMAN STEUERNAGEL

CHIMERA

Book Two of Fractured Orbit

*First Edition*

*Copyright © 2023 by Herman Steuernagel*

*This is a work of fiction. Names, characters, places, and incidents either are the product of the author's imagination or are used fictitiously. Any resemblance to actual persons, living or dead, events or locales is entirely coincidental.*

*All international rights reserved. No part of this publication may be reproduced, stored or transmitted in any form or by any means, electronic, mechanical, photocopying, recording, scanning, or otherwise without written permission from the publisher. It is illegal to copy this book, post it to a website, or distribute it by any other means whether digital or printed without permission in writing from the copyright owner.*

ISBN: 978-1-990505-12-6 (hardback)

ISBN: 978-1-990505-11-9 (paperback)

ISBN: 978-1-990505-09-6 (ebook)

Cover by Covers by Christian

Edited by Novel Approach Manuscript Services

*https://www.hermansteuernagel.com*

Hello reader,

If you're here, you've no doubt already read *Eclipse*, so I want to ensure there are no surprises going into its sequels. As we get deeper into the Loop and the tragedies it contains the series does grow somewhat darker. As in *Eclipse*, *Chimera* contains death, murder, conspiracy, and violence.

While *Chimera* maintains a similar tone to *Eclipse*, this book also contains kidnapping, suicidal thoughts, human and sex trafficking, as well as non-consensual surgery and body manipulation.

While these topics are part of the story's narrative, none of them are covered in-depth, described in an overly graphic way, or glorified.

# PROLOGUE

Abigail Monroe
The *Redemption*

REVOLUTION IS RARELY as straightforward as it seems.

History projects an image of change being propelled by a solitary unit, united in cause and in deed, but life is messier than that. Instead, uprisings are usually a combination of a mismatch of entities that have been pushed down long and hard enough to come together in a messy and oddly coalesced group—and, not to mention, a little luck.

Within this group are individuals, each playing a haphazard part that might be neither planned nor cohesive, but will add to the uprising's momentum.

Whether the uprising inevitably succeeds or fails . . . Well, that's where the luck comes into it.

This group is like the chimera of Greek mythology, a monstrous hybrid formed from various beings: a goat, a snake, a lion, and sometimes other creatures that would rattle even the most vivid imaginations. But when their features are combined, they form a formidable entity: one that breathes fire, devastates its enemies, and makes a name for itself that transcends history into myth and legend.

*Chimera.* Abigail Monroe certainly liked the ring of that. She tucked the word away in the back of her mind for future use.

"I wasn't looking to lead a rebellion, Abi. I just wanted off that damned station. Do you know how long it's been since I've had a half decent dram of whiskey? Send me to a hole on one of Jupiter's moons where I can spend the rest of my days in peace."

Marvin Alejandro sat across from Abigail on an unmarked, empty crate. His uniform was rather pedestrian, even for a fraudulent cargo hauler. The color had faded—what was once a flattering stark charcoal had long ago transitioned into a dull gray—and time had frayed the cuffs. Someone on that station should have offered him a replacement *years* ago.

Marvin was thinner than Abigail remembered, but not gaunt. The jacket he wore hung loosely on him and would have been in fashion among the trader markets of The Belt half a decade ago. Perhaps some of the outermost colonies on Saturn's moons would probably still think so. But he had the look of someone who wasn't quite getting enough nutrients rather than the look of someone who'd stopped eating due to depression or sickness. Age had been kind to him, but the wrinkles around his eyes and the sprinkle of gray in his stubble betrayed that nearly a decade had passed since Abigail had last seen the man, though they were the kind of wrinkles one earned from laughter, rather than stress. With that clue alone, she guessed that Marvin had been fortunate enough to find some reprieve aboard the FLOW station. Heavens knew the man deserved it after everything he'd endured before disappearing.

Even though Marvin appeared less willing to jump head-first into action than he had back when they'd first met, he hadn't lost the spring in his step. Youthful passion still burned behind his amber-colored eyes, but those same eyes danced around as though they had forgotten what they had once been passionate about.

The *Redemption* hummed around them. Hours had passed since they had left the *Eclipse*. The two of them sat in a small enclave toward the back of the ship, away from the prying ears of the ship's captain, Mikka—the ex-pirate who was dreamier than Abigail had expected. Something about Mikka's commanding presence and no-nonsense attitude had a way of getting Abigail's blood flowing.

Then, there was the ship's pixie of a co-pilot, Kiara, who possessed an attractive renegade quality of her own, but she was a little *too* no-nonsense for Abigail's taste. There was a fine line between commanding and hostile, and Kiara stepped way over that line, becoming downright abrasive. There was the potential for her posing a problem to Abigail's mission, but it was one she'd have to deal with another day.

It was a shame, too, because by Mikka's own admission, the purple-haired hard-ass was one of the best navigators in the Loop.

At first, Abigail hadn't believed her luck in finding both Mikka Jenax and Marvin Alejandro in the same brushstroke;

two components of the chimera creature that would be instrumental in burning the Syndicate Empire to the ground.

Or at least, so Abigail had been led to believe.

Sometimes the cards were dealt in her favor, even if she had to navigate through the direst of circumstances in order to play them. It had helped that Abigail had stacked the deck, but even she couldn't have expected things to work out as well as they had.

But unfortunately, she wasn't finished yet.

She brought her attention back to Marvin. She had expected the man to be a little more receptive to rejoining the organization he'd founded.

"You won't find a half decent whiskey out here either, love. Jupiter's moons have the worst distilleries in the system, except for where the bootleg bog water they pour in The Belt is made. So, if your sole motivation in joining me was the promise of a good drink, you're gonna be disappointed."

Marvin sighed. "You know that's only half of what I meant. I couldn't pretend anymore. Those people on the station were honest—more so than either of us."

Abigail smiled wryly. "*That's* a low bar if ever I've heard one."

"I couldn't handle lying to them any longer. People deserve to know the truth about what's out here. But I'd barely scratched the surface, and already my meddling was getting them killed. I finished dealing out death a *long* time ago. It's not a part of my past I want to revisit."

*Marvin Alejandro.* Did the poor saps aboard the *Eclipse* have any idea that a man living among them was actually a hero? Doubtful. The man himself had no idea how iconic his status had become in his absence. And by his own account, those living aboard the FLOW stations didn't realize there was anyone else inhabiting the rest of the system.

Once his followers learned he'd risen from the dead, Abigail was confident they would follow him to the edge of the system—and climb into their own graves if he asked it of them.

And before this was all over, that might be *exactly* what awaited them.

"As long as the Syndicate's involved," she said, "you'll never be done with death. No matter what they preach."

"Ain't that the truth."

"Well, isn't it your lucky day? Now you're being given a chance to help them—all those people on the *Eclipse*, the supporters you left behind when you disappeared, and the rest of Loop as well."

"Nobody's going to give two shits that I'm still alive, Abi. I've spent seven years *hiding*. When I got stranded on that damn station, the Resurgence was little more than an idea—a group of disgruntled pirates, mercenaries, and thieves. I have nothing to offer here. Not anymore."

"I still came to haul your ass out of here, didn't I? I may strut around as though I have a heart of stone, but I haven't forgotten what you did for me, and I don't believe for one second the people who have continued your vision will have forgotten either. Sometimes an idea is enough to shape the world—or in this case, the entire system."

Marvin scoffed. "And this Zee fellow you claim sent you —is that what he has? Ideas? Ideas are cheap. I've seen too many people risk their life on foolishness."

Abigail couldn't help but grin. She couldn't tell him everything—not yet. The transformation of his old Lunar hideout in Asteria would already be an overwhelming change, and he'd have to figure out the rest later. It had been her lucky day when she'd found Zee in that Martian tavern. Rarely did she give in to being sympathetic to a poor soul down on his luck, but she'd seen what the lad was capable of—him and that malfunctioning implant that could see things nobody else could.

It was only through sheer luck she realized Zee could see a path leading to the end of the godforsaken empire that had left most of humanity to rot.

But that was a tale for another time.

"He's got so much more than that," she said.

"What, then? *Hope?* That's still an idea. Just one of a fool."

"Zee's our secret weapon. He's seen how this all plays out —and it starts with *you.*"

"Surely you can see this is a hard sell? You're asking me to take his word that I'm somehow important to the defeat of the Empire. If you're going to convince me of that . . ."

"I don't need to *convince* you of anything, love. All I was told to do was find you and bring you home. I *wasn't* told I'd nearly get blown out of orbit in the process, though."

Losing her favorite ship, the *Black Swan*, was still a bit of a sore spot. She'd have to bring that up with Zee when she saw him next.

"Regardless," she persisted, "both you and that delicious pirate driving this thing have a role to play, and being honest, I couldn't care less if you believe it or not."

Marvin shook his head in protest, but his eyes danced, clearly intrigued. "I had dreams of taking on the Empire once, but I was a young man then. Seven years with nothing to do but drink with the locals kinda knocks down a man's drive. It's time to pass the torch."

"Maybe you just need the right inspiration. Perhaps some eager-eyed rebels who need a leader will persuade you."

"I don't think anyone will look to me after being away for so long. Everyone thinks I'm dead."

"The legend of a man grows in his absence. Besides, you're telling me you're going to bugger off to Jupiter before saying hello to the old gang? No '*Hey, guess what, not as dead as you might have thought?*'"

Marvin waved it off. "I suppose not. I guess a few nights on Lunar will help me gain my bearings. But I was actually quite happy to leave the past behind me."

Abigail smirked. "I've gone down that road. Running away from your demons is more difficult than you might think—for you and the captain both."

Marvin shrugged. "Speaking of difficult . . . do you have a plan to get off this ship? I can't imagine the Port Authority will take kindly to a dead man with a lengthy criminal record stepping off of a short-haul flight."

Abigail chuckled. "You *have* been gone awhile. You do realize the list of charges the Syndicate has filed against me? Most of them are dreamed up, mind you. Do you think I'd have made it this far without learning to dodge the PA every now and again?"

Marvin returned the laugh. "You always were full of surprises. Even when you were young. I knew you'd be one to watch with that charm of yours. Just didn't know you'd have fanciful notions of saving the Loop."

"*When* I was young?" Abigail lifted a hand to her chest in feigned offense. "As for my 'fanciful notions,' I blame *you* for putting ideas in my head, old man."

"I did no such thing; I just didn't want you to wind up in the mines. You were so fragile when we found you. You wouldn't have survived the trip."

Abigail rarely showed emotion, and she wasn't about to start now. "You put wild dreams of saving the system in my head when you dreamed up the *Resurgence*. I was young and impressionable: barely thirteen. I had no business being on a mercenary ship, you know. After you left, I had to do a lot of questionable things to survive and keep the perverts at bay. But despite that, I've still been searching for a way to save the system ever since. I just had no idea my quest would lead me back to *you*."

Marvin tapped his fingers on the crate beside him as he shifted in his seat. "So, this Zee . . . He told you to come find me?"

"Zee said, odds were, you were still alive. I didn't allow myself to believe it, but here you are, and he's proven himself to be right once again. He's got a knack for that."

"Odds," Marvin said, his gaze still focused on the crate beside him. "As if life comes down to a random throw of the dice."

"More like a deal of the hand. We're only able to play the cards we're dealt—but Zee can help us stack the deck. The rest comes down to the odds."

"Yes, well . . . What are the odds of us getting out of here still breathing?"

Abigail smiled. "There's a hidden compartment beneath the cargo hold. Captain Gorgeous had already locked me down there once, to hide from the Orbital Guard a couple days ago. During my stay, I discovered she's installed an escape hatch. We just have to wait for the PA to be sufficiently distracted and we'll pop out and be on our merry way."

Marvin raised a skeptical eyebrow. "That easy, huh? It's plans like *those* that make a guy wish he stayed on the station."

Django Alexander
The *Redemption*

HOME.

Django's last glimpse of home was an eternity away. Each agonizing hour since he'd left the *Eclipse* had been filled with soul-crushing darkness and echoed the chilling possibility: he might never see home again.

In an instant, everything he'd expected his life to be had changed. Now, he was caught in between worlds, and he would remain there until the ship he and Eventide had clambered aboard arrived at its destination. It didn't help that he sat in complete and utter darkness.

*How long have we been traveling? Hours? Days?*

It felt as though he and Eventide had been swimming in darkness for an eternity, and each second that ticked by was another insufferable void between everything familiar and the complete unknown.

Sleep should have come easily. The space they were in was blacker than any night, even than those he'd spent within the chambers of the *Eclipse*. But the hard metal flooring was anything but comfortable, causing his bones to creak and his muscles to scream as he struggled to find a comfortable position.

Not to mention that his stomach lurched at the artificial gravity that held him to the floor.

It was a feeling Django had never had the chance to get used to on the station, as the only place on the *Eclipse* that utilized gravity plating was the tram that ran between the Rings.

The artificial G-forces of the plating tugged unnaturally at his insides, inducing nausea. Now, without sight, the pull felt even more pronounced, and Django worried he was going to be sick.

It made the turbulence of their journey that much more grating, as weightlessness threatened to latch onto him for a split second before the plating compensated for whatever direction down should be. Most people would never have noticed the plating's hesitation—it was so subtle that Django sometimes wondered whether he was imagining the sensation, but his stomach told a different story.

He tried not to dwell on it. Growing sick in a darkened cabin with only Eventide for company would make the rest of the trip both embarrassing and unbearable because of the smell.

Instead, Django did his best to sleep. Patterned holes, an inch in diameter, had been drilled into the floor's surface, giving his hands something other than his gut to focus on. Beside him rested a crate. Made with rough wood, it contained slivers that stabbed at him when he leaned against it.

The cabin smelled of must, wet grass, and a nutty odor that could have been barley or another grain. He should have been grateful this shuttle didn't have chickens as part of its load.

Eventide, who had been curled next to him when they left, had moved after the first hour. Her affinity with her own physical space winning over the need for comfort after abandoning everything they had ever known.

*Everyone else is dead. Except Nova, who I'll probably never see again.*

Everything about his sister staying behind on the *Eclipse* worried Django. He prayed to the stars that Commander Benson would leave her alone; that he wouldn't lash out at her as a way of retribution. He had no choice but to trust the guard, Avery Inglewood, who had taken his sister into her care. For some reason, Uncle Marvin had trusted the guard before he'd died, so Django supposed he would have to do the same.

The *Redemption* shook, the vibrations within the cargo hold rattling his skull relentlessly and ensuring sleep wouldn't find him. Without breaking the silence between them, Django had no way of knowing if Eventide was sleeping or not. The warmth of her body lay an arm's reach away, but as always, he wanted to be respectful of her need for space. Eventide needed time to process recent events, and for her, the best way to do that was to be alone with her thoughts.

Besides, the rattle of the walls prevented much in the way of conversation, so the two of them hadn't spoken since leaving the station's shuttle bay. Their shared patience as they waited for whatever lay before them was enough. This was a path neither Django nor Eventide had wanted; a path they hadn't known existed only two days ago.

As far as either of them had been aware, the *Eclipse* was humanity's last refuge. Along with their ancestors, the station's inhabitants had been patiently waiting for the Earth to become habitable once again.

Until one flicker of a viewport had changed everything.

That had only been a few days ago, but it seemed like another life.

Before Commander Benson had murdered his entire family. Before Benson had turned his entire life upside down.

A whirlwind of events had followed, circumstances that had brought Django to where he sat now: on board the space shuttle *Redemption*.

He would have been a bit more willing to explore his surroundings if he didn't have Officer Inglewood's words echoing in his mind: *Don't come out until you've reached the ship's destination, no matter what happens.*

If Django could actually see the hand he held in front of his face, ignoring that warning would have tempted him more. There had to be a way to reach the bridge above, which would give them a better insight into their destination, and perhaps even how much longer they would have to be on board.

But with no way of seeing the surrounding space, Django knew he would just be feeling around in the dark, hoping to come across a doorway or a hatch—and something told him that opening random doors on a transport ship flying through the vacuum of space was a *bad* idea.

Granted, a door could lead to another part of the ship, but it could also lead outside. He supposed there would be safety mechanisms to prevent that from happening, but as this was his first time on a spaceship, he didn't want to take any chances.

Besides, Avery had told them that whoever was piloting this craft wouldn't treat stowaways kindly. But she hadn't seemed to know for certain, and it was always possible that Uncle Marvin had made arrangements ahead of time without telling him.

Before he died.

The pang of his uncle's death still burned. Of all his family members, Django had been closest to Marvin and Nova, and now Marvin was gone, leaving only the double circle pendant hanging cool against Django's chest as a memento. It was Marvin who had convinced Django to leave.

But any further plans he'd held for Django and Eventide had died along with him.

Which left Django with nothing to hold on to other than a pendant and a station guard's word of caution to stay hidden until they reached their destination.

*Wherever* that *might be.*

The best he could hope for now was that help would find them once they landed.

His eyes grew heavy, despite the churning of his stomach

and the discomfort caused by the hard metal floor. He tried to add together how many hours it had been since he had last had a full night's rest, but his brain was already hurting. And he had nothing to judge the passing minutes or seconds other than his own heartbeat.

A SUDDEN JOLT jarred Django awake, shaking him out of a sleep he hadn't realized had overtaken him.

The violent movement was immediately followed by the ship's systems quieting—subtle at first, but noticeable.

It seemed the craft was slowing.

The turbulence had eased off, but Django's stomach was still being pulled in all directions. The shifting momentum suggested the *Redemption* was descending.

Earth was the only destination that made sense to him. If shuttles from the *Eclipse* flew to the planet's surface and back, then this one had to be heading there, too. Despite everything Django had grown up believing to the contrary, his uncle had claimed people still lived on the planet's surface.

Finally being able to step onto Earth's surface was something generations of station dwellers had fantasized about, though none of his ancestors could have possibly imagined the circumstances that had brought Django here.

The uneasiness in his gut lessened as the craft continued to decelerate. A loud *crack* against the ship's hull made him jump, and the rumble of the engines whirred to a stop. Beeps and clicks sounded above them, followed by footsteps clearly in a hurry to disembark.

Wherever this ship was headed, it had arrived.

Voices replaced the ship's noises, though none were even close to being intelligible. Passengers who had the luxury of being on the flight deck above them were talking excitably among themselves.

Django swallowed his fear. For better or worse, he was here now, but at least he was still with Eventide. They just needed to figure out what to do next.

"How are you doing, Evie?" Django didn't allow his voice to rise much above a whisper. If he could hear the voices overhead, it made sense they'd be able to hear *him*, too.

"As good as can be expected, considering. Stiff and sore. This floor makes for a lousy bed."

"You're telling me."

"Did your uncle give you any idea of what to do once we were off the ship? What about any more details on that magical paper of yours?"

Even though Django couldn't see it, there was a smirk to Eventide's voice, but also a hint of sass. She knew damn well there wasn't anything else for them to go on. The paper she was referring to was the note Uncle Marvin had left behind for Django before he died: instructions on when and where to board the *Redemption*.

"No, nothing. We're just going to have to wait and see what the planet has in store for us."

*Hopefully, a new life. A better one. One with Eventide.*

But if he wanted any semblance of that life he had always

dreamed of, he couldn't continue to hold back his feelings for her. He had to let her know.

"Evie," he said, reaching out to put a hand on her shoulder in the darkness. It was a bold move—Eventide wasn't one for physical affection—but she didn't recoil, and if he didn't take his shot now, Django knew he never would.

He repositioned himself on shaky knees, stiffness screaming at him as he did so. Eventide hadn't been kidding: the metal floor had made all of his joints ache, and the endless vibrations of the journey had made it difficult for him to trust his own balance.

He did his best to ignore his bodily protests.

Commander Benson had almost killed them both, and if there was one thing he'd learned in recent days, it was that you never knew how much time you had left. There were so many things he wanted to say to the woman who sat beside him—his best friend and the woman he wanted to be with. And he'd almost missed his chance.

"I'm sorry. For *everything*."

"Hey, now! None of that," Eventide said. "None of this is your fault."

Part of it had been, of course. Django had stuck his nose where it didn't belong, and, to top it all off, he'd punched a station guard in the process. Maybe if he had just let things be, they'd still be on the *Eclipse*.

*No.* He couldn't let himself think that way. Benson had killed his family *before* Django had done anything that would have warranted retribution. The station's commander had also gone out of his way to try to kill both Django and Eventide.

Benson was the one to blame here.

"I know, but I mean . . ." *What do I mean?* "I know how hard you worked to become a technician, and Benson's a bastard for taking that away from you. I just wish things hadn't ended up this way. You deserve better."

"I should have realized . . ." Eventide's voice lowered, her pitch a blend of anger and sadness. "I should have known they'd never let a D-Ringer into the technicians' program. I'm just lucky I got out in time." Despite the darkness, Django could feel her eyes on him. "I'm lucky you were there to get me out."

Django forced an exhale. He had to take the chance before they ventured into this new world. With their future now uncertain, he didn't know if he'd get another shot.

"Look," he said, "I know this isn't what you hoped for. Stars know, it's not what *I* ever wanted. I just wanted to settle down on the station. Work the farm, you know?"

"You might still get to do that. If the Earth's habitable."

He nodded, even though she couldn't see it. "I know, but now . . ."

*How do I say this? How do I tell my best friend I'm in love with her?*

This was the woman he'd been in love with since they were teenagers. Hell, they were barely more than teenagers now. Eventide had been his best friend for as long as he could remember, and that was a line he hadn't dared to cross. There had always been the possibility that admitting his feelings to her could ruin their friendship. That was the last thing he wanted.

But the two of them had just been through hell and back.

Either of them could have died back on the station. Who knew what awaited them on the planet? He'd already come close to losing Eventide for good, multiple times over the past couple days. If he didn't take the chance, he'd regret it for the rest of his life.

Django's heart raced as he tried to form adequate words, a cold sweat building on his palms as he worked out how to express what was in his heart.

"I don't know . . . When I was told I wouldn't be able to see you again, part of me died. You've always been a part of my life, and I don't want to risk losing you again."

As soon as the words left his lips, the ship's engines fired again, their roar drowning out any possibility of further conversation. Django cursed, but even he couldn't hear his own voice.

The ship shook for several minutes and then slowed again, the engines eventually quietening to a dull hum. Django's stomach lurched as the *Redemption* jolted, knocking him off-balance, and he fell into Eventide. She must have been surprised by the movement, too, because she grabbed onto him for support, her arms wrapping around his shoulders as his hands found the small of her back.

Even through her sweater, the muscles of her back were noticeable. Eventide had worked the fields as a teenager, but never to the extent Django had; her athletic build came from the physicality mandated by the technicians training program. The instructors aboard *Eclipse* had worked their recruits hard.

He tried to right himself as the ship shuddered again. This time, the jolt threw Eventide against him, and with his face centimeters from hers, he could smell traces of sweat and her usual fragrance of vanilla.

His nose grazed her cheek, and with no further thought, he planted his lips on hers.

The kiss was everything he had ever imagined it would be. Hesitant at first, but as he wrapped his arms around her and pulled her close, it deepened. Her lips moved against his, her tongue tracing the contours of his mouth. Django moved his hand to the back of her head and ran it over the smoothness of her neck, the softness of her hair.

*This* was where he was meant to be. Everything he had ever wanted was wrapped in this moment. Suddenly, he didn't care if he was on a farm, the B-Ring, or on a spaceship headed for Earth.

He *wanted* the kiss to last forever. This was the moment he had been dreaming of for as long as he could remember. The universe narrowed to this one stolen moment. The weight of their escape, the looming unknowns, all faded. Here, in the darkness of the ship's hold, there was only Eventide. And everything about her was perfect.

Until she pressed her hands on his chest and gently pushed him away. Her touch was caring, but firm.

It was such a slight movement, but even with the compassion behind the gesture, Django's heart collapsed into the blackness of the space they were huddled in. Silence hung between them. There was nothing *to* say.

He had been terrified of this exact moment; the moment where he laid his soul bare, and it was crushed into a million pieces. The seconds that followed dragged on in agony, punctuated only by the hum of the ship and their own labored breathing.

"Django," Eventide finally said, moving further away from him, her voice no more than a whisper. "I can't."

He opened his mouth to speak, but he struggled to find meaningful words to convey the tumult he felt within. His first impulse was to apologize, but Django didn't *feel* sorry. She had kissed him back. She was open to it. *Passionate,* even. Apologizing felt like betraying his feelings.

"I . . ." she stammered, as though looking for the words to say. She scooted herself back, creating a gap between them that was like a chasm—cold and distant.

Django braced himself for what he knew was coming.

"I don't think we should . . ." She sighed heavily as she searched for the right words to say. "I don't think this could ever work."

His gut sank as his heart pounded wildly. Django moved his mouth in protest but found no words. What did she mean? Was she not even willing to *try?*

"Eventide . . ."

There were a hundred things he thought of to say, but every one of them refused to reach his tongue.

"I'm sorry." Her voice was still low, but firmer than before. She somehow sounded so sure and yet so confused at the same time.

A slit of light pierced the darkness at the tail end of the ship, interrupting them. White artificial light flooded the cargo hold, exposing its contents for the first time in hours, revealing the bright blue tint of Eventide's hair and casting unnatural shadows across her pale white skin. But all Django could see was the mascara running down Eventide's cheeks.

*She's crying? Stars, what have I done?*

In that moment, the last scrap of his old life slipped through the cracks of his rough, calloused fingers. He'd ruined everything. He'd crossed a line with his best friend he had sworn he never would.

*But she'll forget this, right? It's just a kiss . . . We'll move on and laugh about it someday.*

His gaze focused on his friend, hoping for some acknowledgment, some sign that everything would be okay. Whenever Eventide had an important decision to make, she usually consulted her deck of playing cards. Whether she was seeking some confirmation in their faces or feeling their edges to help her focus, it was an odd tick for an otherwise level-headed scientist, but it was a superstition that she clung to. But there were no cards flipping through her fingers now. There wasn't even the twitch of her fingers that would have suggested she was mentally running through them to seek clarity. She wouldn't even meet his gaze, instead, focusing outside of the open door.

Django turned to follow her stare.

Suddenly, what had just happened between him and Eventide became a blurry memory; a reality held beneath the surface of a murky tide. Whatever lay outside of the cargo hold door was about to change his life forever. He'd dreamed of *this* moment, too, conjuring visions of lush trees, blue waters, and majestic mountains; hues of blue and green like those that had appeared for several magical minutes on the

*Eclipse*'s malfunctioning viewports before the technicians had restored the illusion of a dead planet.

Django peered over several crates, forcing his aching legs to stand to get a better view. A wave of noise washed through the slit as it opened: voices and shouts of what could have been hundreds of men and women, engines firing and decelerating, the rattles of the ship and other vehicles and equipment, all mixed with an even greater spectrum of sounds that were foreign to him.

Despite everything he'd imagined, there was no green, no blue. Glimpses of steel and other dull metallic surfaces were all he could make out through the open bay. At least two or three other ships were parked nearby. Muffled voices—digitized, as though being broadcast through a speaker system—were amplified over the rest of the noise, yet the walls of the ship filtered out the actual words being said.

Of course, it made sense that the *Redemption* had landed at a port or docking station of some sort—and one much larger and much busier than a single cargo bay of the *Eclipse*. That hold had the capacity for a single ship the size of the *Redemption*—and nothing more. Django imagined that any port planet-side would have the space for dozens, if not *hundreds* of ships.

Two days ago, he would have said such a place couldn't exist.

He barely heard Eventide hissing for him to sit. She appeared to have already gotten over the kiss, fear replacing her upset.

Yet, her words still slapped at him. *I don't think this could ever work.*

With his pulse echoing in his ears, Django pushed his feelings deep down, to that hidden place where the pain of his lost family still resided and where the vow of vengeance against Commander Roy Benson for their deaths persisted.

He swallowed. There was a universe waiting beyond that slit of light, and he wasn't going to miss a single second of it, no matter what Eventide had said. They'd be okay, eventually. Deep down, he had to believe that was true.

The sound of steel plating grinding against itself filled the hold as the bay opened fully.

Metal paneling, similar to the floor of the *Redemption*'s hold, was now visible beneath the ship. A partially silhouetted, tall man appeared, with beady eyes and a haircut that hugged his skull, making him look like some sort of elongated bug. It was hard to tell with the light of the world beyond shining behind him, but Django swore he was wearing a uniform nearly identical in appearance to the guards back on the *Eclipse*. It even had a similar glowing patch on the chest.

"Shit!" The man's eyes met Django's. He ducked out of sight, pushing the steel door closed again and plunging the cargo bay into darkness once more, except for the narrow slit between the hatch door and the shuttle wall that provided just enough light for Django to make out Eventide's features.

Eventide's eyes focused on the opening, but they didn't betray any emotion. She shook her head. "So much for staying hidden. Whatever's coming, it's not going to be good."

"Uncle Marvin only said to stay hidden *until* we reached our destination. We're here, aren't we?"

"We have a problem." A man's voice, filtered by the cargo door, echoed from somewhere outside the shuttle.

Django's heart raced. Had Benson realized they'd escaped? The commander was bound to have figured it out eventually, but Django had hoped for more time—time, at least, to make it off the *Redemption*.

An unintelligible reply followed.

"You'd better see for yourself. I've never had to . . ."

The metal hatch scraped against the wall, cutting the voice off as the bay reopened.

Three guards replaced the lone man. They stood at the end of a ramp that now extended from the cargo hold hatch. Each guard held a long-barrelled weapon, similar to those the guards on the *Eclipse* carried.

Django knew all too well not to mess with the guards. He could still feel the ache in his ribs from where Officer Geoffrey Isaacs had planted a heavy boot.

The uniforms these guards wore were similar, but now that there was ample light reflecting off them, Django could spot the differences. Unlike the station's white uniforms, these were gray, but they were still composed of the familiar armored plating, as though they were expecting resistance. The material appeared thinner than their station counterparts, equipping their wearers with less bulk. Red LED lights edged the shoulder and elbow pads, giving them a similar glow to the familiar red and blue hexagonal logo on their breastplate. The logo differed as well: instead of the four blue rings of the station at its center, a yellow semicircle sat above a gray one facing in the opposite direction, like the sun hanging over a silver planet.

Eventide lifted her arms to the sky, and Django mimicked

her as the guards aimed their long-barrelled energy weapons at them.

*The game's up. Benson's found us.*

If it wasn't for the guards' uniforms, the alien noises coming from outside of the *Redemption,* or the multitude of ships parked nearby, Django would have sworn they had returned to the station.

But this place wasn't home.

"Keep your hands where we can see them!" the foremost guard yelled. He was taller, at least Marvin's height, but a little rounder in the middle. "Stand up! Nice and slow."

Django's breath caught in his throat. His heart pounded so loudly, he was sure the guards must have been able to hear it.

Eventide was on her feet, her arms still in the air, but Django could have sworn her brow furrowed in irritation rather than fear.

"You are under arrest for stowing away aboard a transport vessel. If you resist, we will shoot you. If you run, we will shoot you. Now, walk toward us, keeping your hands in the air. *Slowly.* Do not make any sudden movements!"

Django swallowed. As he shuffled uncomfortably, he felt his father's weapon tucked behind his belt; the one he'd found under his parents' bed when he was cleaning out their belongings back on the station. He was under no illusion that pulling it on these guards was a bad idea, but he didn't want to lose the weapon, either. If he tossed it into the ship somewhere before he was frisked, he might be able to come back and find it later, but there was a good chance the guards would mistake his intentions and open fire, so he thought better of it.

Being caught was bad enough, but being armed? Django hadn't come all this way to take a bolt to the chest over a misunderstanding.

He had fled the station hoping to find safety and an end to their problems, but as the guards authoritatively ascended the ramp with their weapons at the ready, one thing seemed clear: whatever was about to happen in this new world, their problems were far from over.

Mikka Jenax
Shackleton City


"WHAT THE *HELL* is going on here?"

Mikka Jenax was in no mood for the Port Authority's games, and the two bumbling idiots that had marched onto her ship seemed hell-bent on pissing her off.

Not only did they have the audacity to barge onto her bridge—almost before the docking clamps had engaged—but the two officers also trained their energy weapons—military grade SC-097 rifles, no less—on both her and Kiara. Like *they* were the threat here.

Port Authority personnel were slightly more competent than the Orbital Guard, but not by much, as shown by these clowns testing those boundaries.

Thankfully, Abigail and Marvin had disappeared. They were likely still whispering at the back of the cargo hold, like they had been for the entire trip, exchanging secrets about the mysterious pirate who had orchestrated Marvin's extraction.

As per port protocol, Mikka had registered the two passengers for entry, so their presence wouldn't have been a problem on its own. But if Abigail was to find herself on the receiving end of one of those rifles, Mikka knew she'd have a hard time keeping her mouth shut, and the last thing Mikka needed was a run-in with the Authority on top of everything else that had gone wrong this week.

It had only taken a few hours for Mikka and her ragtag crew to fly back to Lunar from the *Eclipse*, but she had been running on a lack of sleep. The past few days hadn't exactly leant themselves well to rest, and it had been—what? Forty-eight hours since she'd slept in a warm bed? Mikka was looking forward to nothing more than a hot shower and a chance to catch her breath.

And the only thing in her way right now was a douchebag customs officer with a gun.

"You registered four crew members for entry into Shackleton City, Captain: three women and one man," the female officer stated disdainfully.

She was about the same age as Mikka; a woman with hard eyes and a crooked nose who had likely lost her fair share of bar fights. It always amazed Mikka how many fights were started by off-duty patrol officers, as though they needed to let out all the pent-up aggression their job prohibited them from unleashing. Though, the amount of civilian beatings the PA dealt out made that sentiment hard for Mikka to believe.

The PA uniforms always seemed like overkill: the retractable helmet embedded beneath the slate gray collars, as though there might be a chance of being sucked into the void of space at any moment. The suit had been designed to seal off the wearer's air supply in the case of an emergency, but there hadn't been a loss of air in any of the moon colonies in recent memory. Not since the early days of construction. But as with all bureaucratic organizations, some protocols lasted long past their necessity.

The double hexagon pattern of their emblems glowed light blue in the relative darkness of the *Redemption*'s cabin. The woman's long auburn hair hung over her shoulders in a peculiar deviation from the approved military style the guards were usually expected to wear. Her colleague, however—the dark-skinned man behind her—followed protocol, with his hair cropped tight to his skull. Both wore an impatient look, as though they suspected Mikka knew exactly why they were there and was intentionally being difficult.

She'd had enough of surprises. *There'd better be a warm bath waiting for me somewhere—although that's probably too much to ask from my arrangement with Aries. Hell, at this point, I'd even settle for a mattress in the corner of a prison cell.*

"That's right. We registered four crew members," Mikka replied, unable to disguise the irritation in her tone. Tiredness clung to her mind, and she was in no mood to refrain from pushing back against authority. "Is there a reason you're up here? If you need any further proof, you'll be scanning us all when we disembark, or have policies changed overnight?"

The woman sneered. "You're either smuggling or you've got stowaways—which makes you either stupid or sloppy. Either way, you're being detained." She touched two fingers to her lapel. "Bring the kids up."

Kiara cleared her throat and straightened her charcoal

bomber jacket by tugging on the bottom of it. "Our two other passengers are at the back of the ship. I'll go get them," she offered.

Mikka cringed. Kiara hadn't been in enough of these situations to be quick on her feet. If she'd simply kept her mouth shut, then Mikka could have argued that the people the guards were referring to were, in fact, Marvin and Abigail—though, it probably wouldn't matter, anyway. The officer was unlikely to just take her word for it. Orbital Guards might have been too lazy to double-check the back of the ship, but the Port Authority didn't mess around. And Mikka was prepared to bet the *Redemption's* entire load of Corielus seed that the stern-faced woman didn't cut corners.

Times were tight, even for the patrols, and it wasn't unheard of for Port Authority guards to plant a couple 'stowaways' in order to extort a bribe from an unsuspecting captain in exchange for turning a blind eye. Trying to contest a charge of people smuggling would be Mikka's word against the Authority, and there was no way she'd be winning that fight.

A few credits in the pocket of the right officer, though, would "convince" them to drop the bogus charge. In Mikka's experience, the bribe usually cost less than the fine, and it was a hell of a lot less paperwork, so pilots caught out by the racket rarely filed complaints.

The officer nodded, and Kiara scurried to the rear of the vessel in search of their absent passengers.

But if these officers were playing it straight . . . well, *that* would complicate things. There was only one place stowaways could have accessed the *Redemption*. Did they know the ship's destination when they'd boarded? Marvin *had* mentioned that he'd tried to convince people he knew on the *Eclipse* to join him in his escape.

"Is this about money?" Mikka said. "Because if it is, just let us know how much it's gonna take for us all to pretend this whole thing never happened."

"I wish it were that simple. But these two? They didn't scan. They're going to cause a hell of a lot more questions than I'm willing to answer to my commanding officer."

"Wait," Mikka interjected. "What do you mean, 'they *didn't* scan?' You mean there's no record of them? That's not possible . . ."

The *Redemption* wasn't exactly big, so it only took Kiara a couple minutes to come back to the main cabin with a wide-eyed look of worry and confusion. It didn't take Mikka more than a passing glance to know that the pirate and her new buddy weren't with her.

Abigail *was* a crafty one indeed. She'd no doubt sniffed out there'd be an inspection upon docking, though how she'd known, Mikka couldn't begin to guess. But the best pirates had their methods, and it was becoming increasingly clear to her that Abigail was one of the best Mikka had come across.

Kiara shook her head at Mikka, unsure of how to react. Mikka nodded and willed her companion to be quiet for the exchange that was to come.

Two further guards joined them via the main access ramp, with two bewildered youths in tow. The pair were both short, and it was hard to tell if they were teenagers or malnourished young adults. The boy had a muscular frame on him—clearly no stranger to manual labor—but the muscle was lean, lacking the bulk that proper protein and nutrients would have provided. The young woman appeared more fit and was strikingly beautiful. She had dyed her hair purple, which was a strange contrast to her otherwise humble appearance. She stood slightly more confidently than the boy and was pretty enough to turn a few heads. But her sunken eyes, chipped fingernails, and pale skin suggested she hadn't been eating properly, either.

Mikka's thoughts immediately went to what Marvin had told her about the residents on the *Eclipse*. Treated only slightly better than those in the Tubes, half a million bodies had been corralled into each of the eleven space stations in orbit since Earth's evacuation. Twelve, if you counted *Infinity*, the station the Syndicate had destroyed a decade ago to hide the truth from its residents.

*Hundreds of thousands wiped out in an instant. All to maintain the illusion that humanity no longer had a home.*

Mikka still shuddered at the revelation Marvin had shared with her earlier that day. How could the Syndicate kill so many of its people? And for what? To make a statement? To feel as though they were still in control?

It was something she intended to address with Aries as soon as she was able. When they last spoke, the commander had alluded to plans of war. He'd hired her with the implication that she'd have some role to play. She imagined he was more likely to get himself killed than effect any real change, but there was more than a small part of her that hoped David Aries held the answer to ending the Loop's misery.

When Mikka had first met Commander David Aries, the humble junkyard watchman had had the compassion to let

Mikka slip by without turning her in for a mountain of pirating charges under her old name . . . Jax Luana. Did Aries know about the *Infinity*?

*Civil war is brewing . . .*

The two youths looked at Mikka with both expectancy and terror. If she couldn't prevent their arrest, the youths would be incarcerated, and probably sent to the mines in The Belt—*if* they were lucky. The looks on their faces confirmed they didn't understand what they had been getting themselves into when they'd hopped on board the *Redemption*. Despite the slight malnutrition, they still looked more capable of surviving the mines than most.

But it wasn't a fate she wished on anyone.

If she had to hazard a guess, Mikka would have put her money on these two knowing Marvin, and since he'd ghosted them at their hour of need, their fate now rested on *her* shoulders.

*Where has that damn man gone?*

Marvin had revealed little about his past, or how he'd ended up on the *Eclipse*, and Abigail hadn't explained why it was so important that she find him and bring him back into the Loop, either.

But those questions would have to wait. Mikka now had his tagalongs to deal with.

"Ah, here they are!" she said in feigned relief, lifting an arm to them as she approached the two newcomers. "Marvin! Abigail! We were wondering where you'd got to. Clearly you were inspecting the cargo one last time before docking?"

The young man's eyes lit up at the mention of Marvin's name. *So, he knows the man. That's something, at least—now*

*I know who to blame, for sure. But will this kid be smart enough to play along?*

"Uncle Marvin?" the boy blurted. "He's alive? I knew I heard his voice!"

Mikka rolled her eyes. *Apparently not.*

The young woman beside him deflated, then kicked him in the shin, her expression signaling that she wanted to deck the man stood beside her.

The boy looked at her, confused, his brow furrowed with a lack of understanding and his face bearing no recognition of what he had done to deserve the kick. Was he naïve? Or just stupid?

"Django, you idiot!" the woman hissed quietly, just loud enough for Mikka to catch.

The look of confusion intensified on Django's face, as it contorted further with the insult laid on top of the kick.

"What?" Django asked. "You think there's someone else named Marvin? If my uncle's alive, he can get us out of this mess."

*Uncle?* Marvin struck Mikka as many things, but 'uncle' wasn't one of them. From what she knew of him, the guy was only really interested in looking out for himself, and given Abigail's mission to extract him, he was hardly excelling on that front.

"All right, kid." The female officer nodded to her colleagues. "Put them in one of the processing cells for now. We'll get them chipped, processed, and ready to ship tomorrow morning. They're in too good a shape to toss out the airlock."

The boy—Django—began to protest, but a swift kick from one of the PA officers subdued him.

"And as for you"—the woman pressed a finger into Mikka's breast, and it took every ounce of Mikka's willpower not to reach up and break that finger. "You two are under arrest for harboring stowaways."

"There's no prison time for stowaways," Kiara said snippily. "It's a *minor* offense."

Mikka bit her cheek. *Oh, sweet, innocent Kiara.*

The male officer stabbed his baton into Kiara's back, sending her to the floor, writhing in pain.

"There's a queue for processing," the woman said, not batting an eye at her partner's behavior. "Wait time's currently a week. You'll be kept in the holding cells until we can ring you through. Let's go."

Shakily, Kiara stood.

Mikka did her best to give her navigator a consoling look. Kiara hadn't had to deal with run-ins with any of the Syndicate forces before. The Port Authority would have processed them, charged them with a fine, and sent them on their way later that afternoon if Kiara hadn't opened her big mouth. But there are some things you just don't learn until you face them, and growing up in the Upper Rim, Kiara had never had to deal with the crookedness of the Syndicate cops.

She could try playing the Commander Aries card again, but that had gotten her nowhere on board the *Eclipse.* The FLOW station's personnel had been clueless when she'd mentioned Aries's name upon delivery. All she'd meant to do was bypass protocol to get the shipment on board, but since the FLOWs were essentially closed off from the rest of the Empire, the name was worthless. The PA guards on Lunar might know who Aries was, at least, but there was no way he'd be willing to pull rank over a landing inspection. Besides, their mission had technically been off-the-books, so there were no ties to the Syndicate Commander of the Lunar colonies.

With the drop-off to *Eclipse* complete, she had fulfilled her end of her bargain with Aries—the first stage, at least. The commander had made it clear he would be sending her on more missions. Hopefully, those would come with fewer surprises.

But that was assuming the commander continued to employ her. Maybe an arrest would be the excuse Aries needed to drop her like a hot sack of shit. Aries had hired Mikka based on her reputation for being discreet. In all her years of pirating, she had evaded arrest—until now. Now, on a simple drop-off, she was about to be placed in a Port Authority holding cell.

Aries had already agreed to handle the fine she'd received from the Orbital Guard two days ago, but an additional fine for harboring stowaways wouldn't come cheap. It probably wouldn't be worth Aries's efforts—or credits—to keep her around.

The commander had promised to take care of her and her mother in exchange for the delivery the *Redemption* had just completed: a single crate, taller than Mikka, and just as wide. She had no idea what the package contained—and she didn't care. What she did care about, however, was the cargo they had brought *back*: crates full of Corielus seed.

*Infinity* Corielus seed.

It was the only remedy to the Lunar sickness malady her mother suffered from, and the only strain that provided pronounced results. With *Infinity* station destroyed, the crop was so rare that the product in their cargo hold was now worth more money than her ship. Mikka guessed it was probably worth more credits than she had ever seen or even imagined.

*Not a bad payload for bringing a single passenger on board.*

*Or* three, *it seems.*

But if the PA arrested them, Mikka had no doubt the Authority would confiscate her cargo. If she was lucky, she'd have the standard forty-eight hours before they removed the goods from her hold. But if the guards realized what they had stumbled upon . . . There was no way her mother would get a gram of the stuff.

No point deluding herself: the officers would surely haul it off for personal profit. Part of her hoped that with Abigail having the foresight to escape before the Authority came knocking, she'd also thought far enough ahead to get the seed off her ship before the officers brought their own crew in.

If Mikka lost both Aries's support *and* the Corielus shipment, this entire venture had been in vain. Her mother would be homeless, and Mikka would have to find another way to pay the bills.

And with a massive fine hanging over her head, she'd once again have to consider selling the *Redemption*.

"Get moving." The guard flashed a pair of electronic cuffs and slapped them over Kiara's wrists. With panic setting in, the navigator's eyes widened as she looked to Mikka for guidance; for her to do something.

Mikka's first instinct was to wind up and punch the guard in the throat; a reflex from her years as a pirate—doing absolutely *anything* to avoid arrest.

But that wouldn't get her anywhere now. Kiara had a family, and Mikka had her mother to think about. It wasn't as if they could go underground and submit to the life of a fugitive.

Neither captain nor navigator had any active charges upheld against them, so Mikka thought it best just to go through the motions and let this shit sort itself out.

"Don't worry," she whispered to Kiara, reassuringly. "I've gotten out of worse situations than this."

The conviction behind her words was partly true. But how she'd escaped hadn't been exactly legal, and it sure as hell wasn't a risk she could afford to take now.

Sighing, she reluctantly allowed the officer to clamp a set of cuffs around her wrists.

Django Alexander
Shackleton City

HOW DOES *such a place even exist?*

Despite the weapon trained on his backside, it was hard for Django not to be in awe of the foreign world around him.

His senses struggled to comprehend his surroundings as the two Authority officers led him and Eventide off the *Redemption* and onto the metal walkway below. Internally, he wrestled with dozens of questions about what had transpired. *Could* Marvin be alive? Why had those two women pretended *he* was Marvin? And why had Eventide kicked him in the shin?

As important as all those questions were, concentrating on any of them was virtually impossible with the world of wonder that commanded his attention. Evie was still avoiding eye contact with him, so he couldn't even look to her for answers.

A multitude of ships filled the vast chamber they now

stood in. Vessels hovered above parking spaces, ready to either takeoff or drop landing gear. Others were being connected to platforms on higher levels by magnetic clamps that locked onto the ships' hulls to keep them upright and steady. Ramps and walkways, like the ones they were being pushed down, led to the crafts, while still more ships were being loaded with cargo of one form or another. A buzz of activity swarmed around them in all directions.

Overwhelming was an understatement.

The port was massive. The ceiling of the port soared, stretching about a hundred meters before funneling into what appeared to be open sky—a scene that, had he not been hastened by two armed escorts, would have stopped Django in his tracks.

A breathtaking marble of blue and green hung above them, illuminated against a black backdrop, with small balls of light hovering around its orbit.

*The Earth.*

The same Earth that had been visible when the view-ports on the Eclipse had malfunctioned: rich in color, free from the browns and grays that had been the norm of human-ity's homeworld for as long as he'd ever known.

A *living* planet.

Django had spent the entire trip aboard the *Redemption* convincing himself that he would be the first in generations of Ringers to set foot on the planet.

*But if we're not on Earth, then where are we? Another space station?*

There had been glimpses of foreign stations and ships during the viewport malfunction. Their current location *could* have been one of those, he supposed, but Django's gut told him this place was somewhere else. Somewhere more elaborate and grand.

The officers were talking between themselves, closely following Eventide and himself. They must have decided that cuffing the two youths was unnecessary, since their hands were still free.

*Why bother with cuffs if you're willing to shoot your prisoner in the back of the head?*

Django had seen firsthand what those blaster weapons could do, and he wasn't planning on testing the officers' willingness to use them. He did wish the officers hadn't taken his father's blaster from him, though. Somehow, he would need to get that back. His last connection to his father. His last connection to home.

*Stowaways,* the uniforms had called them. Django supposed it was true, but how much trouble could they possibly get in for boarding a ship unannounced?

And then the probable worst-case scenario hit him: they would be sent back to the *Eclipse.*

Back to Benson.

*That might as well be a death sentence.*

Just as he'd had the thought, something overhead caught Django's attention. Several cages hung in a space separating the ship's port from the blackness beyond.

*There are people in those cages!*

Not people—*skeletons.* Django swallowed as he did the math of what must have happened to the poor souls.

The *Eclipse,* it appeared, wasn't the only place where the powers that be would send you out the airlock for your crimes

—whether real or otherwise. But why leave their remains out on display? As a warning? A message?

Station Admin had hidden countless murdered souls. Here, it seemed, they flaunted it out in the open.

But the Earth's true condition—its inhabitability—wasn't being hidden here. If the people here knew the truth, what had those skeletons done to end up dead and on display?

Django swallowed, trying not to think about it.

"They would both be fit both for the mines." The female officer answered a question Django hadn't heard. "Have you ever seen a stowaway that looked so well-fed? Never mind *two* of them."

"Hardly anyone off the Rim looks that healthy," the man replied. "You think they're somebody important?"

"Important *stowaways*? That'd be fresh. Plus, anyone that age without chips? Guessing they just got lucky."

"The devil's own luck." The man had a nervous air to his voice. "But more lucky for us, maybe? Unchipped, and in this shape? Buyers will be climbing over themselves to put in a bid."

The woman grunted. "You know I hate pulling kids out of raids. We're bound to get our asses handed to us one of these days."

"Well, maybe if the Syndicate paid enough to afford more than scraps, we wouldn't have to."

"I know, I know. I've got bills just like everyone else. All I'm saying is, I don't like it. It won't help my kids any if I end up executed for stealing Syndicate property."

"Won't do 'em no good starving, either. And these two

should be worth enough to outweigh the risk. Might set us up good for the *year*, even."

Django did his best to look at Eventide without turning his head, but she continued to stare straight ahead, tight-lipped and eyes glazed over; lost in her own world.

*Is she pretending not to hear them? Or is she thinking about how much I screwed up?*

*First, I got us kicked off the station, then I went and kissed her and potentially ruined our friendship. Then, I apparently said the wrong thing about Uncle Marvin on board the ship.*

An echo of pain still shot up his leg with each step.

But *was* Marvin alive? Django didn't want to get his hopes up.

And now it sounded as though they were potentially being sold off for manual labor because of the decisions *he* had made. Django couldn't think of a way their day could get any worse.

"I'm not selling the girl to the mines, though," the woman said decidedly. "We can get better coin for her than that."

"How do you figure?"

"Franco said earlier that the *Inanna's* been docked in Shackleton the past few days. They're scheduled to depart end of today. That's why Commission's pulled so many of us off regular rotation. We're providing extra detail."

"The *Inanna?*" The guard's tone pitched in disbelief. "As in the A-list Domani ship? Why didn't we hear about this before?"

"You think they just announce their arrival? You know the Syndicate keeps their secrets close. 'specially when it comes to the Domani. But it doesn't matter—I say we sell this one to them. They'll be eager to make a deal if they think she's pretty enough."

Django's fury burned beneath his skin. What was this woman implying?

"You think?" The man's eyes moved to Eventide and studied her, up and down. "I've never heard of them accepting stowaways."

"Have you ever heard of an unchipped stowaway with meat on her bones? Look at her—she's *gorgeous*."

"We can hear you, you know," Eventide said defiantly, without breaking her stride.

The male guard chuckled. "You'll do nicely, lovely. Caregivers will even find ways to work on that attitude."

Out of the corner of his eye, Django could see the officer's sausage-shaped fingers reaching for Eventide's bottom.

There had been so many emotions for Django to process since the *Redemption* had docked, but right now, there was only one that mattered: *rage*.

Eventide must have caught the officer's movement, too; her eyes went wide as she tried to whip around. She pulled her arm back, ready to throw a punch, but the officer was faster. He grabbed Eventide's fist, twisting her arm until he had wrapped himself around her. Eventide struggled to break free, but his bulky mass was enough to keep her in place. His weapon had fallen by his side, his arm somehow still moving down toward her backside . . .

"Sa'ab!" the female guard scolded. "Don't be a pig."

A torrent of anger tore through Django, coursing through his muscles before he even had time to process what he was doing.

He had never been a fighter, but Django had wrestled with enough farm equipment to know how to throw his weight behind his arm. Fist connected with jawbone as he hurled himself at the creep. Saliva, blood, and teeth flew in slow motion from the officer's mouth.

Onlookers gasped. A few might even have cheered. Django was only vaguely aware of the gathering of pedestrians beside them; lingering travelers who had been traversing the spaces between the parked ships and walkways.

A crescendo of victory filled his chest and smug satisfaction overcame him as Sa'ab was forced to spit another bloody gob onto the metal walkway.

The victory was short-lived.

Intense electrified pain coursed through Django's body as Sa'ab jabbed him with a handheld pipe-shaped weapon.

Every muscle clenched and screamed out, as though Sa'ab had battered each one with a slug wrench simultaneously. Pain pierced through all thought and emotion, and Django could hear himself screaming, his throat ripped raw with the strain. He quivered and writhed, but he had no control over the noise. It was as if his own body was betraying him.

The pain sent Django to the floor in a helpless heap of noise and convulsions.

Then, just as quickly as it came, the burning fire through his limbs disappeared and the screaming stopped.

He lay face down. The ache in his muscles remained, and the warmth of his own piss soaked his pants. A damp puddle pressed against the cold metal walkway.

As soon as his muscles stopped spasming, his hands were pulled and secured behind his back to the hum of the electric cuffs pressing against his wrists and into his backside. Cold steel pressed into his face, along with a puddle of drool he must have discharged during the attack. Blood streamed from his nose, and judging by the pain at his temple, he must have slammed face-first into the metal floor.

Django tried to blink away whatever was clouding his vision. He couldn't tell if it was blood or tears, or if the impact of the blow had riddled his senses, but the entire world had gone blurry. Eventide's muffled screams were still audible, though growing fainter. The officers must have gagged her.

Had she tried to help? What had they done to her?

Django tried to push himself up, but the stun device had zapped his muscles of all their strength.

Rough hands pulled him to his feet, and Sa'ab let out a masochistic, guttural laugh.

Despite everything—or perhaps, *because* of it—the fury that encompassed Django had yet to dissipate. He channeled every ounce of energy he could muster into reaching Eventide once again, but he only managed to take a step before his legs failed him and he tumbled to the metal grate of the floor below.

Jarring pain struck him again, the blow inducing a ringing in his ears. Django fought to reach up to console his head before remembering that his arms were restrained. A muffled voice in the distance called his name, pressing through the storm of white noise and pain that ballooned inside his head.

"Django! Django!"

He could have sworn it was his Uncle Marvin's voice.

*Shit, I'm dying.* And his uncle was calling his name from beyond the grave.

Eventide's voice followed—unintelligible, pleading. The PA officer grunted, and then all voices fell silent.

These bastards were going to take Eventide with their greaseball hands and lewd grins while he lay in a puddle of his own piss and faded from the galaxy. They were going to take her to these Domani, whatever the hell *they* were.

He had catastrophically screwed up.

*I should never have left the station.*

No, he should have done something else. Anything else. He shouldn't have run. He should have confronted Benson. He should have made a stand for the life they had, and the home he loved.

Django swore Benson would pay for all of this. Never again would he stand on the sidelines and do nothing.

But now, he was here . . . and he didn't even know where *here* was. Some port, somewhere. Somewhere further from the Earth than the *Eclipse*. And instead of being able to start a new life—a new life with Eventide—he was getting the shit kicked out of him while his best friend was being manhandled.

This wouldn't be how their story ended—not as long as he drew breath.

"I'll take her to the *Inanna*; see if they'll take her," the woman said as the haze in Django's head began to clear. "You find a ship that'll take this one before he causes us any more trouble."

"How can you be sure they'll take her?" Sa'ab said. "For all the trouble she's caused, maybe I should take her instead?

Her boyfriend here couldn't have been satisfying her. I'll show her what a real man's all about."

Django's stomach roiled, but pain still paralyzed him. His forearms shook as he desperately struggled to move them from behind his back, and his shoulders trembled as he tried to push his face off the metal floor.

"Your wife and kids know what a filthy dipshit you are?" the female officer asked. "Stop thinking with your dick for a minute. This could be the sale of a lifetime."

"*Ugh*." The male officer wrinkled his nose. "She smells like cabbage, anyway."

"Yeah," the woman replied. "You're not wrong about that. You take piss-pants here and get him ready to ship out, and I'll get her cleaned and ready for display. We can file the paperwork for their disappearance later."

"Well, don't expect me to be cleaning up his piss. The haulers can hose him down."

"Get him on the first ship out of here, Sa'ab. He's already drawn too much attention."

Django
Shackleton City


BLURS OF COLOR and shapes consumed Django's vision as Sa'ab dragged him across the grated metal flooring and into a corridor cut off from the rest of the port. His face slid across the ground, the officer not even bothering to lift him enough to avoid pulling his face through the puddles and catching on the walkway's sharp metal rivets.

His head throbbed in blistering pain, and blood covered his brow.

Django struggled to lift his head, trying to avoid the sharp circular holes drilled into the floor, but his neck muscles were still weak from the electrical weapon Sa'ab had used on him. Instead, his skin, hair and muscle dragged across the walkway, like a cheese grater rubbing against his flesh.

He faded in and out of consciousness, and his face had gone numb.

They had turned down a secondary hallway, leading

further into the shipyard. Echoes of distant voices and commands ruptured Django's moments of consciousness, but none of them offered him help. Instead, they carried on as if the Authority officers hadn't assaulted a pair of innocent youths, tasing and dragging him across the docks and leaving a trail of blood in their wake.

Mobility didn't reawaken in Django's limbs until Sa'ab had stopped. With concentrated effort, he found he could lift his head, but the weight of it felt as though someone had dialed the gravity up to 3 g.

The effects of the beating aside, Django also found himself struggling with hunger. He hadn't eaten in over twenty-four hours; grief had stolen his appetite, and his strength along with it. Hiding in the *Redemption*'s cargo hold had left additional cramps in his muscles. He was hungry, dehydrated, and covered in blood and bodily fluids.

"What's this one?" said a man's voice with a thick accent.

Django was still face down, so he couldn't see the man's face, but the gruff voice was as rough as the metal grates he had been dragged across. "What are you trying to pull, Sa'ab?"

The officer grabbed the scruff of Django's cloak and pulled him roughly to his feet. As his legs tried to find themselves, quivering and threatening to give way at any moment, Django relied on Sa'ab's ironclad grip to keep him upright.

"Not on the books, that's what he is, Bryers. A stowaway. No chip; no record. You won't have to worry about a disparaging family trying to get him back, or the SF or OG hunting him down because of a criminal record. There's no way for anyone to find him. As far as anyone's concerned, this guy doesn't exist."

The man, Bryers, held a datapad in one hand and grabbed Django's arm with the other, holding it up. The man's light-skinned, unshaven face came into focus. Brown eyes focused intently on Django's forearm, followed by thick sausage fingers that clumsily ran themselves along his skin, first lengthways and then across the wrist.

"What's this?" he asked again, running his free hand over his balding scalp. "Ain't never seen an unchipped older than nine. What game are you playing here? Trying to pull one over on me?"

"No games." Sa'ab raised his hands. "That's how we found him."

"So what?" Bryers leaned over Django, the smell of sweat permeating his clothes. The man moved his datapad to the clip at his belt, freeing both hands to lift Django's face. Django winced and tried to back away, but the man secured Django's head from behind and stretched his eyelids with his thick fingers. "These pale tube-dwellers make for shit miners."

Pain surged again as a calloused finger trailed his already scraped face, intensifying the burn. Bryers's hand moved from Django's face, down his neck, and over his shoulders. He patted and squeezed his palm over Django's shoulders, biceps, and arms until he subtly tilted his head, but the movement was enough for Django to catch it. Whatever Bryers had found surprised him.

"Could've at least cleaned the blood and piss off him." Bryers spoke quickly, stringing his words together with an accent Django had never heard before. It was difficult to understand.

"You can play dumb all you want, Bryers, but we both know the lad's value. Unchipped means you can take him anywhere, and nobody's going to ask questions."

"People always asking questions," Bryers replied. "Also means greater risk. Any questions I get asked, I don't have the answers for. But it don't matter to me where they come from or what their story is. This lad's got muscle, but he's still skinny."

"You get a lot of fat cat Rimmers lining up for the mines, do you? Be real, Bryers. How many recruits do you get that *aren't* in shit shape?" Sa'ab persisted. "None, I'll wager. You're the only one off-Rim who *isn't* too skinny. And you haven't come across a kid in this good a shape for years."

Django groaned. He wanted to argue, but his head was still spinning from the bumpy ride.

"I dunno, Sa'ab." Bryers stepped back, reaching for a second datapad that rested on a pedestal anchored to the floor. Django swayed as the two men forced him to support his own weight. "You didn't do yourself any favors bringing him in looking like this. Besides, we're already full, and the PA has clamped down on our quotas . . ."

"Cut the bullshit, Bryers. We play this song and dance every time! Just tell me what you're willing to pay for him."

"One hundred fifty credits."

The officer cackled derisively.

Bryers didn't crack a smile. "You asked what I pay. That's what I pay today."

"Drop the act. He's worth three times that, at least."

"I'll pay you one fifty credits to take him now—or four fifty if you clean him up, hold him, and keep him fed and in prime condition until I get back from Titan four months from now. Then, I can properly add him to my manifest and don't risk getting in shit for not following protocol. There are still rules I have to follow, *Officer*."

"What's this? The mines suddenly getting picky?"

"It's Syndicate rules and you know it! Nobody comes or goes without registering. Every minute you spend dicking around here is one less I have to process him. Plus, thanks to you, I've got to hose him down and get him new clothes before I let him on my ship. If you want premium credits for hauls, you gotta pretend like you give a shit. You're lucky I'm willing to take him at all. The mines are rough, and it don't help if we bring 'em out there already half-dead."

"Miners are a bunch of deadbeats and criminals. They're *all* half-dead."

"You want the credits or not?"

Sa'ab sighed. "Yeah, fine. But give me a receipt, will ya? Or Jules is gonna think I'm holding out on her."

"You know better than that. No paper trail." Bryers shook his head, pulling up his own datapad and making a few keystrokes. "You'll find the credits are already in your account."

Django's head was still in so much of a fog that he didn't see where the two men who grabbed him on either side came from. Based on how they held him under the armpits, it was safe to assume they were both larger than him and had the strength to lift him with little difficulty.

They were taking him somewhere. Somewhere *away*.

*Eventide . . .*

"No." Django choked on the words as fluid filled his mouth. "My friend . . . I can't leave my friend."

"A friend, huh?" Bryers raised an eyebrow at Sa'ab. "Now who's holding out? What did you do with the other one?"

"Pretty little thing," Sa'ab replied. "Jules took her to be appraised by the *Inanna.*"

"The *Inanna?*" Bryers whistled. "You've either got steel balls or a concussion. I hope you treated her nicer than you did this one." He turned to the brutes carrying Django. "Get him strapped in. We've gotta depart."

Most of the conversation with the accented man had gone over Django's head, but he'd understood the part where he and Eventide were being loaded onto different ships.

"I can't leave without my friend," Django called out again before the crew could haul him away. "*Please.* She's all I've got. Bring her here. She's a strong worker. Good with her hands."

Bryers and Sa'ab both chuckled.

"Good to know, kid," Sa'ab said lasciviously, still laughing as he turned to leave. "You should have told Jules about that. It's a transferable skill that'll be useful in your friend's new position."

"Get out of here, Sa'ab," Bryers said impatiently. "You've got what you came for."

Sa'ab grunted, annoyed, and waved a dismissive hand before he left.

Bryers stepped carefully toward Django, who was still being held upright by the armpits. The man's gaze softened.

"Listen, friend." Bryers smelled of cologne and soap. The

man was overweight, his olive green shirt and dark brown vest barely stretching over his potbelly, but he carried himself as though his appearance didn't affect his confidence. What remained of his thinning brown hair was parted to the side, styled with an excess amount of greasy product, and his face was clean-shaven. "What's your name, kid?"

"Django."

Bryers raised an eyebrow and squinted. "Listen, Django, if your friend's got half a shot of being recruited to the *Inanna*, there's no way in hell I can afford her. Trust me, they treat their Domani like gold. And it'll be a damn sight nicer than any hellhole neighborhood the two of you pulled yourselves out of. And a hell of a lot nicer than the place you're going."

Bryers then nodded to his men. "Clean him up and find him some clothes. After that, lock him in with the others."

Mikka
Shackleton City

MIKKA MISSED the prison the Syndicate Front had held her in several days ago. At least she'd had a private cell in *their* dungeon.

Here, in the Port Authority processing center, waiting detainees were crammed into a tight space with dozens of other women and men. Most of them were probably innocent of any crime more treacherous than her and Kiara's, although, from the barely contained snarls here and there, that didn't necessarily apply to everyone.

It was going to be a rough week if they were meant to sleep in such a crowded space. The regolith walls smelled of burnt gunpowder, as though they'd never been treated for toxicity, meaning that every inhalation could be doing damage to her lungs, the sharp specks of dust cloying at her throat pricking at the soft tissues of her respiratory system. Mikka hoped that even though the smell hadn't been contained, at least the surfaces had been treated for breathability, but she wasn't holding her breath. She had often wondered if inadequate regolith treatments led to Lunar sickness. It would certainly explain why the condition was more prevalent in the Tubes.

Alongside the acrid metallic and sulfuric smell of regolith, the pungent odor of human waste permeated the space. There was only one toilet in the far corner—and it was constantly in use. Consequently, some prisoners had given up on waiting their turn, squatting in the darker corners of the room with no regard for privacy or hygiene.

The whole situation was inhumane, made worse by the fact that this was only a space for those waiting for paperwork to be filed. If this was anything to go by, those guilty of more heinous crimes, or something as banal as insulting the Empire, were probably condemned to deal with a lot worse.

Mikka had no problem standing for hours, but sleeping standing up would be a challenge—and there was no way she'd be able to keep upright for seven days. It had already been over twenty-four hours, and her legs were begging for reprieve, but she certainly wasn't going to lie down in the shit and dirt that coated the floor.

Kiara was already shuffling from one foot to the other, eyeing patches of dirt for a spot where someone hadn't pissed lately.

The navigator's nose hadn't unwrinkled since they'd entered the rancid space. Bodies pushed up against her, and men leered as she defensively crossed her arms over her chest to prevent them from taking advantage of the close quarters.

Somewhere toward the back of the cell, a baby shrieked.

Mikka grimaced. The conditions were horrid for an adult, but allowing kids to be boxed in this hellhole was barbaric.

A hand grasped hers and squeezed tightly. Mikka instinctively pulled the arm in, ready to launch a fist into the person's gut, but she stopped short.

It was Kiara.

Her eyes danced in fear, pulling herself in toward Mikka for protection.

It took Mikka a moment to realize why the woman had suddenly become so tactile. Steps away, a string-thin man had approached Kiara with a grin that was as hideous as it was disgusting and eagerness in his eyes. Three shades of yellow coated his teeth, and he turned his lip up in a snarl. His skin clung to his bones like damp fabric, with not an ounce of muscle or fat to speak of.

An outstretched hand lingered, but Kiara would have been vocal—and likely physical—in response if he had successfully grabbed her. The man was foul, but he was spindly, and Kiara could've kicked his ass if she had the mind to.

The navigator could fully hold her own, but right now, Kiara was in shock. It was their situation, more than this asswipe, that was compromising her decision-making abilities. Mikka wouldn't hold it against her; everyone had their off days, and Kiara had pulled Mikka's ass out of the fire more than once in the past eight years.

"You want to lose that hand, Slim?" Mikka spat, pulling Kiara further behind her. "If not, I suggest you keep it to yourself."

It was the second time she'd uttered the same threat in

the past week, and if Mikka had had her knife, she wouldn't hesitate to find a place for it between the pervert's ribs.

She was tired of dealing with this shit, but it was a sad reality of a crumbling empire. People were getting bolder in taking what they wanted, and desperate people with nothing left to lose were as ubiquitous as stars in the night sky. It sucked that the Loop was full of assholes.

"What's it to you? Is she your girlfriend?" Slim sneered.

*Great! A pervert and a homophobe.*

Mikka gritted her teeth. "She sure as hell ain't yours."

The letch raised his hands in mock surrender, his mouth forming a sickly smile. "Hey, if you're a couple, I don't mind. I've got plenty for the both of you."

*Not a chance in hell.*

The man's expression turned monstrous as he lunged toward them.

Mikka rolled her eyes and threw a fist, cracking against solid jawbone.

A whelp left Slim's lips as his head flew back. Mikka didn't wait for him to recover before sinking a second fist into his gut.

The skinny man held a reflexive hand to his stomach, catching the breath that Mikka had knocked out of him. He spat, and a wad of blood landed on the dirt, miraculously missing the detainees nearest to him. The brownish-red splatter congealed on the urine-encrusted floor.

The rest of the crowd dispersed, realizing that they didn't want to get involved in whatever scrap was about to unfold, leaving a widened circle around them.

"*You filthy bitch!*" Rage filled the pervert's eyes as he

straightened, ignoring the welt that was sure to be growing on his belly and the probable organ damage he was suffering from within—there hadn't been a lot of meat separating Mikka's fist from his insides. "You like it rough, do you? I'll show you!"

Faced with Slim's fury, Mikka braced herself for another round.

Turned out, Slim could talk a good game, but his strength ended there.

He must have miscalculated how much her jab had dazzled his senses, because he stumbled before he even reached her, landing on all fours a short distance away. He pushed his face up, hungrily eyeing Mikka, determined not to be bested by a woman.

Big mistake.

Slim pushed himself forward—face-first into Mikka's kneecap as she brought it up with full force.

Blood spurted as the man's nose exploded. Screams filled the cell as his head snapped back and he tumbled onto his backside.

Even then, Slim refused to stay down. He pushed himself up again, blood flowing freely from the mangled spot where his nose had been.

The pervert didn't take more than two steps before a guard cleared a path from the cell door. A silver wand flashed, contacting with the brute's side and sending him to the ground once again in a fit of convulsions.

With Slim writhing in the disgusting dirt, the guard lowered his baton and called for one of his colleagues for help.

Mikka stood still, fully aware that the guard wouldn't hesitate to electrocute someone else with his weapon. Even though his gaze was on Slim, he held the baton out in her direction, as though she might turn on him. For all the guard knew, she could have instigated the brawl, although she suspected he probably just enjoyed watching prisoners squirm.

The other detainees had done their best to distance themselves from both the incident and the guard by pushing into each other and against the regolith walls, as though they'd had an abundance of space before the attack. Fear glistened in the eyes of many, not so much because of Slim throwing himself at Mikka or Mikka's ability to defend herself, but the baton the Port Authority guard held.

Mikka stood firm in the cell's center. Kiara stood hesitantly by her side, eyeing the crowd and mentally backing away with them.

Slim twitched a few final times as the guard stood over him, waiting to be sure the man was down. Mikka thought he might be dead—*hoped* for it. But then the worm's chest rose as he gasped for breath. His limbs twitched, and he slowly pushed himself up onto all fours and stayed there, heaving, as if the effort had taken all of his strength.

Mikka guessed as much. She had been on the receiving end of those batons before, and it was no party. The guy must have been hopped up on some heavy narcotics to remain conscious after the beating he'd just received. Blood still flowed down his face, and a small pool had formed on the dirt where he'd landed.

"Grab him." The guard still held his baton pointed at

Mikka, but he nodded his head toward Slim. "Bring him downstairs."

*Into the pit.* Slim wouldn't get the privilege of a cell. He might never be seen again.

Two more guards materialized and grabbed the man on either side, cuffing him. The man's will dissolved and his body hunched over as they dragged him out, still on his knees. His face didn't relent, though; his lips were still painted with a sneer, and he glared at Mikka on his way out.

The interceding guard then waved his baton in Mikka's direction. "As for you . . . Come with me. Bring your friend."

Every muscle in Mikka's body had tensed, waiting for the guard to attack. Being escorted out did little to relieve the tension.

Kiara let out an involuntary whine.

The ship's navigator wasn't usually so unsettled. Kiara was typically laid-back and easygoing; a breath of fresh air to Mikka's habitual irritability. It was so easy to forget this was all foreign territory for the navigator, who had spent a lifetime desperately avoiding trouble.

Admittedly, prison was also an unfamiliar experience for Mikka. She had gone over a decade without so much as being kept overnight in a brig for drunken misconduct, yet this was the second cell she'd been held in within the past twenty-four hours.

Maybe she was losing her touch.

As for trouble?

She and trouble were old friends.

"It'll be all right," she whispered to Kiara, even though

she wasn't sure if she actually believed it herself. "If we were really up against it, he would have hit us with that baton."

Kiara gulped as she nodded, but she didn't look convinced.

The guard turned and exited the cell, then looked back to prompt them to follow.

"They're not cuffing us," Mikka whispered. "Let's keep it that way."

She hastily followed. Another guard, who had been standing in the hall watching the action, followed them.

While Slim and his escort had gone down the corridor to the left, the lead guard Mikka and Kiara were to follow turned to the right. Mikka scanned the hallway as they entered. Dim yellow and blue incandescent lighting provided some illumination, but it wasn't much.

Escape wasn't an option. Even if they were somehow able to bypass their two chaperones, dozens of security cameras lined the ceiling above them. The Syndicate had fitted their facilities with the most state-of-the-art surveillance at their disposal, enabling them to monitor everything from infrared to ultraviolet, as well as sound and seismic waves. And Port Authority detention centers were the lowest of the low security facilities in the Syndicate's network.

The cameras were as much a statement as they were about functionality.

The hallway stretched out in both directions, but aside from a single door at either end, there were no exits. Through the dim light, Mikka could barely make out that there were three more guards who stood at attention in the direction Slim was being led. And in case Slim had any more fight left in him, each guard held a high-powered energy rifle at the ready.

Despite moving her and Kiara without restraints, the guards were evidently taking no chances. It wouldn't have surprised Mikka if the whole thing was a setup. Someone foolishly trying to make a break for it would give the bored jailers an excuse to beat the shit out of them.

The Port Authority dealt strictly with goods and travelers entering and leaving Lunar's jurisdiction. Mars, Ceres, Europa, and Io were policed by similar forces under the same name.

The Orbital Guard, or OG, was a horribly named arm of the Syndicate regime. They patrolled most of the space routes between Earth and its colonies. Essentially, they were glorified traffic cops, handing out fines and occasionally confiscating contraband goods.

The guards who had invaded Mikka's home in the Tubes and had taken her before Commander Aries represented the Syndicate Front. The highest level of law enforcement in the Empire, they handled special cases and persons of interest. Aries had used the SF to track her down for his own ends, but they typically conducted undercover and more sensitive operations.

Detainees on Lunar's surface who were found guilty of more serious charges would be transferred into the custody of the LPF, the Lunar Police Force, to be tried and convicted within the satellite's jurisdiction. Their authority oversaw petty theft, mischief, and run-of-the-mill murder, and with that came constant opportunities for the LPF to harass and assault citizens. Their real purpose was the protection of

Upper Rim citizens, but of course, the LPF spokespeople would never admit to this in an official capacity. Actions spoke louder than words, however, and anyone with barely two credits to rub together knew to avoid interacting with the LPF.

Mikka risked a glance back at the others in the cell. The PA would assign many of them criminal records for trying to enter or leave Lunar without authorization, but most of them were good people caught up in a bad situation. Like so many others on Lunar's surface and throughout the Loop, they were so desperate to leave their current depravity that they really had nothing to lose by sneaking onto a departing ship. Desperation would always lead people to places they'd otherwise never go.

It surprised Mikka how calm she felt. Her mind should have been trying to convince her of a thousand different reasons why her situation was dire; reasons she should have been panicking rather than seeing which way the dice landed. She had thrown all her chips in with the commander of the Syndicate Front and then had promptly left the table. Aries was one of only a few people who knew Mikka's former name: the notorious pirate Jax Luana. Her criminal record under that name had been extensive enough that if the Port Authority discovered her true identity, she would be lucky if she spent the rest of her days in the pit with Slim. Most likely, she would be transferred to the SF, who would strap her in a cage above the space docks and open the airlock above her head.

Their air, their rules.

The Empire could hold Mikka up as an example of what

would happen when someone tried to live outside of their regulations; outside of the structure based on nothing more than the location they happened to be born.

Mikka knew she should have been worried, but inside, her mind was calm. *Relaxed*, even.

Maybe it was simply exhaustion. In the past few days, she had lost absolutely everything she had worked so hard to obtain: her new life, her new career, her mother's safety. Perhaps subconsciously, she was now resigning herself to whatever disappointment might come next.

The guards led Mikka and Kiara through several series of doors. The walls changed from the craggy unfinished regolith to refined and smooth rock, and finally to paneled and high-end graphite finishing. They were led past administrative offices and busy Authority officers booking in other tired and dejected souls, whose rail-thin figures betrayed that their biggest crime was hunger.

"Where are we going?" Kiara whispered.

"Outside," Mikka replied, keeping her answer intentionally vague. Surely they weren't being released? Harboring stowaways carried a stiff penalty, and it wasn't an offense the Port Authority would overlook without good reason.

*Unless . . .*

The guards pushed through the main access doors to the facility, allowing filtered sunlight to dance across Mikka's face for the first time in over twenty-four hours.

The sun was harsh on the Upper Rim, which was partly what had made Shackleton the perfect site for a settlement. Perpetual daylight hours allowed for round-the-clock solar power—an infinite source in the otherwise unpredictable environment of space.

Mikka reached up to shield her eyes from the intensity of the rays, filtered through the force field that surrounded the city. Earth's blue glow was visible on the horizon, the sun reflecting off its deep blue oceans.

Her eyes took a moment to adjust, but she recognized the voice.

"Once again, I'm disappointed." Commander David Aries stood smugly at the side of the street next to the PA detention center. "This is twice I've had to request your release."

"Don't get used to it," Mikka quipped. "It's not something I intend to make a habit of."

Nearly a dozen armed Syndicate Front soldiers surrounded Aries. Their posture and sleek silver uniforms made the PA guards look like amateurs in comparison.

Aries gestured to the Port Authority. "You are dismissed," he said. "We'll take them from here."

Mikka

Shackleton City

MIKKA HATED RELYING ON ANYONE, and being bailed out by Aries not once, but *twice*, made her skin crawl.

The ride back to the Syndicate Front headquarters was quiet. *Uncomfortably* quiet. Mikka distracted herself by focusing on what lay outside the window, but it was hard not to feel the tension.

Kiara, at least, had calmed down. She, too, contented herself with staring out the vehicle's window, watching the skyscrapers of the inner city approach and then pass by as they entered Shackleton's downtown core.

Neither of them dared to speak a word.

Mikka didn't recognize the make or model of the car Aries had sent for them. To be fair, she'd rarely had the opportunity to ride in one. Like all vehicles on Lunar, it was EV; lithium, along with copious other metals mined from the Belt, in combination with the moon's endless supply of solar energy, allowed for nearly endless transportation capabilities in the Upper Rim.

Ganymede, Jupiter's largest moon, served as the Syndicate's industrial powerhouse, producing most of the Loop's vehicles and other heavy-duty equipment. Its exports were both used by the Syndicate and sold off to private companies servicing the mines of The Belt and the neighboring moons of Jupiter and Saturn. While vehicles were provided to the families of Syndicate leaders and transport cars filled the streets in cities on Mars and the moons of Io and Ganymede, they were much rarer on Lunar. Here, they were reserved for only those who held the most elite positions within the Empire.

Syndicate leaders simultaneously claimed energy was available in near unlimited quantities while restricting its public use outside of the Upper Rim, citing that there lacked the necessary power storage modules and thus transportation could not be assured for people who didn't contribute their fair share to society. Mikka had never received a straight answer as to which of the Syndicate's opposing statements were true: whether there was indeed a shortage of energy storage, or if the Syndicate was just supplying it disproportionately.

But she was willing to take a wild guess.

Aries, as familiar as he pretended to be, didn't ride in the same car as Mikka and Kiara, of course. He had his own private entourage keeping him company. Mikka and Kiara rode with two soldiers, under watch but no longer at gunpoint. The soldiers had even removed their intimidating and tinted combat helmets, revealing hard and uncompromising faces.

The commander's absence, to Mikka's own surprise, had disappointed her. This was the second time the man had rescued her—three times, if she counted when he had allowed her to buy the *Redemption* unencumbered. Never once had anyone so much as given up a seat on a public tram for her, and yet this man had stuck his neck out for her time and time again.

It hadn't gone unnoticed.

On the one hand, Aries was part of the Syndicate, which, if Marvin's tale was true, was the same empire that had made the despicable call to destroy the *Infinity* FLOW station to cover up their own lies, killing hundreds of thousands of innocent people.

But Aries was also someone who had stuck his neck out for *her*. He'd helped smooth the way for her to purchase the *Redemption*. He'd helped *her* mother. And now he'd bailed her out for the second time.

For most of her life, Mikka had had to fight to get the most basic of scraps from anyone. It was the reason she'd become a pirate. If nobody else was willing to help her, *she* would help herself.

But now, for the first time, someone else had taken notice of her. Someone else was keeping her from scrabbling in the dirt.

The one thing Mikka couldn't shake, though, was his motive. What did Aries hope to gain by helping her?

With no answers readily apparent, Mikka instead tried to focus on the surrounding city. Shackleton was home to dozens of skyscrapers—mostly Syndicate-owned buildings, and some filled with empty offices. Others were residential towers for the families of people who worked either directly or indirectly for the Syndicate. Although nearly everyone in the Loop worked for the Syndicate in one way or another, the people here were just the ones the Syndicate deemed worthy of comfort.

Mikka had fought hard to separate herself from the void of the Upper Rim and the delusion of countless Lunar residents who believed they were making a difference to more than just credit balance, while in reality, they were just aiding an empire that thrived on pushing down millions of its subjects. Each of them had been brainwashed by the Syndicate into believing their efforts aided in the prosperity of them all.

Mikka related to the people who called the Tubes home—and there were *millions* of them, hidden away from the residents of the Upper Rim. Not just in Shackleton, but also in Tranquility, Aldrin, New America . . . The list went on. Each of the residents who lived above Lunar's surface benefited from those below.

During her stint as a pirate, Mikka had worked tirelessly to move income from the haves to the have nots, but the effort had been like dropping a grain of sand into a Europan ocean in the hopes of creating an island of refuge. The solution was far bigger than the contributions made by one person.

Cautious though Mikka was around his motives, Commander Aries had offered her an olive branch for change. At the time, she had shrugged it off, but the more she sat on it, the more she realized the Loop was overdue for restructure.

Snatches of their conversation from the day before flashed through her mind.

*Imagine what Lunar would look like if we didn't send eighty percent of our wealth back to the planet? Imagine what we could achieve if we made our own policies?*

*Civil war is coming . . .*

Mikka was abruptly shaken from her thoughts as the car arrived at the SF-HQ tower. The building was far enough away from the skyscrapers of Shackleton's downtown that its personnel would not have to interact with the city's residents, and yet still close enough to enjoy the amenities offered by the city's core.

Gold was the Syndicate's preference for displaying their affluence. The practice stemmed from an old Earth tradition, when the mineral was once considered rare. Among the asteroid belt, the commodity wasn't scarce, but harvesting it required the necessary resources to travel there, as well as a willing buyer. The vast quantities used by the Syndicate was still as powerful a symbol of wealth as ever, and along with the wanton coalescence of silver, onyx, jade, and marble across its architecture and designs, the Syndicate liked to emulate ancient Earth dynasties.

Mikka's eyes immediately scanned the massive entrance doors of the SF-HQ tower. Framed by thick bands of gold, the doors themselves were a lustrous silver alloy inlaid with onyx patterns that depicted far-off constellations the Empire could only dream of reaching.

But the limit of the Empire's spread was hindered only by

technological advancements. The Syndicate was nothing if not ambitious.

*Thank the stars they haven't spread their evil any farther than the moons of Saturn.*

No substantial populations of humanity had managed to develop a foothold that far out. While persistent rumors suggested some tried to live off the grid beyond Saturn's orbit, securing a consistent supply of oxygen, water, and food would be exceptionally challenging.

Beside the building's entrance, water features cascaded over beds of crushed marble, casting a gentle reflection of the gleaming building façade.

As Mikka cast her gaze upward, following the endless tower into the black sky above, ornate balconies protruded at various levels, with railings made of intertwined gold and silver with onyx filling the gaps, giving each a sense of depth and luxury. The windows of the tower sparkled distinctively, infused with diamond dust. Every aspect of the building screamed of the Syndicate's unparalleled opulence and power.

But as Mikka and the millions like her were testament to, humanity could exist without precious gems and metals. The only resources that truly mattered were the same no matter which planet, moon, asteroid, or space station you found yourself on: water, oxygen, hydrogen, nitrogen, helium, and either uranium or possibly argon that could be used for fuel, and nitrates for fertilizer.

If the Empire ever lost sight of that, it was game over for everybody.

It was a quick trip through the now vaguely familiar

headquarters building, up the elevator and through the hallways back to Aries's office. This was the second time in as many days Mikka had been escorted around the Front's headquarters; the second time in two days where she would need to decide whether or not to trust Commander David Aries.

Aries was already in his office, seated comfortably in a plush chair with a whisky in hand, as though he had been waiting for hours.

The uncertainty in Kiara's demeanor returned as she looked around the office with both curiosity and fear. It wasn't surprising, really; there had to be more wealth in the Syndicate Commander's office than the average resident would see in their entire lifetime.

Mikka made a mental note to give her colleague a lecture on the importance of appearances. *Strength* was the only virtue the Syndicate respected, and if they sensed weakness, the Empire would eat you alive.

"You keep interesting company, Miss Jenax."

"Right to business, then?" she replied coolly.

Aries paused, mid-sip, his eyebrows twitching bemusedly. "I'm sorry, did you want me to ask you how your day's been?"

Mikka crossed her arms. "Might be nice."

"Given where I found you, I think I can guess," Aries said, setting his glass down. "Tell me, though, how is it that a smuggler who has evaded arrest and certain execution for almost a decade comes to be stopped and arrested by a handful of Port Authority officers after conducting one *routine* delivery?"

Mikka swallowed. "It wasn't a big deal," she said. "A

couple kids snuck into our storage hold and didn't have the decency not to get caught."

"Not a big deal for your average rum runner." Aries didn't raise his voice, but his tone was firm. "But my instructions were clear: I needed *absolute* discretion on these missions. I've brought you in because you're the best. I hope I wasn't mistaken in that assumption."

Mikka's face grew warm. Her arrest hadn't been her fault, but it would reflect poorly if she tried to pass the blame. "I guess I'm a little rusty. We'll be more careful next time."

Aries nodded, as though her assurances closed the matter. "Now, back to my original statement . . . When you said you wanted to choose your crew, I didn't think you'd choose such . . . *colorful* company."

Mikka shrugged and offered him a wry smirk. "You never said we were exclusive. I can't let you have all the fun, now can I?"

Though Mikka had told Aries she would pick her crewmates, she had intentionally left out that she'd choose Abigail Monroe. The pirate was wanted by the Syndicate Front, the Orbital Guard, and another dozen levels of law enforcement hierarchy throughout the system.

*Would Aries press charges against me for helping a fugitive?* Apart from their agreement, there was nothing standing in his way.

Kiara grew tense next to her. The woman had the most to lose, and she had warned Mikka multiple times before bringing Abigail on board.

Mikka, however, had known the risks, and she opted to

proceed anyway because of what Abigail had offered her: the chance for her mother to get better.

To Mikka, *that* was all that mattered.

Aries hit a few keys on his console and a holographic image appeared before them.

Mikka fully expected Abigail Monroe's likeness to appear, but instead, the projection showed a man in his twenties. The bulk of his shoulders and arms suggested an athletic build. His smug grin and defiant stare revealed the unwarranted confidence of a man who had yet to be worn down by the harsh realities of the system. A man with dreams. The wild strands of his short black hair were sticking out at all angles as though he had run his hand through it in frustration, but there was also the hint of a mischievous grin on his lips.

"Do you know this man?" Aries asked, studying Mikka's face as if trying to gauge her reaction.

The image wasn't recent; it had to have been at least a decade old, but there was no mistaking who it was. The man in the holo held the same rugged charm, but he was less tired; less worn down by life. He was after the world and believed that nothing could stand in his way.

*The arrogance of youth.*

Marvin Alejandro—or at least, who he had once been.

*What would a holo of me from a decade ago look like? Did I stand the same way, full of dreams and ambitions, before the system wore me down?*

Unfortunately for him, there wasn't much Aries would find out about Alejandro from her. Mikka knew sparingly little. Abigail had told her a few things, but not much, and certainly not anything interesting enough for Marvin to have been on the Syndicate's radar after a decade-long absence.

Kiara, unfortunately, was not a master at hiding her emotions, and her bottom lip quivered. She shuffled her feet, looking anywhere but at the commander's face, as though simply recognizing someone would be reason enough for him to send her out the airlock. Kiara was crafty and had perhaps pieced together some clues about Marvin that Mikka had not, but most likely, she was just nervous about being put on the spot.

*Mental note*: never *let Kiara play poker.*

Aries's face twisted into a sly grin at Kiara's display.

*You can navigate us from one planet to another, Ki, but when it comes to playing your cards close to your vest, your delivery could use a little work.*

Mikka sighed and fought the urge to punch Kiara in the shoulder. Keeping the upper hand with her navigator around was proving to be a challenge.

Aries swiped a command on his console, which brought up a list and various text boxes around the image of Marvin.

"This man," the commander said, "is the subject of one of the system's oldest unsolved missing persons cases. Nobody has seen Marvin Alejandro since the *Infinity* went dark. It was assumed he was on board when the station's life support systems failed."

"Is that so?" Mikka said, feigning disinterest. "Well, I didn't do a background check; I took him in on the good word of a friend of mine. As per our agreement, I get to choose my crew. I agreed to join you for the long term, but my assumption was my companions are free to come and go as they choose."

"It's not that simple," Aries said pointedly. "Alejandro's one of the most wanted terrorists in the Loop."

Mikka swallowed. Abigail definitely hadn't told her *that*.

"Have either of you heard of an underground terrorist group called the Resurgence?" Aries asked.

Mikka shook her head. "No, sir."

Kiara mirrored the reaction, her mouth tight as she chewed on her lip.

"On the one hand, I'm glad to hear it. Alejandro's involved, but I've been able to gather surprisingly little intel on the group."

"Marvin's been MIA for seven years," Mikka said. "He told us so himself. There was no way for him to contact anyone outside the *Eclipse* until Abigail went looking for him. I doubt he's involved in any recent plans."

Aries continued as though Mikka had said nothing. "The others aboard your vessel are no less enigmatic." The commander pressed another button on his console and a holographic image of Abigail accompanied Marvin's. "Abigail Monroe. Wanted pirate. Charges against her are relatively minor—petty theft, mostly—but recent reports indicate she was involved in a raid on a Syndicate shipyard on Callisto about a month ago. Along with several other terrorists, Monroe escaped with extremely sensitive and classified equipment."

Mikka didn't let her surprise reach her face. She didn't know what Abigail was planning, and she didn't care to. Mikka was a smuggler, not a freedom fighter.

"It's clear these two are working together, but I wanted to see if either of them mentioned anything to you about *what* they were scheming?"

Mikka shrugged. "Abigail speaks mostly in riddles. She's a pirate with a passion for gambling and drinking, to the point of being a cliché. As for Marvin, you seem to know more about him than I do. They're familiar with each another, but I was just there to captain the ship, not to ask questions. If they have some grand plan, they didn't breathe a word of it to me."

Aries nodded, his gaze fixed on the holo-projections. "What about the two youths hiding in the cargo hold? Despite my digging, they might as well be ghosts. No names. No details. The PA didn't even process them properly. I was hoping you could shed some light for me. Are they working with Alejandro, too? What do you know about them?"

"Practically nothing. I never even really met them. The Authority hauled them onto my bridge for a total of two minutes before they threw us in that piss-stained cell you found us in. They're young. The boy, Django, thinks Alejandro is his uncle. Sounded like they might have boarded the *Redemption* on Marvin's instructions."

Aries clasped his hands behind his back and walked to one of the giant paned windows that overlooked the city. They were tinted dark so that the incoming light from the sun didn't affect the holo-screens, but the glass was still clear enough to see Shackleton splayed out before them.

"His *uncle?* Very interesting." Aries pursed his lips, deep in thought, as though that tidbit of information might be a missing piece to a puzzle he'd been working on, but didn't quite know where it fit.

"The PA also mentioned they were unchipped," Mikka added. "I'm not sure if that's just PA incompetence or if the FLOWs use another set of protocols they're not used to scanning for."

Aries's expression didn't change. "*That* could be useful. If that's the case, Alejandro likely knows as well. I've sent a few of my men to pull both youths out of the PA holding cells. I'll keep what you've said here in mind."

Aries closed the holo-image of Abigail, then leaned over his screen. Mikka's intel had shaken his previously cool demeanor. He faced the screen, staring blankly, not looking at its contents.

Mikka exchanged a confused glance with Kiara. Two stowaways shouldn't have been anything more than an inconvenience to a senior Syndicate Front officer; a passing curiosity, at most. Being unchipped was unheard of, but it was hardly universe-shattering for a commanding officer.

Something else was clearly gnawing at him.

After several minutes of him standing, looking out the window in silence, Mikka had had enough. "Are we free to go?" she asked.

"What?" Aries looked up, as though surprised Mikka and Kiara were still there. "Oh, yes." He waved a dismissive hand. "I've arranged quarters for you both. And while I remember, Miss Ryson's caregiver will be provided a room there as well.

That surprised Mikka. They hadn't discussed benefits for Kiara. But if anyone deserved a string of good luck, it was her.

"You have another assignment for us, then?" Mikka asked.

"Yes, of course," Aries answered, still not focused on them. "I'll give you more details when we meet again tonight."

Mikka frowned. "Tonight?"

"I'd like you to accompany me to dinner, Miss Jenax. I'll have an outfit sent to your quarters and a car to pick you up at twenty hundred hours. Miss Ryson is free to spend the evening with her children."

Mikka's heart skipped a beat. Dinner with David Aries? She wasn't sure whether she should be excited or terrified.

# CHAPTER SEVEN

Django
Unknown

AT LEAST ON THE *REDEMPTION*, Django had been able to move his limbs. Now, he found himself on yet another ship, this time with his arms restrained, and if he could manage shuffling his butt without disturbing the people who sat beside him, he would consider it a win.

Django swallowed, but his saliva provided little relief for the back of his parched throat. The bit of moisture he conjured scratching on the way down. The air aboard this vessel was drier than it had ever been aboard the *Eclipse*. His head pounded, and Django wasn't sure whether it was from being dragged along the floor or being hosed down with a pressure that must have been calibrated to clean the hulls of spacecraft, as it nearly removed just as much skin as it did dirt.

He had tried to turn his head when they'd aimed the hose

at his face, but even so, the force of the jet had made the scrapes hurt like hell.

From what Django had gathered, the man who'd bought him owned a slave-trading vessel, and probably more than one. Working that out had been the easy part. The hard part was being afraid to ask where they were going, or what would be expected of him upon arrival.

Bryers's men had tossed Django on board. There were at least four of them, all currently watching him from the aisles along either side of the vessel. These men hadn't been as rough with Django as Sa'ab, but that was like saying sawdust tasted better than glass.

Django was hardly concerned with the scrapes on his face; they would heal with time. What worried him more was how long he'd gone with no food or water. He had worked enough long hot days in the fields to recognize the signs of dehydration.

His legs had cramped more than once, seizing on and off as he'd tried to flex them to keep circulation moving. Django constantly tried to shuffle them as much as he could, leaning from one side to the other to allow the blood to circulate, but there simply wasn't enough room to do so effectively. And no amount of movement was a substitute for water.

Metal cuffs dug into his wrists—a much cruder form of restraint than the energy cuffs the station guards had put him in on the *Eclipse*, but no less effective.

And much more painful.

What did it say that he was growing a *preference* for different types of handcuffs?

The pair could have been made of ice for all the chills

they sent down his spine, though it was hard to tell how much of that sensation was prompted by the cuffs' material, as his hands had gone numb hours ago from being suspended in front of him.

Django's body ached and, no matter which way he turned, his joints screamed. He couldn't remember the last decent night of sleep he had gotten, and his body was demanding rest.

But the restraints made sleeping all but impossible.

Fatigue consumed him, enough that Django had managed to nod off more than once, only to be jolted awake within minutes as the ship jumped or shuddered.

All of that was superficial, though. If anything, it was a welcome distraction from the agony he was suffering.

He'd failed Eventide—and once again, he faced the possibility that he might never see her again.

But this time, it was so much worse.

Two nights ago, he'd been plagued with the same possibility, that he might be cut off from being able to visit the B-Ring on the *Eclipse*, and that Eventide would no longer be permitted to venture to the D-Ring to see him.

At least in that scenario, he knew where she was. Hell, he knew where *he* was. Because now, there seemed to be no way for him to find her.

*No, I won't let that happen. I'll find a way out of here and figure out where they took her.*

Anger flooded him so fully that, more than once, Django thought he was going to puke. There was nowhere for him to displace his pent-up rage; the fury that threatened to consume him, begging to be released from his bonds.

But there was nothing Django could do to satisfy that particular beast. For now, his only option was to distract himself from the evil scenarios his mind conjured of all the things the creeps on the *Inanna* might do to Eventide while he wasn't there to protect her.

Of all the things he would do to them once he found them.

The guards had attached his cuffs to a metal bar that ran the width of the bench Django sat on. Bars separated each row of duplicate metal benches, each bench wide enough to sit a half dozen prisoners side by side. The space was dominated by at least twenty rows of slaves, all sitting in silence. If there were whispers among them, they were not audible over the roar of the ship's engines.

Though not cast in complete darkness, as the ride in the *Redemption* had been, this ship's hold was still poorly lit, and Django couldn't see either end of the cabin. The dim yellow glow of the hold provided just enough light to make out the features of the prisoners nearest to him, their faces dancing in the shadows.

On his left sat a large man. He wasn't overweight, per se, but the man's arms were wider than the torso of most people he had met on the *Eclipse.* His oversized shoulders and triceps pressed into Django, pushing him as far as his restraints would allow. The man's tank top provided a full view of his taupe brown arms that bordered on gray and the markings that ran along them. Glowing green designs highlighted their bulge, drawing attention to them as a warning to anyone who might think twice about attacking him. They were tattoos of some sort, but not like any Django had seen aboard the *Eclipse.*

*Since when did tattoos glow?*

The man's arms were also laced with cuts in multiple places along his skin; dark lines that ran along his muscles from his fingers to his shoulders. His face still held a semblance of youth—free of wrinkles and with a youthful air —that led Django to believe the man wasn't more than a couple years older than himself.

As uncomfortable as Django was crammed into such a tight space, this man must have been in agony, hunched over on a bench that barely contained his frame and secured in cuffs that were nowhere near large enough to contain his wrists without cutting into them.

Django tried not to stare at the rings of dried blood and scars surrounding the flesh at his wrists. Evidently, this wasn't the man's first time in inadequately sized cuffs.

Had the man ended up here in circumstances like his own? What about the others? What were their crimes? Had they, too, tried to sneak on board a ship, or had something else cost them their freedom? Were there people here from other stations? Others who had also attempted to escape?

Nobody on the *Eclipse* had looked like this man. He was too large, too burly, and the scars that blended in with his tattoos told stories of fights that would never have been tolerated on the station. Someone with this man's build would have stood out from the crowd.

Muscle pressed up against the dark brown shirt the guards had given to Django after they'd removed his bloodied and piss-stained attire.

Despite the ship being frigidly cold, the shirt clung to

him, moist with sweat—both his own and that of the man next to him. But it was likely that only the body heat of his neighbors offered any warmth. If there was a bit more light, he'd likely have seen his own breath.

The man gave an occasional grunt as the shuttle jumped or shuddered at some unseen interference from outside, but otherwise, he was as silent as the rest of the ship's passengers. His eyes were closed, and his mouth moved as though in silent prayer to an unknown deity.

On Django's right sat a pale-skinned woman, who, though she didn't appear to be frail, was thankfully far more petite. Despite the long hours they had been strapped in for the flight, this woman still held her head up high, as though she were a passenger and not a prisoner.

Hidden behind the woman's green eyes was strength, determination, and beauty; three traits that captivated Django, threatening to pull him in and never let go.

They were the same green as the Earth's surface, now that Django actually knew what the planet truly looked like, and they shone in the ship's dim light, like the tattoos of his other neighbor. Her hair was long, bright red, and wavy. Perhaps she had dyed it, like the blue and purple tints the residents of the Upper Rings often sported, but as far as Django could tell, it was her natural hair color.

Her clothing was simple, flecked with smudges of gray dirt that suggested her captors had forced her to lie on the ground at some point. Burgundy armbands covered the marks on her wrists that were barely visible around the edges of the cloth, making it difficult to confirm whether she, too, was a seasoned captive.

"Do you think the mines are really as bad as people say?" she whispered, breaking the hours-long silence. "Everyone says they're worse than a death sentence."

Django tried to adjust his arms in front of him into a more comfortable position, but it was a useless endeavor. *The mines?* Images from the histories of men in white tank tops, headlamps, and pickaxes came to mind, but surely the reality of such places in the far reaches of space were a different beast.

"I don't know," he replied. "I've never even heard of these mines before."

"You've *never* heard of the mines?" the woman asked incredulously before rolling her eyes. "It's okay if you don't want to talk to me. You don't have to be a jerk about it."

Django's cheeks flushed. He didn't want to appear stupid, but he also didn't know how much he should share with this stranger.

"I don't know much about what happens on the planet. I've been . . . a little sheltered."

The woman's face twisted into a smirk that wiped away the fear that had once been in her eyes.

"You think we're going to *Earth?*" she whispered, glancing around as though afraid the other passengers sitting beside them would overhear her. "Are you stupid, or just insane?"

Django didn't know how to respond. He certainly wasn't stupid, but after everything that had happened to him over the past few days, insane didn't seem that far out of reach.

"I don't get out much."

*Understatement of the century.*

The twisted look didn't leave the woman's face. "What's your name, space cadet?"

Although he wasn't entirely sure how, he got the sense she was making fun of him by using that nickname, but he responded anyway. "Django."

"I'm Rowyn. I'd shake your hand, but . . ." She nodded at her cuffs. There was a glint in her eye that hadn't been there a few moments before.

There was something oddly familiar about Rowyn. The deviousness behind her smile seemed to suggest she already knew more about him than she let on, but perhaps he was just trying to find some common ground in his unfamiliar surroundings.

At least someone was being nice to him for a change.

"What is this ship? Where exactly *are* we going?"

Rowyn's questioning look returned, as though she didn't quite believe anyone could be *that* stupid. Django swallowed his feelings of inferiority. If he was going to figure his situation out and get back to Eventide, he needed answers, and for those, he needed to accept that he might look like a fool. Maybe if he had asked more questions aboard the *Eclipse,* he wouldn't have found himself where he was now.

*Then again, I'd probably be dead.*

In all honesty, Django wasn't sure which was worse: being dead, or knowing that Eventide was lost in the expanse of space without him, having the stars-knew-what done to her.

"I'm still not sure whether you're being serious, or if you're just an asshole."

He sighed. "Please. Explain it to me like I know nothing."

"You hit your head?" Rowyn was still uncertain, but she smirked, as though believing he was toying with her.

"Something like that," he answered. The cuts to his face would no doubt lend credibility to that story. "I really have no idea where I am, so if you could answer my questions, it would really help me out. What is this ship, and where are we headed?"

*And how can I get off here and find Eventide?*

Rowyn's face grew serious and her eyes widened. "All right, I'll play along."

She averted her eyes for a moment, as though trying to decide where to start. "This is a mining vessel. Someone sold you." Rowyn paused and looked Django up and down, as though expecting a response. When he said nothing, she carried on. "Your life is now owned by the cartel that contracts this vessel and controls a series of asteroid mines, harvesting assets for the Syndicate Empire. We're flying to the asteroid belt that runs between Mars and Jupiter, also known as The Belt. That is where we will spend the rest of our brief lives. The exact place we land could be any number of rocks, but it'll likely be Ceres or somewhere close by. Most of this lot are in decent shape. It wouldn't surprise me if we're headed to Psyche 16."

*Asteroid belt.*

It wasn't just the Earth and Moon that were inhabited?

"What does the Syndicate mine? And why The Belt?"

"What do you think? Just about anything that makes the system function; mostly water, helium, hydrogen—but some rocks are also rich in lithium, gold, cobalt, platinum . . . It all depends on whichever Council priority is in favor this week.

The Belt offers the Syndicate the resources it needs to fund their empire, but in the end, it doesn't matter. Nobody working the mines survives more than a couple years, if they're lucky."

The ship shuddered, jolting the prisoners in their seats.

"We'll see about that," Django said determinedly.

"There's no way out of the mines, kid. The Front would shoot you for even trying. It's *suicide*."

*Why is everyone calling me 'kid?' I'm at least as old as she is!*

"They've taken everything from me," he said, his eyes aflame with a momentary wave of grief. "I'm not going out without a fight."

"Makes no difference to me," Rowyn replied. "Where we're going, we probably won't have time to make friends. Get yourself killed. If you don't wanna listen, it's on you."

*Friends.* The thought of having someone to help navigate this unfamiliar universe smacked Django upside the head. He hoped he wasn't being naïve—maybe she was just trying to pass the time—he didn't want to blow an opportunity to create an ally. He needed to get out and find Eventide, and he knew he wouldn't be able to do that alone.

"Look, I'm not stupid. I'm just a little disoriented."

That much was true, at least, and he knew that if he wanted to continue building this woman's trust, he'd need to divulge a little more about himself.

"My parents just died," he said solemnly. "Murdered. I was forced to leave my home, and my sister stayed behind. And my best friend . . . The guards at the port sold her to another ship. I've lost *everything*."

Saying it out loud suddenly made it all seem so much more real. All the events of the past few days felt like a fever dream Django had yet to wake up from.

He surveyed the chamber they were in, reality hitting him anew. Realizations of his current situation came hurtling toward him at lightning speed.

The dim lighting.

The dozens of bodies chained to their seats.

His parents dead.

Eventide missing.

His home thousands of kilometers behind him.

Even the dream of setting foot on the blue planet he'd once believed was lost had been dashed. Instead, life had tossed him further away, into space, past the Moon and toward the asteroid belt.

He was truly alone, and all the things that had made Django the man he was were lost.

*Are you stupid, or just insane?*

Both, *I guess.*

A fresh pang of sorrow at Uncle Marvin's absence swept over him. *He* could have guided Django through this new world. He could have maneuvered around the Port Authority and found them someplace safe, and then Django wouldn't have been separated from Eventide and she wouldn't have been forced to fend for herself on a ship full of perverts.

*What about before all this? What if I'd just stayed put?*

He might not have had Eventide, but he would still have had a warm bed in his quarters. She would have been happy as a technician and could have started a family with her partner, Faron Lu, while Django lived a happy life in the dirt of the space station farms . . .

*I don't think this could ever work.*

The cold metal of his handcuffs pressed against his wrists, and Django allowed the sensation to bring him back to the present. Though the *Eclipse* might have been comfortable—or as close to a semblance of it as Django had ever known—it had all been a lie. His entire life had been a lie. His family would still be dead, and maybe Eventide, too. It would only have been a matter of time before her work as a technician had exposed her to the truth about Earth, and Evie would never have been able to accept and continue the lie. Instead of setting her free, the truth would have killed her.

*It still might have.*

Django narrowed his eyes; he couldn't afford to think like that. He needed to get back his head back in the game, and he had some catching up to do if he was going to survive this place. The only way was to go was forward, to figure out how to get off this damned ship and find his way back to Eventide.

But she didn't have feelings for him. He'd always known it was a risk, telling her the truth, but if he hadn't, eventually it would have torn them apart. And no matter what—no matter how much the rejection hurt—she was still his best friend. That wouldn't change, and she was out there, alone, because of *him.*

He had to find her. He owed her that much.

"For what it's worth, I'm sorry. I had no idea. I . . ." Rowyn sighed. "I've lost people, too. We all have. Those of us here on this ship—a lot of us, anyway—we're like family. We've been working to make a difference, but we got sloppy.

We're lucky the SF officers got greedy; sold us instead of bringing us in. The Syndicate's really going down the pipes if the Front is resorting to trafficking. Then again, I guess it shouldn't be all that surprising."

Django didn't understand most of what Rowyn said, but the compassion in her voice, the sadness in her eyes as she mentioned the people she'd lost . . . Maybe he wasn't as alone as he thought.

"What about you?" he asked. "Do you have a family?"

A pained look crossed Rowyn's face, and he immediately regretted asking. On reflection, it was too personal a question for someone he'd just met.

"My parents were anti-Syndicate activists," Rowyn said soberly. "They organized protests, rallying their friends, colleagues, anyone who would listen, to help them make their dissatisfaction known. It's not exactly hard to convince a sector of the Lower Tubes that they're hard done by; they're all people with nothing to lose. Mom and Dad knew they had targets on their backs, but as more people sided with them, their protests continued to grow bolder.

"My parents didn't believe in using violence. Others saw protest as a low-risk way of venting their frustrations, which was why their movement grew as large as it did. I don't think they ever intended it to; they never even gave it a name. It flew under the Syndicate's radar, at least, *at first*. Of course, it wasn't enough; there was only so much Mom and Dad could do with rallies, poetry readings, and leaflets; only so much that peace could achieve. Eventually, people's frustrations spilled over and they took to the Upper streets. It was a dumb move, but it was inevitable. When people lose loved ones and are struggling to put food on their tables, the level of anger can't be contained to complaints in private quarters any longer. Eventually, it erupts.

"But there was no structure to the protest movement; it was just an angry mob. My parents were smarter than that, too; they knew better. I don't know why they allowed themselves to get caught up in it all.

"They didn't even last an hour once they got above ground. The SF soldiers didn't leave any survivors. It's more common now, but back then, it was the first time in forever that anyone had dared to publicly defy the Empire. The newscasts, of course, reported that the military had been used to preserve justice and order. Like anyone sitting in their cushy apartments has ever known either of those things! The Upper Rim just doesn't want to face the reality of what's living beneath their feet. Most of them would be more horrified by a swell of Tube residents in their streets and would rather the Front kill us all than admit their lives are built on our broken backs, you know?"

Django nodded slightly, even though he knew nothing of what she was talking about. He got the general idea, though, and he couldn't help but draw parallels with the social hierarchy aboard the *Eclipse*. The residents of the D-Ring hadn't resorted to violence yet, but disdain emanated from the higher Rings. The scornful looks the security on the B-Ring had given him and his sister still haunted him.

Wherever these places were that Rowyn was speaking about, they had formed a similar social order, it seemed, and, like himself, she had been at the bottom.

Rowyn sniffed as though she were fighting back tears, but none had formed in her eyes.

"My older brother, Gavin, was supposed to take me in," she continued. "There was no way I could afford a place of my own, so it seemed like it'd be a good idea. He's training to be a guard for the Front—one of the few ways we can forge a better life for ourselves. Either sell our bodies or sell our souls, you know? I thought living with him would be a good way to get my foot in the door, find something more secure. A future better than what we had growing up in the Tubes. Gavin had managed it. Why couldn't I do the same?"

"It was good of him to take you in," Django said. His thoughts went to his own sister, Nova. He had tried to take her in, too; tried to step up when his parents died.

But Benson had taken her away from him.

Rowyn spat. "He's a bastard. I would have been better off dying on the streets. Not two weeks after the riot, we were having supper at his table. I felt woozy, but I thought it was just the stress of everything catching up to me, so I excused myself to go to bed. Next thing I know, I've collapsed, unable to move my arms and legs. Completely incapacitated. Gavin picks me up, takes me to the docks, and tries to sell me to a damned Domani cruiser. Can you believe that? My own *brother?*

"But, for whatever reason, the Domani didn't take me. Maybe I'm too hideous or they've got a thing against redheads, or maybe Gavin ran his mouth like he always does. Either way, when I came to, I found myself in a back alley brothel, the kind that uses up their girls until there's nothing left for them to give." Her eyes flashed. "You asked me about family? No, I have no family."

"That's *awful!*" Django managed. Her own brother! He couldn't imagine doing anything so despicable to Nova, nor anyone else on the *Eclipse*. Everyone he had known, on the D-Ring, at least, had always strived to help one another. Especially family. "And you're not hideous, by the way."

That seemed to earn a smile from Rowyn. She shook her head, her gaze focused on her cuffs. "I should have known. Gavin and I, we'd never been that close. He works for the Front, for crying out loud, while I was destined to follow in our parents' footsteps, fighting the Syndicate. But that's what you do for family, isn't it? You put your trust in them, until they give you a reason *not* to.

"Thankfully, the day I was sold to the brothel, Taku was leading a raid on the place. Lucky for me, rescuing the helpless and giving them a new lease on life is his thing. He might be paranoid, but he's got a good heart. He introduced me to the Resurgence; taught me that family doesn't have to be defined by blood, and that together, we can accomplish *anything*." She smiled wistfully. "Made me think I had evaded the wrath of the gods who decided I should be born on the soulless rock that is Lunar. Made me think I could make a difference."

Django nodded along as though he knew who Taku was.

"Until *this*, at least." She nodded to the rest of the ship. "We worked so hard to build up the Resurgence. I know it'll go on without us. But I've always assumed it was my purpose, that I'd be there when the uprising happens, but I guess *this* is how it ends."

Django surveyed the surrounding ship again. Their situation felt hopeless. He remembered stories he'd learned in school about people shipped across Earth's oceans in a similar way, captured and forced into slavery. Many of them didn't even survive the journey. Would the haulers aboard this ship treat their prisoners any differently?

Django shook off his train of thought. It seemed illogical that the miners would go to the effort of collecting people to work in their mines, only to allow them to die in transport.

Not to mention cruel.

*Seems like a lot of that going about, though . . .*

"Maybe it doesn't have to be," he replied hopefully. "I'm not giving up on finding a way out of here."

No matter what, he wouldn't accept defeat while Eventide was still out there.

*She's still my friend. And what's happening to her is my fault.*

Rowyn sniffed derisively. "You don't get it, do you? There's *no* way back from the mines, space cadet. It just doesn't happen."

The ship shuddered again, this time more violently than before. Someone beyond Django's sightline called out and the few security guards who had been walking the aisles now scrambled toward the prow.

Immediately alert, Rowyn strained her neck to see what was going on.

Django was curious, but nothing in this new world made much sense to him, anyway. Lights at the front of the cabin flickered, making it difficult to focus on anything, and a haze billowed from a door that Django could only assume led to the ship's bridge.

It took a few seconds for him to realize smoke was pouring into the cabin.

*Is the ship on fire?*

Django tried to wriggle out of his cuffs, to no avail. He sucked in air, panic swelling in the pit of his stomach. Of all the ways he expected to die, being handcuffed to a burning ship wasn't near the top of the list.

A reverberating *pop* caused everyone in the hold to jump, immediately followed by several more. Django winced and, on instinct, ducked as much as he could. The other captives around him did the same.

It was then he realized the source of the noise . . .

Gunfire.

Django Alexander
Unknown

BLACK MASKS OBSCURED the faces of the three gunmen who pushed their way through the smoke-filled corridor. They carried weapons that were no longer supposed to exist; weapons that were said to have disappeared with the Climate Wars.

*Guns. Old-fashioned guns, complete with bullets.*

Every guard aboard the *Eclipse* had carried an energy weapon. Even the blaster pistol Django had found hidden under his parents' bed fired bolts, not bullets.

Bullets were something from old stories of bank robberies and the wars of ancient history, where people fought over prejudices, dominating natural resources, or living space; land that had yet to be radiated.

Projectile weaponry was supposed to be a thing of the past, but then, of course, nothing outside of the *Eclipse* was supposed to exist.

He dropped his head down between his arms, as low as he could, taking his lead from the people around him. His body strained against the tightness in his muscles. He didn't scream in fear like others in the hold, but he had no desire to take a bullet in the head, either.

Beside him, Rowyn let out a curse and muttered something to herself that Django couldn't make out. Shouts from the masked men called for the security guards to get down. The piercing shriek of energy weapons discharging clashed with the thunderous reprisal of ballistic firepower.

The violent exchange was over in minutes. Blasters stopped firing, as did the bullets. The shouts of the ship's guards ceased, and only the prisoners' cries echoed throughout the hold.

Django hesitantly lifted his head to survey the damage. He was no firearms expert, but surely bullets were no match for energy weapons.

Through the haze of smoke, three people remained standing.

But none of them were the guards.

Django's mind spun out of control. *Is this good? Bad?*

It felt terrible, but Django couldn't see how much worse it could get from being imprisoned and sent to a distant mine.

Suddenly, the events aboard *Eclipse* seemed logical by comparison. There were no men, women, and children chained up to be shipped to the stars-knew-where. There was no battle of energy weapons versus bullets, and there were certainly no masked people breaching the hull for a lethal raid.

"Quieten down and listen up, everyone! We're not here to harm you. We're the Resurgence."

*Resurgence.* Rowyn had said that word earlier. Maybe these were *her* people.

The man who had addressed the hold stood only a few rows away. Another newcomer had positioned themselves toward the door that presumably led to the bridge, holding their weapon with both hands, as though afraid they might drop it. The third invader must have stood toward the ship's stern.

"My name is Taku," the man continued. At the mention of his name, Django noticed Rowyn shifting in her seat. "We've now taken control of this vessel."

A cheer erupted among the passengers, and it was only then that Django looked up. Smiles beamed on the faces of the other prisoners, including Rowyn. They all looked at each other with similar, elated expressions, as if this was the savior they'd been hoping for.

Django still didn't know what to think, so he simply sat and studied the new situation. Rowyn had said Taku had rescued her once before. This *had* to be good news.

But Taku still wore his mask and gripped his weapon with two hands, as though he was expecting the prisoners might turn on him as well.

"They actually tracked us down," Rowyn said, inspirited. "Taku's full of surprises."

Waves of other voices soon drowned out her excitement, a loud clamor as the relieved passengers released hours of pent up energy.

Taku raised a hand for the ruckus to quieten, a smile

visible beneath his mask's mouth-hole, and Django flinched as bright lights overhead illuminated the chamber, assaulting his tired eyes that had grown accustomed to the darkness.

Taku removed his mask and tussled his dyed bleach blond hair, which contrasted with his dark beige skin tone. Shadows danced across his face, the flood of light high-lighting a scar that ran above his right eyebrow.

Now unmasked, Taku once again addressed the hold. "Your entire lives, you have been kept down. That ends now. The Resurgence offers hope and freedom. We are the end of the Syndicate. We are the four horsemen; the harbingers of their demise. And we will return to Earth. Some of you are our friends already, and we welcome you back. Others haven't heard of us, but soon, the name 'Resurgence' will be on everyone's tongue.

"You were bound for the mines of Psyche 16—most of you, only because you were in the wrong place at the wrong time, and all of you because the fates dictated that you were born in orbit rather than on the surface. If you're looking for a way to get your revenge, you've found it.

"If you're not a fighter and you have left loved ones behind, you can go back to your families knowing that we will fight in your name. For the chance for you to dream. For the chance for you to *hope* that one day, you will be free of the shackles the Syndicate has placed upon you."

Murmurs of assent filled the hold.

The handcuffs securing each of the prisoners clicked open. The bottom of the cuffs were stiff, sticking out from the row in front of them, so Django's hands remained resting on them. They had lost all feeling, to the point where he was unsure if he could lift them from the cuffs.

Others around him were rubbing their hands in relief. He tried to throw his shoulders enough to force his hands from their former restraints, but he was unable to gain enough momentum, being so close to Rowyn and the big man beside him.

"Need a hand there, space cadet?" Rowyn offered with a chuckle, massaging her wrist with her other hand in an attempt to restore her own circulation.

Before he could answer, she reached over and grabbed his forearms. Her hands were cool and calloused, as though they had spent many hours tending to the fields, but her touch was gentle, betraying the amused smirk on her face.

She freed his hands just in time to avoid the large man as he stood up, pushing Django into Rowyn.

"Whoa, Wilder! Easy there, big guy!"

Rowyn pulled Django toward her to keep him from toppling over. She was surprisingly strong for her small stature, and she pressed her body against his in a way that suggested she didn't mind the close proximity.

Embarrassed, Django tried to regain his footing on his own and re-establish some distance between himself and Rowyn, but he was unable to achieve more than a centimeter or two. Her body was comparatively cool against his skin, unlike the heated bulk of the man mountain Rowyn had called Wilder.

"Sorry, Rowyn," the large man said. "I don't think I've ever been so stiff."

"Wilder!" Taku shouted above the clamor of the prisoners standing up and relieving their sore limbs for the first time in hours.

Django froze, his eyes locked onto the man who had given him his freedom. His eyes were intense, as though high on the thrill of taking over the ship, and he still gripped his rifle intently.

"Taku," the big man replied.

"His name is Wilder?" Django didn't mean to voice the question out loud.

The burly man scowled, but then his face brightened. "Nickname," he clarified.

Taku was all smiles as he approached them. "I was worried they'd have killed you before trying to wrestle you into those cuffs!"

"They weren't going to let these guns go to waste," Wilder replied, raising his arms to draw attention to his impressive biceps.

Taku grinned and nodded. "We'll be back in a few hours. I would love to hear about any information you gleaned from your mission."

"We were unprepared," Wilder replied. "Syndicate's tightened security after the raid on Titan. We'll have to use more stealth than brawn in the future."

Taku laughed. "Don't go getting any ideas about retiring. We're not getting rid of you just yet." Then he turned to Rowyn. "It's good to have you back, Ro. Don't ever scare me like that again."

He clasped an affectionate hand to her shoulder before moving on.

AS THE HAULER carved its way through the expanse back toward Lunar, the atmosphere on board was strikingly different from that of their outbound journey. The ship's interior was awash with the glow of overhead lights, casting an intense illumination on its occupants. Gone was the heavy tension, now replaced by a palpable sense of camaraderie.

Django, although weighed down by fatigue, found himself buoyed by the surrounding energy. He tried to discern more about the people he now found himself, but the animated conversations of those nearby were filled with inside jokes and shared experiences, riddled with jargon from this strange new system.

The hundred or so passengers who filled the cargo hold chatted away, their voices echoing off the ship's metal panels, merging into a single, unintelligible roar.

With little to contribute, Django mostly sat and listened, trying to decipher whatever information he could. He managed to glean some insights from Rowyn, though the details she provided seemed alien to his limited understanding. She revealed her allegiance to the Resurgence movement, and through her, he began to understand that this faction had a singular goal: to dismantle the imposing Syndicate Empire that had cast such a long shadow over many lives.

Wilder had moved deeper into the ship with Taku, and the two of them huddled together just out of Django's earshot.

Rowyn eyed the pair with a worried glare.

"How did you end up here?" Django asked. "On this ship, with these other rebels?"

Rowyn sighed as she brushed a strand of red hair from her face. "We got sloppy. Overconfidence nearly did us all in. The Table—what we call the council of Resurgence leaders— sent us to raid a top-secret Syndicate base on Callisto. A small legion of us were supposed to commandeer a few dozen prototype vessels—experimental military ships that can travel between Mars and Earth in a *week*. Overall, the mission was a success, but we couldn't account for all variables. A series of errors saw our group split up. Some were able to escape with a handful of the ships we were after. Those of us who were left behind were captured. I don't know why the Syndicate soldiers didn't just execute us. They could have. Instead, they knocked us unconscious and sold us off."

"Sounds like corrupt law enforcement is a common theme here," Django said.

Rowyn nodded. "The military and the police are paid well, but the allure of making an extra credit is still enticing. If they think they can get away with it, officers will sell a pris- oner into the slave trade rather than tossing them in a cell. People like you and me, who have a bit of muscle on their bones, we're worth big money; otherwise, they wouldn't bother. The cartel-run mines pay the traders well for people capable of the work. If the authorities didn't sell us off under the table, the Syndicate would have at a premium. The mines don't care where their workers come from. We're victims of our own health."

Django nodded, mulling over Rowyn's words, trying to put the pieces together and wrap his head around the scope of this new universe he'd found himself in. "Did you say your raid was on Callisto? As in Jupiter's moon? Isn't that on the other side of the asteroid belt? Why would Sa'ab drag you back to Earth's moon first?"

Rowyn shrugged, raising an eyebrow. "Where are you from? Most people call it Lunar . . ." She waved it off without waiting for an answer. "Sa'ab probably had another delivery here, or was picking up additional transport. Hell, the 'roid we're aiming for could be on the other side of orbit. Rocks do move out here, ya know."

"But that means you've been on this ship for what . . . months?" Django tried to do some quick math in his head. He didn't know what the tech in this system was capable of, but he estimated a trip from Earth to Callisto would take more time than he'd want to spend tied up on the hauler ship. Hell, even getting to the asteroid belt would have been a long ride.

"Probably two months," she replied indifferently. "It's not like they gave us a calendar back here. We'll find out for sure once we land. It would have been another month or more to get out to the mines."

Django supposed it didn't matter in the end. He was only vaguely interested in the technological capabilities this society possessed. Eventide would have been more enamored by it. All he was concerned about was whether their journey was now taking them back in the right direction, back to where he could begin his search for Eventide.

Without warning, the ship shook violently, slamming Django's head against titanium paneling. Rowyn grabbed onto a bench for support.

"We're entering the gravity field," she explained, sensing

Django's concern as she pushed herself to her feet. "It's nothing to worry about. But we should have been strapped in. We must have lost track of time."

She smirked at him as she pulled herself onto a bench and buckled in.

*I guess it's better than handcuffs.*

Django rubbed the tenderness at the back of his head from where it had struck the bulkhead and followed Rowyn's lead, not wanting to get tossed around again.

"The team will escort us to a transition house once we land," Rowyn explained as Django fumbled with his belt. "You should get your head looked at when we get there."

"Transition house?"

"We want to make it difficult for the Syndicate soldiers to follow us. A TH gives us a chance to stop, assess and throw off anyone who might be on our tail. It's difficult bringing a ship in undetected."

"So, we're not out of the vacuum yet?" he asked.

"Not even close."

The ship shook again, but this time most passengers were ready, having strapped in, or were at least sitting down. Even so, more than one who hadn't were thrown off-balance and found themselves colliding with the paneled floor.

Taku had disappeared elsewhere on the ship. Wilder stumbled along the rows of prisoners-turned-passengers, making his way back to his original seat. His face pale.

Rowyn's face reflected concern. "What's going on?"

"PA ship's apparently spotted us," Wilder said, strapping himself in. "Prepare for a bumpy ride."

"Wait," Django said. A million worst-case scenarios

coursed through his head. "What does that mean? Are they firing at us? Are we going to crash?"

"Keep your voice down, space cadet!" Rowyn hissed. "You're going to start a panic, and that's the last thing we need right now." She turned to Wilder. "What are we looking at?"

"Taku's got the team making an expedited landing. We need to lose them before we dock, and this hauler isn't exactly built for acrobatics. We're headed for Rupes Altai. If we can lose them along the embankment, we can hopefully make it to Spencer's Landing without them following us."

Taku appeared in the aisle. Determination marked his face, but there was an air of desperation surrounding him. Django didn't need to be told that the situation in the cockpit wasn't going according to plan.

"You two," he said, signaling to Wilder and Rowyn. "I need you up front. If we're going to shake these PA bastards, I'm going to need your help."

"What's happened?" Rowyn asked, concern evident on her face, even as she unstrapped herself from her seat, eager to jump at Taku's command.

"We hit a sizeable chunk of debris on the way in. It's chaos up on the bridge. The pilot was too busy trying to avoid the PA and steered us right into it. Communications are down, Rowyn; I need you to check on those systems, see if you can find us a workaround. Wilder." Taku's voice turned more urgent. "I need you up front. Now. One of the pilots got knocked out."

Wilder swiftly unbuckled, then paused. "Django, come

with me. If things go bad, an extra pair of hands would be useful."

Taku hesitated, assessing Django with a scrutinizing gaze.

"*This* is Django?" he asked, in a way that made Django think that somehow the man had heard of him . . . and expected something other than the wide-eyed farmer who sat in front of him.

Taku pursed his lips, seemingly unimpressed, as he continued his survey. "Fine, but stay out of the way unless Wilder says otherwise."

Django, surprised but eager, quickly followed Wilder and Taku through the dimly lit, narrow passageways, his heart pounding. As they stepped into the cockpit, the change in ambiance was palpable. The spacious chamber was bathed in a mosaic of soft, amber glows emanating from an array of faded screens, buttons, and switches that had seen better days. Despite its size, the place felt cramped. Cables snaked haphazardly around the room, and heavy-duty tape had been used to patch up minor breaches in the paneling. A mild, lingering scent of burnt wiring wafted in the stale, recycled air. An old, scuffed pilot's seat, the leather of which had long lost its sheen, sat before a wide, slightly scratched viewport. But it was what lay outside that took Django's breath away—an expansive view of the lunar landscape, marked by the imposing rise that couldn't have been anything but the Rupes Altai.

Half a dozen members of the Resurgence were spread throughout the room, each attending to their designated stations with urgency. The tech seemed archaic compared to the designs and systems on the *Eclipse*, and there was a sense of ruggedness about this old hauler's bridge.

There was no sign of the crew who had manned the ship before the Resurgence boarded, leaving Django to only guess at their fate.

A woman, who Django assumed was the mission's pilot, was slumped over in the cockpit's corner, unconscious. The co-pilot, a wide-eyed young man who was struggling to maneuver the ship alone, looked relieved to see Wilder.

Wilder immediately took the controls, leveling the ship and offering words of reassurance. "It's okay, Anderson. We've gotten out of dicier situations than this."

Anderson visibly breathed a sigh of relief. "This ship doesn't handle well. Plus, I've never had heat on my tail before."

"Don't overthink it. You've been through enough simulations to know how this goes."

Anderson straightened, buoyed by the large man's words.

"We need to use the Rupes Altai's shadows," Taku instructed, his voice tense but steady. "Fly low—but not so close that we kick up dust. We don't want to leave an obvious trail. Once we're deep enough, veer sharply into that canyon." He pointed toward a serpentine trench within the ridge's shadowy embrace. "We'll detach the shuttle we arrived on and crash it into an open plain as a decoy. The dust plume will distract the PA long enough for us to get clear."

Wilder nodded.

Django couldn't help but notice the outline of another ship on a holo-projection descending from the ceiling.

As the ship descended into shadow, the grandeur of the ridge became overwhelmingly apparent. Stretching for hundreds of kilometers, it was no wonder Taku believed it to be the perfect place to lose the Authority. Peaks stretched into the darkness of the starry sky, reflecting sunlight off their surface.

Wilder worked the controls at his station as the ship banked sharply alongside the cliffside. Django fought to keep nausea at bay as the ship's g-force increased with the descent.

Everyone else in the room held onto whatever was nearby as the ship's artificial gravity struggled to keep up with the maneuver.

The walls of the chasm were jagged and irregular, with boulders and rocky outcroppings jutting out threateningly. The ship edged its way along these natural boundaries, its rising walls inducing a sense of claustrophobia Django hadn't realized he possessed.

"Kill the engines," Taku ordered. "Are they still following us?"

The holo-projections had gone dark, with the giant rock wall separating them from their pursuers and the rest of Lunar.

"It's hard to tell," Anderson replied. "This cliff obscures our instruments as much as it does theirs."

"I'm not picking up anything on comms, either," Rowyn chimed in. "If they haven't given up, they're being quiet about it."

Tense moments passed, the only sound the hum of the ship's systems, as they waited for confirmation that the threat had passed.

"Follow the Altai for as long as it makes sense," Taku said. "Then keep us as low to the ground as you can until we reach Spencer's Landing. But keep an eye out. If we catch the PA's eye again, we can't be seen pulling into the dock. Rowyn, keep monitoring the PA channels. Let me know if you pick up anything that indicates they've spotted us."

Wilder grunted a reply. Rowyn responded with a thumbs-up.

Django couldn't peel his eyes from the viewport. There was so much land ahead of them; so much rock and terrain to cover. How anyone could spot them in the wide stretch of emptiness was beyond his comprehension.

The realization made him feel small and insignificant. As though nothing he could possibly do in this vast system would ever make a difference.

AS TAKU HAD SUGGESTED, Wilder and the Resurgence team had slowly steered their ship across the gray, lifeless surface of Lunar, tentatively hugging craters and canyons. Fortunately, the PA seemed to have given up their chase of the rogue ship, and the team navigated toward Spencer's Landing with no further interruptions.

Once the ship docked, its passengers didn't need to be told to disembark. They were grateful for the chance to stretch their legs and set foot on land once again. The stream of people caught Django, Rowyn, and Wilder, pushing them toward the exit.

Django had expected to return to the space dock from

which they'd departed, but the hangar bore a closer resemblance to a cave. An opening above them allowed a stream of sunlight to cascade into the subterranean chamber. The hole was large enough for several ships to pass in and out, but from above, it merely appeared to be another cavity in the moon's cratered surface.

"What is this place?" he asked inquisitively.

Rowyn smiled knowingly. "We can't very well go through inspection with a stolen ship and a hundred passengers scheduled for arrival at Psyche 16, now can we?"

Django shrugged. That made sense, but it was yet another reminder that he was a foreigner in this world.

Even if it wasn't the port that the slave vessel had set out from, it was *a* port, large enough for a dozen or more ships.

Instead of the open sky nightmare of the main docks, rectangular pockets of light streamed through the openings in the rock above them. These gateways in the rock were just large enough for ships to travel through, clearly intended for discretion against anyone observing from above.

"So, this is some sort of secret docking facility?" Django asked. "One controlled by the Resurgence?"

"More like a private landing pad," Wilder replied. "The owners are sympathizers. It helps that the entrances are discreet." Then he smiled and said with a wink, "Most of our secret bases are on Lunar's dark side."

Taku shot Wilder a harsh look, and Rowyn grimaced. That particular piece of information wasn't supposed to be shared.

The group streamed down the ship's ramp with the rest of the new arrivals. At the end of a boardwalk, near several chambers dug into the moon rock, three figures stood waiting. As though waiting for family members returning from an expected journey and not captives being rescued.

If only he had any family left to wait for him.

Taku pushed his way to the front of the group, barking commands the entire way.

As the three figures came into view, Django had to do a double take to ensure he wasn't hallucinating. There was no way the scene before him was real and not the by-product of a concussion from slamming his skull against the slave ship's bulkhead.

Taku was talking excitedly with one man, clasping him on the soldier and bringing him in for an embrace, as though they were old war buddies.

A man Django immediately recognized.

Uncle Marvin.

Mikka
Shackleton City

MIKKA NEEDED a hot shower after visiting Aries's office. There was something about the encounter that had both made her skin crawl and got her blood flowing. On some level, the commander was clearly getting to her.

*Maybe I should make it a cold one.*

Either way, it had been two days since the *Redemption* had landed on Lunar, and Mikka was conscious she was starting to smell.

Skyscrapers towered above her and Kiara as they walked through the streets of Shackleton City. Tightly packed buildings and narrow pathways were illuminated by vibrant neon signs, advertising everything imaginable. The potent scent of molten metal lingered in the air, accompanied by the occasional waft of sewage.

The orange banners of the city hung from balconies and flagpoles alike, defying the absence of Lunar's natural gravity that should have been one sixth of its current strength; instead, enhanced artificial gravity pulled them closer to the ground, proclaiming the dominion the Syndicate held over the forces of nature.

As they meandered toward the residential building housing their temporary quarters, Mikka was lost deep in her thoughts. She wasn't sure which made her sicker to her stomach: that she had aided a known terrorist or that David Aries had asked her out on a date.

*Was it even a date?* Maybe she was reading too much into things. Perhaps he just wanted to discuss business. Another delivery, perhaps? *That* would make much more sense.

It wasn't as though she'd hadn't fantasized about Aries before. In a very literal sense of the word, he had been her savior, right back when he'd let her slip past his watch in the trash heap, elegantly nicknamed the Boneyard, and had allowed her to purchase and restore the *Redemption.* Him turning a blind eye then had allowed her to put her pirating days behind her and work legitimate contracts for the past eight years.

But eight years was a long time, and Aries held a new position now. He was as much of a ruthless tyrant as any other Syndicate leader, no matter what he claimed motivated his ambitions. A pair of broad, muscular shoulders couldn't change that.

"I still don't understand what he gets out of this."

Kiara had been distant since they'd left Syndicate HQ, but now she seemed to want to speak her mind. Mikka could sympathize with the struggle tearing at her navigator's thoughts; it closely mirrored the same conflict that raged in her own mind. "Taking care of your mother. Taking care of my girls. If you're obligated to be his . . . *employee* or whatever, that's one thing—but what happens if *I* don't want to be? If I wanted to back out, what happens then? Does he take everything back?"

"Usually, employee benefits end when the contract does. You know how these things go."

"Well, Betsy messaged me. Says she's never seen any place like this apartment. You know I'll do anything for my kids, Meeks."

Betsy was the caregiver to Kiara's two girls, a woman who Kiara trusted and paid a fair wage. In the past, it had been a struggle for Mikka and Kiara to earn enough to pay for both Mikka's mother and Betsy and still have enough left over for themselves, but somehow, they'd managed it.

"And that's *why* he's doing it," Mikka assured her. "I requested you as my second in command. He wants to ensure you stick around to keep me happy. That's the difference between these larger government gigs and working in the shadows for privateers. A few benefits and a little security."

"Something about it still doesn't feel right," Kiara said resolutely. "Nobody's ever done shit for us before—not like this. There's always a catch . . ."

Mikka grinned. "Maybe all our hard work is finally paying off?"

Kiara scoffed. "There's no way you believe that. What has the Syndicate ever done for *you*? The same as it's done for anyone else: *nothing*. This contract makes me uneasy, Meeks. I really wish you'd step down."

"*You* can do whatever you want," Mikka said breezily.

"But you remember that fine Monroe got slapped on my ship? Aries got me out of that. I *owe* him. And that's on top of him helping me to break out the *Redemption* without turning me in and the place he's set up for Mom. For the first time in my life, I'm able to provide a decent home for her. I can't just turn my back on that. It's the whole reason I quit being a pirate."

Kiara cocked her head and gave Mikka a questioning look, reminding her the navigator was the one person who knew it wasn't the *whole* reason she'd given up piracy. Wisely, Kiara chose not to contradict her.

Instead, she changed tack. "You don't even know what kind of arrangement he's got her in. And what exactly are you going to do? He does you one favor and now you're his Domani forever?"

Mikka snorted disdainfully. "Do you see me tickling his boys? I've got no other choice, Ki. Without his help, I wouldn't be able to keep the *Redemption*, which means Mom would be as good as dead."

"For Pluto's sake, Meeks! You keep bragging about how you were once the best goddamn space pirate in the Loop! Surely you can come up with something better than this. Some other way to help her out that doesn't involve Aries's handouts."

"I *was* the best pirate, Ki. Past tense. If anything, I think the last few days have proven my skills aren't what they used to be. Forget what I said before—you *know* the real reason I had to leave, and who had to pay the price for that. I nearly lost everything. I can't let people down like that again."

"You've let one event define the past decade. Maybe it's time to move on."

"I *am* moving on. *This* is me moving on. Look, I appreciate you have your concerns, and I'd be lying if I said I had none myself, but right now, what I need is a job. And it's a hell of a lot better of a chance than most people get. Hell, it's more than I *deserve*."

"Sell your soul to the devil for a dime. What's it going to cost you in the end?"

"I lost my soul a long time ago, Ki. I'm still trying to cover the debt."

Kiara sighed. "We all make bad decisions. It's part of being human. But those decisions don't define us; it's how we respond that makes us who we are."

Kiara was right, to a point; she couldn't let her past continue to pull her down, not when there were so many good things happening. But she also couldn't jeopardize the present, not when the choice impacted more than just her.

Finally, she said, "Everything I've worked for over the past eight years has been about redemption. I know I'll never atone for my sins, but I have to try. For all the shit I've had to pull through, I finally feel like it's paying off. This could be how I make a *real* difference. I can't screw this up."

Mikka ran a hand through her coarse hair as they pushed their way past the constructs of the Upper Rim. It always amazed Mikka that she had spent most of her life living on Lunar's surface, and yet the Upper Rim still felt alien to her. Given how different it was to the Tubes, it might as well have been another planet.

Mikka preferred the crowds in some of the other colonies.

Ceres, Mars, and Europa all had a vibe that somehow seemed more real. The people there had worked hard to earn the little they had.

Men and women in suits of all colors and Lunar high fashion passed by. High towers stretched to the depths of the black sky, their paneled walls lit with holo-screens advertising everything from paella to alcohol and one-night-only Domani. Cocktail lounges were a favorite on the Upper Rim, and for those with wilder tastes, illegal drugs were easy to find if you knew where to ask.

"Doesn't it make you sick?" Kiara asked, nodding to the billboards. "The excess? The greed? The Upper Rim waste their credits on vices when all those beneath the surface would step over their dead relative for a scrap of food. *This* is the world your friend Aries helped to build."

"You know it does," Mikka replied. "You think I've suddenly stopped seeing it or something? But nothing I've done in my life has shifted things one way or the other to help change this."

A holo-screen advertisement sprang to life as they passed. Two semi-transparent wrestlers—large shirtless men tattooed in luminescent ink—pitched head-to-head in a life-sized grapple filled the walkway, as though the match was happening right before their eyes. Both men appeared evenly matched until one made a flashy move, revealing a cybernetic arm that was used to toss his opponent to the ground in a crushing blow.

The ad was for a body mod artist. The augment would have been illegal in any Syndicate-approved fighting league, of course, but there were plenty of back alley brawls that encouraged a little technological assistance. Without the watchful eyes of the regulators, anything that enhanced the spectacle tempted patrons to up their bets, and there were plenty of credits to be made in underground fight clubs.

Aries's receptionist had given Mikka two addresses before she had left his office—two separate residential buildings in Aldrin Square. One was for her new quarters, though, if she were being honest, Mikka would have been just as comfortable sleeping on the *Redemption*. The small ship had been her home for much of the past decade, and it held as much room as she realistically needed.

The second address, however, which was only a few buildings away from the first, was where Aries had secured new homes for both Mikka's mother and Kiara and her kids.

Mikka considered her options. After the week she'd had, she would be prepared to kill for that hot shower—something, admittedly, she couldn't get on the *Redemption*. But first, she needed to see the place Aries had set her mother up in, to make sure she was okay with the new arrangement.

She caught her breath as they approached the address. The high-rise looked much the same as the others surrounding it, blending in with the skyscape. Mikka didn't know what she had been expecting, but the luxury residential block rose majestically into the black sky with lush green leaves decorating its balconies and crisp, clean lighting that set it apart from the gaudy holo-projections of the main street. There were no ads adorning this building; instead, its endless glass windows were pristine, and the greenery must have taken a lot of work and genetic engineering to thrive outside of the farms and orchards that had been specifically engineered to support bio-life.

The building's decadent pillars were reminiscent of architecture Mikka had seen on holo-feed images of Earth. Small statuettes of Roman gods decorated the façade surrounding the entrance, as though the ancient deities protected the inhabitants from vengeful demons of the underworld.

There was even a woman standing guard at the front door, dressed from head to toe in a black, form-fitting catsuit, as though she were about to film one of the spy movies of old. An energy pistol hung at her hip.

Mikka nodded to the guard, who eyed her suspiciously, right until the moment Mikka passed her arm over the keypad on the front door and the automated locking system lit up green. A genderless face projected from the screen, so lifelike that it prompted Mikka to take a step back.

*Almost* lifelike, save for the empty eyes that looked straight into her soul. Mikka hoped it wasn't reading anything deeper than her retina.

"Welcome, Miss Jenax. Your mother is located in Suite 2501," the abiotic face announced.

The holo turned to face Kiara and performed the same scan. Kiara shuddered under the machine's gaze.

"Welcome to your new residence, Ms. Ryson," the holo-projection continued. "Your children, Anna and Isabelle, are waiting for you in Suite 2502. Please proceed to the lift in the center of the lobby."

Kiara eyed Mikka nervously as the glass door to the

building slid open and the guard stepped aside to allow them entry, with no change to her expression.

'Open-plan' would have been an understatement. Decorative cushioned chairs were arranged neatly, separating sections of the floor into casual seating areas. All the furniture was empty, as if waiting to be used, but it appeared so fresh and clean that maybe they never had been. There was no reception desk, but Mikka spotted several mobile holo-screens that she imagined would project the same genderless face that had greeted them outside. Ornate fountains gushed throughout the lobby, washing the space in white noise and a hot humidity that Mikka hadn't encountered outside of a geyser experience on Io. The verdant greenery she could only compare to images of the jungles on Earth she'd seen as a child. Images of Earth, the way it used to be, before the forests had burned during the Climate Wars.

Blue holographic displays pointed the way to the elevator that sat in the center of it all. Bright lights encircled the space in such an obvious manner that Mikka questioned whether the lighting was always present or if it was specifically designed to guide their way.

"This way, please." The voice that had accompanied the face outside emanated from the walls, confirming Mikka's suspicions about the virtual assistant.

The elevator door slid open, and the two women stepped within its maw.

"Is it just me," Kiara said, "or does this building give you the creeps?"

Mikka cleared her throat, but even so, her voice peaked at a higher pitch than she'd intended. "Definitely not just you."

The elevator door closed, and for a moment, a wave of panic washed over her. She didn't enjoy being trapped in such a confined space, especially one she had no control over.

Before she'd finished the thought, though, the doors chimed as they slid open again. "Welcome to the twenty-fifth floor."

"Did we even move?" Kiara thought out loud.

A short hall, as elaborate as the entrance, greeted them. There were two doors on the left, and two doors on the right.

The holo-projected lighting split off in either direction. Each path was labeled. The projected lights to the right lit up in purple and read "Mikka Jenax," while the ones to the left, in blue, read "Kiara Ryson."

"This is some *next-level* shit right here," Kiara said, confounded. She hefted her pack higher onto her shoulders and turned to follow her designated path. "Why do I feel like I'm about to get murdered? I'll see you on the other side, I guess."

The door to Mikka's mother's new apartment slid open before Mikka came to it. 'Next-level' didn't even begin to describe this place. The projected text faded behind her as she entered.

"Mikka? Mikka Jenax?"

A stout woman with wide-set eyes and small hands looked up from a sofa. She held out a tablet projecting a Syndicate newscast and put it aside as she stood, brushing her hands on her outfit and smiling eagerly. The woman embodied the opposite of her mother's previous caregiver, Tabitha; she was so full of positive energy, it literally bubbled out of her. Her smile was warm, and she genuinely appeared happy to see her. "I'm your mother's new carer, Olivia. I've been expecting you."

*I bet you have.* Mikka would have been surprised if the virtual assistant hadn't notified the woman of her arrival.

None of her wildest expectations could have prepared Mikka for the place. It was certainly opulent for an off-the-books contractor. The room itself was bright and open, with ceilings that rose at least twelve feet high. The kitchen and living room were adjoined in the same space. Each section was just as spacious as entire properties down in the Tubes. Behind Olivia, floor-to-ceiling windows covered the two outer walls of the suite, and neon lights and holo-projected images from the streets below cast unnatural colors on an otherwise sunny day. Some screens were so bright that their displays reflected into the apartment itself, reds and blues streaming through the glass and bouncing off the interior screens and walls.

Olivia must have noticed Mikka's distraction with the display and commanded the curtains to close via voice-activated control. A semi-opaque screen slid across the room from either end of the windows, blocking out the bulk of the artificial light and noise while still allowing some of the sun's natural rays to come through. The dancing colors ceased, allowing the white and sharp grays of the room to exude their own radiance.

"You must be eager to see your mother," the woman said, flapping her hands forward and ignoring Mikka's awe. She hopped through the room and waved a hand. "Come."

Not waiting for Mikka, Olivia took off down an unassuming hall that cut deeper into the apartment than seemed possible. There were five doorways: two on either side of the hall and one at the end.

"Your mother's room is the second door on the right."

Olivia's feet barely touched the ground as she skittered along the floor. If Mikka's feet hadn't been firmly planted, she would have thought someone had distorted the apartment's gravity. "My door is first, and the bathroom is at the end of the hall. There's a room for you on the left if you choose to stay here, and the fourth door is for the other caregiver, Maria."

"Two caregivers? Is that necessary?"

Olivia smiled a toothy grin. "Oh, yes. Commander Aries requested your mother receive the finest care, but Maria and I have our own families to take care of, too, so we split the work."

*Two* caregivers. Her mother now had someone looking out for her *at all times*. Until now, she had barely afforded someone checking in twice a day. She fought back the tears that threatened to appear and simply nodded, instead of saying something that would be guaranteed to open the floodgates.

The door to her mother's room opened and the little willpower Mikka had summoned melted like butter.

The room was larger than her mother's entire old apartment. Sunlight streamed through the open window, revealing a bed with a full mattress and teal sheets. Against the wall sat a dark gray sofa, sitting below a shelf that proudly displayed her mother's old knitted projects; a hobby she had been forced to abandon long ago, once the Lunar sickness had taken hold.

But that wasn't what caused the tears to gush down Mikka's face.

From her spot on the couch, her mother looked directly at Mikka, recognition in her eyes, and smiled.

---

"SHE'S STILL NOT TALKING." Olivia rushed to Mikka's mother's side to adjust the pillows that rested behind her. "But recognition has begun creeping through. She definitely seems to know who you are, but she's taking her time to warm to *my* presence."

Her mother was still gaunt, her dark cheeks hollow, nearly skeletal, her brown eyes sunken. Her hair had gone white, but it was clean, at least. Olivia was clearly doing a better job of cleaning the woman than Tabitha ever had. That wicked woman had staged a break-in at her mother's home and called the Front, claiming Mikka had been the offender. Luckily for Mikka, that was the second time David Aries had intervened in her life.

Now, her mother was sitting upright—with recognition in her eyes. When was the last time she had showed any glimmer of awareness?

"How is this possible? She was barely conscious when I left her two days ago. There's no cure for Lunar sickness."

Olivia nodded. "You're right, there isn't. She's not cured, I'm afraid, and she likely won't progress much further. That said, I think she's been trying to speak, asking for water and to use the bathroom."

*A miracle!*

"But how?"

"The seed you've been sending the last couple days. It's had a remarkable effect. To be honest, I've never seen Corielus work so well or so fast. It's almost as if this were a strain from the *Infinity*."

*The seed that I've been sending?*

"I haven't sent any . . ." Then the realization struck her. "How long has it been coming?"

"Just the past two days. We've been giving it to her three times a day," Olivia continued, "and she perked right up even after the first couple doses."

Since the *Redemption* landed.

*Abigail.*

But how? Abigail had abandoned the ship. Mikka had assumed the Port Authority would have impounded the seed and sold it off, or at least cached it in the Syndicate infirmaries on the Upper Rim. If they had realized the seed's source, they could have made a sizeable fortune.

Or had Aries discovered it and shipped it? That couldn't be right. If so, why would Olivia think *she* had been sending it? Regardless of Aries's continued charity toward her, he hardly seemed the type to pass on taking credit.

It was all too much to take in.

Her mother's smile had faded, and she had gone back to staring at something that was invisible to anyone else in the room. But even sitting upright and conscious was ten steps ahead of anything she'd achieved during the past six years.

Mikka smiled and wiped away her tears. David Aries had kept his word and then some. For the first time in a decade, it seemed like everything was going to be okay.

Mikka
Shackleton City

MIKKA COULDN'T REMEMBER the last time she'd been on an actual date.

The clock embedded in the wall panel of her new apartment blinked 19:30.

She brought her glass of wine to her lips and let the tart liquid slide down her throat. The bottle had been waiting for her when she'd arrived as a welcome home gift of sorts. She took another swig for good measure and felt the alcohol go straight to her head. She knew it was a mistake drinking before her date even started; Aries was wily, and she needed a clear head to avoid agreeing to anything she hadn't thought through. But in truth, she was beyond nervous, and the wine helped to calm her. Drinking was how she maintained her cool in tight situations, though it sometimes led to brash decisions.

And sometimes it led to horrible mistakes.

Mikka smoothed out the wrinkles in the scarlet dress Aries had picked out for her. The outfit was ridiculous. Not that it didn't look good—she looked *fabulous*—but the dress was easily more expensive than any other article of clothing she had ever owned. Come to think of it, it was probably more expensive than anything she'd ever owned, the *Redemption* aside. She shuddered to think of how many people those credits could have helped. A dress from one of the Rim's high-end designers would have cost enough credits to feed several families living in the Tubes for a *month*.

It was criminal. All for a dress.

But it was a simple enough decision to put the thing on. If she hoped to receive more direct answers from Aries, she needed to impress him somehow, and if she had to wear an expensive dress and high heels to dinner to accomplish that, then so be it.

She couldn't help but admire herself in the mirror as she walked by. Hell, she'd spill her secrets for someone who cleaned up this good. Hopefully, Aries felt the same.

Not that Mikka knew what secrets she expected to learn. The commander had already committed her to a verbal contract, though perhaps she could get a better sense of her role in his plans. She would find it hard to believe Aries had waited ten years to approach her based on her good looks alone.

There was something else at play here.

Allowing herself to get comfortable with him was a bad idea. Getting more deeply involved with Aries and his plans to undermine the Syndicate Empire—whatever they were—was a mistake. But after seeing the residence he'd provided for her mother, how could she refuse something as benign as dinner? So, she'd pushed the thought aside and decided to make the most of the situation. She would use whatever Aries was after to her own advantage, allowing his hospitality to take care of her mother for as long as possible. Or as long as the *Infinity* seed continued to be delivered, at least.

Besides, the apartment Aries had provided for *her* was no less exquisite. It was smaller, admittedly, with only one bedroom, but it wasn't like she needed the space, and she much preferred the view overlooking the edge of Shackleton crater and the forests on its outskirts that were cultivated for oxygen production.

Mikka looked at the clock again. 19:35. She was ready early. Aries had said he would send a car for her at 20:00, so she had time to kill. Just enough to drink her glass of wine and drown some of the butterflies that had made their way into her stomach.

A few minutes later, a buzzing noise alerted her to someone at the door. It had to be the ride Aries had sent for her, but it was over twenty minutes early. Lucky she'd got ready early; she would have hated to make him wait for twenty minutes while she finished putting on her eyeliner.

Mikka threw back the rest of her wine—there was no point in pretending she wasn't going to be at least a little buzzed over dinner—and then lifted a napkin from beside the bar to wipe the lipstick that had smeared from her glass. She walked over to the door and pressed her forearm to the panel. "This is Mikka," she said in as sweet of a voice as she could muster.

"Good to hear your voice, love. Would you mind buzzing us in?"

Mikka froze with her hand on the panel. Her gaze instinctively flitted around the lavish apartment apprehensively, as though somebody would reveal themselves, waiting for this moment. As if Syndicate Front guards might be ready to jump out of the couch cushions.

She hit the entry button without comment, too shocked to respond. Too *worried* that someone might recognize the wanted pirate standing at her door.

An apartment paid for by the very people hunting her down.

"What the hell are you doing here?" Mikka asked exasperatedly as Abigail Monroe strode nonchalantly into the room.

"Nice to see you too, love." Abigail stopped and arched a thin, white eyebrow in surprise. "And I've gotta say, I like what's going on *here*." Abigail's hand hovered over Mikka's chest. The dress was a little more revealing than Mikka would have chosen to wear, but she couldn't say she'd given it much thought until Abigail had pointed it out.

She rolled her eyes, although she wasn't sure whether it was at Monroe for highlighting it or Aries for picking it out for her.

"You can't be here . . ."

"Why? Didn't you miss me? You worried about the Front showing up? In case you hadn't noticed, I'm quite adept at giving them the slip."

"Oh, I noticed, all right. You've been MIA since we

landed. You abandoned me and Kiara to the PA." She wanted to both strangle and hug the pirate at once.

Abigail let her gaze wander around the suite. "You seem to have done all right for yourself. Besides, you may remember, there's a bounty on my head. What did you expect me to do? I don't think your commander friend would have let me get away with as much . . ." She waved her hand above her head in a circular motion, gesturing to the entire suite. "*Flair.*"

Mikka gritted her teeth. "Aries had to haul our asses out of detainment! And all because your pal Marvin decided to smuggle stowaways aboard my ship!"

Abigail nodded absently as she surveyed the room. "Yes, something we only found out about afterwards, actually. Marvin was quite upset to learn they'd been hauled off. He's off to find the boy now."

"The boy? Django? What about the young woman who was with him?"

"Sold to a Domani trader—and a pretty high-end one, by all accounts. She'll be a bit harder to trace, but I'm sure he'll find her, too."

*Domani? Those PA bastards must be dipping their hands in the cookie jar again.*

That would make it tough to find her. The Domani business could be more secretive than the FLOW stations. Aries had mentioned that he had intended to talk to Django, but if the Authority officers had sold the woman, it was likely they had sold him, too.

Aries would have the resources to find them if he felt a

reason to bother, but Mikka suspected two missing persons wouldn't be much more than a passing curiosity to him.

"So, why are you all glammed up, love? Date tonight? Should I be jealous?"

Mikka raised an eyebrow, unsure of whether the pirate was serious or not. "I do have a date. So, if you don't mind . . ."

"I don't mind at all, love. We've all got to scratch those urges while we're still young."

Movement behind the pirate caught Mikka's eye. A young man—a boy, really; younger than Django, fifteen at most—peered around the door behind Abigail with a peculiar mix of uncertainty and confidence.

Abigail followed her gaze. "Ah! Yes, I nearly forgot. This is Zee."

"Zee?"

The boy's dark hair only partially covered the painted blue stripes that ran across his scalp and met at the edges of his forehead. Two thin stripes also cut down his cheeks, running vertically under each eye. One stripe was black, leading to his right eye, with no iris—just an eerie black abyss that appeared to be all pupil. The other line across his left cheek glowed yellow, as though revealing a fire burning within the boy's face. The glow carried through to his eye, though it then dimmed into a muted halo, framing an iris that was unnaturally blue.

David Aries had a tattoo-implant under his left eye, a small triangle that glowed, but it was a mere reflector compared to the illumination this marking provided. It had to have been an implant, but Mikka had never seen anything like it, and while Aries's implant likely improved his eyesight, she couldn't imagine what the glow behind this youth's eye might accomplish, or why it was juxtaposed so heavily against the darkness of his right.

"Zee was the brains behind tracking you down the first time we met," Abigail said, leaning against the wall panel. "He's got a nose for talent, so to speak."

"Tracking *me*?" Mikka crossed her arms and leaned back. "I seem to remember you putting out a distress call shortly before your ship *exploded*. You had less than twenty minutes before the escape pod cooked you in the Earth's atmosphere. You're telling me this kid *orchestrated* that?"

"Water under the bridge." Abigail waved a hand dismissively as she continued to scan the apartment with lustful eyes. "These are some *nice* digs, love. It's amazing what the Syndicate's blood money can stretch to these days."

"Aries isn't like that." Mikka surprised herself by how quickly she jumped to the commander's defence, but she believed the sentiment behind her words. "He's working to change things."

"*Right.*" Abigail scoffed. "Change things for whose benefit?"

"And what would you know?" Mikka snapped.

"Aries won't bring unity, only hardship." The boy, Zee, spoke for the first time. His soft voice had an ominous tone—hollow, as though he wasn't speaking the words, but someone was speaking *through* him.

"Tell me again about this kid?" Mikka directed her question to Abigail.

"They call him the Wayfinder," she replied. "Off-market

implants installed in a Portuguese market on Io produced some . . . *unforeseen* side effects."

Unintended consequences of implants were common, especially outside of sanctioned, sterile Syndicate clinics. Black market augmentations were a lucrative underground industry, despite the high risk of walking away with a few negative side effects. Brain and nerve damage were the most common with facial augments. Burns were another. She'd seen the consequences countless times, dealt by back-alleyed dealers in the street markets of the system's outer moons and asteroid colonies. This kid had obviously received heavy ocular mods, which were the riskiest to perform. Anyone who sought those on the black market was taking their own life into their hands.

Judging by the age of the kid, it probably hadn't been his decision, and anyone who would force those kinds of implants on a kid or be prepared to perform the surgeries was nothing short of monstrous, in Mikka's opinion. But life was cheap that far out in the system, and it was possible some rich cartel leader on Io had experimented on an abductee before chancing it on themselves. It wouldn't have surprised Mikka if the kid had lost more than one neuron in the process.

"That's the risk you take with that kind of shit," Mikka said. "Why's he here?"

Abigail smiled. "Zee's the way forward. He sees outcomes. Statistics. Think of him like a walking algorithm."

"The 'way forward' to *what*, Abi? Listen, my ride is going to be here soon. Can whatever this is wait until later?"

Zee reached over and gripped Mikka's arm, pulling his face in line with hers and his one dark eye meeting her own.

His blue eye had disappeared, leaving a seemingly empty socket bathed in yellow light. At this proximity, it was too bright for Mikka to look at.

"Don't trust Aries," he warned.

There wasn't worry or panic on the kid's face as he issued the advice. He was simply reporting something dangerous, like '*don't step outside the airlock without your helmet on.*'

"Listen, Abi, as fascinating as this is . . ." Mikka said, shaking the kid off her arm. "What did you come here for?"

"First, let me ask you something, love: What are you after? You've got the meds for your mom. You've got this swanky new apartment. What gives? Why are you still dancing to the Syndicate's tune?"

"Are you serious? Where do you think all of this is *coming* from? I'm indebted to Aries," Mikka replied indignantly, side-eying Zee in the process. "He's helped me a couple times, and now he's calling in the favor. In return, he's providing for my mother. I work for him now."

"Sweetheart . . ." Abigail said softly, putting a hand between Zee and Mikka. She must have sensed that Mikka wasn't loving the invasion of her personal space, as she pulled Zee a few feet away. "I know you stumbled across me up there, but it was no accident. Zee saw it all. You, Marvin, the kids . . . They're all involved in this. I told you then that luck had favored me that day, and I meant it. Your decisions will determine the fate of this war and the future of humanity."

Mikka snorted derisively. *What the hell is she talking about?*

"Is that what this is?" she fired back. "Recruitment? I already told you, my pirating days are over. I have more sins to atone for than one life can bear." She took a deep breath, tired of having to defend herself on that particular point. "I'm done racking up debt on my soul. Aries has offered me a job that takes care of my mother. I can live out my days knowing I've done that much, at least."

Abigail stood her ground. "You and I both know a few deliveries and a romp in the hay aren't going to cover your sins."

Mikka would have throttled Abigail if there wasn't a fifteen-year-old boy standing by as witness.

"Join me. Join *us*. We're going to make a difference. You don't have to work for the man who's going to heap ruin onto this system."

"And what *exactly* are you going to do?" Mikka asked. "You think a few pirates are going to change the world, Abi? You need to give up the rum; it's rotting your brain! You can fight the Empire, but it'll sure as shit come back and bite you in the ass. The Syndicate has had *centuries* to build up their defences. You think a few pirates are a match for that? I've been there, done that. Tried to steal from the rich and give to the poor. Got my ass handed to me and a lot of good people killed because of it. I have no interest in doing that again."

"Many people will be killed," Zee said, the glow in his left eye pulsing. "There's no escaping that."

"Love," Abigail stepped in. "This isn't just a few pirate ships. Why do you think we pulled Marvin out of the *Eclipse*?"

"Marvin's a terrorist. And if I'd have known who he was, I would have left him where we found him. I would *never* have agreed to let him board my ship."

"He's the leader of the Resurgence. Hell, he's the *founder*. We need him. And if it weren't for Zee, we'd never have known he was still alive. I didn't know how it would all pan out at the time, but getting you to go to the *Eclipse* was no accident. Zee saw it all."

"The Resurgence is just another terrorist group, Abi. Inciting riots has never gotten anyone anywhere except out the airlock. I'd rather be a pirate."

"It's not like that. The Resurgence isn't about terror; it's about *freedom*. It's a whole movement. They've been prepping to take the new Prefect down, the Earth's leaders, the Council, the whole damn bloody Syndicate! Marvin's got a trump card in one of those kids we snagged along with us. The wheels of his plan are already in motion."

Mikka crossed her arms. "Those kids that were sold to slavers, you mean?"

"A minor setback. Like I said, Marvin's on it."

"Are you hearing yourself? You've recruited a kid from Io, two kids from a FLOW—and you expect *what* from me? That I'm going to turn my back on all this to go back to running? Hell, the people you're going up against blew your ship out of the sky! If I hadn't come along to save your pasty ass, we wouldn't be having this conversation!"

"I've told you, love, you're just not listening. The Empire *must* fall. And a turncoat Syndicate commander won't do the trick. You're just replacing one tyrant with another."

"Aries hasn't told me what his plans are yet. But at least *he* has the backing of soldiers, troops, supplies . . . You're talking about a *system-wide* uprising. That's not something a handful of rebels will be able to pull off."

"I wasn't saying it'd be easy—but it would be preferable."

"You really think it's possible? Taking out a few leaders isn't going to bend the will of the powers that be. The Syndicate will just elect a new Council."

"The future's just a matter of playing the odds, love. You let us worry about that for now."

"Look, we're going round in circles. Why are you here, Abi? What are you asking me to do?"

"You need to kill David Aries."

If this hadn't been the only time Mikka had seen Abigail Monroe straight-faced, she would have thought the pirate was kidding. She nearly laughed.

"I thought you said this kid can see the future. If that's true, you already know the likelihood of that happening."

Zee looked up, the light in his glowing eye striking, the depth of his black pupil haunting. "You *will* kill Aries, Mikka Jenax. But by the time you're convinced it's the right path, you'll wish you had done it sooner."

Django
Spencer's Landing, Lunar

"THAT MAN IS MY UNCLE!" Django shouted to Rowyn. She stood right next to him, but he still wasn't sure if she'd heard.

His heart raced as he tried to squeeze between his fellow passengers, but they were already tightly pushing against one another along the ramp.

In the distance, a sharp buzzing sent an echo through the port. The entire group grew suddenly quiet, everyone pausing in their forward advance, but the calm lasted only for a moment before the volume exploded to new heights and the rush of the crowd renewed. The group flowed forward at a pace that threatened to trample anyone who couldn't maintain their footing.

Whatever had caused the sound, it wasn't good.

Resurgence fighters who had been standing at ease beside Marvin ran toward the far side of the chamber, in the direction the noise was coming from. Two others appeared from the depths of the rock tunnels and ran the opposite way.

Marvin stood firm as Taku approached and they exchanged tense words that were too distant for Django to hear.

Marvin nodded and ran ahead, signaling for the group to follow him as he maneuvered through a gap in the rock wall, only wide enough for two or three people to pass through at a time. Taku didn't follow, or at least, not right away, instead organizing the swell of passengers into groups of three and sending them through behind Marvin, telling them to hurry.

Someone was coming, and Django could only guess they weren't thrilled about the Resurgence diverting a cargo hauler filled with prisoners away from the mines.

Rowyn cursed under her breath, confirming his thoughts. "Someone's tracked us here."

"Who? Why?"

"Maybe the Front, but more likely private guns, Corpo Patrol, hired by the cartels who run the mines. It was only a matter of time before they figured out their shipment got rerouted back to the surface."

As quickly as the group moved down the ramp and into the tunnels beyond, it still felt like it was taking forever for the crowd to get where they needed to go, and with every passing second, the weapons' fire grew louder.

Django could hear multiple blaster discharges in the distance now, interspersed with a few salvos of gunfire.

Despite his best efforts, Django remained at the back of the group. Along with Rowyn and Wilder, who seemed to be prioritizing the people around them ahead of their own safety, they were some of the last to make it to the opening. He managed a glance over his shoulder and saw the backs of several men and women who were firing weapons into a space out of Django's line of sight, but the resultant flashes of light told him that whoever they were fighting couldn't be far away.

Taku shoved Django roughly through the door, along with a couple of people who trailed behind them.

"Let's go!" Taku shouted from the fissure, his call directed at the fighters who were now being pushed back toward the entrance.

"It's too late!" the closest soldier, a man probably no older than Django, yelled back. He wore a helmet with the visor pulled down, but his dark lips and bearded chin were visible, as was the panic that caused his entire body to shake. "We need to buy you some time, Taku. Just go! We'll lead them away!"

Taku gave a thumbs-up. "Hold them off for as long as you can, then get to the transition house. And make sure you're not followed."

The man grunted and disappeared from view. Django had a sinking feeling they wouldn't be seeing him again.

Taku touched his wrist to several spots around the cave's entrance, prompting small red indicator lights to activate at each spot he touched.

"Everyone, get as far in as you can!" he ordered. "We need to get that door closed!"

*They're sealing us in.* Whatever Taku had just activated was going to bring the entrance down, shutting out their pursuers and closing off their ability to follow them.

Worried that they'd be trapped, Django searched the space feverishly, hoping for another exit. At the far end of the enclave, a tunnel opened out into darkness, blasted from the regolith rock. Even though they hadn't been activated, Django could tell someone had lined the hole with even more charges. No one could accuse the Resurgence of not planning well enough to cut off anyone following their escape.

*Clever. I just hope it's enough . . .*

The space they funneled into was vast, more reminiscent of a grand hall than a simple cave, and was large enough to hold the hundred or so people who crammed into its space. Artificially carved from the moon's subsurface, the cavern bore the marks of machinery and deliberate design, rather than natural processes. The ceiling was high, with ridges and grooves left behind as evidence of the drilling that had shaped it. Luminescent strips adhered to the walls emanated an intermittent, soft, bluish glow. These strips, appearing worn and well-used, were likely remnants from the early days of excavation, but they still served their purpose. Here and there, temporary structures had been erected—tents, supply crates, and mobile workstations—suggesting the space had seen multiple uses over the years.

Taku closed the door behind them and waited, his shoulder pressed against the iron as though his bodyweight might be the crucial factor in preventing the door from succumbing to the explosion.

Django couldn't pay any more attention to him, though; there was only one man in the room he cared to talk to. He pushed his way through the throng of people, once again huddled together and waiting for further instructions, a buzz of uncertainty hanging over them like a black cloud. Behind them, toward the back of the cave, his uncle stood, peering over the crowd until his eyes landed on Taku, the weight of his gaze evaluating the actions of the man who had sealed them into this chamber.

"Uncle Marvin! Uncle Marvin!" Django shouted as best he could over the confusion of the crowd. He hadn't realized how tense he'd been until the relief of seeing his uncle again flowed through him. "I thought you were dead!"

Django cast aside any sense of dignity—which wasn't exactly an uncommon occurrence for a D-Ringer—and opened his arms to rush his uncle into an embrace. Warm tears streamed freely down his face, but he didn't care. He didn't care that there were a hundred people watching. For one of the few times in his life he could remember, Django let his emotional guard down and embraced the complete euphoria of confirming the man who had helped him to escape from the *Eclipse*, the man he called 'uncle', was still alive.

He wasn't alone any longer. Finally, he had someone to turn to who could shed some light on the foreign world he had stepped into. Someone he could turn to, to find Evie.

Django worked his way to the front of the group and was only a few feet away when he finally caught Marvin's eye. His gaze filled with both relief and concern, but his hand shot up before Django could get close enough to lock in his bearhug. A wave of disappointment struck him in the chest, harsher and more violent than the pain inflicted by Sa'ab's electrified baton.

"*Later,*" Marvin mouthed with a sharp glare.

Django slowed to a stop, his mouth moving in disbelief and his heart racing. He didn't know whether he should be disappointed, embarrassed, or just confused.

"I thought . . . I thought you were dead . . ." Django's voice was barely more than a whisper against the clamor of the crowd.

An intense blast sounded from beyond the doorway, followed by a tremor that struck the entire room. Dust fell from the ceiling, but there didn't appear to be any pressure against the door that Taku couldn't handle. Once the shaking stopped, he stepped away from it, a boyish smile indicating how proud he was of his efforts.

Marvin puffed out his chest and Django thought he was about to tell him something else, but instead he turned to address the room.

"Friends, it's been a long time." Marvin held up his hands, and the former prisoners all erupted in a cheer. "Some of you may remember me. Many of you will at least *recognize* me. Some of you won't have any memory of me at all, but there will be plenty of time for us to get to know one another. I'm back—and I'm here to stay."

Whoops and whistles of support sprung from the crowd, Rowyn included, while others, like Wilder, clapped effusively at the announcement.

More bursts of gunfire accented the address from behind the now-sealed doorway, reminding everyone present that their celebrations came at the expense of someone else's willingness to fight for them.

"Taku has graciously invited me back into the fold, along with the rest of the Resurgence leaders," Marvin continued.

"I hope in time that you can lend me your trust, as you do for them. In return, I offer you my life."

There was an uncertainty in Marvin's eyes. If Django hadn't known the man since he was a kid, he probably wouldn't have seen his uncle's eyes darting back and forth; probably wouldn't have seen his fingers twitching or his feet shuffling slightly.

Django stood there, his mouth agape. *Marvin's one of the resistance leaders?*

It didn't make sense. His uncle had been a shuttle pilot, delivering goods from *Eclipse* to the surface, but had been forced to retire after the radiation had affected his cognitive ability; or so Django had been told. On board the *Eclipse,* Marvin had worked in the cargo bay.

*This* man was a revolutionary?

Uncle Marvin certainly couldn't have had the time, or the ability, to be *leading* any sort of rebellion from the Moon's underground. Could he? Sure, his uncle had some wild tales, but were they all true? Or had they only been a small part of the truth?

Marvin had never mentioned he was any sort of leader. He hadn't mentioned that there would be dozens of prisoners who would cheer for him when he returned, a full seven years after he'd left them.

This wasn't the reception of a missing pilot; this was the welcoming home of a hero.

"It's been far too long," Marvin continued. "I was trapped, unable to return until now, but we will have time to discuss that later. Taku and the Founders' Table have been filling me in on what's been happening, and I'm very impressed with all your efforts. I know there will be questions, but this is neither the time, nor the place. Right now, we need to get back to base. We haven't bought ourselves much time, so, please, speed and determination will be your friends today.

"For those of you who are not part of the Resurgence and have no wish to be, you'll be free to go once we get further into the tunnel. If you choose to make that decision, there will be no changing your mind. You will be sealed off from the rest of us and forced to go your own way. But if you'll just trust me for the next few hours, I'll do my best to convey you all to safety."

Without waiting for a response, Marvin waved to Taku and then disappeared through the doorway at the back of the room.

Taku nodded and gestured for the crowd to follow Marvin into the opening.

Django stood still, watching the blind follow the blind. The man who claimed to be his uncle had disappeared into a hole in the wall that led to a dark cavern in a place Django wouldn't have even imagined existed the day before.

It took a moment to register the hand that had landed on his bicep, and the second on his shoulder. Suddenly, Rowyn's voice was in his ear. Her warm breath danced along the side of his face before her voice reached him.

"Are you all right, space cadet? You look like you've seen a ghost."

Shivers ran through him, and though the rest of the room rushed by, Rowyn's presence created a bubble, separate from the ocean of reality that flowed around them. Her green eyes bore into him, her touch sending a shock through his arm and shoulder. The burgundy armbands she wore seemed to pulsate with a charge, as if electrifying the air between them. She smiled, and the feeling intensified.

Django shrugged it off as a figment of his imagination. There was only one thing he wanted to know. "Who do you think that man is?"

Rowyn raised a brow. "That's Marvin Alejandro. He's the leader of the Resurgence. Been missing for seven years. But you knew that, right? You ran after him. You were shouting at him. I'm guessing you know him?"

Django nodded. "Yeah. He's my uncle."

---

"WE NEED TO MOVE."

Wilder faced Django and Rowyn with intensity in his eyes, but fear had replaced his earlier excitement.

Shouts and blaster fire from beyond the collapsed entrance grew steadily louder until the barrage was competing with the whoops of excitement as the crowd emptied into the corridor.

Django's vision rested on the exit, and he felt himself going into shock as he tried to parse out the man leading them.

*Marvin Alejandro. Leader of the Resurgence.*

The scant amount of lighting the room contained flickered just before everything shook, as if something had detonated somewhere in a far-off place, its seismic effects reaching them in ripples. Some who lingered close by stirred at the disturbance, as regolith dust rained down from above.

"What was that?" Django asked.

"Our men have fallen," Rowyn said intuitively, eyeing the steel door that marked their entry point to the cavern. "Or this is the second wave of the assault. Either way, they're blasting their way toward us."

"Come on." Wilder's large and sweaty palm rested against Django's back, urging him toward the hole in the wall. "We've got to move. We don't want to be here when those bastards break through."

Rowyn didn't need to be told twice. She jogged to the entrance and stood beside Taku, whose face was growing red with agitation.

Django only had one option: go forward with these people he had just met. To follow his uncle—*if* he could still call the man that.

With the chamber now clear, Django wasn't sure what he was waiting for. The mystery of who his uncle truly was had paralyzed him.

"I'm not going to wait all day, boy!" Taku shouted. "I've got to seal this up before the Front gets through that wall."

"Come on, Django!" Rowyn said, confusion breaking in her voice. "You can figure out whatever problems you have on the other side of this. You're going to die if you stay here!"

"Won't they just keep blasting through this entrance?" Django asked. "How is this going to stop them?"

"If you hurry your butts, this tunnel will collapse to a point much further down." Impatience dripped from Taku's voice. "It'll take them days to get anywhere, but if we don't go now, it won't matter. Make the call, or I'll have to bring all this down on your head."

His time was up. Wilder gave Django a final push, and he was all but thrown into the darkened tunnel, nearly tripping as the smooth cut tile underfoot turned into roughly chewed stone.

Rowyn rolled her eyes and took off into the darkness. She was done waiting for him.

Explosions shook the cavern as though they were right on top of him, and Django hunched his shoulders to avoid what he assumed was his impending doom.

"*Move!*" Taku shouted. "I've got to bring the ceiling down! *Now!*"

Red lights winked on all the way along the tunnel, giving Django a marker as to how far he needed to run in order to escape everything literally caving in on his head. He picked up his pace to a sprint. There was a good two hundred meters, maybe more, to cover.

Wilder ran ahead, having no problems with the accelerated pace over the rocky path. Rowyn likewise glided down the tunnel effortlessly, a good hundred meters ahead of them.

Django pushed as hard as he could. He'd never considered himself out of shape, but he'd never had much of a reason to run, either.

He wheezed as he sucked in the dust-filled air, the sharp crystals of disrupted regolith coating his lungs. Anyone who inhaled the stuff daily must have had serious lung damage.

Taku passed him halfway through his run and then looked back at him intently, mouthing for Django to hurry.

Django didn't even know if he was past the last indicator

light when the rumble behind him culminated in a roar. A cloud of dust enveloped the lights as, one by one, the detonators brought the tunnel down.

Django found strength he didn't know he had, pushing harder to ensure he'd outrun the last of the charges. He wouldn't be much help to Eventide if he was buried alive.

So focused on what he was running from, Django wasn't paying attention to what was in front of him, and he almost ran straight into a wall. He caught himself inches from a faceplant, at a point where the tunnel forked left and right. A moment of panic gripped his already fatigued lungs. In his determination to escape the blast, he hadn't been paying attention to the group ahead of him and hadn't seen which way they went.

The fear only lasted a moment. Out of the corner of his eye, Rowyn appeared and grabbed his hand, yanking him to the right.

Whatever lay ahead for him, there was no going back now.

Django
Underground tunnels, Lunar

DJANGO'S LEGS cried out in pain with every step, protesting the hours of walking he had completed on little sleep and even less water. The few members of the group who held small flashlights ahead offered glowing pinpricks of relief in the tunnel's gloom, but otherwise, there was nothing to break up the monotony of the trek.

The excitement of Marvin's return had subsided and now a weight pressed down upon the group, prompting them to continue in uncomfortable silence. Hushed murmurs and crunching boots were the only noises the group made. With the tunnel behind them sealed, the shouts and explosions had ended along with it.

The stretch before them was endless, taunting them with thoughts that they might have traded one prison for another—and the first hadn't involved endless walking.

Hours ago, they had come to another fork in the road,

where Taku had told the escapees who didn't want to throw their lot in with the Resurgence to break off and go their separate way. A large chunk of the group did so, which surprised Django a little. Though he'd only just begun to experience this new world beyond the *Eclipse*, even he had surmised that it was a lot harder to get by on your own.

There were only a couple dozen of them left now, out of the hundred that had begun the journey. Django still had no idea where they were going, so he focused on just keeping one foot in front of the other.

There wasn't a single part of Django that didn't ache. His back and joints were still tired from being forced to sit at unnatural angles, both aboard the slave hauler and on the *Redemption,* and his feet ached from the hours of walking across the uneven terrain. It had taken him a while to adjust to the tunnel's path; his feet were more accustomed to walking on the tiled and carpeted flooring of the space station. Even in the fields of the *Eclipse*'s agricultural complex, he had rarely been forced to walk through the dirt, and when he did, the ground was evenly plowed and cultivated, not rough and hazardous.

Uncle Marvin led the group headed for the Resurgence hideout. Regardless of the discomfort he felt, this was the path Django had to follow. It was the only path that would lead him to Eventide.

A few hundred meters after Taku had closed off their entrance, the tunnel had changed. It had gone from an evenly spaced borehole to a tunnel that constantly varied in size and shape, and without asking, Django could only guess that they had moved from a path that had been blasted from the rock by Marvin and his disciples into a tunnel that was of natural formation.

Sleep-deprived and exhausted, Django wasn't sure if he'd be able to make it any farther. There was nothing but other bodies in front of him, moving at a steady pace, but it was a pace that was becoming increasingly harder for him to maintain.

Wilder and Rowyn walked on either side of him, each taking turns to talk to him. They offered him encouragement that they were almost there when they noticed him stumble a little more frequently, when his head drooped and his body sagged. Under the fatigue, despair grasped for him, reaching through the pit of everything that had occurred to him until it was all he felt. It consumed him, like the vacuum of space had claimed his family. This endless, bleak, black tunnel would be the last thing he'd ever see.

If he had nothing else, Django had these two new friends; companions in a strange world who were willing to stand by him despite only having known him for a day. With the exception of Eventide, he didn't know if he'd even had friends like that on the station. And there was a comfort in pushing forward, knowing that there were others cheering you on.

Uncle Marvin was at the front of the group, but Django hadn't had a chance to speak with him yet. It was frustrating, but for most of the journey, Marvin had traveled ahead of them, discussing the way ahead with unseen scouts. He had quietly reported his findings to Taku, who took the information in with a satisfied nod. Beyond that, Taku was making the most of the long stretch of uninterrupted time to fill Marvin in on seven years of Resurgence operations.

Django struggled to make out bits and pieces of their conversations, but his head hurt, and everything was muddied. Even the encouragements from Wilder and Rowyn were hard to focus on. The edges of his vision faded in and out, but he hardly noticed; there was nothing for him to see but rocks. His feet had gone numb, and he was only vaguely aware that he was still moving them, one in front of the other, by the assumption they continued to keep him upright. It wasn't until firm hands gripped Django's shoulders that he realized the group had come to a halt.

Through tired eyes, Django surveyed the chamber they had entered. Others had already found a place to sit on makeshift stools and beds. The person who had grabbed him —possibly Wilder—helped him to sit on a plush surface. It was soft, cushioned like a bed, but it was far too low to be like any sort of bed Django had ever slept on. Sweat and musk clung to the travelers, and Django supposed he probably stank, too.

Water met his lips, and reflexively, he drank. The cool liquid tasted of slate and old coins, but it didn't matter; it quenched a thirst that had been lingering for days. Django hadn't had a drop of water since leaving the *Eclipse.* Knowing the human body can only survive without water for about three days, Django reckoned he had to be pushing that now, if he didn't count the blast from the hose used to clean him off in the port. It was a miracle he'd remained standing for as long as he had.

"Take it easy, kid," a tired male voice said. It wasn't one

Django recognized. "There's plenty here to go around. You don't want to overdo it."

Django removed his mouth from the jug he'd been embracing and gasped vigorously for breath.

As the world came back into focus, he could see they had arrived at a building of some sort. Somewhere along their journey, the group must have climbed out of the tunnels, perhaps up a slight incline toward the end that had taken them to the Moon's surface and on into the shelter. But Django didn't remember climbing. In fact, he remembered little of anything.

*The Moon's surface.* The thought still struck him as incredible.

The world moved around him, as though he were still trudging through the tunnels, but between water and rest, his faculties were slowly returning—even if the room was spinning slightly. He sat on top of a mattress resting on the floor, in a sea of a dozen others that were placed around the room to offer the escapees comfort. The room itself was three or four times the size of the ship they had escaped, and here, there were several doorways that led to other rooms.

A soft blue light caressed those who had followed Marvin and Taku to this place. Even after hours in near darkness, the light was subdued, but it was enough to make out the features of his fellow escapees.

Each of them appeared more exhausted than the last. There were men and women, young and old, in a variety of ethnicities.

Other than Rowyn and Wilder, Django hadn't attempted to learn a thing about any of them. Being honest, he hadn't had the chance. But now he shared a sort of commonality with the couple dozen people who had stayed with Marvin, Taku, and the others. They either didn't have other lives to get back to or had found a larger sense of purpose here, among the Resurgence.

"Why have we stopped?" His voice cracked, despite the few gulps of water he had just swallowed, and he looked longingly at the jug that was still making its rounds through the room.

"Glad you're feeling better, space cadet," Rowyn said, crouching down to meet Django at his level. She reached up and brushed a stray strand of hair out of his face with her fingers. He could smell the leather-like material of her burgundy sleeves, and light reflected off their faded golden circles, causing him to wince.

Rowyn jerked her hand away, mistaking the reaction. "Sorry, I didn't mean to . . ." She trailed off, as though unsure how to finish.

"No, it's not that . . ."

A figure stepped through a doorframe, grabbing their attention and interrupting Django's words. Even silhouetted by bright yellow light from the adjacent room, Django recognized his uncle.

"Friends, get some rest. You've been through a long ordeal today. I wish I could tell you our struggle is over, but no friendship worth its salt can be built on lies. We'll go over what your presence here means in the morning."

The man stepped into the room, allowing the cooler light to both illuminate and draw the color from his face. He was both exactly the same and completely different to the Uncle Marvin Django had known since he was a kid. The same hair that wasn't quite parted but still styled to one side, the same stubbled beard, the same goatee . . . But this man no longer epitomized his uncle's warmth. His eyes were no longer hazy with drink; no longer darting over his shoulder as though worried someone was watching him. Instead, he was confident, charismatic, and held the attention of every single person as though he had been speaking that way his entire life.

Marvin strutted through the room as any commander would have done through a space station, boots clicking on the tile, surveying those in his care as though they might be soldiers under his command returning from a long deployment.

His uncle approached, a smile crossing his face, and put his hands on his hips. "I see you've finally made some friends."

The warmth Django associated with his uncle had suddenly returned. This was the man he had been at his older sister's wedding; a man more likely to issue a joke than a command.

Django felt some of the tension he had been holding in his shoulders release. He hadn't been aware of its presence, but he knew where it came from. He still wasn't sure what to make of his uncle being in this place; being this *person*.

"I thought you'd died . . ." Django blurted. Tears formed in his eyes that he was too tired to hold back. "I thought I'd lost you."

"Can we talk in private, Django?" Marvin asked. If he

were going through any similar emotional battles, he hid them well. "Are you feeling well enough to stand?"

Django pushed himself up from the mattress while Rowyn extended a hand to help him with his balance. He resisted taking it at first, but as he struggled to find the strength to steady his own weight, he relented and grabbed hold, and she pulled him up with surprising strength. He wobbled until his legs eventually found their stability again. They were tired, but Django was no stranger to a prolonged day on his feet.

It was all the sitting he wasn't used to.

Marvin nodded, as though he expected nothing less, and beckoned Django to follow him as he walked to the doorway he had entered through a few minutes before.

Django stepped cautiously, allowing his legs to find their bearings and his gaze to pass over the others who had joined them in the Resurgence's mystery location. "What is this place?" he asked.

"This is a transition house," Marvin explained. "It's a safe haven for Resurgence personnel, but it's not somewhere we ever stay for long. This place allows us time to research potential recruits before we disclose to them where our base of operations is. It reduces the chance of a spy infiltrating our facilities and gives us time to shake anyone else who might be following us."

They crossed into the next room. The light shifted from cool blue LEDs to a warm yellow. Here, it was more apparent that the transition house's walls were constructed from dark gray stone, as if hewn from the Moon's surface itself, but in a way that was much more refined than the rugged regolith tunnels the group had traversed through to get here.

They hadn't reached the surface at all, Django realized. Perhaps this place was still underground, carved into the rock itself.

The room was nothing elaborate. It was smaller than the main space, with several chairs suitable for lounging, but each of them had seen years of unmaintained wear. The fabric frayed at their edges, and spots on the seats had worn down so far that Django was surprised the stuffing wasn't poking through them. On the *Eclipse*, residents would never have allowed the furniture to get to this state of disrepair, not even on the D-Ring. Someone would have taken the initiative to reupholster them. But in a place that was likely full of resources, everything appeared to be falling apart.

Marvin turned then, a colossal grin on his face—the face of the uncle Django had known and loved since he was eleven years old. Suddenly, Django was that kid again, with a need for someone to look out for him and keep him safe. The man opened his arms and Django unabashedly fell into them.

There was a warmth to the embrace that felt like home, with Marvin's familiar vest pressed up against Django's cheek. But there were subtle differences, too. The familiar smell of dirt and alcohol had faded, but traces still remained, buried deep in the fibers of Marvin's clothing, like they had been there for so long that they had become part of the cloth.

There were newer smells, too: the burnt gunpowder smell that seemed synonymous with the rest of the Moon was especially strong, as though Marvin had been rolling around in dust, and a hint of vanilla and apples, which caused Django's stomach to growl.

Without the strength to hold them back, tears rushed freely down his face, the trauma of the last few days releasing through the open floodgates. Tears of sadness for everything he'd lost. Tears of joy at confirming his uncle was still alive. Tears of insufferable loss through the realization that everything he had once believed to be true was gone.

"I don't understand," Django said as he regained his faculties. Or at least, he thought he had. Everything came out in a rush of anger, sadness, and confusion. "Everything's completely fallen apart. You let us believe you were dead! Why? Eventide and I were nearly killed trying to follow that note you left. And now I'm stuck here. Here! On the *Moon*, of all places! The Earth is inhabited, but there are people out here. Not just here—Mars, Europa, Io, all over! But I left my home to be here because of you! I had to leave Nova with Benson, some slave trader has abducted Eventide, and I was about to be shipped to some regolith mine in the asteroid belt! Then, I find out you're alive; that these people all supposedly know you; and that you're some leader in a resistance against an empire I had no clue was even out there! I can't even keep everything that's changed straight anymore! You *can't* just pretend this is normal! You can't say you're happy to see me when nothing I've ever known is real. I . . . I don't even know the real *you!*"

The smile faded from Marvin's face as his eyes darted back toward the main room. After a moment, he nodded.

"I guess I owe you an explanation."

# CHAPTER THIRTEEN

Mikka

Shackleton City — Earthrise Restauranté

MIKKA FELT as out of place as a battle-scarred spaceship docked at a luxurious orbital gala, where the elite danced gracefully to the strains of Tchaikovsky, with Domani serving champagne.

In Mikka's estimation, the Earthrise Restauranté had to be the fanciest, most elegant establishment on the surface of Lunar. She certainly couldn't recall ever entering a place any more refined.

*Come to think of it, it* might *be Tchaikovsky playing* over the speaker. Mikka had always confused the *1812 Overture* with Dvorak's *New World*, though it had been a long time since she'd last heard either. And since when did she even know the names of ancient Earth composers?

She'd once dated a guy, many lifetimes ago, who'd had a thing for classical music. Mikka hadn't thought the tidbits she had picked up during that time would stick, but chords and notes came back to her in a rush as the brass and drums of the movement bellowed over the concealed loudspeaker, as though she was marching into battle rather than doing her best to balance on high-heeled shoes on her way to dinner.

Commander David Aries sat at a crystalline table on the far side of the dining room. With no regard for subtlety, a half dozen guards formed a perimeter around his section, separating him from the rest of the patrons.

The table at which he sat had been carefully selected to be far enough away from anyone who might be tempted to eavesdrop. The guards, each standing a few meters from the table, ensured their privacy while also remaining out of earshot.

Mikka spotted several more men wearing discreet black suits who stood at the entrances. It was hard not to draw attention to themselves as they eyed each diner as though any of them could be a potential assassin.

Mikka did her best to stride through the restaurant without breaking her neck. The shoes she wore were a scarlet red that perfectly matched her dress, though personally, she thought the four-inch heels were overkill. She'd never been to an establishment with a dress code that required such footwear before, and she couldn't for the life of her fathom why women in the Upper Rim tortured themselves in this way.

She still felt guilty for wearing an outfit that would have cost enough credits to feed a family in the Tubes, in a room that could have housed several dozen of them. How did people on the Rim justify the lavishness of their spending while the residents below them fought so desperately to live?

Someone had polished the gray tile floor with such intensity that Mikka could make out the reflection of her shoes and shimmering dress on its surface. It was damn near as smooth as glass, without a trace of regolith dust. Her heels clicked apprehensively as she approached the table, Aries's security watching her every step. Two more guards who had escorted her on the car ride to the restaurant still followed close behind her.

*Who's more at risk here? Me or Aries?* She found herself grinning as she contemplated the answer.

Any of the dozen guards wouldn't hesitate to snap her neck if it came to it. But that wouldn't matter if she shoved a knife in between Aries's ribs first.

The blinds had been closed to keep out the natural sunlight and the artificial lights had been dimmed, providing the illusion of a setting sun. It wasn't quite the same, of course, but it set a mood that the Upper Rim restaurant was clearly aiming to achieve. Lit candles on the edge of the room allowed some ambient light, while miniscule pinpricks of light decorated the ceiling, mimicking the stars that would have been above them if the city didn't rest in perpetual light.

Of course, having lived in the Tubes for most of her life, the darkness was like an old friend.

Night was a luxury to the residents on the surface and light a luxury to those underground. It seemed, no matter where you lived, you always longed for something different.

Mikka swept past other patrons, poking at their dinners with precision and poise, as though critiquing their food rather than consuming it. They were high-ranking Syndicate officials, mostly, she noticed, still dressed in their SF and LPF uniforms. Others were dressed from head to toe in business suits and dresses that weren't a million miles from her own; off-duty officials, wealthy entrepreneurs, or black-market profiteers.

David Aries looked at the window, focusing on the closed blinds as though they were wide open and he could see the sunlight reflecting off the skyscrapers. The commander had changed from the long jacket he usually wore, settling instead for a charcoal gray suit and a gunmetal gray tie. He resembled the businessmen rather than the military captains and officers, though he was much more attractive than any of them.

Aries's eyes met hers as she approached, likely alerted to her presence by the clicking of her heels. These were not the shoes of a pirate; they would make sneaking up on someone practically impossible.

A smile lit his face. Not the same smile he gave that was all kinds of wrong when he was telling a half-truth or a fact with a hidden meaning, but a genuine one. Mikka would almost have said it was warm and inviting; the type of smile that someone who cares about you breaks into whenever you walk through the door at the end of a long day. Nobody had ever smiled at her like that before.

Perhaps she was imagining things, or maybe she wasn't as good at reading people as she believed.

Her conversation with Monroe crept back into her thoughts. *Don't trust Aries.*

But if not him, then *who*? A pirate and a kid whose brain had been fried by an implant? A mercenary with two runaway kids from a FLOW station?

Mikka had killed people before, of course. As a pirate,

eventually you're faced with the decision of 'kill or be killed.' But to act on what Abi and Zee had asked of her? She wasn't a murderer. *That*, allegedly, was Marvin Alejandro's department. She'd never taken a life without reason, and she wasn't about to start now.

Aries stood and moved to slide out the chair on the opposite side of the intimate table. "Thank you for joining me," he said as she sat.

"Did I have a choice?"

"Are you here out of obligation?" Aries asked with a pout. "I hope that's not the case."

"Honestly, I didn't think I could've said no—but that doesn't mean I didn't choose to be here." Mikka let a smile touch her lips.

A waitress stopped by to take her drinks order. She ordered a whiskey, neat. "The best you have."

The waitress nodded with a bemused look and hurried off.

"Awfully bold of you to assume I'm paying for that," Aries quipped. His voice was playful, but his eyes suggested there was a shred of truth to his words.

"You're providing a home for me, a caregiver for my mother, but a few credits for a whiskey is over the line?"

"In a place like this? A glass of Earthrise's best whiskey can run a steeper price than your apartment for a month."

She couldn't imagine the monthly rent for the penthouse alone. It probably exceeded the running costs for the *Redemption*. "I can order something else . . ." she said, aghast at the prospect of what exorbitant vintage the server might bring out.

"Don't worry. What they'll bring is expensive, but they won't bring the antiques. You need to ask for those specifically. Just remember, this isn't your usual underground tavern."

The server returned with a glass of golden elixir. Aromas of peat and cedar hit Mikka before she even lifted the glass, and she didn't have to know how much it cost to realize it was more credits than she would have been able to afford. She suspected it might even top some of the bootlegged ancient Earth whisky she'd smuggled during her pirating days.

"I've taken the liberty of ordering us dinner," Aries announced. "I hope that's okay?"

"If you're picking up the check, who am I to complain?"

A handful of waiting staff returned. Their black suits screamed the kind of refinement that residents of the Tubes could never have imagined, let alone afford. The uniforms looked brand new, like they hadn't been passed down and mended over the years. Nor were they embedded with grit or riddled with holes. That was normal for the Rim, but there was more to it than that. The stitching of the fabrics was more precise; the buttons made of a metal that glistened in the artificial light.

The group of attendants set up a makeshift table beside their own and set plates of food upon it. The array wasn't an exorbitant amount for the Upper Rim, but it would have been a banquet for anybody in the Tubes, complete with an exotic variety of unfamiliar slices and pockets of delicacies.

Smells of salt and brine wafted from a platter of alien seasoned white meat.

"What's this?" she asked.

Aries gave a wry smirk. "Supper."

He was enjoying her naivety, and it wasn't like Mikka to feel so far from her element.

"Yes, but *what* is it? I've never seen anything like this before. Like some sort of fowl, but lighter in color and has an odor. It smells somehow both delicious and awful at the same time."

"This, Mikka, is seafood. Shipped to us in extremely limited quantities. Syndicate leaders are some of the only individuals that have access to it. Earthrise brought it in specifically upon my request."

Mikka snorted. "You ordered this to *impress* me?"

Aries smiled broadly and shook his head. "I ordered this to make you *think*. To show you my motivation for what I have to do. Please, dig in." He plunged his own fork into the flakey white meat and took a bite.

"Everyone has their price, I guess. Me? I prefer cold, hard credits." Mikka couldn't keep the sass from her voice.

"You're missing the point. When have you ever heard of there being a sea other than on Earth?"

Mikka furrowed her brow, uncertain of where the man's point was taking them. "Europa has oceans and rivers, but I haven't heard of anyone setting up a 'seafood' farm there. I suppose it's not impossible, though. The waters of Enceladus are believed to be extensive, but they're buried so far beneath the ice that they're inaccessible."

"I want you to take a moment to think about this, Mikka," he said, pointing his fork in her direction. "If the only place we can procure seafood is on Earth, then there's something fundamentally wrong about what you've been told about the Syndicate and its people."

Mikka paused. The answer should have been right in front of her. Most of Earth was unfit to sustain life, but it had been healing. The Syndicate had admitted to that. Every year, the reported zones deemed habitable grew in size, but only to the benefit of those who were planet-born. The authorities kept the rest of humanity off-planet to ensure the trend continued.

*Everyone but the Syndicate leaders.*

Her mouth fell open as the realization struck her. "*Somebody* has to be catching the seafood."

Aries snapped his middle finger on his thumb, pointing his index finger at her. "Bingo."

He set down his fork and leaned forward, his forearms resting on the table. "The Syndicate pump breathable air into habitats on multiple worlds. We've conquered extreme temperatures and environments wherever we go. But have you never stopped to wonder how we can colonize half the solar system but fail to fix radiation fallout from two *centuries* ago? We can grow crops on the rocky and frozen wastelands of Ganymede, but detoxifying Earth's soil is too steep a mountain to climb?"

Mikka had never really thought about it before, but what the commander was saying made sense. "But why?" she asked. "Why keep so many of us off-world if people are allowed to live down there for agriculture? I can't see the Syndicate elite lifting their own fingers."

"That, I don't know," Aries said. "Believe it or not, I have as little access to what happens on Earth as you do. Three nights ago, I told you 'SF Commander of Shackleton City' wasn't as prestigious a title as you made it out to be. I wasn't kidding.

"But what I do know is this: those of us off-planet are growing tired of being kept in the dark. We grow weary of our people being ignored."

Mikka chuckled. The man couldn't be serious. "What, then? You plan on exposing their secrets? What good will that do?"

"That won't do anything; not as things are. Everyone knows the Syndicate lies. The Earth controls everything. Every single thing we do—the food we grow, the minerals we harvest, the goods we produce—it all flows to the planet. The only thing we get to keep is ice for our water and oxygen, and that's because the Earth has plenty of that; but they tax us on it, anyway. If we want to change things, we have to stop the flow of goods down to the surface."

"You think the Syndicate is just going to allow that? I know you have a lot of resources at your disposal, but even you won't be able to stop the armada that'll come for you if you try to erect blockades."

"There's more to it than that." Aries leaned forward, a sparkle in his eye, and Mikka could suddenly see the little boy this man once was. "There must be change at the top. *From within.*"

It was curious, thinking about Aries as a child. They had all been young at one point. Nobody started out as a commander or a pirate, a soldier or a thief. Some were born in the Tubes, destined to struggle for their short, arduous lives, while others were born in a place of privilege where they could work their way up to becoming commander of a military base, even from the humble beginnings of a junkyard watchman. They all started out as curious children, but because of chance, fate, or whatever else a person wanted to believe in, some were born beneath Lunar's surface, fighting for survival, while others were born with every opportunity to climb the ranks, to reach whatever point society said was okay for that person.

Though it seemed even David Aries had limits as to how high he could climb. Still, he had his sights set even higher.

Commander Aries wanted to be the damned Prefect!

"Was this your plan all along?"

"What do you mean?" The twinkle in his eye didn't fade, but his expression dimmed from excited to confused.

"When we first met, you were a watchman on a floating scrap heap. Now, you're commanding Syndicate forces in Shackleton. When we met the other day, I was impressed you'd managed to work your way up to this position. You'd advanced so far in such a short amount of time. I thought you were ambitious, but now I see you're still not satisfied. You're ready to take on the whole damn system! When did your dreams go from building a better life for yourself to becoming emperor?"

His smile vanished, as though it hadn't been there at all, and the sparkle in his eyes glazed over as David Aries shifted uncomfortably. It was an odd gesture for a man who exclusively displayed confidence and self-importance. Even as a watchman at the Boneyard, this man had shown no sign of humility.

Watching him squirm was so uncomfortable that Mikka

considered apologizing, but she stayed quiet, waiting to see what this display was really about.

Aries cleared his throat, the hesitation vanishing and his original confidence returning—but it returned cautiously, as though on guard against being shot down again. "You cut right to the chase, Miss Jenax. I don't believe anyone has ever asked me that before."

"How many people within your circle know you managed the Boneyard? Though it can't be a secret, I'm sure it's not a detail you share openly. It's not exactly becoming of a man who wants to set himself up as supreme leader."

Aries's smile returned, but the warmth had faded, closer now to the suspicious grin he'd flashed in his office. She was pressing the right buttons, that was for sure, though she wasn't entirely certain she *should* be testing him in this way. She didn't yet know his intentions with her, and the spark he was showing could have been anything from amusement to desire.

"Insightful as always," he said. "That's exactly what drew me to you."

"Oh, really?" she said, taking a sip of her whiskey and savoring the alcohol as it burned her esophagus. *Damn! This is a good drink.* "I thought you were a sucker for a pretty face."

"I grew up on the Rim," Aries said, ignoring the bait. "But I wasn't as privileged as most in the Front. The poorer districts of Upper Shackleton face the crippling comparisons with Lunar's most well-to-do as their neighbor."

"Am I supposed to feel sorry for you?" Mikka quipped. "While you were comparing credit balances, those of us in the Tubes were so desperate for food we were stealing your garbage. And that was on the days we got lucky."

Aries lifted a hand. "As hard as it is to believe, I realize that now. But human nature is to compare ourselves with those of a higher social status, not lower. We're always wishing for that which we don't have, and we have a harder time focusing on what we do.

"Anyway, my father always thought things could be different. He truly believed we were one generation away from being able to return home to Earth. He believed I would be among the first generation to set foot on the homeworld. He was a hobby climate scientist with no influence on anything, but he spent his time crunching numbers and studying data. From what he pieced together, the Earth, though still fragile, had nearly healed. But as he dug deeper and analyzed everything available to him, he realized there were stark differences between the projections the Syndicate was giving us and the readings from the equipment set up on the planet. He was adamant his numbers weren't wrong.

"But he *was* naïve." Aries's face dimmed as he fixed his gaze on his plate, his eyes not actually looking at it. "He thought that if he approached the Council, they would realize their error; that they'd merely miscalculated the data. He thought the information was the key to bringing an end to the exploitation of the Loop. If the Earth was on its way to healing, some of that wealth could go back to the people working for it."

"And let me guess, they didn't take well to that idea?"

"He could only come to one conclusion: the Syndicate's lying to us."

"No shit." Mikka didn't hide her sarcastic tone.

"It's one thing to *assume* the empire is lying, or at least, working in its own interest. It's quite another to see the numbers. To this day, the Syndicate tells us it will be a hundred and fifty years before humans can return to the planet. That number hasn't changed in a hundred and fifty years, and it'll be that forever more. They have no intention of letting us back. Not now. Not ever."

"What does that have to do with your ambitions?"

Aries's lips tightened. "My father never came home from that meeting, and my mother said nothing. Not one thing. It was as if one day, he existed, and the next, he never had. I didn't understand it then, but I know now that she was scared. She was terrified the Syndicate would come after his family; that we might pay the same price for the information he'd discovered. Not only did the Syndicate kill him, but they also closed off the data points he had used, so nobody else could access how the Earth is really faring. Even now, I still don't know the extent of healing that's occurred since my father pulled the numbers thirty years ago. Nobody does."

Mikka's thoughts scrambled for the words to say. She might have misjudged Aries completely. "So, you decided to avenge your father from the inside? To prove the validity of what he discovered?"

Aries nodded. The uncomfortable shifting returned.

*He's never told anybody this before,* she realized.

He lowered his voice. "I won't let the Syndicate get away with what they did to my father. They will pay for their crimes, and the rest of the Loop will reap the benefits. Soon, the Council will not get to decide who is and is not allowed to visit Earth. Humanity will be able to return home."

Suddenly, it all made sense: the kindly Boneyard operator and the apartments he'd provided for both her and Kiara. David Aries actually gave a shit.

Which made Zee's words even more haunting. Even more preposterous.

*You need to kill David Aries.*

The commander who sat before her might be the only real shot the Loop had at starting again. He was someone who had seen what it was like at the bottom of the ladder and had both the desire and access to resources that could change it now that he'd reached the top.

Aries, for everything he'd been through, everything he hoped and aspired to be, wasn't someone Mikka needed to fear, and he was more than she'd ever hoped for. He wasn't just going to be her savior; he'd be the savior of the entire empire.

Abigail and the Wayfinder had the wrong woman. They had pegged Aries for a villain. Instead, he was going to be the hero.

Mikka met his eyes. "So, why bring me here? What's my role in all this?"

His smile returned, more charming than devious. "We're going to hit the Syndicate where it hurts. Let me show you."

# CHAPTER FOURTEEN

Mikka
Shackleton City

MIKKA AND ARIES finished their dinner and then continued on to the commander's next stop of the evening. The seafood hadn't been to Mikka's taste, but there were other courses she had enjoyed.

Delicate Martian moss crisps boasted a subtly sweet and earthy flavor. Titan ice snails, a delicacy of Saturn's largest moon, were served in a light, aromatic broth that shimmered with bioluminescent hues. From the asteroid belt came spiced rock ferns, which were surprisingly tender and juicy. To finish, they indulged in a dessert of Ganymede's glacier jelly, a cool, translucent treat that melted on the tongue with hints of mint and wintergreen. The spread was more than just a culinary marvel, it was a showcase of the worlds the Syndicate had claimed dominion over.

Advancements hoarded by the elite. Few residing on any

of those worlds would ever have sampled even a morsel of the dishes Mikka'd been presented with tonight.

Of course, she had seen Syndicate extravagance before, but never had anyone invited her to partake. Every bite felt like a betrayal, turning against the people who still lived in the Tubes, who wouldn't see this much food in an entire month, let alone one meal.

"You can't feel guilty," Aries had said. "Nothing gets accomplished that way. You didn't choose to be invited to this dinner any more than the poor choose to be desperate for food. The only thing we can do is help to bridge the gap."

That was true enough. Change had to come from within, and unless that change was meaningful, it was like putting a bandage on a broken limb. But it still didn't feel right.

"If nobody feels guilty," she'd replied, "then nothing will change."

A swarm of guards had escorted them from the Earthrise Restauranté down a series of elevators until they reached a railcar shuttle. It seemed strange to Mikka that the commander would choose to take public transportation anywhere, even while being escorted, but once she saw the exterior of the transit car itself was black with a glossy, sleek finish, similar to the uniforms worn by Aries's private bodyguards, the pieces began to fit.

Syndicate markings—the double hexagon with the star of the Syndicate Front in its center—disclosed the vehicle was not public transport after all, but privately owned and used exclusively by the commander and his guard. Handy, if they needed to move through the city unobstructed by anyone on the street level.

Or in the event of an attack.

The ride itself was uneventful. The transit car was just large enough to comfortably hold the commander, herself, and the six guards who accompanied them. Aries's coolness had returned, small talk and deep confessions left behind at the restaurant to be replaced only with silence.

It took all of Mikka's effort not to shrink into her seat under the weight of the six sets of eyes that bore into her. There was no doubt in the security officers' minds who the threat in this vehicle was, and it wasn't the commander.

Aries either didn't notice the treatment or expected nothing less. His own gaze lingered out of the transit car, as though he could see anything in the tunnels that whipped past, distant and pensive.

*What is he plotting inside that big brain of his?*

Once they disembarked, Mikka recognized where they were—partially, at least. The extensive, cavernous hall reminded her of the bay where she had parked the *Redemption*, suggesting they must have been near the docks.

Banners and standards decorated the facility filled with Syndicate blue and the insignia of both the Port Authority and the Syndicate Front. Unlike the rest of the port, however, this area was not only quiet, but completely vacant. Only a few guards whose uniforms carried no affiliations stood at ease along the walkway that stretched endlessly through the massive bay.

This port had to be five, if not ten, times larger than the main public space dock. Hundreds of black ships lined the promenade, their paneling mimicking the transit car they had arrived in: black, sleek, and glossy.

*Perhaps Aries is going all out to rebrand his arm of the Syndicate?*

Mikka didn't have to be told this was the Syndicate's fighter fleet—or part of it, at least. Highly sophisticated ships rarely saw action, if ever, and there wasn't enough conflict within the Loop to warrant such a display of firepower.

"Why does the Syndicate have such an extensive fleet?" she inquired. "There's nobody that could even come close to matching this."

"That's exactly why Alejandro and other terrorists like him will ultimately fail." Aries didn't slow his step as he followed the promenade around the outside edge of the nearest building. "This is only a fraction of what the Empire possesses. It would crush any uprising in a matter of hours."

He said it so matter-of-factly, but nobody had yet informed her of what Alejandro's plan *actually* was.

"What does Marvin mean to do?"

Whatever he was up to, Abigail was also involved. Based on the display of power all around her, it seemed whatever they were planning wouldn't be enough.

"What does any terrorist mean to do? Sow seeds of chaos. Disrupt our way of life."

Mikka tried to not react to the statement. *Whose* way of life would be disrupted, exactly?

*Those with something to lose.*

"But all the resources that must have gone into building these . . ." Mikka said, nodding toward the fighters. "The Syndicate could put those resources to providing relief to the Tubes."

She tried to do a rough count of how many millions of

credits the Syndicate must have spent constructing the war machines, but she quickly gave up. They had built a space force worth *millions*, in an empire without enemies, in the same city where hundreds of thousands couldn't afford to eat. Even sacrificing a handful of these ships would have provided untold relief.

"Does the Syndicate even have enough pilots to fly these?"

Mikka was embarrassed to admit that she didn't even know how vast the Syndicate's forces actually were. How many soldiers did they command? How many pilots? The number of ships before her suggested hundreds.

"We do," he replied coldly. "That and more. Which is why the new Prefect wants to ramp up production."

"Ramp *up* production?"

"This Prefect's rumored to be even more hardline than his father. He's secured his rule by stoking old prejudices. He wants to ensure Earth remains only for the planet-born."

"But we were *all* planet-born at one point. Didn't we originate in the same place?"

"That doesn't matter to the Prefect and his supporters," Aries said. "All they know is hate. And greed. They'll use us for our resources, though, unless we do something about it. I've reached out and established loyalty with an extensive network of soldiers that are either Lunar- or Mars-born, as well as those born elsewhere in the Loop. We'll have the resources to commandeer these units if we get the timing right. Force the Syndicate into a fair fight. But this isn't what I wanted to show you."

*A fair fight.*

For all his talk of helping others, Mikka kept forgetting that Aries was planning on bringing war to the Loop. Sure, he might increase his chances of winning if he commanded these ships, but would it be enough? Humanity hadn't seen war since leaving Earth, and the Climate Wars nearly destroyed them all.

They made a series of turns before entering a warehouse. Overhead lights flicked on as they entered, illuminating the stacks of crates and boxes piled stories high within. Smaller warehouse bays branched from the main inventory. They walked past multiple doorways leading to rooms that seemed to be filled with an endless supply of munitions, the smell hitting Mikka: flint and sulphur, gunpowder, and a burnt metallic smell that she guessed were blaster charges waiting to be installed.

They didn't walk through the labyrinth where the bulk of the boxes were kept. Aries was steering her away from them, as though she hadn't already worked out what they were.

Instead, he led Mikka into a separate, smaller side room, nearly hidden at the rear of this Empire-exclusive facility. The room was compact enough to have once been an office, or maybe a large storage closet, but the ceiling was much lower, only three meters or so above her head. Someone had arranged the crates within into five groups, each containing four units. The boxes were familiar—identical in appearance to the unit she had delivered to the *Eclipse*.

"Don't tell me you're sending the stations *weapons?*"

Getting the FLOW stations involved would be a death sentence. Anyone suspected of the conspiracy would be sitting ducks to the Empire's wrath. The Syndicate had already proven with the *Infinity* how much value they placed in the FLOW stations. They'd already killed hundreds of thousands of innocent people to preserve their secrets.

Aries's face lit up with his trademark smirk. "And *what*, exactly, would you expect a space station to do with weapons that could affect their relationship with the Syndicate?"

Her response tumbled coldly from her lips. "Judging by this warehouse, you're planning a coup."

"Intuitive as always, Miss Jenax. But I'm happy to learn I'm not completely predictable. I've still got a few surprises up my sleeve." He motioned to one of his guards. "Open it."

The guard wasted no time, punching in a series of numbers into the keypad attached to one of the crates. The latch on the box hissed open, and the guard lifted the crate's top.

With the lid pulled back, Aries gestured for Mikka to step up onto the platform. "When you left port for the *Eclipse*, you asked what you were delivering. I never answered you because your first shipment was a test of your loyalty. I didn't believe you would run, but it never hurts to be sure."

Mikka peered inside the wooden box. She didn't know what she expected to find, but she prepared herself to gaze upon a stockpile of explosives. What lay inside the box, however, was not weapons, and she shook her head a few times to ensure she wasn't imagining the contents.

The crate contained white sacks stacked one on top of the other, each stamped with 'COURTESY OF YOUR FRIENDS ON LUNAR' along with the Lunar territorial logo—two intertwined hexagons surrounding a gray semi-circle opposite a larger yellow semi-circle.

The box was filled to the brim with the packages.

"I don't understand . . ." she said. "What are these?"

"Pick one up," Aries encouraged. "Open it and see."

Skeptical, Mikka did as she was told. The contents shifted, and she could immediately tell what it contained.

"You're sending them *food?* Why? They grow food up there."

"You still don't understand," Aries replied. "It's not about the food. It's more about the message it sends."

Mikka cocked her head to one side. "The stations grow most of the Loop's food. What good does sending it back to them do?"

"You're familiar with the rumors that FLOW station residents believe they are the only survivors of the climate catastrophe of the mid-twenty-first century?"

"Of course, but I'd always assumed it was a pile of hot garbage until we picked Marvin up from the *Eclipse.*"

"Almost everything the FLOW stations ship out is raw goods. They believe they are sending plant and animal life to the surface to rebuild the Earth's ecosystem. Instead, most of it gets shipped here, to Lunar, and to substations where it's processed, packaged, and shipped out to our citizens. The FLOW stations never see packages like this."

The realization struck Mikka like a slap to the face. Aries was discreetly telling the stations that there was life outside; that their shipments weren't going where they thought they were.

"Wouldn't there be easier ways to do this? Why not try

hacking the stations' comms network and broadcasting a transmission?"

"A transmission would be too easy to trace back to the source, and there would be no guarantees it would work. The stations have their own internal comms. The only external communications channels are through Station Admin; token commanders with no real power who cling to the stations under their jurisdiction like a fistful of grain. They would jam the message before it ever reached anyone."

That would explain why it took Marvin so long to contact someone to establish a means of escape.

"But why food?"

"You might find it hard to believe, but the FLOW station residents who grow the food for most of the Loop actually receive little of it. It's not as bad for them as it is for the Lower Tubes, but it's not far off. A message can be intercepted before it is passed around, but a bag of food will make its way through the lower decks, and with it, tales of where it came from and the markings on the bag."

Mikka took another look at the sack of foodstuff before setting it back down. "'Produced on Substation 37, on behalf of the Syndicate Empire.'"

It seemed like a good idea, in theory, but Mikka suspected there was more to the plan than David was letting on.

"Marvin claimed the Syndicate destroyed the *Infinity* because its people found out the truth. What if they do the same to the rest of them?"

"The Syndicate can't afford to lose another station. The Empire was forced to cut rations when *Infinity* went down, and FLOW stations also feed the elite. If they all go down, they'll starve. There aren't enough fisheries or laborers on the surface—or throughout the system, for that matter—to make up the difference. The Syndicate has no choice but to make concessions. Without willing slaves growing their food, there's no other option."

The pieces came together in Mikka's head. *This* was how Aries was making a difference. Ever since she first stepped onto a pirate freighter as a teenager, she had dreamed of doing the same, but she'd held no actual power to help more than a handful of citizens at a time. Aries was talking about changing the entire regime.

"Why are you showing me this? To convince me? I wouldn't think you'd need the approval of your contractors."

Aries laughed; a more genuine laugh than Mikka believed she'd ever heard from the man. It melted a layer of ice she hadn't realized she had constructed, and beneath waited a woman Mikka had forgotten existed.

The commander took a step closer to Mikka and lifted a hand to the back of her head. "I thought it was obvious, but I guess I'll have to make my intentions clearer."

He leaned in, his fingers running through her hair as his lips met hers.

Mikka welcomed their warmth and the pull of his embrace . . . and the last of any reservations she held melted away.

# CHAPTER FIFTEEN

Django
Lunar transition house


THE MAN who called himself Uncle Marvin stood before Django, his hands clasped behind his back as he paced the room and took several deep breaths, as though trying to determine where to start.

"You have no idea how happy I am to see you made it to the shuttle," he finally said. "Though not without some injury, I see."

Marvin hovered a finger over Django's face, concern marking his brow.

"I never would have believed the guards on the *Eclipse* could be considered hospitable," Django replied.

Marvin laughed. "There was a reason I confided in Avery Inglewood."

He walked to the center of the room, giving off an air of presenting a speech to a diplomat rather than talking to his nephew. "I was worried Avery wouldn't find the note, or that you wouldn't understand the message."

"With all your talk of leaving the station, it didn't take a genius to work out what it could mean."

Marvin nodded, as though that had been his intention all along.

"Who are you really?" Django asked. "Were you *ever* a pilot? Why were you aboard the *Eclipse?*"

Marvin pointed to a seat against the wall; an ugly yellow chair with frayed edges that had worn down over so many years that it was now more white than yellow. It had seen better days, much like the rest of the furniture in the transition house.

"This might take a while," Marvin said. "Grab a seat."

He moved to a small table that rested against the wall and grabbed a small jug of water that rested on its surface. He filled a cup and handed it to Django with a smirk. "I'd offer you something stronger, but we're lucky to even have water here." He smirked. "I remember how much you enjoyed the ale."

The dank taste of the horrid beverage Marvin had handed Django at his sister's wedding still lingered on his tongue.

"Life changes in ways we don't expect." Marvin echoed his own words from several days ago. Django had lost his family that day, while Marvin, it seemed, had been given his old life back.

Marvin grabbed a seat opposite and gestured again. "We can't go anywhere until our scouts confirm the Lunar Police haven't tracked us here. Probably means we're here until morning. You might as well get some rest. You look like you haven't slept in a week."

"I haven't," he concurred. "Not properly, at least."

Django dragged his feet to the chair and slumped over. Marvin was right: if he stayed awake long enough to have a conversation, it would be an accomplishment.

"Now, about your questions . . ."

"Oh, I've got plenty. Like, why has everyone I've ever known lied to me? Why is almost everyone I've ever loved dead? And how can I find where those bastards took Eventide?"

Marvin nodded and took a sip of his own water. "That's fair, lad. But let's start with who I really am, and we can fill in some of the blanks later. I'll try to answer any questions you have after that. Fair?"

Django shrugged.

"My real name is Marvin Alejandro. Obviously, I had to assume a new identity when I arrived aboard the *Eclipse*, and so I found a name that was similar. Your parents were sympathetic to my cause. I got extremely lucky."

"My parents knew who you really were?"

That seemed incomprehensible to Django. His parents had never given any indication that Marvin had been anything other than who he claimed to be. The story on the station had always been that life as a shuttle pilot had exposed Marvin to an excessive amount of radiation and he'd needed to stay on board for both medical and mental health reasons.

"They knew who I *wasn't*, at least, and that was all that mattered. I didn't go into detail about all of this." He waved around the room, implying the transition house and the Resurgence itself. "But over the course of the seven years I lived on the *Eclipse*, you and your parents became the only family I had. I had few friends. I kept my distance in case this day might come, but I still resigned myself to the fact that I might never have found the chance to leave."

"Why couldn't you have left? Couldn't you have just stolen a shuttle? Snuck on board a ship that was hauling goods from the station?"

"There are many reasons, but escaping is not as easy a task as you made it look. Besides, I think part of me was happy to have a place where I could have some peace; where I wasn't constantly looking over my shoulder. I grew comfortable, but in doing so, I put all of you in danger."

"How did you get on the *Eclipse* in the first place, if you weren't a shuttle pilot delivering goods to the surface?"

"Has anyone ever told you about the *Infinity*?"

"You mentioned it just before . . ." Django sighed. "Just before you supposedly died. But I didn't understand what you were talking about back then."

"Well, let's just say the people aboard the *Infinity* discovered the truth, just the same as you did. The *whole* station. The Syndicate decided that it was in their best interests to destroy the station to maintain their secrets. I'm the only survivor."

*The entire station?* That would have been *hundreds of thousands* of people. How was that possible?

"I was working a job on that station and managed to escape by hiding out in a shuttle that happened to be headed your way. If I hadn't, I wouldn't be here right now."

"But . . ." Django struggled to wrap his head around the story. "The *Infinity* . . . It was . . ."

"Destroyed." Marvin finished the sentence Django couldn't. "*Infinity*, like the *Eclipse*, was one of twelve space stations that our ancestors built before they were forced to leave Earth."

"So, that much is true? We left Earth because of the wars?" Django tried to hide the hope in his voice. He needed to know something—*anything*—he had believed was still true.

"For the most part. Instead of one station, like you were told, there were twelve. And the plan didn't initially include hiding the planet's true state. That came much later."

"Did our ancestors really destroy the Earth? Or has it been habitable this whole time?"

"They damaged it. Or at least, their actions did. By the time they put any countermeasures in place to reverse the damage, it was too late. This much, you know from your history lessons. Millions of people were displaced; millions more lost access to drinkable water. Soon, countries were at war over access to clean water and land that could still grow food. Both were in short supply. The people revolted, and countries invaded other countries. Desperation led to irrational decisions.

"The irony is, once the wars began in full force, they destroyed much of what our ancestors were fighting over. Soon, the powers that be realized if they didn't put an end to the conflict, there'd be nothing left for anyone. Mass escape shuttles evacuated anyone who wasn't deemed important enough to stay on the planet."

"What made a person important?" Django asked.

"Their wealth."

"Like the Admin," Django said. "Of course, people like Benson would feel entitled enough to remain when nobody else could."

Marvin smirked. "Station Admin are just a speck in the asteroid belt. Benson is just as stuck on that station as anyone else."

*Trapped or not, Benson killed my family. While his pompous ass lounges in his lavish A-Ring.*

"How many people were left?"

"The Earth's population had nearly reached ten billion when the conflict began. Once it was all said and done, only a few *million* people survived. Most of the Earth was a radioactive wasteland. The wealthy took over a few remote spots that had been the least impacted and built their own oasis cities in Iceland, New Zealand, and a few other places that had escaped the worst of the fallout. The elite divided civilian survivors up into twelve equal groups for deportation. These groups would become the founding populations of the FLOW stations.

"The stations themselves were built before the wars, designed to be waypoints to the stars. A step between the Earth and its colonies on Lunar and Mars. But once the Climate Wars ended, they were modified and repurposed to hold humanity hostage."

"Were some people sent here, then?" Django asked. "To the Moon?"

Marvin shook his head. "Colonies had already been established here. Those living off-planet weren't forced into a station, but they weren't allowed to return to the surface, either."

Django rubbed his temples. It was a lot to take in. "As much as this is an interesting history lesson, what does this have to do with you? With the Resurgence?"

"I'm getting to that, but it's important you know what happened in our past so that you understand the Resurgence's purpose and what brings me here."

Django sighed, but he nodded for his uncle to continue.

"The authorities that remained on the planet after the war converged into what is now known as the Syndicate Empire. They claimed dominion over what remained of humanity, but instead of helping to forge a better path forward, they extorted their own people for the resources they produce, and it's been that way ever since. Why do you think you were constantly sending produce and livestock to the surface? It wasn't to heal the planet, Django. It was to provide for the people who live there."

"I'd pieced that much together," Django said. "I'm just struggling to see where the Resurgence comes into it."

Marvin tapped his fingers as though he were growing irritated with being pressed to provide details quicker. He sighed.

"The Resurgence is a movement. It started out as a few young activists, but has seen incredible growth over the past decade. Ever since I left, the group has been slowly biding its time, stashing away resources and building up a community that can take on the Syndicate. The Resurgence was formed to bring them down so that we can restore control over our resources."

"Why can't the Syndicate spread the resources out equally?"

"Because that's not how they think. Look at your station, for example."

'*Your station*,' Django thought. *A few days ago, it was* your *station, too.*

"Admin saw the most benefit on the station, right? The folks in the D-Ring worked the hardest, and most didn't even get their own bed."

Though Django's living conditions were better than that, Marvin had a point.

"The A- and B-Rings hold the most sway," Marvin continued, "and used the most resources, despite more people living on the D-Ring."

"Okay," Django said, running a hand through his hair. "So, what's your point?"

"The Syndicate works in the same way. Think of their leaders on Earth as the A-Ring. The most wealth, but the fewest people. Everything that's mined or manufactured either in the stations, on the Moon, Mars, or the asteroids, the profits go to Earth, and they redistribute it as they see fit.

"The FLOW stations are the D-Ring. You were pulling the weight of the entire system and didn't even know it. The stations grow the food, manufacture goods, and provide the Syndicate with the means to fund their empire. Some colonies further out carry some of the load, but the FLOW stations are the Syndicate's bread and butter. Literally."

"So, this group, the Resurgence, you were a part of them before you came to live on the *Eclipse*?"

"I formed the group," Marvin replied. "I was surprised to

learn it still existed after all these years, but my allies never gave up on the cause. They've just never felt it was the right time to strike. Until now, anyway."

"So, the Resurgence is some kind of private army?"

"In some ways, that's true, but combat operations aren't our key strategy. Right now, we're devising a plan to take out a few of the right people in positions of authority and then move in to fill in the void. We wouldn't get far in an all-out battle against the Syndicate. No matter how prepared we think we are, they are far better armed and have far more resources at their disposal. If we're going to take the Syndicate down, we need to do it from the *inside*."

Django had always thought his uncle had some wild ideas, but it turned out he'd been holding back. Everything he'd said in the last five minutes was nothing short of *crazy*.

Finally, he replied, "Are you going after Benson? Because if you are, count me in."

Marvin let out the loud belly laugh Django remembered from his youth. "You haven't been paying attention, lad! Benson isn't important. He's a pawn in a bigger machine. If we gain control of the Syndicate, we gain control of the stations."

"Benson might not be important to you, but he's taken everything from me. I can't let him get away with that."

"When we last talked, you nearly bit my head off for suggesting you leave the *Eclipse*. Now, you're talking about revenge against the station commander?"

Django waved a hand around the room. "My world isn't what it was a few days ago. I had to kill a man to escape! Benson's the reason I'm out here. The reason . . ."

The words caught in his throat. Everything that had happened over the last week was finally catching up with him.

"The reason what?" Marvin asked, concerned.

"Eventide." Her name caught in his throat. How many days had it been since they'd been separated? Django shook his head, fighting back the tears. The Syndicate, Marvin, even Benson—none of it mattered if he couldn't track her down. "I need to find her."

"I know," Marvin said consolingly. "I was able to track you down. Eventide was a little harder to find, but we know she was taken aboard a Domani ship."

"The *Inanna*," Django confirmed.

Marvin nodded. "But the Empire keeps tight-lipped about its Domani, especially the ones on that ship. We don't know where the *Inanna* was headed yet. Don't worry, though —we'll find her."

Django's lips tightened; he could feel his resolve hardening. "The way that PA bastard was talking, she's going to need our help soon. The things they might be doing to her . . ." He couldn't finish the thought. It was too much.

Marvin moved from his seat and crouched down beside Django, lifting an arm and placing it on his shoulder.

"Listen, kid." Beneath the mask of bravado and confidence, he was still Django's uncle. This *was* still the man Django knew. Concern hovered in his eyes, the same look he had given Django the night of Celeste's wedding, filled with a thousand mysteries and a hundred ideas, but also compassion and fatherly wisdom. "I won't lie. Horrible things happen to the men and women aboard that ship. But life out here, off the station, is pretty horrible for everyone. If it makes you feel any better, the Domani, especially aboard the *Inanna*, are better taken care of than almost anyone else in the system, except for Earth. maybe. The *Inanna*'s a very prestigious vessel. But I know that's a small comfort. I'm working to find out if some of the connections I once had are still alive. It won't be easy to track her down, but we'll find her. Just understand, this could take time, and patience will be our ally. Pulling her out won't be like getting you off the hauler. It's going to take precision."

A rock formed in Django's gut. It seemed to be too much to hope for, but his uncle's offer was the miracle he needed. For all the secrets Marvin held, Django had nobody else he could trust.

"But in return, Django, I'd like to ask something of you."

Django looked past the tears that had formed in his eyes, pushing them back to enable him to focus on his uncle's face. The new Marvin had returned, the firm leader replacing the compassionate uncle. He was in there somewhere, but he was a ghost of himself.

"What could you possibly need from *me?*" Django asked. "I have no credits, no belongings. *Nothing.* How could I possibly help?"

"It's not what you *have* . . ." Marvin said. "It's what you *don't.*"

"What do you mean? I don't . . ."

Marvin grabbed Django's arm a little too enthusiastically, twisting it so that his forearm faced upward. "*This*, my boy."

He pointed to Django's forearm.

"My arm?" Django's heart raced. "You want to cut off my

arm?"

He'd heard of ancient cultures requiring sacrifices such as this as a test of loyalty. Would he be willing to go that far to prove his devotion to his uncle?

*Not that far.*

"What?" Marvin's face twisted in both horror and amusement. "No! What's wrong with you?" He flipped over his own arm. A small flashing light emitted from beneath his skin.

Eventide had had a similar implant inserted when she joined the technicians program: credentials that allowed her to access the maintenance corridors and otherwise restricted areas of the *Eclipse*. As a boy, Django had always been fascinated with the lights coming from Marvin's arm and had later assumed the device existed because, as a shuttle pilot, he also needed access to otherwise off-limit areas.

"You're unchipped," Marvin continued. "The Syndicate install implants in just about everyone in the Empire, except for people born on the stations. They mostly serve the same purpose as an I.D. badge, but they also serve as authentication for tech and equipment."

"So what?" Django asked. "You want me to get one of these?"

"In a manner of speaking," Marvin said. "The Syndicate designs these things so that they're impossible to remove without doing severe damage to the holder's arm. It means the Syndicate guards can spot anyone who has tried to remove their chip straight away. We can mask them to avoid detection—pirates use several methods to get around access points—but we can't alter the devices themselves."

"There's no way to hack into them and change the coding without replacing them?"

"They're encrypted with a synthetic DNA to user DNA handshake. It's one of the few devices that are impossible to skim or fake. Once the chip embeds its code in your bios, the passkey has to be adjusted through the receiving device to allow you access. There's nothing about a person's code that can be changed. It's a mark for life. And if the holder tears it out or cuts off their arm, the encryption still exists. The person is dead to the system and their body will reject a second chip."

"And you want to install one of these things in *me*? If you can't remove it without destroying my arm . . ."

"My crew has informed me Resurgence techs have been able to create a master key. A chip that can access any Syndicate system.

Django didn't know anything about the Syndicate systems, but even to him, the concept sounded too good to be true.

"How did they manage to do that?" he asked.

Marvin paused for a moment, a thoughtful look crossing his face. "It wasn't by accident. A few years ago, whispers circulated about a defunct Syndicate project aimed at creating a 'Universal Authenticator'—a chip for the Syndicate's elite that would bypass normal protocols and grant them access to any system, any tech, anywhere. There are systems that require two, some even three levels of authentication. Anyone with the kind of chip the project was proposing would have unlimited access to every system in the Empire. The Syndicate scrapped it due to the potential risks and vulnerabilities, fearing it would fall into the wrong hands. Never mind that the systems had been segregated for that very reason."

A wry grin formed on his face before he continued. "Their concerns weren't unwarranted, it seems. Resurgence technicians got a hold of the blueprints and prototypes of that project and reassemble the scrambled encryption, creating the master key. It's said to be capable of interacting seamlessly with any Syndicate system, overriding the unique synthetic DNA handshake protocol.

"The only problem is, there was only one encryption code that would work, so the experiment cannot be duplicated. We've got one shot."

Django eyed him skeptically. "I know nothing about this world, uncle. And you want to put this . . . master key . . . in me?"

"Without a holder, the key is useless," Marvin confirmed. "Outside the FLOW stations, it's impossible to find an adult who hasn't been chipped. Without someone like you, we'd have to find and train someone from childhood, and we just don't have that kind of time."

"Look, Uncle Marvin, I'm glad you're alive. I'm glad you got out in time to do all of this, but . . ."

An intrusive beeping interrupted Django. It reminded him of timers he had used back on the *Eclipse* to alert the workers in the fields to any mechanical issues detected with the irrigation system.

Marvin threw up a hand to keep Django from continuing with his sentence. "*Shit,*" he said. "That's the scouts. Someone's found us. We'll continue this discussion later."

# CHAPTER SIXTEEN

Django

Lunar transition house

CHAOS STRUCK THE TRANSITION HOUSE.

Marvin leapt from his squatting position before Django could fully comprehend what was happening.

Django sat on the yellow chair, frozen with indecision and clueless as to what he should do. *Run* would have been his first guess. But in which direction? And where could they go?

He was at Marvin's mercy for now.

"Louis! Petrik!" Marvin yelled into the next room, to two of the Resurgence members Django hadn't spoken to yet. "Take those who can move through the shaft. See if you can lose these guys on the way to the second transition house. And be on the lookout! If the scouts or I can't divert them for long enough, they'll be on your tail.

"Rowyn!" Marvin continued. "Get those unable to run into the shelter. We don't have much time."

Rowyn was already on the move, darting to a patch of discolored regolith flooring and scraping aside dirt to reveal a trapdoor. She pulled it up, continuing to surprise Django with the amount of strength she possessed for someone of such petite stature. Pushing aside the panel, she revealed a staircase that led still further underground. "Anyone unable to run, please head down the stairs," she announced to the stream of people that began to flood the room. "If anyone needs more help, I'll make my way around and help escort you down."

Marvin wasn't done giving orders. "Amy and Vlad, take your teams through the east tunnel and try to divert the LPF from the main group. Lead them as far down as you can. If you can't take them out, at least try to shake them.

"Taku, Wilder, Estevan, Lemongrass. You'll stay here with me to fight off anyone who makes it this far. Everyone else, follow Louis and Petrik and get the hell out of here."

The able-bodied members of the group were up and filing out of the house and down the corridor in a fast but orderly fashion. Django expected there to be grunts of dissatisfaction after only having just arrived and finally being able to rest, but other than the people who were physically incapable of carrying on, there were no complaints.

Those who couldn't stand were being escorted by stronger companions into the hidden stairwell Rowyn had revealed, their arms draped over those who had been designated to be their support as they shuffled along.

Louis, a lean man with black tattoos lining his medium brown skin, already stood by an entrance. Petrik, meanwhile, was hurrying the people who were deciding whether to stay or go. A dark green shirt clung to his short but muscular frame, complimenting the desert-like skin tone of his bulky arms.

Both were calm in their commands, their movements encouraging haste but consciously not inducing panic.

"It's a long trek to the next transition," Petrik stated calmly. "And we're going to need to move fast. If you're not sure you're up to the effort, stay here. Rowyn will ensure your safety, but we'll need to seal the escape route quickly."

The Resurgence member hesitated as he said the words. There were no guarantees, only the hope that they wouldn't be discovered.

Django surveyed the people hurriedly leaving and those feebly being carried down the stairs. He didn't fall into either camp.

These people were his only connection to finding Eventide, and he knew he only had one option.

"I'm staying to fight with you." Django approached Marvin, licking the dryness away from his lips. "I'm not going to another transition house."

Marvin was busy inspecting a weapon. It looked to be another ballistic rifle rather than the blaster pistols the guards on the station and in the port carried. Marvin didn't pause as he replied, "It's not safe. Go with Louis and Petrik. They'll make sure you're taken care of."

"I don't need to be taken care of. I can fight."

"Do you think I just put all these resources at risk to bail you off that hauler for *fun*? I'm not putting you in harm's way. End of story."

Django paused, studying his uncle as the man passed

weapons to the fellow fighters who had committed to staying. "You *came* for me? You knew I was here?"

Marvin finally met Django's eyes, weapon in hand. "I didn't know when we landed, or I would've pulled you out before the PA got you."

"So, Rowyn? Wilder? You didn't take that hauler for them?"

Marvin nodded as he handed off the weapon he was holding and picked up another. "That was how I convinced the others to come get you," he said. "But I wasn't willing to let you go without a fight. I'm still not."

"Eventide's still out there. We can't give up on her, either."

Marvin's frame stiffened as he stopped what he was doing completely. "We're not giving up on her, lad. But getting yourself killed won't help any."

"Let him fight." Taku appeared beside them, a variety of sheathed blades hanging from a belt around his waist. Multiple weapons were strapped to his back, including a mid-sized blaster, which he slung from his shoulder and pushed toward Django. "You ever use one of these, kid?"

Django nodded as he wrapped his fingers around the weapon. It was lighter than the one he'd fired aboard the *Eclipse*, the one he'd used to shoot the station guard, but otherwise it was nearly identical.

Marvin's eyes flashed at his comrade, but Taku stood his ground. "We can't afford to turn anyone away," he said resolutely. "It'll be a good test of the boy's loyalty."

Marvin's face turned more serious. "If we lose him, Taku . . ."

"And if one of us goes down? You might be willing to be a martyr again, but the Resurgence needs me. It's a no win. We shouldn't have been the ones on this mission, but we came because of *him*. Let him earn his place."

Worry danced in Marvin's eyes, but Taku ignored him, grabbed a leather belt from a pile of supplies and pushed it toward Django that stowed two sheathed knives.

The belt was heavier than it looked, but he'd carried heavier items for far longer in the fields. Django tied it around himself quickly.

"I'm staying with you," Django said firmly. "I'm not losing you again."

"If he gets killed," Marvin still addressed Taku. "We miss our chance."

Taku crossed his arms over his chest. "He's going to have to fight sometime, old man." His tone wasn't confrontational, but he wasn't going to be swayed, either. "None of us are safe. You can't keep him locked away forever."

Marvin sighed, his demeanor shifting as he relented. "I wish you'd change your mind, Django, but I can't stop you from staying. That said, I'd rather not add your death to my list of sins, so please watch your back and listen out for our instructions. These people have been doing this a long time."

"There's not much to know. Just point and shoot." Taku lifted his own weapon and flipped through the panel on its touchscreen and set the mode to standby. Django mirrored the steps to do the same. There were other options, including rate of fire and charge intensity, but Django left those on the default settings.

"Just make sure you don't drain the charge before you need it," Taku continued.

Taku then held up two small black disks with a red band that ran across their circumference. Django recognized them as the same charges Taku had used to bring the tunnel down from the dock. "These detonators are to be used as a last resort. They're not remotely controlled like the ones we set up, so be careful you don't blow an arm off. You can either hurl it at a group of soldiers, or set it up on a wall to cause a collapse. Flip the safety switch to access the primer, then click once to activate the device. Twice will set the timer for five minutes. Hit it a third time and you'll have thirty seconds to get the hell out. Click once more to cancel the timer. You've only got two, so make 'em count."

Django nodded in understanding, but he hoped he didn't have to use the devices. He was sure something would go wrong; that he'd set them off at the wrong time, take out his own leg, or, worse, hurt someone he cared about. But he tucked the two devices into a pouch on his new weapons belt.

A flash of movement to the side of the room caught Django's eye. A man dressed from head to toe in khaki staggered in; an old hat lay limp on his head. Scorched marks soiled his clothing, and Django swore smoke was still coming off them. "Alejandro, the LPF are almost here. Twenty minutes, max."

"Move, people!" Marvin commanded. "This is it. Downstairs or get out of here. Amy, Wilder, make it obvious which way we've gone so that they follow us and not the others."

Marvin wrapped an arm around Django and pulled him in tight. "I know this is a lot to take in, lad, but I really wish you'd leave with the others." His eyes flashed a glimmer of desperation; the same look he had given Django when he'd first tried to convince him to leave the *Eclipse*.

"I can't run. Not anymore. I ran from the station, and look what it got me. Like I said, I'm not going to lose you, too—not without a fight."

Marvin clasped a hand on Django's shoulder. "All right, just be careful. Don't make any rash decisions. Make sure there's someone left who's willing to go after Eventide at the end of all this."

"You swear you'll help her?" Django asked. "I need to know that if something happens to me, she'll still be looked after."

"I swear," Marvin confirmed. "But you know I won't be able to forgive myself if anything happens to you."

"I'm not yours to protect. Not anymore."

"Uncle or not, we all look after each other here. That's what set us apart from the Syndicate."

The alarm increased in volume and intensity as the last of the Resurgence members who were leaving disappeared out the side door.

The tension surrounding them reached a fever pitch, and they were running out of time before the Lunar forces would descend. Django gripped his newly obtained weapon, preparing for the worst.

Rowyn finished helping the last few people through the trapdoor, then pushed the panel back into place, concern etched onto her face.

"Aren't you joining them?" Django asked.

"I need to stay out here and fight," she said. "There's nothing I can do for them in there. The only way they make it out is if we make sure the soldiers can't get to them."

The entire standoff seemed flawed to Django, as though they were winging it and hoping for the best.

Marvin shoved an envelope into Django's hand, tearing him from his thoughts. It bore the same handwriting and seal as the note that Avery Inglewood had passed to him only days before. "This is for if we get separated," he explained. "Don't open it until it's safe."

Marvin didn't stick around to allow Django to ask questions. Their time was up, and he moved into position by the exit.

"Amy!" he called to a woman who, despite appearing to be in her early forties, carried herself as though she could take on whatever army was coming all by herself. "You and Vlad pull the crew out, now! Make as much noise as you can!"

Amy nodded and signaled to her team, who followed her through the open door. Not even two minutes had passed before gunfire echoed back through the tunnels into the transition house.

"They're closer than we thought . . ." Taku murmured, steadying himself. "Whatever happens, we can't let them take this house. We have to protect those still inside the tunnels and seal the exit to the next transition house at all costs. We can't risk the rest of the team being followed."

Wilder grunted, and Rowyn nodded in acceptance of the order.

"What about the people hiding in the cellar?" Django asked. "What happens to them if we blow the exit?"

"Hopefully, it won't come to that, lad," Marvin answered.

"But if it does, the cellar will be cut off from the house as well. It goes far back enough into the rock face that our people will be safe. Someone will come back for them once the threat has passed."

Marvin and Taku stepped into the tunnel that ran along the outside of the house, like a street would have above ground.

Gunfire echoed in the direction Amy had taken her team. The LPF was close.

Marvin moved carefully as he led his team in the direction from which the firing was coming, intent on sealing off the path to the transition house. Taku was right by his side, one of his weapons raised to his shoulder, anticipating a rush of enemies from around the corner ahead. A dozen Resurgence members marched with them, pulling ahead by ten meters or so. Wilder and Rowyn lingered behind with Django.

"Try to keep up," Taku called back. Despite him not having raised his voice, the command echoed through the passageway. "We don't want to get separated."

Rowyn picked up her pace, getting a few steps ahead of Django and Wilder. She held her weapon tenaciously as she closely surveyed the dimly lit passage.

Django brought up the rear with Wilder by his side. His muscles shook as adrenaline coursed through his body. He could tell he wasn't up to his full strength. Maybe he had no business fighting alongside these people, but he had cast his lot now. He wouldn't stop until Eventide was free.

He wasn't going to run. Not again.

A mid-pitched pulse tore through the tunnel, the compression wave nearly knocking Django off his feet.

"Oh, *sh . . .*"

An explosion shook the walls. Fragments of rock rained down from above, silencing his uncle's curse.

"What was that?" Django yelled.

Marvin and Taku steadied their weapons and fired into the darkness ahead of them, striking at an enemy hidden in the shadows.

Another pulse. This one sent Django to his knees, and he covered his ears with his hands. The sensation tore through his head, unleashing a pain in his temple that made him want to reach in and tear his own brain out to make it stop.

The intensity of this blast was far more extreme than the first, sending rocks crashing from the ceiling into the pathway between Django and his uncle.

Right on top of Rowyn.

Eventide Rossi
The *Inanna*

INTENSE, nauseating pain woke Eventide Rossi. Her thoughts drifted through a vast vacuum of confusion, lightyears away from the nearest breath of air, with no shuttle to tether to, and under threat of disappearing completely into the void. Her entire body screamed in agony, as though she'd fallen onto the electrified rails and been run over by the inter-Ring tram aboard the *Eclipse*.

*What the hell happened to me?*

Her face hung through a hole cut at the edge of a table, reminding her of receiving a massage in one of the B-Ring recovery rooms.

*Worst massage ever.*

Massages were supposed to be relaxing—nice, even— despite the necessity of someone else having to touch her.

This *definitely* wasn't that. She wasn't just stiff and sore;

her muscles screamed as though they had been stretched out with a torture device and then pressed through a juicer.

*Was I in an accident?*

The pain didn't contain itself to her muscles or joints, either, or even her skin. It coursed through her *entire* being, as though blades traveled through her veins, her bones, and into her muscles from the inside out. Every fiber of her being felt like it had been torn apart and reconstructed at a molecular level.

She searched her brain for glimpses of what might have happened, but the throbbing was so persistent, she couldn't concentrate, and there were so many pieces missing. Everything was lost in a haze, but Eventide put every ounce of concentration she could muster into remembering.

She had been at Celeste's wedding with Django. Something had happened there.

*A hull breach? Did a meteor storm hit* Eclipse?

That felt close, but it wasn't quite right. It was something like that, something familiar . . . but she knew it was wrong. The pain that radiated through her body kept the information just out of reach.

*Why do I feel so groggy?*

Eventide attempted to ignore the pain, to focus on what else lay around her. It was a trick she had learned while pushing her body to its limits undergoing the station's technicians training. When she had signed up for the role, she hadn't realized how physically demanding the training would be. Weeklong bootcamps were a part of the job, and the station admin demanded that their recruits were in peak physical condition.

A strange requirement for an engineer.

Strange, because she had been secretly training for something else. But what?

The thought seemed to be just beyond her grasp, through a fog she couldn't quite push past.

*If only I could extinguish the fire tearing through me . . .*

She needed to find out where she was. Eventide grimaced into the headrest and forced her eyelids to open.

At first, everything was blurry, sleep crust clinging to her eyes and mixing with the tears that ran over her eyelashes. But she *could* see.

Eventide did her best to blink away the scales, and to her relief, some of the crust flicked off her eyelids. Not all of it, but enough.

Movement outside the edge of her vision caught her attention. Wherever she was, she wasn't alone.

White cloaks swept beneath the table, while white floor tiles were cast in a blinding and sterile white light.

*This is a medical facility.*

Perhaps she *had* been in an accident. She just wished she could remember; or understand anything about her situation. Judging by the pain she was in, perhaps she was lucky to be alive. The chances of surviving a hull breach were extremely low.

*Has anyone else ever survived one?* Not to her recollection. No, this had to be something else.

Eventide allowed her mind to search through the pain, straining for the memories that might provide some answers.

*Where did I go after the wedding?*

Her quarters. Django had visited her in the B-Ring quarters. He wasn't supposed to be there, but he'd come to tell her something. That he . . . *loved* her, maybe?

Then, the idiot had kissed her, proclaiming he had feelings for her.

*Why did he have to do* that?

Eventide had always known, of course, but it wasn't something they'd ever spoken about. Certainly, it wasn't something he'd ever *acted* on. They had been friends for so long, and she wasn't sure if she could ever feel the same way . . .

*Wait . . . That* did *happen, but not in my quarters. We were on a shuttle when he kissed me. We were leaving* Eclipse.

*Why would we ever do that . . .?*

And then it all rushed back to her in a flood. The kiss. The *Redemption*. The arrest.

The *Inanna*.

Memories of being pulled aboard a different ship came back to her. Dozens of men and women, wearing silk outfits that Eventide would have described as pajamas, greeted her. The memories were still fuzzy, but she couldn't forget the outfits and how uncomfortable they'd looked. Each wore the same cut, but in a variety of colors. The outfit's front consisted of two slender strips of fabric that revealed more than Eventide was used to.

*Why were they all so muscular and toned?*

And the nodes implanted in each of their necks . . . Large hexagonal nodules that extruded from their skin by nearly a centimeter. Each of them wore a necklace that connected the two nodes like a battery and swooped down the front of their necks. Some were more elaborate, spreading across their chests and drawing attention to the men's pectoral muscles and the women's breasts. Her neck itched just thinking about it.

She remembered them being friendly. *Too* friendly.

After the ship had taken off, she had been taken to the ship's bar. The other passengers took turns talking to her. Their conversations sickeningly sweet and artificial, as if they were robots. Sweet like candy. Like the drink they had given her.

Their conversations were a blur. But whatever they had told her had horrified her to the point of disbelief.

*What* is *this place?*

Then she remembered everything going fuzzy; a wave of disorientation. And then nothing.

Until she woke on this bed, in more pain than she'd ever imagined possible.

Something had happened at that bar. Something that had caused her to pass out. It was almost as if they had drugged . . .

*The drink.*

Someone must have put something in her drink. But why? And how long had she been unconscious for?

*And why do I feel like I've been hit by a space shuttle?*

"The patient is conscious," a man's voice said from across the room. "Did you give her enough sedative?"

"The standard amount," a woman's voice replied.

"For a woman? That's not sufficient," the man answered. "She's small, but she's got twice the muscle mass of most of the women we pick up. Increase the dosage."

Eventide let out a groan. *What are they doing to me?*

Fire entered her veins as a needle stabbed into her arm. It must have been the sedative, but what kind of sedative hurt that much?

"What . . .?" She groaned again. She wanted to ask a question, but it was hard to form the words. "What are you doing to me?"

Eventide heard the garbled words leave her mouth as though they were spoken by someone else.

Someone intoxicated.

She muttered a curse, but all coherence was lost, drifting on the hypnotic ebb . . .

She should have never left the station, or have let herself be put into a situation like this.

*A situation like . . . what, exactly? What's happening to me?*

Guilt surfaced above the pain, but as soon as it appeared, she pushed it aside.

*No! I'm not to blame here. This is* not *my fault.*

Her brain spun out of control as she tried to focus; tried to fight the sedative that had been pumped into her veins and the fire that accompanied it.

*Why are they doing this?*

Eventide moved to push herself off the table—

Or at least, she tried. But her arms wouldn't cooperate. She gasped, struggling to get air into her lungs.

*I've got to move!*

Maybe she was approaching things the wrong way. Slight movements might be easier for her body to manage, and perhaps they would prime her neural pathways to engage in larger ones.

It was worth a shot.

Eventide focused on her fingertips, straining with the effort . . .

*Easy,* she thought, doing her best to settle the rage building inside of her. *I'm not going to get anywhere if I tire myself out flexing my fingers.*

Her breath steadied as she focused everything she had into reducing her heart rate and silencing her mind. It wasn't hard to achieve, thanks to the sedative, and the pain gradually settled to a dull ache that throbbed within her. There must have been analgesic in that shot, too.

*Have to stay awake . . .*

Her fingertips tingled. Eventide concentrated on just the index finger of her left hand, thinking about what it would be like to move it.

She took a deep breath and visualized the finger moving several times in her mind. If she could just get it to cooperate, she would be one step closer to getting off the table and getting some answers.

*One step closer to leaving this place.*

First time: nothing. She might as well have been willing a spoon to bend with her mind.

Second attempt: the same.

On the third try, she cleared her mind, thinking of nothing but steadying her breath, then worked on the movement of pulling her trigger finger on her left hand, an action she'd performed countless times during weapons training.

She squeezed the imaginary gun's trigger and felt her finger graze the soft surface of a blanket.

*It worked!*

The world entered into a spin. The dose of whatever she'd been injected with was surging at full strength. Eventide fought back tears as the fire spreading through her veins renewed. Surely the sensation had to stop?

Her mind threatening to lose consciousness, she focused on her trigger finger.

*Have to . . . stay awake . . .*

Mikka
  Shackleton City

MIKKA SIPPED COFFEE from a stainless steel mug as she watched the dockworkers loading the last of David Aries's cargo onto the *Redemption*.

The mug wasn't hers; she'd taken it from David's apartment. She felt a shred of guilt at lifting something from his place after the incredible night they'd shared, but she promised herself that she would return it as soon as they got back from their mission. He probably wouldn't even notice it was missing.

*Just watch, I've stolen a Syndicate commander's favorite mug.*

Mikka couldn't remember the last time she'd had a coffee mug that was so new that it added a metallic aftertaste to her drink. But that wasn't the reason she'd taken the mug, nor was it her pirate's predilection to pilfer coming home to roost.

She simply couldn't resist leaving the apartment without at least one more cup of coffee.

Coffee beans were such a hard commodity to come by, as nearly all harvested quantities were shipped to the Earth's surface. The remaining stocks were sent to Syndicate leaders in the cities on Lunar, Mars, and other outposts. For anyone outside of elite Syndicate circles, coffee was either off-limits or bootlegged.

Unsurprisingly, the coffee in David's apartment was some of the finest she'd ever sampled. Smooth and balanced between natural sweetness and gentle acidity, Mikka swore she even tasted notes of chocolate on the finish.

In one of life's little ironies, she and Kiara had made a great deal of credits off the back of black market coffee transport, but if she had known the quality of what she'd been hauling, she might have been more tempted to skim some beans off the top of her deliveries.

Today, she wouldn't be transporting coffee or anything else that was listed in the gray area of what she could legally carry. This mission was purely philanthropic, hauling something helpful for a good cause. Something that would change the fate of the Empire. Possibly forever.

There were twenty crates that needed to be loaded onto the *Redemption*. Mechanized lifts undertook the strenuous labor, a task that, in any other port Mikka had ever found herself in, would've been performed through a combination of manpower and machinery.

Hoists loaded crates of varying shapes and sizes onto different vessels across the port. None of the crates were marked with anything that would betray their contents, but

Mikka would have bet a significant number of credits that most them contained weapons.

Where Aries was shipping arms to, or what his plans for them were once they reached their destination, was anyone's guess. But if Mikka was going to play a part in this game of his, she was going to have to trust the moves he made.

Until yesterday, there wouldn't have been a flaming chance in hell that she would have been able to say she trusted the man with a straight face.

Now, though, she had *every* reason to believe in him.

Aries had arranged for the Redemption to be towed to this side of the port, which Mikka was less than enthused about. Under the auspices of her ship being impounded, it was the only permitted method of bringing a civilian vessel into the restricted area.

Mikka had never thought of the *Redemption* as being particularly spacious, but parking it next to full-scale war machines was almost embarrassing. The dark, ominous ships dwarfed her own; as a short-range hauler, it was only equipped for a crew of six or eight. Its quarters were cozy, but the ship made up for it with plenty of cargo space, particularly for the discreet, more valuable contracts she sought. It was a small enough craft that when she'd first salvaged the ship, Mikka had piloted the craft solo. But navigation was a hell of a lot easier if she had at least one other crew member on board—and partnering with someone as skilled as Kiara was every captain's dream.

The navigator continued to surprise her. As a prime example, back at the apartment building in Aldrin Square, before Mikka had left for her dinner date, Kiara had been crying; something Mikka rarely saw from the woman. The tears might not have been flowing freely, but they were there. Kiara hadn't even attempted to hide them.

Aries had given Kiara's kids something the navigator had only been able to dream of before: safety, security, clean food, and water. Ship's navigator wasn't the worst gig in the Loop, but with all the Syndicate taxes and import fees heaped on haulers like the *Redemption*, Mikka and Kiara barely made enough to make ends meet. It didn't help that Kiara's job meant her kids also needed a full-time sitter.

Now, they had *three*.

Working for a Syndicate commander with a conscience might not have been what either Mikka or Kiara would have imagined as a career path, but now Mikka had no desire to do anything else.

Abigail Monroe could keep her bloody pirate's life and take her little rebellion with Marvin Alejandro and shove it up her ass.

But from the moment Mikka had entered the landing docks, despite the navigator's wave of emotions the day before, it was clear that Kiara didn't share her views on this one.

"This is too much, Meeks."

Kiara stood beside her, her open mouth almost to the floor. For as long as Kiara remained under contract, Aries had granted the navigator the same access as Mikka.

"What does the Syndicate need with all these ships?" Kiara asked, expressing the same thought Mikka had ruminated less than twenty-four hours ago. "There's nobody else out there! Who are they planning to fight?"

"They want to ensure nobody threatens the Empire's stability," Mikka replied. "They're stationed here for our protection. Who knows, maybe they'll be used to better life here for us one day."

"For *our* protection?" Kiara scoffed. "More like their own!"

Mikka nodded. After all, that *had* been the intent of the Empire. "We'll see."

"'We'll see?' What's gotten into you?"

"David has a plan," she said. "He's going to turn this Empire around."

Kiara looked at her with an icy glare. "He's '*David*' now? I don't know what he told you at dinner, but it's obvious you're thinking with your crotch."

It was a step too far, but Kiara couldn't possibly have known that Mikka had spent the night with the commander, and she sure as hell wanted to keep it that way.

Ever since David Aries had helped her slip away from the Boneyard eight years ago, she had fantasized that the man would later take her into his chambers. She had never imagined that he would one day become a commander, plot a revolution, bring her into his plan—and then into his bedroom.

But here she was, and for once in her life, things seemed to be going right for a change.

Small steps forward. And the future had never looked so bright.

*How much* does *Kiara know?* The navigator was intuitive, but to divine that Mikka had spent the night with Aries? That would be borderline mind reading.

Mikka shook her head. She was getting ahead of herself. There was one telltale sign Kiara didn't know where she had spent the night; the woman hadn't upped and quit yet.

But be that as it may, Mikka couldn't let the disrespect lie. "What do you know of it?" she asked, a little harsher than she intended, but no more than she meant.

"I see the way you two look at each other. Now, you're defending a Syndicate armada, of all things! The man's got inside your head." Kiara tapped her own temple to emphasize her point. "There's enough firepower here to blow Shackleton clean off the surface. Don't get caught up in this little fantasy of yours and forget where you came from. There's no enemy to fight. They built these ships to keep *us* in line."

"He's not like them, Kiara . . ."

"What's gotten into you? Powerful men don't relinquish their power easily; they always thirst for more. You know this."

"After all he's done for you," Mikka said evenly, "I'd like to think you'd be a little more willing to keep an open mind."

Kiara rolled her eyes. "'An open mind?' Do you hear yourself?"

"Come on." Mikka pushed her way forward toward the *Redemption*, her nostrils flaring. "We need to go over our preflight checks."

There was no sense in arguing. Kiara wouldn't understand. *Couldn't* understand. But why not?

*Why can't Kiara see everything that David has been doing?*

He was trying to right the wrongs of the Syndicate; start fresh from within. David had supplied the means to take care of Kiara's kids, too. How could she not see that the man was different?

"*Stop!*" Kiara shouted above the noise of the machinery, the mechanics, and the clangs of metal on metal that echoed through the docks. "What the actual *fuck*, Mikka?"

Mikka stopped in her tracks. Though the air was usually blue aboard the *Redemption*, it was rare for Kiara to swear *at* her.

"You were a bloody *pirate!* That in itself against every ethos of the Syndicate! Three days ago, you were furious about how they've treated the people in the Tubes. Your mother just about died because of the policies of *this* man. *Why* are you defending him? This fleet of ships could obliterate every base on Lunar, and Mars, too, probably, and you're just going to keep on doing deliveries for him like you're not getting tangled in this web of . . . of *whatever* it is he's planning. This isn't like you!"

Maybe it was a bit much to take in all at once. Even Mikka had to admit, it was a quick about-face after all the years of running. But she was done with that. In one night, Commander Aries had convinced her that he was different from the rest of the Syndicate leaders; that he was going to bring about change. But Kiara had reason to be skeptical. She hadn't heard Aries's motivations for his ascent to power. She hadn't seen the packages of food they were about to deliver to the FLOW stations.

"For one, He bailed us out of the OG's bullshit fine that nearly cost me the *Redemption*, which, might I remind you, would have left you unemployed! He's given Mom a home! He's given *you* a home!"

Kiara's eyes watered. "Do a few generous acts cancel a *century* of heinous crimes? What price will we pay for those gifts?"

Mikka took a deep breath to calm herself. "He confided in me last night, at dinner. He told me some things about his past; about his motivations and why he wants to see the Empire fall."

Kiara's gaze shifted, subtly changing. Even before she spoke, Mikka could tell the navigator wasn't buying it. Kiara would never believe a man like Aries could change, no matter what he did for her. They had both seen the unrelenting hardship of a system run by the Syndicate Empire. Had Mikka not been with Aries the night before, witnessing first-hand the man he *could* be, she wouldn't have believed it herself.

"He's playing you, Mikka. Feeding you out of the palm of his hand like a trained sparrow."

Mikka had to bite her tongue. If this had come at any other point in their business relationship, she might have thrown a fist at Kiara's jaw at best, or told her to find a new ship at worst. But Mikka meant it about Kiara being the best navigator she had ever come across. She couldn't afford to lose her.

If Kiara would stick around for long enough, Mikka could convince her she was right. For this to work, she had no other choice.

If Aries could convince Mikka, it was possible to convince *anyone*, even Kiara.

But until that happened, she couldn't afford to have Kiara

sabotage the mission. She needed to know that her navigator wouldn't act against her.

"Do you trust me or not?" Mikka asked. "I can't afford to have a liability on this mission."

This payload was the key to everything. The path to preventing the most bloodshed.

*This mission would change everything.*

"I trusted you until the moment you let that pirate aboard our ship. Ever since then, I don't know who you are anymore. It's been one bad decision after another."

Mikka bristled. "Well, the good thing is, you don't need to like our orders, Kiara. You just have to follow them."

"Do you even know what we're delivering?" Kiara asked. "You saw their confusion when we dropped the last package off on the *Eclipse*."

Mikka smiled, seeing a way to reach her friend's heart. "It's food."

"What do you mean, 'food?' FLOW stations are farms. Why are we delivering something they already grow?"

"You think the Syndicate leaves them with their fair share?"

Kiara paused. She was too upset to agree, but the understanding look in her eyes confirmed Mikka had made her point.

"Aries is planning to reveal the truth to the FLOW stations. You heard Marvin: they all believe they're the last remnants of humanity. This will open their eyes; cause them to question their reality and stop sending their produce to the elite on the surface. Once the station residents realize the

Syndicate has been lying to them, the Empire will be forced to play fair or risk losing their main food source."

Kiara crossed her arms. "I know you have a crush on this man, Meeks, but you're being manipulated. I hope you see that before it's too late."

Mikka scoffed, rolling her eyes and crossing her arms defensively. Kiara still didn't get it. Trust was a commodity hard to come by. What more could Aries do to prove himself? To prove the vision of the Empire he'd shown Mikka?

If Kiara couldn't trust *her,* at least, then maybe they didn't have the relationship Mikka thought they did.

Done with the conversation, Mikka stormed away before she said something she couldn't take back.

Mikka

The *Redemption*

THERE WAS no time for delays.

It took nearly an hour for the Syndicate ground crew to finish loading the crates into the *Redemption*'s cargo hold. Despite Aries's intention to accomplish his mission quickly, he was only willing to designate a skeleton crew to handle the goods. It made sense, considering that he wanted to keep things discreet, but it was difficult for Mikka not to grow anxious as she watched the minutes tick by.

Though Mikka's usual contracts were never particularly large, the twenty crates, stacked two high, easily lined up against one of the ship's bulkheads. As per standard shipping protocols, magnetic clamps held the boxes in place so that even if the *Redemption*'s artificial gravity failed, the cargo wouldn't be sent hurling across the ship.

Mikka watched the last of the crates being loaded up

with mechanized lifts, every tick of the clock an agonizing eternity.

She knew she was overthinking it, but they were already behind schedule and they hadn't even left the port yet. Experience told her that this wouldn't be the only delay, either. Just because the *Redemption* was now registered on the Syndicate network with the special permissions it would need to bypass any Orbital Guard inspections, it didn't mean there wouldn't be other delays.

Aries wanted the deliveries to be completed within the next week, and despite the FLOW stations all being within Earth's orbit, the logistics of getting to and docking at each one, without lengthy discussions at checkpoints and arranging the appropriate appointments at each station, never mind filling out the required paperwork, meant they would have to keep a steady pace. Having to complete manifests for a shipment that was supposed to remain off-the-books still aggravated Mikka, but forged documents would raise fewer questions than none at all.

Once the preflight checks were complete, Mikka and Kiara boarded the craft and fired up the launch sequence. With the time they'd already wasted, they would be lucky if they got to their first destination before docking hours had ended. Mikka didn't welcome the idea that they might launch now, only to have to spend the night on the *Redemption*.

Not when spending the night with David was the alternative.

But they couldn't wait until tomorrow, either. Even if they dropped off one consignment, it'd be a start.

As it was, docking at each FLOW station was going to be

a long trip. Kiara was still fuming and hadn't said a word to Mikka since their altercation in the loading bay.

Mikka punched in her codes with trepidation. The last thing she wanted was to be delayed any further by the two of them getting into another fight. They had their mission. Kiara might not have trusted Aries's intentions, but she had agreed to the job. Nevertheless, it might have been too late for the navigator to back out, but Kiara could still make their trip a difficult one.

Mikka would let the matter lie as long as Kiara did. It was her mission—and her ship—and she had shut down any talk of dissent. The matter was over and done with, as far as she was concerned. She didn't need Kiara to be friendly, as long as she did her job like a professional.

Once they were given clearance from ground control, the *Redemption*'s ion drive fired up and propelled them out of the reaches of Lunar's gravity, past the force field that protected its inhabitants from the endless void of space.

The *Redemption* rumbled around them, bringing a smile to Mikka's face. There was nothing like being on the shuttle again. Her time with Aries had been fun, but being on land made her restless. Being aboard her ship was where she felt most at home.

"Where's our first stop?" Mikka had memorized the itinerary, but she sought to cut the tension by carrying on as normal.

"Space station *Freedom*, ETA ninety minutes. Sit back and enjoy the ride."

Kiara finished punching in the coordinates on her console, then took her own advice and leaned back, resting her head on her hands, elbows out. Her thick black boots thudded onto the dash, causing Mikka to wince.

When Kiara had first joined the *Redemption,* the careless action had nearly made Mikka toss the navigator out on her ass. Mikka didn't want black scuff marks, dirt, and regolith dust clogging up her controls, especially since she took extreme care in cleaning and maintaining the craft to top-notch condition. But once Kiara proved herself to be responsible and took care of the equipment better than if it were her own, Mikka eventually let the action slide.

Today, though, Mikka didn't put it past Kiara to be doing it just to grind her gears. She wouldn't take the bait, though. If anything, Kiara was giving herself more cleaning to do later.

Instead, Mikka let her gaze drift to the stars outside their viewport and tried to clear her head. Watching the other ships and shuttles scurry about the Loop was almost distracting enough to keep her mind from drifting back to David Aries.

*Almost.*

The time passed quickly as Mikka wrestled with her thoughts and emotions about the man who had won her over. Everything she had worked so hard to achieve—security for her mother, a well-paying job that didn't have her skirting around the law for once, not to mention someone to pull into her arms, a man of power—was all coming together. Never had Mikka expected even her wildest dreams to come true. And best of all, she still got to fly her ship.

There was no need to waste away in a Syndicate tower. She still had a purpose to be out among the stars. Any of these little side missions Aries had for her, she'd be more than happy to fulfill.

It seemed like no time at all before the FLOW station grew larger in the ship's viewport, and Mikka breathed a sigh of relief that the flight to *Freedom* had been uneventful.

*As smooth as can be. If only all my jobs were this easy.*

"Have you been in contact with the crew yet?"

They had barely said two words to each other since they had left Lunar. Kiara had seemed content to monitor the frequencies of the orbit and Mikka wasn't in the mood to talk.

"Just now." Kiara lifted a finger, signaling for her to wait a moment. She lifted her other hand to her ear as though she were having a hard time hearing whoever was on the other end.

Kiara shook her head. "They're saying there is no scheduled pickup on the manifest." Her fingers moved swiftly over the console. "Copy, *Freedom*. We're not picking up. We're dropping off."

Mikka cursed silently. She'd been worried this might be a problem. On the *Eclipse*, they'd had the benefit of having Abigail along for the pickup Marvin had arranged for the *Black Swan*. They had already been on board when they'd convinced the *Eclipse*'s crew to accept the delivery. Here, they were going to struggle just to get on board.

"Open the main channel," Mikka commanded. "We don't have time for this."

Kiara nodded and hit a few strokes on her control panel, then snapped and pointed a finger gun at Mikka to indicate that the channel was live.

"*Freedom*, this is Captain Mikka Jenax of the shuttle

*Redemption.* We have a delivery from the surface for you. I know it's a little unorthodox, but the commander is expecting this. It's incredibly important to the station, and I know he won't be happy if you turn us around."

Kiara let out a huff and rolled her eyes. Mikka hated lying, but she had to believe what Marvin had told her about the station's beliefs. As far as the people on the station in front of them knew, they were the last vestiges of humanity in the system, and all their efforts focused on sending supplies down to their dead planet in the hope of one day reversing the effects of the war. The *Freedom*'s personnel wouldn't understand any excuse that conflicted with that.

"All right . . . *Captain.*" There was a tone in the communications officer's voice that suggested he hadn't heard the word 'Captain' being used before.

*Of course he hasn't. Shuttle haulers that go between this station and the docks probably refer to themselves as 'pilots.' This is probably the first time he's ever had to interact with one.*

She was botching the mission already, and this was only the first run. If the station turned her around, or sought to get authorization from their commander, *Freedom* might refuse them from boarding altogether.

"This is Comms Officer Lionel Bongard," the voice continued. "Give me a second. I need to refer this to my supervisor."

"This isn't going well," Kiara stated flatly. "Your boyfriend should have smoothed over the protocol for us to deliver these shipments. FLOW stations literally only ever ship *out.*"

"I'm well aware of that," Mikka said, trying to keep the annoyance out of her tone but guessing she was failing miserably. "But Aries can't have these shipments traced back to him. Any rebellion aboard the stations has to appear as though it's organic."

"And if the uprisings don't come?" Kiara asked. "What then?"

"Right now, we've been hired for *this* part of the plan. Let's focus on that for now."

"*Aye, aye, Captain.*" Kiara tossed a mock salute in Mikka's direction, but her eyes were already studying something else on her holo-screens.

Mikka held her breath as she waited for a response on the other end of the channel. Every second of silence seemed like an eternity. What *would* she do if the *Freedom* turned them around? How would she get the goods to the station then? Would Aries think she wasn't up to the task? What would it mean for her role? What would it mean for her mother?

*What would it mean for us?*

Only now did the hold Aries had on her life creep into Mikka's thoughts. If she let him down, she let her mother down as well.

She shook off the thought as she cemented her stance. *That* wasn't going to happen. David wouldn't do that to her.

*He's different*, she reminded herself. *He's proven that.*

"Jenax, can you confirm what you're delivering and verify that it's not contaminated?"

*Contaminated?*

Then the realization struck her.

*Of course.*

If the planet was still irradiated from the wars, the FLOW stations would naturally be concerned that *anything* from the planet might be the same. How many blunders could she make in one conversation?

"I sure as hell wouldn't have it on my ship if it was," she said, hoping an air of confidence would see her through. "As for the contents, that's not my department. I'm guessing it's research of some kind; probably has to do with how far the planet's healing has progressed. But nobody tells me these things. I'm expected to do my job, and that's it. We get loaded up and shipped out, same as we do when we're on the station."

That, at least, the man would be able to understand.

The ship's hum, along with the beeps of the internal computers, filled the silence as Mikka waited for the comms officer to respond. Kiara's chair squeaked as she turned in it.

*I really need to fix that . . .*

"You're not one of the regulars, Jenax. I'm fairly new to this position, but I've gotten to know most of the other pilots."

Kiara exchanged a worried glance with Mikka.

"What are you saying?" Mikka asked. "Where else would I be from?"

"I suppose . . ." The comms officer left the thought unfinished, but the conflict going on in his head was almost audible. Mikka was a stranger who had said a few things that didn't seem quite right, but as far as the officer was concerned, there was nowhere else she *could* be coming from. His gut was wrestling with his brain.

"Listen, Lionel," Mikka said, deciding he had deliberated for long enough. "I don't know what you think we're trying to pull, or why we'd be bringing anything other than what Admin has instructed us to. You can make all the checks you want. Give the commander a shout, too. I know he's a very busy man, but I'm sure he won't mind being interrupted by a delivery."

Another long pause. Mikka didn't mind this one as much. She was confident the comms officer wouldn't risk bothering the station commander. She doubted the crewman even had access to Administration, and his supervisor probably didn't, either. Reporting his suspicions would involve a long chain of requests to reach the man at the top and, somewhere along the line, risked the communications officer being reprimanded for wasting Admin's time.

At least, she hoped that was how it played out.

Eventually, the crewman sighed. "All right, *Redemption*, you're approved for docking. We have you scheduled for boarding at 0900 hours. Please stand by until then."

A faint click confirmed the frequency being closed and Mikka felt the tension leave her neck and shoulders as she smiled self-assuredly.

Until she realized what their delivery time would be

"0900?" she repeated. The computer's clock blinked 17:35.

*That lazy bastard wasn't stalling because he's not sure of our origin. He just doesn't want to pull in a ship at the end of the day.*

"Son of a . . ." She let the curse trail off.

It looked like they'd be spending the night. It wasn't ideal, but when they showed up unannounced, Mikka couldn't expect much more from a station with a small loading bay.

"Hurry up and wait," Kiara quipped. One of them had to say it.

"We might as well make ourselves comfortable. Set us up in the overnight queue and cut the engines."

"Sure thing, Captain. We've . . ." Kiara trailed off.

"What is it?"

Kiara furrowed her brow at the screen. "There's a ship headed toward us at maximum burn. It could just be a coincidence . . . but it seems to adjust accordingly whenever I alter course."

"Can you get a read on what type of vessel it is?" Mikka asked, a second before a deafening siren assaulted her ears.

"What in the fractured orbit . . .?" Kiara cursed, just barely audible between the wails of the alarm. More curses followed as Kiara dashed from one screen to another.

"Computer, decrease alarm volume to ten percent! I can tell there's a damned emergency!"

The *Redemption* shook violently, throwing Mikka into one of the bridge's command consoles.

Kiara picked herself up off the floor and jabbed in several keystrokes into the holographic inputs. "We're under attack!"

Django
Lunar transition house

DJANGO'S SCREAM carried on long after the rock had settled.

Rowyn had been there. *Right there.* Ahead of both him and Wilder. Running determinedly, increasing the distance between them, encouraging them to hurry.

Then, in a sudden avalanche of rock, she was gone.

As the dust settled, Django stood in disbelief in the now-barricaded tunnel. A large arm wrapped around his shoulder. He struggled to push it off, but trying to move Wilder's arm was like trying to move a tree trunk; his grip was steadfast.

A cloth descended over his face and Django panicked, trying to push it off, before he realized Wilder was providing a filter for the dust so that it didn't enter his lungs. He grabbed the cloth so that he could hold it up himself, but he didn't stop trying to break free from Wilder's grip.

The grasp was intended to be comforting; an embrace meant to calm him down and ease his pain.

Django wasn't ready to mourn.

Not until he saw Rowyn's lifeless body. Until then, there was still a chance she was alive.

"Let go!" Django yelled.

"Django, we have to leave!"

"No! We need to help Rowyn!"

He wouldn't let another friend die. He wasn't going to run. That's what got him into this mess.

*That's why Eventide's gone.*

"There's no way she would have survived that much rock falling on her! Sorry, she was my friend, too, but . . ." Wilder drifted off, as though considering what to do. "We can't waste time."

"'Waste!'" Django wrestled free of Wilder's loosening grip. "This is our *friend* you're talking about! You don't want to save her because it would be a *waste* of time?"

Wilder put up his hands placatingly. "*Nobody* could have survived that! And you heard what Alejandro said—we have to seal that exit! That's our top priority now! If we don't, then the Syndicate will kill the others, or worse, they could follow them all the way to the base."

Blaster fire sounded behind them as if to emphasize his point.

"Look, if they can shake those soldiers—which they *will*—Marvin and Taku will be waiting for us at the next transition house. If we get stuck here, if the soldiers enter that tunnel, put them all at risk." Worry tracked across his face, and he sighed, defeated. "I'm sorry, Django, but we can't let them follow the others."

Django refused to back down. "If the roles were reversed, she would help you."

Wilder flinched. That struck a nerve. Rowyn would have come back for him, and he knew it.

Django pressed on with a desperate hope. "Marvin said you look after each other. He said that's what makes the Resurgence different from the Syndicate."

Beads of sweat and dirt coated Wilder's brow as he scratched his temple. His chest heaved. Was his exhaustion because of their most recent effort, or did it have more to do with the dilemma he faced?

"Is that true or not?"

Wilder took a step back, biting his lip. "Of course it's true." A pained look set upon his face. "But we can't sacrifice everyone else to save Rowyn. She's my best friend. There's not a single person who means more to me than her. But if we don't go, we risk the Syndicate finding our base, killing every-one, and jeopardizing everything the Resurgence has worked for. That's not what Rowyn would want."

The dust was settling quicker than Django would have expected, and he took a few deep breaths into the cloth that Wilder had given him.

"You go, then," Django said. "But I have to try."

"I can't leave you, bro . . ."

"But you can leave *her?*" Django's shout echoed through the tunnel walls, bouncing along the passage into the distance. "Do what you want, but I'm staying! I'm not running away again while another of my friends dies! *Go!* Blow the charge. But I'm not going *anywhere* until I find her."

Wilder muttered a word Django didn't understand—it was definitely a curse—before grunting and running back into the transition house.

Of course, Django didn't want his uncle's movement to fall, but he couldn't leave Rowyn behind, either. Not if there was even the slightest chance of her being alive.

If she was dead, then he would be alone again, but at least he wouldn't have to live with the pain of having abandoned another friend.

Django tied the cloth around his face so that he didn't have to breathe in the regolith dust as he got to work, then grabbed at the rubble with his bare hands. The debris wasn't as easy to move as he'd expected; the rock was sharp and hard to grab. It scratched and cut his calloused hands as he heaved mounds of debris out of his way, tearing at his fingers, wrists, and forearms.

"I'll find you, Rowyn! I promise."

The process was slow and difficult. His already tired limbs protested as Django hauled rocks and dirt to the side. The effort quickly become painful, and he wished he had gloves to protect his hands. To make matters worse, shards of sharp regolith further aggravated the bloody scratches and cuts on his hands.

The sounds of the attack grew closer, even as the pulses of blasters echoing in the chambers beyond became less frequent. The shouts of soldiers increased in volume, and Django suspected he didn't have long before they found him.

*And then what? What do I do? Go down firing in a blaze of glory?*

He couldn't take on an entire legion of armed soldiers himself.

"Rowyn!" he called out once he had made a dent in clearing the debris. "Rowyn, can you hear me? I'm coming!"

A faint cry, muffled by rock, called back to him.

*She's alive!*

A renewed bout of energy overtook him as he pressed onward, shoveling dirt and rock at double the pace as before. Tears flowed over the dirt on his cheeks; his hands had gone numb. He was so close . . . He had to get her out of there.

"Django? Is that you?" The voice became more distinct as the debris cleared.

*She can talk!*

"It's me. Are you okay?"

"I think so, but I can't move."

"Hang on! I'm coming!"

Seconds ticked by as Django continued to dig deeper. It didn't take long before he could see Rowyn lying on the ground, several large stones stacked around her like a small cave. If the chunks of rock had fallen differently in either direction, they would have crushed her completely. Django was relieved he wasn't looking upon the aftermath of that and pushed the image from his mind.

Rowyn was here, and she was okay. His heart leapt. All the pain had been worth it.

"I can see you! Just hang on! I'll get you out of there."

Her eyes met his, tears trapped within them. Gray soot covered her face, the whites of her eyes catching the light from the tunnel, making her appear like a specter in the darkness.

"Django, something's trapping my leg. Even if you pull me out, I don't think I'll be able to walk on it. Please, go on without me." Desperation cut through her plea.

*"I'm not leaving you!"*

Rage tore through him again as Django shouldered boulders out of his way. He wasn't going to abandon her here, even if he had to carry her out.

The cavern shook and Django jumped, shielding his face with his hand as the quake brought pebbles, dust, and a few loose rocks down around him. The boulders around Rowyn shifted, and she let out a scream as they threatened to collapse in on her anew.

"What was that?" Rowyn asked.

"Probably Wilder caving in the exit to the transition house."

She nodded as though it made perfect sense.

"But you stayed behind!" Her eyes went wide as the realization struck her. "You *idiot!* You should have gone with him! Now, we're both going to die!"

"Not if I can help it."

"How are we getting out of here?" she asked. "Both of the exit tunnels are sealed."

"We go back the way we came."

"Through the guards?"

"Let's worry about that once you're free. I'm almost there."

She looked up at him with her striking green eyes and a grimace of pain. Saving her was worth the risk.

But more than anything, Django wished he'd done the same for Eventide.

It didn't matter what Uncle Marvin said: losing Eventide *had* been his fault. He had messed up. He hadn't stood up for her as he should have. Sure, he'd been tased, but then he'd given up.

*Why did I do that? I could have run after Sa'ab when he handed me off to the slave ship. I could have made a break for it while I was being hosed down.*

*I should have stopped us from being abducted in the first place.*

Maybe if they had stood their ground on the *Eclipse,* he and Eventide could have taken on Benson together and revealed the truth to everyone.

Instead, he had left Evie to fend for herself.

The same thing wouldn't happen to Rowyn, even if it meant being stranded in an underground tunnel with nobody else to help. He would find a way out.

From now on, he would fight tooth and nail for the ones he loved.

Rowyn shuddered as she inhaled deeply.

"What is it? Are you okay?"

Another long pause. *Is she thinking about telling me to leave again?* Maybe she was more injured than he had originally thought.

"Thank you for coming back for me."

Warmth flowed through his chest. Marvin had come back for *him*; the least he could do was pay that favor forward to one of the few people who'd helped him navigate the bizarre world he'd entered.

But there was something else about Rowyn; something comfortable about her that he didn't want to lose.

Something that reminded him of home.

Maybe that was why he felt so strongly about getting her out of here.

"We're Resurgence, right?" The words came out naturally, but they took him aback. He hadn't thought of himself as being part of the movement until that moment. "It's what we do."

A chinking sound beside him caused him to jump.

A shovel had been planted into the dirt, the handle of which was being held by an incredibly sweaty and dirty Wilder.

"We all look after each other." A white, toothy grin formed in stark contrast to his dark, dust-covered face.

Wilder reached over with his large hand extended and open. Django grabbed the arm and pulled the big man in close.

"What are you doing?" Django said. "I thought you were going to blow the tunnel?"

"I did." Wilder's expression didn't change, but his eyes said the words for him.

"You trapped yourself on this side with us?"

Wilder's smile faded slightly as he nodded. "Yeah. You were right. I couldn't leave Rowyn here. I can't believe it took a newbie to remind me of what we're fighting for." He tussled Django's hair before firming his grip on the shovel and putting it to work.

Django shook his head and smiled. "You could have at

least told me there were shovels! I've been on my hands and knees here! We're almost done."

"I forgot about them until I saw them in the house. That's what made me realize I was being selfish."

"You were going to *leave* me here?" Rowyn shouted, sounding less than impressed, but with a hint of sarcasm lining her voice.

"He came back." Django gave Wilder a knowing grin. "That's all that matters now. We're in this together."

# CHAPTER TWENTY-ONE

Django
  Lunar Tubes


WILDER GRABBED Rowyn under the armpits and gently pulled her toward him as Django slotted the shovel beneath the boulder pinning her leg.

"Careful!" Rowyn cautioned. "No sudden moves, or this whole place comes crashing down on us."

Django and Wilder had cleared out as much of the rubble as they thought was safe to reach Rowyn. Any more, and they were afraid of removing a cornerstone piece that would dislodge the rest of the rocks, crushing them all.

Django carefully shifted his weight to use the shovel like a lever. They only needed to raise the rock a fraction to slide Rowyn out.

Sweat trickled down Django's face as he pulled down on the shovel's handle. But still the rock held fast.

"It's not budging."

"Use your body weight," Wilder advised.

"What do you *think* I'm doing? It's not budging."

"Maybe it's because you're too small!"

"Would you like to come try this?"

Wilder chuckled and set Rowyn back on the ground as shouts echoed anew from the passage behind them.

"They're just about here!" Rowyn hissed. "Forget this! Leave me here!"

"Not a chance, princess." Wilder chuckled. "You're stuck with us now. *Pull*, Django!"

Wilder leaned into the end of the shovel and the rock moved—but only an inch.

As Wilder primed himself for another attempt, Django took his cue and wrapped his arms underneath Rowyn's armpits. She clasped her hands around his forearms, and as Wilder leaned into the shovel again, Django pulled.

Rowyn groaned in agony, her fingers embedding themselves in Django's arm. He winced, but kept pulling until she was free of the rock's grasp.

"Can you move it?" he asked, despite knowing the answer. There was no way around it: her leg was clearly in a dire state.

Rowyn shook her head as her face contorted in pain.

Blood soaked her pant leg, and Django was afraid to inspect it closer. He'd never coped well with blood.

"We're going to have to play doctors and nurses later," Wilder grunted as he lifted Rowyn upright. "Hang on tight!" He hoisted the petite woman up and over his shoulder, ignoring her protests. "Let's go!"

They raced paced the entrance to the now collapsed transition house. Nothing but rubble filled the space where they had rested a short time ago, and unless you knew otherwise, it was impossible to tell there had once been a path of escape in that direction.

Dim yellow LED striplights lit the tunnel ahead. As the three friends raced forward, they passed smaller caves on either side of them.

*One of these has to be another way out . . .*

"Do you know where you're going?" Django huffed. He still wasn't used to running and was already exhausted from the longest day he'd ever experienced. "Why don't we just go down one of these?"

"There's a safety tunnel ahead we might be able to take. The rest of these are dead ends." Wilder was hardly breaking a sweat, even with Rowyn slung over his shoulder. "They're decoys meant to confuse anyone following us."

Suddenly, Django was relieved he didn't have to navigate these tunnels alone. If Wilder hadn't come back for them, who knew how many wrong turns he would have taken? Would he even have been able to carry Rowyn? Probably not given the state he was in.

A flash of light ahead of them brought them to a standstill. Flashlights waving in the dark revealed the soldiers' positions ahead, about to turn a corner.

Wilder grunted. "They're closing in. Get into the nearest tunnel!" Without waiting to see if Django heeded the advice, he darted into a nearby cavern, disappearing into darkness.

They waited in the shadows, the sound of Django's heavy breathing filling the space.

"They're coming from the main tunnel on the right," Wilder assessed. "We need to head to the left."

"So, what do we do?" Rowyn prompted. She had climbed down from Wilder's shoulder and stood on her right leg. The left dangled limply, soaked with blood, and she twitched as though it was causing her a lot more pain than she had let on. "Wait for them to pass us?"

Wilder shook his head. "There's no guarantee they'll come this way. If there's only a few of them, they'll have no reason to turn. If it's a bigger group, odds are, they'll split up to cover more ground."

"So, we sneak up behind them?" Django asked. "Take them from behind?"

"We risk more coming," Rowyn said. "Then they'll have us surrounded."

"We've got to do *something*," said Wilder. "You've got to get that leg looked at."

"We need a distraction," Django surmised. "I'll lure them down this way and lead them back the way we came. Once they're past, you take Rowyn and get her out of here."

"And what about you, numb nuts?" Wilder said. "What happened to sticking together?"

"Don't worry about me. Just get Rowyn to safety. I'll find you guys later."

"I don't like this at all, Django. We've got each other's backs, remember?"

"Look, Rowyn can't walk, and I can't carry her. Sorry, but I'm not arguing this one."

Unwilling to discuss it further, Django stepped out into the main tunnel. Behind him, Wilder and Rowyn protested earnestly. But they didn't move to stop him.

"They're coming!" Django hissed. "Watch for your window!"

With that, he broke into a sprint toward the fork in the rock where the voices were now clearly coming from.

The small recess where Wilder and Rowyn stood was only fifty meters from the left turn they needed to take. Lights waved along the side of the wall as the soldiers scouted ahead with their flashlights.

Django had a small window of opportunity to make this work. He had to give his friends their best shot at escape.

He reached for his weapons belt and removed the detonators Taku had given him. He clicked them once each and pressed them against the wall beside the opening Wilder and Rowyn would need to head through.

The soldiers were within view now, the beams of their flashlights strobing across his face and their shouts erupting through the cave.

"Hey! Stop right there!"

Django froze, gauging the distance between himself and the approaching guards. They still had a good few hundred meters to run, but they were coming fast. He shot his hands up over his head, palms out. He wasn't going to draw a weapon.

Not yet.

"Who are you? What are you doing down here?"

Django let out a sigh of relief. He had been worried the soldiers would shoot him first without asking questions. He didn't answer, though; he couldn't think of anything that would sound both convincing and wouldn't get him shot. Besides, he couldn't stop to chat. Not here.

"Are you deaf, kid? You shouldn't be down here."

At least they viewed him as a lost youth, and not a threat. That was good; he could use it to his advantage. Django feigned the most innocent, childlike face he could muster.

"I'm sorry." He took off running.

"Hey, kid! Wait!"

The soldiers came running after him. Just as he'd hoped.

Django ran without looking back. He needed to draw the soldiers away from Rowyn and Wilder's hiding place.

His legs felt like jelly. They didn't want to cooperate, but he forced one foot in front of the other, carried by pure adrenaline.

He ran a hundred yards, soldiers yelling at him from behind the whole time. Another fifty yards, and they were right on his tail.

He just hoped they'd all followed him.

Django slowed and put his hands on his head, turning around so that the soldiers could see he wasn't a threat. A surprising side of him wished he could just pull out his blaster and unload, but doing so would put his friends at risk. He was much better off keeping it concealed.

"That's far enough!" one of the soldiers said, his gray helmet raised over his head, hiding his features. "We're not going to hurt ya, kid."

Django doubted that was true, but for the moment, he had them sufficiently distracted.

"I've been separated from my friends," he said. "I think they've gone on without me."

The soldiers snickered. "And who are your friends? The Resurgence? Those terrorists? Are your parents with them?"

*My parents are dead.* It was an odd thing to strike him in that moment of life or death, but he had to push past it, to play along.

"Please," Django said. "I just want to find my way back to them."

Movement behind the soldiers caught his eye as Wilder took off. Rowyn hung on his back this time, her arms wrapped around his barrel chest. Wilder must have decided he'd be faster this way.

"Stop right there!"

Soldiers toward the rear of the group had also seen the movement and raised their weapons in response.

The sound of blasters filled the space, but not from any of the Syndicate men. Energy blasts were coming *toward* them.

From Wilder.

Wilder held an energy pistol and was firing wildly as he closed the gap to the exit.

*So much for a clean getaway!*

Django dropped to the ground. He wasn't about to get caught in the crossfire, and he had to show the Syndicate that he wasn't going to fight them or he'd end up dead.

He lay face-first as the soldiers lifted their weapons toward his friends.

"Come on. Come on," Django chanted breathily, hoping his efforts hadn't been in vain.

Wilder disappeared around the corner as the Syndicate soldiers unleashed a barrage of energy bolts.

The shots went wide, hitting the wall behind them in a cloud of regolith dust.

"Get them!" the lead soldier shouted, motioning for his men to pursue as Django looked on helplessly.

All he could do was hope he had timed everything correctly.

"This one's armed!" another soldier shouted. "What do we do with him, Sarge?"

"Cuff him and take his weapons. He was smart enough to surrender, at least. Maybe we can learn something from him."

Django's gaze hadn't left the tunnel exit where his friends had disappeared. His eyes remained locked on the rock face even as the soldiers dragged him to his feet and slapped electronic cuffs onto his wrists.

Everything went quiet for a second.

Right before the blast wave hit them.

The direct blast of the detonators sent dead and wounded soldiers sprawling to the ground as the entrance to the tunnel collapsed.

Django let out a sigh of relief. His friends had escaped, and these soldiers wouldn't be able to follow them. What that meant for *him*, though, he was yet to find out.

Eventide

The *Inanna*

BRIGHT LIGHT WAS ALL that existed.

Unlike the last time she woke, Eventide remembered *exactly* what had happened. Memories of past events flooded her consciousness: where she was, her struggle to stay awake, and her last thoughts as her eyes had grown heavy against her will.

*Against my will.* Just like everything else done to her on this godforsaken ship. The epitome of hell.

Even though she didn't know how yet, Eventide knew that whatever her captors had done to her was about to make things a lot worse.

The pain she had felt the last time she awoke was gone. No, not gone. Dulled.

What had caused the pain to begin with was still a mystery, but Eventide wasn't sure she was ready to discover the answer just yet. Whatever it was, she wasn't going to like it, and her primary focus needed to be escape.

Echoes of the sensations she'd felt on the table the first time she awoke still called to her. They were faint, but they were there, reminding her of the agony she'd experienced. Her captors must have given her painkillers. Damn powerful ones to have numbed the excruciating pain she'd felt earlier.

*How long have I been asleep?*

Her eyelids slowly opened, mitigating the assault on her vision as the brightness enveloped her.

Eventide squinted, willing her eyes to adjust, and the surrounding room slowly came into focus—stark white, which made the intensity of the light that much harsher. Holoscreens cast projections around the room. She tried to focus on the data they held, but through the inertia of sleep and drugs, they appeared as little more than a blur of text and graphs.

Beneath her fingertips rested the soft caress of a blanket and a spongy cushion that supported her.

*Good, I can move. And at least I'm lying on an actual bed, not an operating table.*

The sensation of the fabric was foreign against her fingers, as though she was feeling with somebody else's hands. Whatever painkillers she was on had desensitized her nerves.

Stars, she hoped that was only temporary.

Eventide lay on her back, still in a medical lab, but a more comfortable enclosure than before. Other than the holoscreen data, there was no equipment, no staff, and nothing to suggest that persons unknown were actively doing anything to her. At least, for the moment. This room seemed more suitable for monitoring than for procedures.

But something was still off . . .

Her fingers and toes wiggled as Eventide willed them to. They felt strange, another by-product of the painkillers, but they still responded.

*Okay, so no biotic arms. That's a good start.*

She tried to turn her head but couldn't. Her eyes flitted left and right, but she couldn't lift her head from the bed. It felt as if there was a weight on her forehead, holding her down.

Panic welled inside her and she fought to keep her heart rate under control.

*Paralysis from the neck up isn't a thing, right? Why am I being restrained like this?*

"It's best not to struggle." A woman's voice came from somewhere to the right, in a thick accent Eventide couldn't place.

A variety of accents had been commonplace aboard the *Eclipse*. The histories said that when humanity fled the Earth, deportation affected people from a multitude of countries. But the pioneers of the station were no longer restrained by the borders that had once divided them. There were no more countries. The station was all humanity had.

But Eventide now knew the histories were wrong.

Her mind scrambled to place the woman's accent but came up blank. Were there still countries on Earth? Did people still see themselves in terms of race and borders? Was she now on the planet's surface?

Eventide hadn't noticed there being anyone else in the

room, but it made sense if she hadn't been able to turn her head.

"What . . ." Her voice cracked, her mouth dry. She swallowed and tried again. "What did you do to me?"

"You'll be okay. I haven't lost a patient in a very long time."

"What did you *do?*" she repeated.

"You'll have some swelling and a lot of bruising for a few weeks. Most of the soreness will be from the muscle stimulation and nodule implants; that's normal. But the pain you're feeling now is from the chip installation. It's risky at your age: your body's immune system is fully developed, so it's constantly warring with the bio-integrations until they can find a symbiosis. Many adults don't survive the procedure—or so the textbooks say. Coming across an unchipped adult is unheard of these days. It was touch and go for a bit, but you have the best care here, and your body is strong. You're on the home stretch now."

"'Chip installation?'" Eventide murmured. She closed her eyes again. The lights were too bright, and she wanted to focus on the woman's voice. Drool spilled from the sides of her mouth, the painkillers evidently affecting the use of her tongue. She pawed at her face, attempting to remove the spittle, but her hand flapped around her mouth, merely spreading it around instead.

"Now that you're awake, I'd like to know: how did you manage to go so long without a security chip? You had a key pass embedded in your arm, but from what I can tell, that served a different purpose. It was an older model; one that doesn't integrate with your biomechanics. Just an electronic pass, like something my parents would have had."

*In my arm?* The woman must have been talking about the implant that enabled her to access the maintenance tunnels and high clearance levels of the *Eclipse. Has this doctor replaced it? What does she mean about integrating with my bios?*

"I'm a technician." Eventide's voice grew stronger, though it was still hoarse. "It was an access chip."

The woman pursed her lips as though thinking, pulled up a datapad, and studied it as though it listed something she couldn't quite explain.

"You're in better shape than most people who come through here, so someone's been feeding you, at least. You had nice muscle development, even before the enhancements, so you've not been hiding away in the Tubes. In fact, I've never had anyone on my operating table that started out so fit. You could be my finest work of art yet."

*Work of art?*

"But it makes no sense. If you are Syndicate-born, your parents are legally obligated to chip you at birth. Please, tell me, where are you from?"

"Space station," Eventide said, matter-of-fact. There was no use in hiding it. Whoever these people were, they already had her strapped to a hospital bed and had subjected her to some sort of procedure.

*What else can they do to me?*

"Pfft . . . A FLOW station. Come on now, if you're going to make something up, at least make it believable."

It might have been the drugs, but Eventide wasn't sure

why her home would be something to lie about. She wished she could turn her head to see the woman's face. Perhaps she was making fun of her, but Eventide didn't think so. The woman sounded sincere.

"I'm . . . not making . . . it up," she said, struggling for breath with each word. "*Eclipse.*"

The ensuing silence led Eventide to think the woman might have left. Eventually, she spoke. "That's . . . That's not possible. Well, I suppose anything *is* possible, but I've never heard of anyone *leaving* a station. I understand you might not want to divulge where your home colony is, but I assure you, the rumors about us aren't true. Your family history is safe with us. We don't use that type of information against our Domani. Haven't for decades. We've had no need to."

The woman, dressed in white scrubs, came into Eventide's view for the first time. Her tanned skin and youthful face made her appear to be in her mid-thirties, but there was an air about her that made her seem older than that. Wavy brown hair reached to her shoulders, in an array of shades that couldn't be natural. Smile lines were visible, but they were dulled, as though someone had erased them. Only her dark brown eyes gave her true age away—they were filled with experience and fatigue that betrayed the smoothness of her face.

The woman had a little more weight on her than Eventide was used to seeing on a person—not in an overweight sense, but she appeared healthy, as though unaffected by food rations. Her smile was charming—comforting, almost—but within the woman's intense eyes, the comfort was drowning in a weighty sea of cynicism. Her gaze focused on Eventide in a way that made her insides itch, even more than the painkillers already did.

"I find it hard to believe, but if it's true, you'd be best to keep that information to yourself." The woman looked up and scanned the room as though she was worried about who else might be present. "It would explain why you're such an anomaly. We know little about the stations, but we know the Syndicate. They won't take kindly if they find out you escaped."

An endless parade of questions ran through Eventide's mind, but she struggled to form any of them into a single coherent thought. Nothing made sense.

"Who . . . are . . . you?"

Speech was still an effort. Eventide hoped that her strength would return as the effects of the sedative wore off, but the procedure she had undergone had weakened her substantially.

"I'm Doctor Amelia Morales," the woman replied. "I know you have no reason to trust me, but I *am* trying to protect you. There's something about you I've never seen in any other patient, and I have to figure out why that is. Keep the information about your origins to yourself. Don't trust anyone else here, or anyone they show you to. As far as the Caregivers know, you're a girl from the mines. Do you understand?"

Eventide had no idea what this woman was talking about, but nodded anyway.

The doctor continued. "Now, I've installed your new biometrics chip and your implants. It will take some time for you to recover, but you will get your strength back."

*Implants?*

"*No!*" she yelled, but the word only escaped her lips in a hoarse whisper.

Eventide's mind flashed back to the night she had boarded the *Inanna*, before she'd been drugged with whatever blue concoction they had given her. The men and women dancing around in their silk pajamas, ornate necklaces adorning their chests . . .

Necklaces connected to the nodes on the back of their necks.

She grappled at her neck, but she felt nothing but her own skin above her collarbone.

Following Eventide's train of thought, Morales said, "They'll give you the necklace later. Right now, you only have the nodes implanted."

"What . . . What are they? What do they do?"

Eventide's hands tried to find them, reaching for her neck, but she couldn't position her fingers beneath her head.

"They feed into your nervous system." Morales held a syringe, flicking it to remove the air bubbles that had formed within the blue liquid it contained.

*Blue like the drink . . . She's going to sedate me again!*

"The implants enable the clients to control both your pleasure and pain centers." The woman's words were casual, as though she were telling Eventide that the nodes allowed her to select whether she wanted rice or pasta with her evening meal. "Now, hold still. This will keep the pain at bay while your body tries to adapt. You need to rest."

*Control pleasure and pain . . .*

Eventide's mouth moved in silent horror.

"It does *what?*" Her voice returned, the unexpected intensity of its volume prompting her body to rebel.

She *had* to get out of this hospital bed, get away from these *monsters*—but she couldn't move.

Eventide's arms flailed, but her legs, torso, and head were all secured to the bed, ensuring that no matter how hard she struggled, she wasn't going anywhere.

Morales ignored her battle against the restraints. "Clients will control how much pleasure or pain they give you in response to your actions. Perform well, and they can release large quantities of dopamine into your neocortex, giving you pleasure like you've never experienced before. Disappoint them, and they can release pain signals directly into your brain stem."

Fury coursed through Eventide's body, the warmth of her wrath overriding the effects of the painkillers. She tried again to push herself off the bed, but the restraints wrapped around her torso kept her pinned, and her head was locked in place as though in a vise.

"I've stabilized your body until the connection can heal. Be careful with your arms if you don't want me to secure those as well. If you rip the sensors out, it could lead to either paralysis or death."

Tears flowed from Eventide's face, her cheeks and neck growing damp. "Why? *Why* would you do this?"

Morales looked at her for a moment, her face twitching as though confused by the question. "All Domani receive the implants," she said. "It's how the Caregivers can guarantee their customer's satisfaction. You'll be able to move again in a couple days. Until then, get some rest. You're lucky to be here. There are many in the Loop who have tried and failed to be accepted aboard the *Inanna*. It's a better life than most are afforded."

*But they* chose *to come here. I chose none of this!*

Eventide fought to wrestle the tears away. She needed to save her strength. This wouldn't be the end of her story.

# CHAPTER TWENTY-THREE



Eventide

The *Inanna*

MORALES HAD BEEN RIGHT: Eventide had regained most of her kinetic ability within a couple days. It wasn't pleasant, but by the time the doctor removed her restraints, she was more than ready to get out of bed.

A dull pain still ebbed through her. The back of her neck was tender, and her veins itched with the substance Morales had injected her with.

Somebody new stood beside her now: a young woman, with light brown skin and eyes and hair to match. This woman was at least a couple years younger than Eventide, and she was stunning. Her face was adorned with more makeup than Eventide had ever seen on one person, but the effect didn't come across as gaudy. The contouring and layers complemented the most flattering angles and structure of her face.

The pajamas she wore were of the same design worn by

every other person on the ship—the *Domani,* Morales had called them. The outfit was essentially a silk jumpsuit with two strips of fabric that strapped down her front and backside and over her shoulders, accenting the woman's finely toned arms, breasts, and washboard stomach.

She held up a blue outfit that mirrored her own. "Get dressed," the woman said. "And then I'll show you to your quarters."

With the effects of the drugs lessening, Eventide was feeling more like herself again. "What? You people don't say hello around here?"

"Hello." The woman smiled in a way that was bizarrely contradictory; rigid, like the smile on a doll, but beaming, as though the woman hadn't picked up on Eventide's sarcasm.

Eventide lifted the piece of sapphire blue fabric the woman handed to her and turned her nose up. Being blue, it would complement her hair, at least, but that was beside the point. The pants were loose-fitting; those were okay, she guessed. *Ugly, but whatever.*

But Eventide was far from a fan of the two strips of fabric that crossed over the chest. It would barely cover her.

She'd worn a hooded sweatshirt when she was off duty for a reason. It was comfortable. The technician uniforms were fine. But this? *This* was demeaning. Eventide harbored no ill will toward women who felt comfortable wearing outfits like this—if it was their own choice—but these Domani certainly wouldn't *force* her to wear it.

"I'm not wearing that," she said resolutely, tossing the garments back.

The woman's eyes widened with shock, and then her

brow lifted as though confused. "You must, Eventide. All Domani wear these."

*I must?*

It was a plea more than a demand. Still, Eventide wasn't interested in a wardrobe change.

"How do you know my name?" she asked.

The woman looked embarrassed, like she had done something she shouldn't have, but her smile returned as quickly as it had dissipated. "You spoke it in your sleep. The sedative you were given is powerful. You told us your name and mentioned a man, Django. He sounds *lovely!* I hope he will join us here."

*Django.* A wave of guilt washed over her. She was here, and Django was still out there, somewhere. But where? It took her a moment to recall when the Port Authority officers had said Django was being taken.

*The mines.*

Django wasn't a stranger to manual labor; he could handle grunt work. But the idiot was likely to get himself shot trying to rescue *her.* She was going to have to find him first.

The only way to do that? Learn as much as she could about the *Inanna* and how to escape.

"Well, seeing as you know my name," Eventide said, "what's yours?"

"I'm Yunni." The woman looked at her with the same unnerving smile, barely blinking as she looked at Eventide expectantly.

"Yunni," Eventide repeated, trying to ignore the creepy vibes the woman was radiating. "Last I knew, I was boarding a ship. We're still on a ship, right?"

"Yes," Yunni replied, her eyes still wide and curious. "The *Inanna*."

"How long have you been on this ship?"

"Six months."

"Did you choose to be here, or were you forced against your will, like me?"

Yunni's face scrunched, as though baffled. "I don't understand. You don't want to be here?"

"No, I don't *want* to be here. I was arrested on some bull-shit charge when our ship docked, and a guard turned me over to this . . . *bordello*."

The confusion on Yunni's face intensified. "If you hadn't become Domani, you would have been sent to the mines, executed, or taken by some other ship. Here, we are treated well, and the Caregivers find us a good place to live, with someone wealthy. There's no better position in the Loop. And the *Inanna* is the best Domani ship of them all."

Eventide raised an eyebrow and studied the woman. It was amazing how sincere she was in her plea, as though Yunni was trying to will Eventide into understanding.

*Stars, is life so bad here that people dream of being sold as a prostitute? Is that the highest achievement they can hope for?*

All Eventide knew of sex workers, she had learned from the histories. If there were any aboard the *Eclipse*, Eventide certainly hadn't been aware of them.

*Damn, that's what these people are, isn't it?*

She held no ill will for anyone who had chosen to be on this ship. Maybe Yunni had. Or maybe she'd been brain-washed to believe she *wanted* this lifestyle.

But Eventide *hadn't* chosen it. She'd spent her entire life training to be a technician, and she wasn't about to give that up because some dimwit guard saw an opportunity to make a few credits.

"You need to get dressed," Yunni said, disrupting Eventide's thoughts. "If you don't put this on, you'll have nothing to wear!"

Eventide looked down at herself on the bed. Someone had draped a thin blanket over her while she slept. She had been so disoriented, she hadn't realized she was nearly naked. Thankfully, she was wearing underwear—but it wasn't *her* underwear. Her captors had *given* her some to match that dreaded outfit—but nothing else.

Except for a golden necklace with a silver amulet that lay across her collarbone.

*The implants!* She put that thought to the side for the moment.

"Where are *my* clothes?" She held back a hiss. This wasn't Yunni's fault; they were both victims of these 'Caregivers'. Maybe they ran the ship?

Yunni, perhaps, believed she didn't have any other options, and maybe she didn't—but that made her a victim.

But Eventide wasn't going to just sit back and resign herself to that outcome.

Yunni's face continued to contort with bewilderment. "These *are* your clothes." She reached over and gave them a shake, as though Eventide didn't understand *which* clothes the woman had been referring to.

"*Ugh!*" Eventide groaned. "Are you trying to be difficult? I want *my* clothes. The ones I was wearing when I arrived on this ship."

"Oh!" Yunni said, understanding dawning on her face for the first time. "Your old clothes were destroyed. Like your old life, they are no longer yours. You now belong to the *Inanna*."

Eventide didn't hold back the hiss this time. "I don't *belong* to anyone."

Yunni blinked, but her sweet expression didn't change. "You belong to the *Inanna* until they find you a client. Then, you will be transferred."

"I will not be *owned!*" Eventide let out a low growl. "And I don't want to wear this outfit."

"These are the only clothes I have for you." Yunni's tone was firmer now. Perhaps she was growing tired of Eventide's pushback. "If you don't put these on, you'll have to walk around the ship in your underwear, and I have to say, *that* isn't recommended." The girl smiled as though it had been a joke she was quite proud of.

Eventide sighed. She was almost inclined to walk around the ship naked just to prove a point. She mulled it over for a moment, but thought better of it. If she wanted to escape, she was going to have to assess her situation and figure out a plan. That was going to be hard enough wearing the ridiculous pajamas. There were no benefits to drawing attention to herself.

"*Fine,*" she relented.

The logical part of her brain was spinning. All she *wanted* to do was storm out of her room and demand her release. But how far would that get her?

Eventide allowed her hand to drift to the cold amulet that lay across her chest: a disc the size of her palm with a stone at its center.

She could tell right away that it wasn't a stone at all, but an electronic device of some sort. *That* was good to know; maybe she could use it to her advantage later.

Was this device shielded from heat? Radiation? Electromagnetic pulses? Or was it emitting some sort of radio waves that would eventually fry her brain?

Eventide knew too little of the world outside the *Eclipse* to make assumptions about what her captors would and wouldn't have developed the devices to achieve.

She needed to learn more, if she could, before poking around at it. Who knew what kind of fail-safes might have been built into the design? She'd have to keep her guard up and be crafty about how she went about discovering the shackles' vulnerabilities.

Carefully, she trailed her fingers to the two nodes the butcher doctor had embedded in the back of her neck and shivered. Even with the slightest touch, they burned into her flesh. Eventide didn't dare put any amount of pressure on them, and sleeping with them was going to be difficult if the painkillers wore off.

Doctor Morales had mentioned it would be dangerous to remove the device. Perhaps *lethal.* Had that just been a scare tactic?

Bioengineering wasn't much more than a footnote in Eventide's science textbooks. Their ancestors had deemed it too dangerous a concept to entertain. It appeared the Caregivers didn't feel the same way.

*Someone will be able to remove them. I hope.*

Her feet hit the cold tile floor beside the bed and she sucked in a sharp breath at the shock. Yunni still stood there, eyeing the outfit, unfazed that another woman stood in front of her, almost naked.

Eventide stretched out her arm and paused as she grabbed the fabric. She froze, her gaze resting on her forearm.

It wasn't *her* forearm.

It was *an* arm, attached to her body and made of flesh and blood, and she had full feeling in it, so it wasn't mechanical like she'd feared earlier. In fact, it looked like it *could* have been her arm, had she undergone a radical workout regime, smoothed her skin, cleansed her pores, and removed her body hair.

Her eyes moved over the rest of her body in a disoriented study. Something was different about . . . *all of her.*

"Is everything okay?" Yunni asked.

"No . . . My arm . . . It's . . ."

There was muscle development that hadn't been there before. Her biceps, triceps, and shoulders were all toned. Not massive, like the bodybuilders of ancient Earth, but like she'd been hitting her PT extra hard.

She examined the rest of her body. Her quads and calves now had muscle definition Eventide had only dreamed of before. Though she'd never been out of shape, and her training was rigorous enough, she'd never managed the caloric intake to build this sort of muscle.

"What did they do to me?"

"What do you mean?" Yunni asked again. "Is something wrong?"

Yunni wasn't cut the same way. Her body was toned and fit, but Eventide's body looked as though she were an athlete.

"My body didn't look like this. It wasn't this way before I

got here," Eventide explained. "Why do I have so much muscle?"

"Part of your enhancements," Yunni said with a shrug. "If you want to be Domani, you have to be in prime shape."

*I don't* want to be Domani!

"You're saying my *implants* are enhancing my muscles?" Eventide pointed to the amulet on her chest. "How? I've never heard of such technology . . ."

Yunni gave what was fast becoming her trademarked confused look. "Your necklace? No, a necklace couldn't do that. I think it was the surgery, but I don't know how it works. What does it matter? You're here now."

Of course Yunni didn't know how it worked. She was happy enough just having a warm bed.

Eventide sighed and begrudgingly slipped the pajamas over her alien body.

The clothes were soft and comfortable, which she immediately hated. What she hated more was that there was nothing keeping her contained, like it would take nothing at all for her to fall out.

She twisted and bent to test the limits of her new attire. The movement quickly reminded her of how stiff and sore her body was, but, unbelievably, the outfit magically seemed to stay in place.

A pair of sandals sat next to her bed, and she slipped them on. Like the pajamas, they were minimalist in design—slip-ons with crisscross straps that slid over the top of her feet. The soles were lined with some sort of soft yet sturdy material. It was like standing on a cloud.

Eventide did a few quick stretches, trying to loosen up

the muscles that were protesting being out of bed. "How long have I been in here?"

"A week now."

"'A *week!*'" The surrounding room spun, and Eventide had to hold onto her bed for support so that she wouldn't fall over. "I've been in bed for a week?"

"Yes. It is an intensive surgery. You need time to recover. You've done very well. Most of us are in bed for a month."

A week was way too long, especially in a society that traveled via spaceship. How far into the cosmos had humans settled? How fast could they travel?

Django could be anywhere by now. Was he still imprisoned, sent to the mines? Or had he escaped? Maybe slave ships were slow, and he hadn't arrived there yet.

*Or maybe he's already dead . . .*

Eventide immediately chastised herself for thinking that way.

Knowing Django, he wouldn't have given up on her. He wasn't usually a man of action, but he had a soft spot for her. She almost chuckled as she thought back to him punching the guard who had run his mouth off about her on the *Eclipse*. Random acts of violence were out of character for him, but it was the first time she could think of Django stepping outside of his comfort zone to do something for her.

Maybe she'd been underestimating him when she'd told him she didn't think things could ever work between them.

And she didn't want those to be some of the last words she ever said to him.

"Are you ready, Eventide?" Yunni asked. "I need to show you to your quarters."

Eventide sighed. *Am I ready? I'm ready to get the hell off the* Inanna.

But she would bide her time—for now.

"I suppose. Except . . ." Her hands fidgeted around the edges of her outfit. "I had a pack of playing cards on me when I arrived. You wouldn't happen to know if it was destroyed along with my clothes, would you?"

# CHAPTER TWENTY-FOUR

Eventide

The *Inanna*

FOR THE MOST PART, the *Inanna* reminded Eventide of the *Eclipse*, but the interior design was more ornate and the technology far more advanced.

*As though they've had a couple hundred years to improve their systems.*

Would she even be able to understand the computer schematics if she had an opportunity to study them?

There were other aesthetic differences, of course. LED lights that would have been blue on the *Eclipse* alternated between purple and red on this ship, depending on which corridor Eventide wandered down. The ship's floors were completely carpeted, which was impractical for a spacefaring vessel. These were not the dull utilitarian rugs that adorned a handful of places on the *Eclipse*, but a thick, plush beige carpet. She imagined walking barefoot would be comfortable and, in fact, she could feel the soft surface on the sides of her feet as her sandals sunk into it.

There was no way the entire ship could have been decorated in this fashion. It would have been a hazard in places like the bridge and Engineering.

If she had to guess, the Caregivers were restricting the Domanis' access to certain areas of the ship. This seemed highly curated toward a group of people someone was trying to keep comfortable.

Eventide hated that the ship both reminded her of home and yet felt so utterly foreign.

The most striking difference between the two were the aromas that enveloped Eventide and embedded themselves in her hair and clothes. Compared to the B-Ring on the *Eclipse,* the smell was far less . . . *sterile.* It wasn't that the *Inanna* didn't seem clean, but instead of bleach and disinfectant, the air was infused with a sweet, floral aroma. Was it rose petal or cherry blossom?

*Who am I kidding?* She had no idea. She was lucky to have guessed 'flowers.'

Django would know instantly what flowers gave off this particular scent, and he wouldn't have hesitated in telling her, listing their unique properties, how many specimens they had in the *Eclipse's* seed vault, how long it would be until the Earth could grow them again . . .

He also wouldn't have hesitated to laugh at her for guessing 'cherry blossom' when the answer was likely an obscure strain of chrysanthemum that only blossomed in a certain ancient country on the fourth of May.

She didn't wish Django was aboard the *Inanna* with her,

of course, but Eventide certainly wished she was with him—somewhere else, almost *anywhere* else. And without two stupid implants protruding from the back of her neck, and without being taken against her will, likely to be sold for sex or worse . . .

*The implants can control pleasure or pain.*

Eventide grimaced and then shuddered. She had read enough of Earth's history to know how demented people could be, especially toward those they viewed as property instead of as equals.

Several other people passed them as they ventured down the hall, all wearing the same silk pajamas in varying colors, identifying them as Domani.

It struck Eventide that every person on the ship, other than Doctor Morales, seemed to be under the age of twenty-five. In fact, now that she thought of it, she was one of the older people aboard the vessel. Yunni couldn't have been much older than eighteen.

But Eventide had to stop thinking about the other prisoners here, and start thinking about her own means of escape. If she paid attention, perhaps she could find a way off this ship and be on her way.

Then, something else struck her; something that was in stark contrast to the *Eclipse*.

"Where are the guards, Yunni?"

"Guards?" Yunni asked in her puzzled tone. "Don't worry, Eventide, you are safe here. There is no need for guards."

"But what if one of the Domani does something? Is there nobody here to stop it?"

"There is much we are permitted to do under the rules. There's no need to guard us."

"But what if someone was to break the rules?"

Yunni's face twitched as it struggled to maintain the happy composure she'd adopted until that point. "Why would we want to do something outside of the rules?" she stated, as though it was the most illogical thing Eventide could have said. "The Caregivers give us everything we need. None of us have the desire to do anything we shouldn't.

"Treat each other with kindness. Follow the guidance of the Caregivers. Treat ourselves with compassion. These are easy rules to follow."

"How can you be sure?"

All trace of joy darkened from Yunni's face. "If we break the rules, we are punished."

Eventide pointed to the back of her neck. "Through our collars?"

Yunni looked as though she was about to throw up. "We don't talk about it."

The pieces fell into place. There was no reason to hire physical guards if the fear of pain kept everyone in line. She sighed.

"But what's the deal here?" She wasn't sure she wanted to know, but she had to find out. If she knew what she was up against, perhaps it would help her figure out a way to get off the ship and back to Django. "What happens to us?"

Yunni's face softened, its glow returning.

*It's like this woman only has two moods: elation and despair.*

At the thought of their purpose aboard the *Inanna*, Yunni

didn't scrunch her face as though the question was absurd. She nodded as though she had been expecting it all along, then grinned as though thrilled by the topic.

"The *Inanna* docks at Syndicate ports and takes appointments with highly esteemed clients. Mars, space docks, Lunar's crater cities and the most highly sought-after positions are on Earth. High-ranking officials take Domani in, and we remain there until they are done with us."

"Done with us?" Eventide's mouth dropped in horror. "And then what? They throw us out with the trash?"

"The average life span in the Lunar Tubes is sixteen. On Mars, it's twenty-four. In the asteroid mines, it's far less. Most only live for a year, maybe two. The average life span for a Domani is thirty-four, and for most of our later years, we are cared for but not required to perform regular duties. Some who please their clients live much longer. We are lucky for the opportunity we have."

*Oh, hell no!*

Yunni's statement raised more questions than it answered. Mars? Asteroid belt? How far out had humans traveled? And why were their life expectancies so short?

And she'd be damned if she would ever consider being kidnapped, mutilated, and passed off to some deviant client as 'lucky.'

It was as though Yunni was reciting information from the Domani handbook. *Maybe she was. What did they do to indoctrinate these people?*

"You'll learn more at orientation."

*Orientation. I'll finally be able to get some answers. Maybe learn more about this ship.*

"Are Domani ever released from service? Do they ever get to be free?"

Yunni's face contorted once again. "I don't understand."

Before Eventide could push any further, Yunni stopped in front of an enormous set of sliding doors. She didn't see a keypad or a scanner, but as Eventide stepped closer, the door slid open.

"These are your quarters," Yunni announced.

"Can anyone just walk in?" It was bad enough she had to wear a ridiculous outfit that showed everyone her cleavage, but to have no privacy at all on this ship? Nowhere to go without the constant dread of someone walking in on her at any hour of the day or night?

"No, only you."

"You didn't enter a code or scan anything . . ." Eventide persisted.

Yunni pointed to the nodes protruding from her own neck. "The ship knows who you are through this. It knows when you are at your door."

Eventide swallowed. *The implants are sending the ship biometric data.*

"So, we're being tracked?"

Yunni shrugged as if to say either she didn't know or she didn't care, and she waved a hand, gesturing for her to enter the room.

Seeking answers from this woman was pointless.

The door to her quarters slid open. Eventide didn't know where to look first. The lights were dim as they entered, which only added to the ambiance of the quarters. Like a candlelit dinner, the Caregivers had set the room up as though they expected every night to be a romantic one. The cabin was at least two times the size of Eventide's quarters on the B-Ring, and she suspected even Commander Benson himself didn't have quarters this large.

Four couches faced each other in the center of the room. *Four.*

Each would comfortably seat three people. Clearly, this was a shared space, and Eventide would have roommates. She looked around for signs of the room's other inhabitants but, at first glance, couldn't find any.

In between the couches was a square glass coffee table, which also doubled as a holographic projector.

Eventide let her gaze float upward. The ceiling had to be nearly twenty feet high, and viewports looking out into the dark expanse of space spanned the entire height. Directly above the coffee table, a crystal chandelier hung from the ceiling.

The wall on Eventide's right appeared to be one giant screen, while the opposite wall held a large painting of a landscape on a world Eventide didn't recognize. The image featured an onyx-black sky despite sunlight streaming onto the grasses and plains that rested on the surface. High walls in the distance revealed that there might have been a biodome or barrier at the edge of the inhabitable world.

*That can't be Earth, can it?*

On *Eclipse,* the Admin had never shown the residents a recent photograph of the planet's surface, only the charred and dead remains of wars and pestilence that had occurred centuries ago. But if it wasn't a representation of Earth, where was it? The painting in no way resembled what Eventide imagined Mars to look like, with red, rocky terrain, nor did it appear to be the gray regolith surface of the Moon.

Square ridges along the side of the wall contained some sort of plant life, and, again, she wished Django was there to help identify the greenery. Hell, she wished Django could see this place. He had balked at the extravagance of the B-Ring quarters. He would absolutely lose his mind here.

"Yunni, how many of us live in this room?"

Eventide wouldn't have believed Yunni's grin could have gotten any wider, but any time Eventide asked about the ship or its residents, her excitement reached new levels.

"These are *your* quarters," she said. "Only *you* live here."

There had to be a mistake. This place was far too luxurious for only one person, never mind being the living space of someone being held against their will.

An odd wave of pleasure rolled over her. For a moment, it was as though she truly belonged in this space; as if the room was the most wonderful place she'd ever been in.

*Well, it is, isn't it?*

For a few seconds, her senses betrayed her. Everything about this place felt right.

Until she shook the thought off.

*Yes, these quarters are impressive, but don't get lost in the frivolity of it all. You don't belong here.*

"Orientation begins in two hours. Shower and get dressed. There are clean outfits in your bedroom. Someone will be here to collect you when it's time."

Without waiting for a reply, Yunni turned and left. Eventide got the sense the woman was eager to leave, as though she'd already spent too much time with the strange woman who asked too many questions.

Now that she stood within it, Eventide could understand the appeal of life in a room like this; how the promise of a life of luxury would appeal to those who had come from places where it was a struggle to survive. Hell, this room alone would even appeal to the residents on the B-Ring, and *that* had been a tremendous upgrade from her quarters in the D-Ring.

But Yunni's responses were something different entirely. The woman clearly couldn't understand why someone would question being taken against their will; that anyone would challenge having probes shoved into their skull to lock them into a life of debauchery in exchange for a spacious room and skimpy silk pajamas.

She sighed. Beyond the room's viewports, both the Earth and the Moon were visible, but they were small and far away. Somewhere circling that blue orb was her home.

*Is that what it is now? How can it be after all the lies they told us? Do I even have a home anymore?*

And then she realized she did. His name was Django Alexander, and Eventide wasn't sure if she would ever see him again.

Mikka

The *Redemption*

"GET US OUT OF RANGE!"

The *Redemption* shook as Mikka jumped into action, sprinting to the bridge's central console and activating the weapons control systems.

"What the hell do you think I'm *trying* to do?" Kiara snapped back.

Over the years, Mikka had rigged the vessel with only minimal weapons systems, trying to maintain a light arsenal. The *Redemption*'s energy cannons and compact pulse missiles weren't enough firepower to be much more than a deterrent to the thieves and pirates that plundered the space lanes of the Syndicate's colonies, but the fewer arms Mikka had at her disposal, the less grief the Orbital Guard would give her.

But it also meant the ship wasn't a match for any vessel presenting a serious threat.

Mikka pulled up a visual of the attacking ship on the *Redemption*'s targeting screen. "What the hell *is* that thing?"

Even though the strange craft was about ten times the size of the *Redemption*, this ship was nearly flat. Not quite a box, but slanted at the front, and sleeker than any conventional ship design Mikka had ever come across, as though aerodynamics would help in the vacuum of space. Mikka could only guess the angular contours had something to do with some sort of sensor evasion, but then, it could have just been for aesthetic appeal.

"I've never seen anything like it," Kiara admitted. "And whatever it is, it outguns us. We might be able to outmaneuver their navigation controls, but it looks like it's got a pretty powerful ion drive, built for long hauls."

"Pull it up, full holos."

The ship's bridge shimmered into semi-transparency around them as holo-projectors gave them a three-sixty view of the *Redemption*'s surroundings. Earth sat below them, to their starboard side, but they were engaged in a high enough orbit that the planet's proximity sensors wouldn't pick them up if they weren't looking.

But the FLOW station *Freedom* would sure as hell be able to.

And Mikka was prepared to bet the station administration would immediately report any firefight within sensor range straight to the Syndicate. Regardless of the *Redemption*'s mission, the Syndicate wouldn't take too kindly to a firefight.

There was no point in appealing to the Syndicate directly. With her new credentials, it was possible they might assist her rather than arrest her, but Mikka couldn't risk it. David had requested discretion, and she hated the idea of him having to bail her out for a third time in one week.

Besides, she couldn't help her ever-present urge to keep a low profile and evade law enforcement. Some habits were hard to break.

The *Redemption* shuddered again. The supply vessel's shielding was absorbing the impact for now, but they wouldn't hold out under sustained firepower.

"Magnify. Bring it in five hundred percent."

The image of the attacking ship expanded from a speck in the distance to a meter-high panel toward the rear of the bridge. The ship carried no markings. No viewports. Nothing protruding from its surface at all, as though it had been built for atmospheric entry without breaking a sweat.

Like a flat silver bullet.

Whoever had built this ship had done so for stealth—and for combat.

Even if Mikka contacted the OG herself, that ship would likely blow the *Redemption* to bits long before anyone came to their aid.

As if to prove her point, two more beams arced their way. Kiara spun on the controls and Mikka stumbled, nearly toppling over as the gravity plating failed to compensate for the inertia of Kiara's radical spin.

A fresh surge of alarms filled the bridge, drowning out Kiara's curses as she sent the *Redemption* into another impromptu roll. The impact sent Mikka hurtling to the deck this time, as the ship completed a full three-sixty spin. The

*Redemption* could handle itself, but its gravity plating wasn't built for that kind of maneuvering.

Kiara watched the pursuing vessel somersault behind them through her feed. The navigator ignored the holo-projector as her fingers flew over the control console, monitoring each of the signatures the ship was putting out and responding accordingly.

"Divert us away from the station!" Mikka shouted. "We can't allow it to get caught in the crossfire!"

The *Redemption* suddenly felt sluggish when compared with the graceful bird on their tail.

"I'm working on it!" Kiara fired back. "But she's got a lot of juice on us. We won't get far at this rate."

*The worst part is, I don't think they're even trying yet.*

"We've got to give it more power than this, Ki."

"If you've got any ideas, go for it!" Kiara shouted over the ship's alarms. "All I can do is try to outmaneuver its attacks!"

Kiara's hands flew over the controls at an incredible pace. She was sweating, and Mikka could almost see the tension in the navigator's back muscles as she hunched over the console.

Mikka ran back to her own console and limited whatever systems she thought they could temporarily put on hold. She reduced the temperature down to ten degrees Celsius; gravity to 0.5G; and air generation to fifty percent. Things were going to get uncomfortable.

She could set the oxygen to zero and they'd be fine with what was circulating in the ship for a couple hours. Mikka contemplated the move for a moment, but they needed to think rationally, and a drastic cutoff to their air supply was likely to end badly. If they got knocked unconscious, Mikka didn't want to suffocate if she didn't come round in time to turn the taps back on.

She hesitated before disengaging the power to the secondary systems. If their main power supply failed, they would be in trouble, but if their attacker blew them to bits, having the *Redemption*'s back-up systems online wouldn't matter.

"I'm rerouting as much power to navigation as I can," Mikka said. "Hopefully, that will boost our engines. Use the rest for your death rolls!"

"I hope it's enough!"

"I'm guessing when you said we can outmaneuver them, you meant . . ."

Kiara grimaced. "Barely avoid getting blown into space dust."

"*Shit!* Can you tell who it is? Syndicate?"

"If it is, they're special forces. There's no markings or signatures I'm able to read off that thing."

"Pirates?"

"It's possible, but that is *one hell* of a trophy ship. It's got to be an experimental vessel of some kind. There's no ship in the Loop with an ion drive that could match what I'm seeing. I bet they could make it to Mars in a *week*."

"Who the hell is it?"

"I don't know, but I'm pretty sure we're not getting out of here without a fight," Kiara said, as the ship shook again.

Mikka barely heard her. She was busy powering up the few energy weapons they had on board. They weren't likely to do much damage, but she had to try *something*.

"Hate to break it to you, but we're already in the middle of one," she said.

A burst of energy lit up their holo-screen as the first wave of firepower dispersed. The streams of energy soared for several seconds before impacting with the silver shell.

"Did that even do *anything?*" Mikka yelled.

"I can't tell!" Kiara replied. "Their stats are unreadable, but it didn't slow it down any."

"*Gah!*" Mikka exclaimed. "I'm arming one of our tactical missiles. We need to put the brakes on that thing!"

The *Redemption* was equipped with three missiles, and one EMP pulse for emergency use only. The munitions didn't come cheap, even on the black market, and so far, Mikka had thwarted any pirates she'd faced without them.

"I'd hold off until they close in on us," Kiara advised, "or they're just going to shoot it down before it reaches them."

Kiara was right. And a replacement would run at about a thousand credits each.

*If we last that long.*

"Has there been any increase in our speed?" Mikka asked. "Are we gaining any ground?"

"Our speed? Yes. Their speed? Also, yes. They've compensated; matched us every time. And to be honest, it seems like she's holding back on us."

*Damn!*

The *Redemption* swerved again, and in the bridge's reduced gravity, Mikka's boots left the deck in a small hop before she regained her footing. Kiara grabbed onto her nav station to keep from floating away and then buckled herself in.

Mikka needed some good news. "How are our shield plates holding?"

"Right now, they're at ninety percent power, but that's only because we've been able to steer away from the worst of their blows. But one, maybe two well-placed hits are all we'll be able to take. They've got military grade weapons, and our shield plating wasn't exactly designed with them in mind!"

*Military grade.*

Mikka cursed as she surveyed the ship coming ever closer. *Who the hell is this, and why were they firing on* us?

"Let me know when they're close enough for me to fire."

Kiara hissed something under her breath that Mikka didn't catch, but she got the gist of it.

It wasn't good.

"What's going on now?"

"They've brought company!"

Mikka scanned the holo-screen, but she couldn't make out much. An orbital space dock loomed below them, while another FLOW station drifted in the distance, along with tiny pinpricks of light that marked the flight paths of cruisers and carriers along orbital routes.

"I'm not seeing . . ."

Mikka froze. From the direction of the *Freedom*, a light rapidly approached from the ether. Its propulsion had to be twice the speed of the initial vessel. "*What the . . .?*"

"They came out of nowhere!"

"There's more than *one*?"

A second ship plunged from behind the first, as though both had been hiding in plain sight.

"I'm counting three hostiles swarming us now. The first

two are pulling out ahead of us. They're doing their best to cut off an escape!"

"Why didn't we pick them up on our sensors?" Mikka pressed, trying to get a read on the enemy ships as she spoke.

But she already knew the answer.

"They're not showing up! It's like they're invisible!"

The ship shuddered again.

"Are they *all* firing at us?"

"Just the one, so far," Kiara responded. "The other two are still out of range, but they won't be for long."

Mikka rubbed her face. The likelihood of the attack being random had gone out the viewport. Either she'd pissed off the wrong person, or someone had discovered her association with Aries and wasn't too happy about it.

*But did they really have to send the best top secret ships in the fleet out after us? All for delivering a few kilos of rice?*

Of course they did. Mikka had proven herself to be crafty over the years and, at one time or another, had outsmarted every other ship in the Syndicate armada.

Which meant she could outwit them again.

Somehow.

She rattled through the options in her head. They were too far from anything to take cover. Too far from anyone to call for help. Too outgunned to fight. Too outmatched to run.

"How quickly are they able to turn those things around?" Mikka asked.

"Damned if I know, but I don't think that's going to be our issue . . . Wait . . . No, no, *no!* I'm not here for crazy ass maneuvers, Jenax! Death rolls are about my limit! Just get me home in time for my holo-shows with a glass of wine your fair emperor has so graciously afforded me."

"So, *now* you're on his side?"

"I'm on the side of whoever doesn't get me killed."

"Give me another option and I'll consider it."

"What about your pretty boy? Surely Aries has got ships that can swoop in and save the day?"

"Can you read any that are close by?"

"No," Kiara sulked. "But I didn't pick up these two, either."

"So, what then? Send out a blind distress call? Look, Aries wanted this mission to be discreet. I don't think sending out a locator beacon is quite what he had in mind . . ."

"I hate to break it to you, but this shit ain't going to be discreet for long if we can't throw off these fighters. Can we open a frequency?" Kiara suggested, her eyes wide with panic. "Maybe talk our way out of this one?"

It was the longest of long shots. Mikka hated negotiating with anyone who had opened fire on her, but it seemed like a less reckless move than what she had been about to propose. That was something her old self would have done, the pirate buried deep she had tried so hard to leave behind. Jax Luana, a woman now dead to her.

But Mikka would keep the maneuver to herself for the moment. Kiara's idea seemed like the better alternative.

"Do it," Mikka said. "Though I feel like if they were in the mood to talk, they would have tried that before opening fire on us."

"If they don't respond, I'm all ears for whatever suicidal

idea you've come up with." Kiara swiped a hand over her holo-screen. "It's open."

"This is Mikka Jenax, captain of the *Redemption*. Unknown vessels, why are you firing on us?"

Silence followed.

"Unknown vessel. We are a cargo ship with authorized clearance. We think there might have been some kind of mistake. Please respond."

"A fourth ship has appeared," Kiara interjected. "Looks like it was hiding out behind the others."

*Damn it!*

"And the lead ship is powering up its weapons."

Mikka closed the comms channel. "I guess we have our answer . . ."

"All right. What's your crazy idea, Jenax?"

*Only one thing left to do.*

"Take us around as quickly as you can and head for the lead ship. See if you can get us there before the others get within firing range."

Kiara's jaw dropped. "You're not thinking about *ramming* them, are you? I wasn't serious when I called your plan 'suicidal.'"

"Get under the ship."

Kiara met Mikka's gaze with a blank stare.

"Do you trust me?" Mikka pressed.

"It's not a matter of trust. It's a matter of whether we die before I get us there."

"Guess it's time to find out if you really are the best in the Loop."

For a moment, Mikka wasn't sure if Kiara was going to

respond, her gaping stare unwavering. Then, Kiara turned back to the controls and took two deep breaths. "Locking in the flight path."

Mikka would have smiled if she was more confident her plan was going to work. "Hold on and evade their fire the best you can."

Taking her own advice, Mikka strapped herself into the captain's chair. She was under no illusion that Kiara wouldn't have to execute some fancy acrobatic moves to pull this off.

The change in g-force was instantaneous, and Mikka was glad she had buckled in. The *Redemption* arced in nearly a full one-eighty, tossing both captain and navigator as much as their restraints would allow. Mikka's stomach roiled, and she was once again thankful she had a solid stomach for gravitational shifting. She'd worked with many a crew member who would have tossed their lunch under such an intense maneuver.

Kiara hit another set of commands on her panel and the ship lurched forward. Another sudden shift in g-force plowed Mikka in the chest, pressing her back into her seat and stretching the skin on her face before the gravity plating could compensate.

It was hard not to duck as energy bolts came at them head-on through the holo-projected image that still occupied the bridge. Mikka considered turning the screen off as the *Redemption* catapulted headfirst into the lion's den, but she wanted to have a closer look at the highly advanced ship that was trying to fry her ass.

Kiara masterfully steered the *Redemption* between the

blasts. The oncoming craft was relentless in its attack, set on blowing Mikka and her navigator out of orbit.

"It's not slowing!" Kiara exclaimed. "They've anticipated we're setting up to ram them!"

"That's exactly what I *want* them to think," Mikka replied. "Their shields would vaporize us on impact, which is why they're not altering course. Don't hit the brakes until the last minute. I want to sit as close to them as their shields will allow."

Mikka braced herself. As good as Kiara was, there was still a high chance this would end in disaster. But to catch an attacker off guard, you had to do something unpredictable. They would only have one shot at this.

"Care to fill me in on what we're doing once we get there?"

"We're throwing a Hail Mary play. Just prepare to punch it again."

"We're doing a what now?"

"An old Earth term. A last-ditch effort. Look, just get us into position."

Mikka held her breath, her stomach duplicating the rolls of the ship. Errant energy bolts struck them more than once, but they just grazed the *Redemption*'s shield plating, fortunately away from any critical systems.

*This might actually work . . .*

Mikka tried not to think about how much the maneuver was going to cost her. *Aries better be willing to reimburse me for repairs when this is finished.*

The other three ships pulled into range just before they reached their target and let out a barrage of energy blasts. At least one bolt struck true, rattling the ship and sending sparks flying throughout the cabin.

"They've penetrated the plating!" Kiara shouted. "Our hull absorbed that one, but I don't think we'll be able to take much of that."

"You've got to avoid them, or this will never work!"

"I'm doing my best!" Kiara barked.

"*Do better!*" Mikka yelled as the *Redemption* took another hit. Mikka was thankful she had recently spent the credits she had on upgrading the ship's hull integrity. Until now, she had been worried the modifications had been unnecessary.

"Hold steady . . ." Mikka said.

"Pulling into position now. We're close enough that the other ships are holding their fire."

Mikka let out a sigh of relief. "Just keep that ship between us and the others until we make our move."

The holo of the lead ship hung above them. Its monstrous size dwarfed the *Redemption*. It wasn't the largest ship Mikka had encountered, but it was damn near close.

"What kind of ship is this?" Kiara asked her.

The moment of reprieve allowed her to finally gape at the monstrosity. She unbuckled and half-floated from her seat in the reduced gravity. She couldn't help but stare in awe at the smooth, silver vessel above them.

"The kind that's meant to travel far and fast, probably to the colonies further out in the system," Mikka surmised. "But it's a specification I've never seen before."

"Playing space barnacle is only going to give us a few

minutes," Kiara said, uncertainty causing her voice to shake. "What's the next step, Meeks?"

The sheer enormity of the vessel made Mikka doubt her plan, but they had no other option.

"We've got three missiles and one pulse equipped. We're going to unload everything we've got and then hightail it out of here."

"You think *our* missiles will get through whatever shielding they have equipped? Their weapons and engines are far superior to ours; I think it's safe to assume their defenses would be stronger as well."

"We're out of bloody options here, Kiara. Launch our missiles at the incoming ships—target their weapons systems if you can—then immediately launch the Pulse above us."

"The Pulse will take out our systems as well," Kiara said. "We'll be sitting ducks."

"We've got a big shield above us," Mikka reasoned. "And I'm banking on it taking that huge vessel longer to become operational than we will."

Kiara shook her head as she pulled up the weapons control screens. "I sure hope you're right."

Mikka smirked. "Have I ever steered you wrong before?"

"Not until recently."

Mikka's smile didn't fade. She'd missed this; these moments when everything was on the line. The thrill of a close encounter. The rush of possible capture. The plunge into the unknown. She had left it all behind for the security of a regular paycheck and a life above reproach, but damn, she had given up the rush of *living*.

"Stand by. The second the systems are back online, I

want you to set a course for the nearest space dock. We'll contact Aries from there and see if he can give us some insight into just what the hell is going on."

The control panel beeped at her as Kiara tried to pull up the weapons systems. A flashing red banner alongside a cartoon holo-image of a frowning face taunted her.

The message read: *OFFLINE. SORRY, LOVE.*

"You have *got* to be shitting me!"

Mikka

*The Redemption*

MIKKA SLAMMED her fist on the console.

"What's going on?" Kiara yelled over the alarms.

The control panel beeped and then powered down as if the *Redemption* had no weapons at all.

The ship above them jerked away. Mikka nearly stumbled, surprised at the sudden movement, but she held her ground.

*How is that ship able to move so fast?*

"Our weapons are offline!" Mikka slammed her fist down a second time. The impact sent a shot of pain through her arm as it reverberated against the solid surface, and she cursed the ship as though the pain was its fault.

Streams of energy descended upon them, their impact landing true, throwing the *Redemption* into a frenzy. Alarms blared and lights flashed as sparks rained down. The impact threw Mikka off-balance this time.

"*What?*" Kiara cried, panic marring her voice.

"Can you get us out of here?"

Kiara tried to swipe her navigation screen, shaking her head as she did so. "Nothing. The entire system's frozen! What the hell is going on?"

"That bitch locked us out of our own ship. Hold our position and open a channel to the lead ship!"

Kiara's face puckered as she tilted her head. "Which *bitch*?" She didn't wait for an answer, hitting a control on her console and nodding to confirm that she'd opened a channel.

"Abi, if you punch a hole in my ship, there's going to be hell to pay!"

Kiara's eyes widened as the realization struck her.

"Well, hello to you, too, love." The pirate's voice echoed through the ship, sass dripping from the woman's familiar tone. "Did you miss me?"

The pirate's voice grated on every molecule of Mikka's being. "You haven't been gone long enough. Try again in another hundred years or so. Though I suspect the answer will still be the same."

"There she is! There's the loveable charmer they promised me when I went looking for you."

"I see you found yourself a new ride," Mikka replied. "And as far as we can tell, they're more advanced than anything else in the Loop. Who'd you steal them from?"

"Do you like it? This is my new ship, the *Chimera*. It's going to come in handy."

"I'd like it a lot more if it weren't trying to blow the *Redemption* out of orbit."

"Oh, I was never actually going to hurt that pretty face, love."

"You mind explaining what that shitstorm was, then? 'Cause it sure as hell didn't feel like a romp in the hay."

"That could be arranged . . ."

Kiara rolled her eyes. "What the hell have you done to our ship, pirate?"

"I just needed to slow you down," Abigail replied. "I leave nothing to chance. It's the only way to win the game. Zee, of course, calculated that you were probably going to go along with Aries's plan, even after we tried to convince you otherwise. Fortune dictates we lay waste to your ability to do so."

"Who the hell is Zee?" Kiara snapped.

Mikka gritted her teeth. Her shoulders tightened as she tried to direct her fury constructively. "What do you want, Abi?"

"Oh, nothing really. We just need to pull you out of the game for a bit. It seems your role here might have some rather . . . *dire* consequences."

"I'm not playing any *games* with you. Can we talk this out so we can be on our way?"

"Oh, it's too late for that, I'm afraid."

"You have the audacity to fire upon *my* ship and then proceed to tell me it's too late for *me*?"

"Sounds about right."

"So, what? You're going to shoot us down? You killed our weapons so you could destroy us?"

"I've told you before, love, I don't kill unless I have to. I'm not about to change that now. Besides, Zee tells me you're important to the Syndicate's collapse. We'll need to keep you around. The *Chimera* has just a large enough hold that your purple-haired pilot *should* be able to guide you inside. Just don't scrape the paint on your way in."

Mikka ignored the questioning look Kiara gave her and motioned a finger across her own neck, intimating to mute the channel.

Kiara hit the button, then turned to Mikka. "What the hell is going on?" she asked. "Who is Zee?"

Mikka rolled her eyes and used the reduced gravity levels to pull herself across the bridge to check the *Redemption*'s status. Outside of the locked controls and a few damaged hull plates, all systems were operating within normal parameters—or at least, the reduced parameters Mikka had set them to.

She had no doubt that if Abigail had wanted to disable any critical systems, she would already have done so.

"Some damn fortune teller Monroe's allied herself with. It seems for once, you and her agree on something: I shouldn't be so eager to help David."

Kiara smirked. "Careful, you're going to make me like her."

Mikka felt a twinge of relief that some of Kiara's personality was making a comeback, but it was short-lived in the circumstances.

"If we could gain access to our systems, would you be able to get us out of here before they blast a hole in our hull?"

Mikka hoped the pirate would do her best to keep them alive, but keeping her ship in a salvageable state was another question.

Kiara didn't answer right away. She glued her wide eyes to her console's screen, analyzing every possible flight path.

"I don't see a way. I'm sorry."

"*Damn.*" Mikka wracked her brain. She had no weapons to speak of; a smaller, slower ship; and no way out. If she damaged the *Redemption* trying to escape, Aries might finance the repair, but they would have to make it back to Lunar first and their mission would be delayed for weeks. Of course, if the pirates damaged their engines, they'd be sitting ducks.

Even if they made it back to Lunar, that would be strike three. Aries would have every reason to pull them off the mission altogether.

"What about communications? Can we get a message back to Lunar? Maybe we can buy enough time for Aries to direct patrols our way."

"Negative," Kiara replied. "They're jamming all communications except ship-to-ship. Those ships have triangulated us and blocked all outbound transmissions beyond a two-klick radius. To be honest, I'm surprised I could even mute the channel. Whatever that pirate did, she's locked us out of the entire bloody ship!"

*Abigail could have done that before she fired the first shot, but she engaged first.*

"She's toying with us," Mikka said. "I bet she did something to the controls when she was last on board. Now, she's enjoying watching us sweat it out."

"I think you're right," Kiara agreed. "I just don't know how we didn't catch it sooner."

"She's a crafty one. We didn't know we had to look for it."

"Maybe *you* let your guard down, but I sure as hell didn't trust her. I should have been keeping a closer eye on her, and I knew it! Still, I'd like to review our security protocols once we dock. It's doesn't sit right with me that our ship's systems were compromised so easily."

"One problem at a time. We've got to get out of here first. Unmute me." Mikka paced across the bridge.

Kiara nodded to confirm the frequency was live again.

"Abi, I know you believe your new toy has some kind of sixth sense, but this is getting out of hand. All we're out here doing is making a few deliveries to the FLOW stations, just as we did when we transported you to the *Eclipse*. Now, please, let us go about our business. Or, if you prefer, we can talk it over a glass of rum once we're done."

"That ship has sailed," Abigail said. "I wanted to talk when we were on Lunar's surface, and you didn't want to listen to me then. Now we've had to resort to more . . . *drastic* measures. Prepare to come aboard. And don't make this any harder than it needs to be."

"Not like we have much of a choice," Kiara quipped as she muted the channel again.

Mikka sighed. "As much as I hate to admit it, I think we're going to have to surrender now and escape later."

"Damn it, Meeks!" Kiara sighed as she frantically tapped at her screen, scrolling for an alternative option—*any* other option. "What if we get on board and they shoot us? Take our ship and our cargo. They get rid of the problem. *Monroe* might not be a killer, but I know nothing about this Zee or anyone else riding with her."

"Fortune teller or not, Zee's just a kid," Mikka said. "I

don't think he fully understands what he's gotten himself into—or if he even had a choice. And Abi's crew will follow her orders. I think we have to take her at her word. If she wanted to kill us, she'd have done it already. And as much as I hate to admit it, the *Redemption* is a scrap heap compared to what Monroe's flying. I don't think they'd bother saving her."

"What about the cargo? What if they destroy it?"

"A few crates of rice and beans? This isn't our regular run; the cargo's worth jack on its own. The payoff is in the *delivery*. Take or destroy it; we're not that far from Lunar. We head back and load up again."

"*If* Aries trusts us for another round."

And there was the rub. No matter their personal relationship, Aries had hired Mikka for this gig under the pretext of discretion. It wasn't as if he would send an armada with her for round two. Once again, the fate of her and her mother rested on Mikka's ability to complete the job assigned to her.

And once again, she was failing miserably.

Mikka had no other choice: she was on her own. But she had been on her own her entire life; it wasn't as though she needed some moonbase commander to come to her aid every time she was in trouble.

She almost laughed out loud as she recalled the number of tight spots she had wormed her way out of. No pirate ever survived in the Loop without a bit of cunning.

"I've faced worse than this," she said, trying to negate some of the fear in Kiara's eyes. "We just need the right opportunity. We go in, we assess the situation, and we form a new plan. Open the frequency."

Kiara shook her head as she tapped her display screen. "I hope you're right."

"Prepare a pot of tea, Abi. Looks like we're coming aboard."

"I thought you'd see things my way."

As Mikka cut the channel again, rage building against Abigail's arrogance, she told herself to focus. She had already provided her mother with the care she deserved; now, it was time to do the same for her own soul. Ending the Syndicate stranglehold on the colonies was her one chance at atonement.

She wasn't about to blow it.

# CHAPTER TWENTY-SEVEN

Eventide

The *Inanna*

HOT WATER CASCADED over Eventide's stark body.

*How long has it been since I've actually felt clean?*

She allowed the torrent to flow over her head, being careful when the pressure came too close to her neck. The implants were still tender, and she didn't want to aggravate them any further. Questions circled in her mind as to how the devices had been embedded in her skull, and to what part of her nervous system they were attached. But mostly, she needed to know if she could remove them; if this science experiment that had been performed on her was reversible.

Tears flowed with the shower's water stream, and Eventide let them fall.

On the one hand, she stood in the most amazing shower. The water was hot, and the jets came at her from all angles. It was the closest thing she could imagine to what rain must have been like on Earth.

Despite that, she couldn't enjoy it, because on the other hand, she'd lost everything. Not just her home, nor the career she had worked so hard for, but *herself*. The prongs that protruded from her neck had stripped her of her identity, and apparently even her own autonomy over pain and pleasure. The more she thought about it, the more it made her sick to her stomach.

*Maybe I'd be better off ripping them out and ending it all.*

The tears continued to flow, mixing with water to wash over her body.

But she wasn't ready to give up. She had lost something she had never thought could be taken away from her, and she was more alone than she'd ever been, but she wasn't beaten yet.

Her mind somersaulted, trying to avoid embracing the new reality that now smacked her in the face.

*How can* this *even be real?*

Eventide turned the water off and finished getting ready. The Caregivers had filled her closet with the same damn pajamas—a dozen of the exact same outfit, all in blue.

*At least they suit my hair.* She felt a shred of satisfaction at the thought, but it quickly dissipated.

Something about the complementary colors did seem unsettlingly satisfying, but Eventide dismissed the thought. It didn't matter what her uniform looked like.

This was still a prison.

As Yunni had promised, a chime announced her visitors precisely two hours after she had arrived at her new quarters. Eventide was exhausted, and she certainly didn't want to go anywhere, but she forced herself to answer the door.

The tribute waiting for her was nothing like the starry-eyed Yunni.

Two men and one woman waited in the hallway. One man was dressed as she was. His garment was ruby red, but otherwise matched the same shape and style of Eventide's own.

*Maybe the colors mean something?*

The man's hair was also red, but that couldn't have been the determining factor. Yunni's robes were silver, and that certainly wasn't her hair color.

The man was roughly Eventide's age and held the same distant look in his eyes as the rest of the Domani she'd encountered. His skin, though pale, was abnormally smooth and free of any blemishes, freckles, or moles. His physique was toned, too, but that was to be expected if all Domani underwent similar surgical procedures. This man was the only one of the three who offered even a trace of a smile.

The second man was another story entirely. Despite Yunni's insistence that there was no need for the *Inanna* to have guards on board, this man couldn't have been described as anything else. His broad shoulders led into arms as thick as her waist, and his barrel chest was taut rather than flabby. His long black and silver jacket hung open, with only a thick belt keeping it together. Beneath the jacket, he wore a black padded shirt that hinted at some sort of protective armor.

On his back and on his hip, he sported a variety of weapons, one of which Eventide recognized as a blaster similar to the FL-87s carried by the guards aboard the *Eclipse.* His belt held a baton, a large knife, and a second concealed energy weapon.

The woman, despite having to be at least into her late fifties, still had the smooth complexion of youth; the same unnatural look of the Domani and Doctor Morales. She wore a black suit, reminding Eventide of what Admin would have worn on the A-Ring. She was short, barely Eventide's height, and she puckered her lips as though she had just tasted something sour. Her eyes burned a deep brown that made her pupils seem to disappear into her irises.

"You will come with us to Orientation," the woman said.

"And you are?"

"I am Caregiver Lin." The woman's demeanor didn't break from 'annoyed sourpuss.' Her voice held a twinge of yet another accent Eventide had never heard before. There had been two hundred years of history kept from her for unfamiliar accents and dialects to emerge. At least she'd been able to understand what everyone was saying so far.

"I will be your Caregiver for the duration of your stay on the *Inanna*," Lin continued. "You may direct any questions you have to me. Lars, here," she gestured to the big man beside her, "is assigned for your protection and will ensure your safety during your stay."

*I doubt that. He's here to keep me in line, more like.*

"And this is Orin." Lin pointed to the red-haired youth on her left. "He's also a new recruit. Expect to be seeing a lot of each other."

"I'm excited to meet you, Eventide Rossi," Orin said in a robotic tone. He stuck out a fist eagerly while looking at her with the same dumb grin as Yunni.

Eventide looked at the fist and then back at Orin. It appeared he was waiting for her to do something in return.

She hesitantly lifted her own fist to meet his, unsure if that was the proper reaction, but he gingerly lowered his fist as soon as they connected.

"Enough of that!" Lin admonished. "First rule: there is to be *no* physical contact between Domani. Save it for the clients."

*Clients.* Eventide's stomach lurched.

Orin looked sheepish and whispered an apology.

Eventide swallowed. "What if we don't want to be touched by . . . clients?"

Lin raised a puzzled eyebrow. "All Domani desire physical contact."

"I don't," Eventide emphasized. "Not even from people I like."

Lin paused, as though Eventide's reaction was out of the ordinary. Was everyone else here so willing to be obedient?

"You are the property of the *Inanna*." Somehow, Lin's face scrunched even further. "You will behave accordingly."

Eventide gritted her teeth and resisted the urge to test who the guard was *really* there to protect. "I am *nobody's* property."

*First priority is to find a way out of here.* She sucked in a deep breath, which calmed her down, but she was sure it must have seemed like exasperation to Lin.

*Not far from the truth.*

"I will need to speak to Doctor Morales about this." Lin typed some notes on her datapad.

Eventide gasped as a thousand needles stabbed her in the brain; a piercing pain unlike anything she'd ever experienced. She would have cried out, but she found herself unable to.

*What are they doing to my brain?*

"You will learn your place soon enough. Come now, follow me."

The needles disappeared as quickly as they had arrived, and Doctor Morales's words hit Eventide anew.

*Control your pleasure and your pain.*

*Did Lin cause the stabbing pain because I stood up to her?*

Was that why all the other Domani seemed so placid? Were they conditioned to avoid punishment? Or had the Caregivers eradicated all fight within them?

Something about Lin's reaction suggested that wasn't what had happened.

Lin had been *surprised*.

If defiance was something that had to be shocked out of the Domani upon arrival, there would have been a look of determination on Lin's face, not confusion.

Eventide knew one thing: she wouldn't sit around and wait to be sold to some horny *client*.

---

AS MUCH AS Eventide had hoped she would finally get answers, the orientation consisted of little more than displaying a map of the ship—or a partial one, at least—a guide to the typical schedule of visitors to the *Inanna*, and a chance to meet others like her who had been recently abducted.

There were about a dozen others, nearly evenly split between men and women. Despite there being much talk among them of brother- and sisterhood and support for each other, no introductions were made, and any interactions had felt hesitant and forced.

It appeared, though, that Eventide was the only one to notice. All the other Domani maintained their serene smiles and seemed quite pleased with the experience.

Eventide spotted Yunni among the attendees, though the woman had told her she wasn't a new recruit. Somehow, she had earned a supervisory role within the Domani. Perhaps she had been so overly happy to be on board that she'd earned a privileged position.

At least her attention was no longer on Eventide.

Lin's other lackey, Orin, had chosen a seat obnoxiously close to Eventide and looked at her with the wide-eyed stare of a child excited to be attending their first day of school.

In fact, every other person going through orientation was beaming with excitement.

Several individuals who were obviously not part of the Domani stood in the corners of the room. They didn't wear the revealing outfits, nor did they share the same starry-eyed look of delight. Mistress Lin stood straight as a board, her lips still puckered as though she were chewing on a lemon. Lars stood beside her.

*My own personal bodyguard.*

The man was busy flexing his muscles, stretching out the plastic-like fabric of his own bodysuit with a self-amused smile on his face. Eventide rolled her eyes.

Doctor Morales stood on the other side of Lars. Expressionless, the woman surveyed the seated Domani as she might a room full of houseplants—with only curious interest, perhaps assessing whether her little experiments on each of them had been successful. The wicked woman was likely scheming what sort of device she could implant in them next.

Yunni ended up explaining the ship's layout. The information she shared was surface level and couldn't possibly have covered most of what lurked within the ship's hull.

Quarters. Dining hall. Games room. Library. Exercise facility.

The rest of the ship was either off-limits or not important enough to mention.

Eventide raised a hand.

"Yes, Eventide?" Yunni nodded toward her. "You have a question?"

"Where is the engine room?"

The ship would have one, plus an engineering section that controlled the engines. Either would be infinitely more interesting than anything she'd seen so far. Eventide was, after all, an engineer, and she had no interest in spending her free time playing games and lifting weights. Aside from the horror of the place, it wasn't lost on her that she was aboard a freaking spaceship. There was so much she could learn.

As she voiced the question and allowed the revelation to take hold, a wave of excitement struck her. *Extreme* excitement. Maybe this misfortune might provide her with a once-in-a-lifetime opportunity. For as long as she was being held against her will, it made sense for her to learn as much as she could about spacefaring ships and their propulsion drives.

Before humanity had left the Earth, they were still relying mostly on hydrocarbon fuel to power their spacecraft, but over the course of two hundred years, surely that inefficient and destructive fuel source had been substituted.

Yunni wore her standard confused look. "We don't need to visit the engines." She looked toward Lin, as if for support.

"But I'd like to see them," Eventide pushed. If she was going to be stuck here, she might as well do something useful with her time.

*I'm not staying here.*

"The engine rooms are off-limits to the Domani," Lin chimed in. "All ship's operations are off-limits. I suppose that leads us to the next part of the presentation. Thank you, Yunni. I'll take it from here."

At the mention of her name by the Caregiver, Yunni's face lit up. Eventide couldn't tell if she was happy to have the pressure taken off, to hear her own name, or if this was just part of the woman's constant general state of ridiculous elation.

Lin stepped to the front of the room, taking Yunni's place. "Each of you is here because you were found in a state of distress. In those moments, someone saw more potential in you than you could achieve in your existing social standing."

*Yeah, and the potential to make a few quick credits.*

"You now have an opportunity to do something almost nobody else in the Syndicate Empire can do. You will rise above the rank of your birth and live among the wealthy. It is a privilege and an honor, and I hope you realize how rare a position you find yourselves in." Lin's gaze honed in on Eventide. "I suggest you don't screw this up."

Lin smiled, and a few of the other attendees laughed as though the Caregiver had made a joke rather than a thinly veiled threat.

"What happens if we do?"

Eventide's gaze met Lin's, and she did her best to match the Caregiver's intensity. She hadn't become the first D-Ringer to pass technicians training on the *Eclipse* by being timid. Despite the need to go along with things for the moment, she wasn't going to shy away from pushing a few buttons along the way.

For a split second, Lin looked taken aback. A quiver to her lips and a slight twitch of the eyebrow suggested she wasn't asked questions like this often. Or ever.

A few of the other recruits giggled, as though it were a continuation of Lin's joke.

*What is wrong with these people?*

Lin glanced toward Doctor Morales, an unspoken question in her eyes, but she returned her focus to the room of Domani, pointedly avoiding looking at Eventide. "Adjusting to a new place can be hard. As many of you are aware from firsthand experience, there are fates worse than death. My fellow Caregivers and I on the *Inanna* are here to help and guide you, to nurture you in your path forward, until you find your way to your future home with one of our esteemed clients. Don't mistake friends for enemies or pleasure for pain. It is possible that we've made mistakes, and that not all of you will be a good fit. Those who are not will be terminated from their time on the *Inanna*."

There was an audible gasp from one recruit across the room. The sound caught Lin's attention, breaking her concentration. The Caretaker craned her head to determine who had made the sound.

Someone else in the crowd was showing signs of opposition to being on this ship. Eventide wanted to know who.

The orientation room wasn't large, but it was full. Eventide followed the small section of Domani who turned to stare at a smaller woman whose copper skin nearly blended in with her outfit. Eventide almost had to do a double take to confirm the woman wasn't sitting there naked. The woman closed her mouth quickly, hurriedly restoring the same half-empty stare the rest of the Domani held.

The shift appeared to satisfy Lin, and she regained her composure. "We are dedicated to finding the right match between Domani and client. If we feel you don't have what it takes to pair with a client, then you will be dismissed. But don't worry, that has never happened under my watch, and I don't intend for it to start now."

Somehow, Eventide didn't believe anyone who was 'dismissed' survived to tell about it.

"That is all for this part of the orientation," Lin said, composing herself. Nobody else in the room seemed to notice her momentary loss of focus. "Yunni will now provide a tour of the ship."

Yunni had mentioned a games room; perhaps that was the best way for Eventide to learn about the other captives. Perhaps she could discover if the gasping woman had any thoughts about her next steps. Maybe together, they could find a way off of this godforsaken ship.

But Eventide imagined she wasn't going to like the answer.

# CHAPTER TWENTY-EIGHT

Eventide

The *Inanna*

INSTEAD OF DRAWING further attention to herself, Eventide resigned to remain silent for the rest of the orientation. Everything about the situation was wrong, but she wouldn't get anywhere by growing the target on her back.

The Domanis' first stop was the games room, which wasn't so much a room, but a complex. There were at least a dozen areas and rooms that were connected for the Domanis' entertainment. There was a running track, volleyball courts, basketball courts, virtual reality rooms, and even a gigantic-sized pool.

Eventide couldn't help but stare at the giant vat of water that just sat there, out in the open. The amount of water sitting in one place was mind-blowing. The showers were impressive, but this? This was a miracle.

What would happen if the gravity ever cut out? *Did* that ever happen? Gravity plating seemed to keep everything in place aboard the spacecraft, but what kept the water contained if that force suddenly stopped working?

The *Redemption* must have employed similar technology. It surprised Eventide that she hadn't already stopped to consider the gravity tech being used. On the *Eclipse*, she had believed artificial gravity plating was rare, which explained why it had only been implemented for the tram in the station's center spindle. Out here, in the wider solar system, perhaps anti-grav wasn't uncommon.

Eventide wanted to ask about it, to learn more about how the technology worked, but she forced herself to bite back the question. She reminded herself that she had already drawn too much attention as it was, and that the Domani weren't exactly a curious lot.

More than ever, for the sake of her own sanity, she needed a plan to get off the ship.

At the end of the tour, Eventide found herself back in her quarters. There was a sick pleasure she felt at the sight of the room. She was glad to be away from the insufferable smiles of the Domani. For all it represented, the room was a safe space amid unwarranted glee and the glares of their captors, offering solace Eventide imagined she wouldn't find anywhere else on the ship.

But it was more than that. There was something about the room that made her feel like she was at home. Her bed, in a small room off to the side of the quarters, was inviting; it was easily the most comfortable thing she'd had ever laid down on. The lights radiated warmth against her skin, in a way that almost made the indecent outfit was wearing worthwhile, like she was bathing in the sun.

*Is this what being on Earth is like? The sun on your skin and a gentle breeze in your hair?*

It was tempting to give into the euphoria the *Inanna* offered. Maybe the Domani and the Caregivers had been right: maybe there wasn't anywhere else that would cater to her as much as this place. Why would she ever want to leave? This could be home.

She stopped herself.

*No.*

Something was wrong.

Why was it so hard to shake the feeling that she belonged here, that this could be the place she needed to be? Here, she didn't have to worry about hull breaches, engine power, or gravitational plates.

*Or Django.*

Warm lights beamed down onto her bed, inviting enough to make her want to retire for the night. A yawn forced its way out.

*Maybe I should just lie down for a few minutes . . .*

Whatever they had done to her had taken its toll.

*Whatever they did to me.*

The thought snapped her to her senses. *This is part of it!* The sensations of belonging. The desire to go to sleep.

*Pleasure and pain.*

Could the implants be manipulating her thoughts? Were they sending signals right now to her brain, to calm and relax her? It would explain the Domanis' constant elation. If that was the case, why hadn't it affected her in the same way?

*But it is affecting me!*

Eventide could feel it in the draw to lie down; in the comfort of her quarters; in the aromas that circulated in the room, scents she had never before smelled, but somehow innately knew what they were: cherry blossom and pear. The room temperature was perfect and kissed her skin in a way Eventide would have thought impossible within the confines of a ship. She'd certainly never felt this way aboard the *Eclipse*.

The *Eclipse*. Home.

*Used to be home*, she reminded herself.

She could never go back. So, why not stay here?

But Eventide knew why. Everything about this place, despite it feeling perfect and more natural than anywhere she'd ever been before, was wrong.

This wasn't the life Eventide had chosen. This wasn't the life she had worked so hard to achieve.

Maybe the other Domani had nothing left to fight for. After a difficult and tiring life, a safe, warm place would be hard to resist.

Somehow, Eventide had fought it.

She could *still* fight it.

But the draw was compelling, and Eventide could tell she would need to make her move soon, or whatever dopamine signals the Caregivers were channeling to her brain were going to win.

She had worked too hard to become a station technician. And even if the role was a lie, it didn't mean the knowledge she'd learned was useless. She could still be an engineer. She could still build a better life.

Aside from that, Django was still out there, and if he was

going to survive in the system that was now revealing itself to them, he would need her help.

She couldn't stick around and wait for the allure of the room to take hold. Before the determination left her for good, Eventide slipped out of her room.

*It knows when you're at your door.*

Yunni's words were hard to forget. With the room logging her coming and going, the Caregivers would know she had left. Would they track her moments throughout the ship? Perhaps, but considering the lack of guards and other security measures, perhaps the Caregivers trusted that the chemical signals being fed into Domani brains would be enough to keep them from trespassing. Lars was supposedly her personal guard, but he was, of course, nowhere to be seen.

Something made Eventide different—but she couldn't be the only one.

Orin, Yunni, and the rest of the Domani at the orientation had the glow of peaceful bliss and belonging, as did the other Domani Eventide passed walking the halls of the *Inanna*. None of the other people on board had shown a single thought that went against the narrative the Caregivers had been imposing upon them.

*Except one.*

The woman who had gasped during the orientation meeting.

At the hint of the disobedient being terminated, the woman had reacted with horror. Every other person in that room had acted as if Lin's words were nothing sinister, as though murdering one of their peers was a perfectly reasonable response to someone who didn't want to follow the ways of the Domani.

Eventide needed to figure out who this woman was. Perhaps, like her, she felt she had a purpose beyond the *Inanna*. Perhaps she would become an ally.

Eventide trod lightly out of her room, her feet sinking into the plush carpet. She couldn't help scanning the corners of the halls, trying to spot cameras or any other evidence confirming she was being watched. But she couldn't see anything obvious.

*Who needs eyes when trackers are embedded inside the people you want to watch?*

The games room promenade contained floor-to-ceiling windows that peered out into the void of space, offering Eventide a perfect starting point.

Perfect, because she needed to assess where in the solar system she was.

The darkness of space was overwhelming. Eventide had always thought so while aboard the *Eclipse,* but at least the big gray and brown marble of Earth had always been below them, its orbit keeping the station firmly tethered to something tangible.

That wasn't the case now. The *Inanna* could have been lost, adrift in the void, for all she knew, with nothing holding them in place except for whatever fuel source propelled the ship between the planets and the far reaches of the solar system.

There were so many questions Eventide would have loved to hear the answers to. And she didn't know if she felt worse about being held against her will or the attempt to keep her ignorant of the reality of her situation.

Eventide snorted at the thought. *That's been my reality my whole life, hasn't it? Lies.*

It took a lifetime of dedication to secure a posting as technician aboard the *Eclipse*, only to discover the job was a lie. Their lives were all lies.

Technicians didn't fix problems; they made them disappear. The hull breaches weren't breaches at all, but a means of getting rid of the noncompliant.

And even when the Admin had disclosed *some* of the truth, they hadn't told Eventide everything. It wasn't just that the Earth had healed more than they were told; people were already *living* down there. Who knew how many? It wasn't just that there were more humans than the half a million that had survived on the *Eclipse*; there were millions of others living on other stations. How many more had colonized the solar system?

Did Admin even know what was real?

Reality had been hidden from her on board the *Eclipse*, and the *Inanna* was no different.

And Eventide sure as hell knew that whatever Django was dealing with, things were being hidden from him as well.

*Does anyone know what's actually happening?*

Was the entire solar system like this? Higher powers masking reality from their subjects? Reality obfuscated from one power structure to the next. Did *anyone* know the truth, or was it lie upon lie all the way to the top of whoever ran this godforsaken empire?

In the distance, Earth grew steadily larger, a blue and

green orb thrust against a backdrop of black. The *Inanna* was making its way toward the planet.

*Will I ever get used to seeing the planet like this? Blues and greens instead of hues of brown and gray?*

Every time was like the first. Celeste's wedding felt like a lifetime ago, the rich colors of Earth revealing themselves in a moment of chance that catapulted her and Django into this nightmare.

Eventide should have already known something was wrong back then, back when she had been studying to be a technician. Her exams had hinted at it, the answers skewed to ensure the candidates showed loyalty to the station and its administration above anything else.

But no amount of training or vague clues could have prepared her for the truth.

Once again, Eventide found herself in the position of being privy to the truth hidden from the masses. Somehow, she was the only initiate aware that she and the rest of the Domani were being emotionally manipulated through the receivers connected to their neocortices.

It wasn't fair for any of them, and somehow she'd reveal the truth. All of it.

But not today.

The problem was far more overwhelming than Eventide could comprehend. She hadn't even known life existed beyond the station walls until recently, and she hadn't come down to the *Inanna*'s viewing area to wane about politics or kept secrets. Before she could worry about bigger things, she had to get herself off the *Inanna*.

She wished she knew more about this new reality she faced—this 'Loop', as Dr. Morales had called it.

Eventide sighed.

A flash of movement out of the corner of her eye caused her to freeze. She slowly turned around, but the complex was empty. She was either too late or seeing things.

*Was someone there?*

Shadows danced across the atrium floor as lights from interactive panels and entertainment units flashed along the otherwise darkened floor and walls. But as far as Eventide could tell, she was alone.

It must have been a trick of the light, flickering in the dark, but she couldn't shake the feeling someone was watching her. She stood frozen by the window, waiting for anything to disprove her hypothesis that she was seeing things.

The *Inanna* was an unfamiliar place that made unfamiliar noises. She was jumping at shadows, no doubt, but if she was going to get off the ship, she had to keep her wits about her.

What would Django say if he found out *she* was the nervous one around flickering display panels?

*He'd probably die of laughter.*

First, she had to figure out what her options were. It wasn't like she could open the airlock and step into the void of space.

Hopefully, the *Inanna* had been equipped with escape pods. If she could find Engineering, she could . . .

She paused. *What could I do?* They were in the middle of space. Nothing but emptiness surrounded them for hundreds of thousands of kilometers. She could point the escape pod at the Earth—but then what?

*I don't even know what's down there.*

Eventide's heart sank. It wasn't going to work, was it? She wasn't getting off the ship. Even if she found a craft, something likely impossible for a Domani, she would still need to commandeer it and figure out how to launch it from the ship without detection. Once outbound, she would have to figure out where to actually *go*, never mind navigating whatever other obstacles the system held for her.

As much as Eventide hated to admit it, she would be much better off waiting until the ship docked and planning an escape then.

Unless she succumbed to the subliminal forces tugging at her emotions, trying to convince her that the *Inanna* was where she truly belonged . . .

Movement flashed again to one side of the rec room. She was sure she saw it this time, but again, by the time she turned, all was still. Several doors at the edge of the room stood silently, taunting her.

But one of those doors *had* moved.

All Domani were supposed to be in their quarters, and if the draw Eventide had felt to hers was any indication of the signal's power, all the other Domani would be safe and sound beneath their sheets.

Had a guard been stationed on the promenade in case one of them resisted the siren's call?

*There are no guards.*

She recalled Yunni's words from earlier in the day, but they weren't true. Lars, the escort who had walked with her and Lin to Orientation, was supposedly assigned to protect Eventide.

She scoffed. *The man's been MIA since Orientation. He clearly cares more about Lin's safety than mine.*

No, if the guards had truly been there for the Domanis' protection, they would have been stationed outside of the quarters —and Eventide hadn't seen any.

But someone *was* there.

Her heart raced, pounding so hard that she thought the sound of her pulse alone would give her position away—if the damn implants in her neck hadn't already. Her back dripped with sweat, but Eventide hadn't gotten as far as she had by letting her fear control her.

But damn, if only the dopamine her implants released would take effect . . .

Something told her that panic kept it at bay. *Is fear an emotion the Domani ever experience? Or are they so wrapped in their cocoons of chemical signals that they've forgotten how to be afraid?*

The thought made her want to embrace the fear that threatened to immobilize her. That way, at least, she'd know the feelings were her own.

The rational part of her brain told her she should return to her room and pretend that she had never left. But there was another part that needed to know whether there was a guard or a Domani stalking her in the shadows.

Someone else was awake, and she needed to know who.

Eventide moved toward the door that had shuddered. If she remembered correctly from Orientation, it was the ship's study, though what exactly the Domani were supposed to be studying was beyond her. There was no access to any learning materials that were of any value, only entertainment, and the room served more like a lounge.

Eventide touched the controls on the wall panel to prompt the door to slide open, taking care not to get the biochip in her arm too close to the display. She still wasn't sure to what extent her implants would enable the Caregivers to track her movements, but if her biochip interfaced with the door panel, it would give her away completely.

The door slid open silently. Thankfully, they didn't make the same hissing noise as those on the *Eclipse*.

Then she caught her breath and wished she'd never left her quarters.

Orin lay on the study's carpeted floor.

In a pool of his own blood.

# CHAPTER TWENTY-NINE

Django
Shackleton City

AT LEAST I'M *not dead*.

In the moments after the tunnel collapsed, Django had been certain he had sealed his own fate. He'd dropped to the ground, hands behind his head, waiting for one of the surviving soldiers to execute him.

"What now?" one of them had said. "Do we kill this one?"

There had been a pause as their leader considered his options. "Did you know the two who escaped?"

Django didn't have to look up to know the guard had directed the question at him.

"No." Django had surprised himself at how quickly and easily the lie had come, but he'd braced himself to receive an energy bolt to the back of his head, anyway.

"Bring him in," the guard said instead. "I'm sure Aries will get more out of him."

The journey to the jail cell had been longer than Django had been expecting. The Resurgence tunnels had purposefully snaked away from the confines of Shackleton City proper.

Django had been left in the cell for what felt like hours now, with nothing to mark the passage of time except an intermittent distant rumble, somewhere far above the prison. So far, his tour of the universe outside of *Eclipse* had comprised a dark cargo hold, a slave ship, underground tunnels complete with a functional hideout, and now a prison cell.

*What a bloody warm welcome!*

Unlike the crowded slave ship, Django was the lone occupant of his cell. White electric lighting glowed from somewhere down the hall, but the room itself had no integral lights.

His cuffs appeared to be grafted from some sort of energy field; something akin to the force field that separated his cell from the hall and the port from the vacuum of space. The technological mysteries he'd encountered bordered on magic.

*Eventide would have a ball trying to decipher how everything works.*

Pain lanced through his chest as he thought of his friend and everything they'd been through. Everything they were *still* going through.

So much had happened over the course of the last mind-bending week, it was hard for him to keep everything straight in his head.

*I don't think this could ever work.*

*Horrible things happen to the men and women aboard that ship.*

Django's forearm chilled where Marvin had run his finger down.

*A master key. A chip that can access any Syndicate system.*

And now, once again, Django found himself alone, facing an uncertain future.

At least he could rest easy knowing he had helped free Rowyn. He hoped she and Wilder had made it to the second transition house by now. Even if these Syndicate soldiers were going to torture him or send him back to the mines, the sacrifice was worth it to help his friends.

It would be too much to expect another rescue attempt. Marvin had only gotten approval to go after the slave ship because the miners had also captured prominent members of the Resurgence. There were no smokescreens for finding him buried deep within a Syndicate prison.

Occasionally, distant screams and not-so-distant groans interrupted the silence of his cell. What crimes had his neighbors committed, and how much time had they already served here?

*How long will I be here for?*

The Port Authority had arrested him simply for boarding a ship without permission. He was now being detained for affiliating with a group of insurgents. There was no way the charge would be taken lightly.

Without warning, blinding light flooded the cell. Two guards disabled the force field and grabbed Django from the floor, forcing him to his feet and shoving him forward as he scrambled to find his footing.

"What's going on?" he stammered, struggling to gain his balance and focus on the newly illuminated world around him. "Where are we going?"

"Shut up!" a gruff male guard on his right admonished. A female guard to his left tightened her grip under his armpit, as though the simple question might be a prelude to an escape attempt.

The route the guards dragged him along was like a maze. They maneuvered through cold, sterile corridors, the hum of fluorescent lights overhead complementing the dull gleam of the metallic walls' dull gleam. They traversed up several flights of stairs before the cold design of the prison level gave way to more opulent surroundings: lavish sitting areas with plush white sofas and polished obsidian tables, sprawling conference rooms with holo-displays, and walls adorned with artwork of lavish landscape paintings that either pictured how Earth had once been before the wars, or how it stood now.

As they continued, soft music played somewhere in the background, an eerie contrast to the silence of Django's cell. The stale odor of poorly recycled air was soon replaced with a fresher, botanical aroma. Hints of Earth-based plants— lavender, jasmine, and even the faintest trace of gardenia. Django knew the plants well, though they were only grown experimentally on the station. They didn't grow plants like these en masse on the *Eclipse* because they were supposedly too fragile to survive the dead planet below.

Django was unable to dwell on his wonder for long, as

each step he took was met with the cold, hard touch of a baton to his side, urging him onward.

They eventually reached a set of gleaming elevator doors framed with gold accents. One of the guards swiped his forearm over an access panel and the doors slid silently open, revealing a spacious, mirrored interior.

Once the elevator car reached its destination, the guards led him into an office encased completely in glass and filled with a dizzying array of holographic displays. Most portrayed facts and figures of one form or another, while other screens displayed the faces of men and women Django didn't recognize, spinning in a translucent state.

A man with a powerful air about him, dressed in a long coat, stood in the center of it all. Django knew little about this world, but whoever this man was, he seemed important.

Or at least, he *believed* himself to be.

He was, without a doubt, a senior Syndicate figure. Flashbacks of Commander Benson streamed through Django's mind. This man's posture was the same: straight-shouldered, with his hands clasped behind his back. His hair was so short that Django couldn't tell if he'd shaved it and it was growing back, or if it had been cut to that length intentionally. He was a large man, nearly as big as Wilder, but twice Wilder's age. Like Wilder, this man also had a tattoo that glowed, but it was only a small yellow triangle beneath his left eye. The mark on this man's face, however, appeared to be functional rather than cosmetic. The faint outline of circuitry caught the light emanating from the holo-screens across the room, as though the tattoo held some sort of cybernetic device.

*In this bizarre hellscape, anything seems possible.*

Wrinkles surrounded the commander's eyes, and creases marked his forehead. Despite this, with the air of confidence and power he exuded, Django supposed many women might have found him attractive.

His uniform was similar to Commander Benson's, except that, even in the light from the array of holo-screens, Django could tell the cloth was newer and more refined. There were more lights or embellishments attached to the suit, and this man wore a long black jacket overtop, as though trying to fight off a chill that didn't exist within the office tower walls.

"We captured him in a raid on a Resurgence safe house," the male guard announced. "They were firing on SF officers."

"I didn't fire a weapon," Django said defensively, even though he *would* have if he'd not been using himself as a distraction. "I was running away from the shooting."

"Then why were you armed, kid?"

"Release him," the man said with a wave of his hand that suggested he couldn't be bothered with arguing.

The guard hesitated for a moment before nodding and swiping a hand over Django's cuffs.

Considering this was the second time Django had found himself in handcuffs since he'd left the station, he was starting to see how such an enhancement would come in handy. Django relaxed his arms as the cuffs deactivated.

"It's Django, isn't it? Welcome to Syndicate Front HQ," the man said. "You've been creating quite the stir since you got here. Considering it's your first time here, you've made some interesting friends."

Django bit his tongue.

"A little birdie told me it was in my best interests to bring you in; that perhaps you could help me with what I'm trying to accomplish. I also suspect you don't possess the full facts when it comes to the crimes of the man you've been associating with."

"Excuse my ignorance, *sir*," Django replied, trying to match the man's confidence. He doubted he was succeeding, but he had to at least appear like he was holding his own. "But I don't know which man you're talking about. I've done nothing but been thrown in and out of prison cells since I got here. I haven't been helping anyone."

"Sir's fine, but you can call me Aries," the man said. "I'm the Syndicate's Commanding Officer of the Lunar colonies."

The title sounded impressive, and by now Django recognized some of the words.

*Commander*, like Benson. Was this man as crooked as his family's killer? It might have been unfair to hold a man's title against him, but Django couldn't help but believe that the man responsible for hunting down his uncle and his friends, and for holding him in a cell, was as much a piece of shit as the station's command.

*Syndicate*, the organization Marvin and the Resurgence were fighting against. Django didn't know much more than Marvin had told him, but he could put enough pieces together to understand that the commander in front of him was responsible for making life in this lunar city unbearable.

He couldn't help but think of Rowyn's brother, a Syndicate officer who had sold his own sister for some quick and easy credits. That was the kind of empire the man before him represented.

"All right . . . *Commander*." It didn't feel quite right for

Django to call the man by his name as he'd suggested, not even his surname. "Why have you brought me here?"

"Do you recognize this woman?" He pointed to a holographic image on a panel in front of him. The screen showed a three-dimensional image of a dark-skinned woman with her dark hair pulled back and arms crossed over her chest, wearing a black leather jacket and a sneer on her face that made even Commander Aries look like a nice guy.

She hadn't seemed so intimidating in person.

"She was on the *Redemption*. The ship I boarded to escape the *Eclipse*."

Aries smirked. "*Escaped*. An interesting term. Reports say the FLOW stations are the safest places in the Loop. No crime, and nobody goes without food or water. Centuries ago, the stations were set up to provide for the system, and in return, we provide their inhabitants with the necessities. Why would you want to *escape*?"

There was something in the commander's tone that led Django to question whether the man really believed what he was saying. The man picked up a glass on the table, a quarter-full of an amber liquid, and took a sip.

"It's a prison," he replied. "A prison its residents don't even know they're in. The only crime we committed was being born in the wrong place."

Aries shrugged. "Aren't we all? Some are born down on Earth with a silver spoon in their mouths, granted access to the entire system. Their only qualification? Being born in the right place at the right time. Others are born in the underground cities our ancestors built within dwarf planets and asteroids, millions of kilometers from their homeworld, on a rock where every day is a struggle. They have no guarantee of food or water, and even air isn't a commodity they take for granted.

"The question isn't what you were given, it's what you did with what you had. This woman, the captain of the *Redemption,* her name is Mikka, and she was born in the Tubes. Her father died when she was young, and it forced her to use her cunning and craftiness to break free of her prison. She did it using means that weren't exactly *legal,* but sometimes we must do what others would frown upon in order to serve the greater good. Do you understand where I'm going with this?"

The words sounded convincing, at least. *Work hard in order to overcome the odds.* Isn't that what Eventide had done on the *Eclipse?* But Django still had his guard up.

"I'm a farmer," Django said. "Or at least, I *was.* I worked hard. I loved my life. Then everything was taken from me. My family is dead. My uncle is not who I thought he was. One of *your* guards stole the only person I have left and shipped her off to who knows where! I understand perfectly well that you can pull yourself up by your bootstraps, until someone else with more money, more power, more *capability* comes along and smashes it all to pieces. What do you even do when your bootstraps are taken from you?

"Commander Benson killed my family and forced me to leave everything I know behind. If I hadn't, I would be dead too."

*Am I saying too much?* It was likely Benson and Aries were on the same side. Perhaps they worked together to press down those beneath them.

But Aries nodded, as though nothing Django was saying struck him as odd.

"What about her?" Django asked, nodded his head at the projection of Mikka. "What does she have to do with any of this?"

"Right now, Mikka is completing a task for me, so sadly, she couldn't be here, but I wanted you to know that it was *her* who vouched for you. She was concerned about your well-being and thought you might be able to help us locate Alejandro."

"Alejandro?"

"You know him as your Uncle Marvin, but he's so much more than that. And I'm certain he hasn't told you all that much about who he *really* is."

Django
Shackleton City

"HOW DID you know who *I* am?" Django asked. "I haven't talked to anyone since the guards brought me in. Nobody took my name or asked me any questions."

"Oh, I have eyes everywhere." Aries grinned, and Django immediately wished he hadn't. He took back the thought that the image of Mikka had appeared more intimidating. "You know, it's not all that common we come across someone of your physique that we're not able to process."

*So I've been told.* Django's hand reflexively moved to his forearm, as though covering it might somehow stop Aries from cutting him open. He immediately moved his hand away and admonished himself for making such an obvious move.

He remained silent, though. Marvin wanting to implant some chip in him was one thing, but there was no way he'd be okay with Commander Aries doing the same. That aside, he thought it best not to make a spectacle.

"We don't hear too much about what happens on board the FLOW stations." If Aries had noticed Django's hand, he didn't acknowledge it. "I'd be interested to learn more sometime."

Aries walked to a console situated at the side of the room and took another sip of his drink. The console was a sleek silver and white portal that had a dizzying amount of colorful LED lights bouncing around it, and it reminded Django of a fancier version of the systems the *Eclipse* used to monitor crop production. This control panel, however, held holo-projections far more elaborate and at much higher resolution than those on the B-Ring.

Three-dimensional projections hovered above the table-shaped computer system. Blue and purple lights flashed around it, with holographic keyboard terminals resting on top as though they were physical inputs rather than beams of photons and quantum signatures. Lines of code and charts that Django had no interest in attempting to decipher rotated above the console, but before he'd even had the chance to, they all disappeared as Aries typed something into the machine.

A projection of his uncle Marvin replaced the previous image of Mikka. It was definitely his uncle, but a younger version of him—possibly by a decade. But there was no mistaking the rugged face.

"What do you know about this man?" Aries lifted his glass again, but kept his eyes poignantly focused on Django, as if watching for any subtle clue that might provide him with unspoken information.

Django hesitated. How much did this man already know about his uncle?

*Hell, how much do I really know?*

*I have eyes everywhere.*

Was this a test?

Clearly, the man wanted some sort of answer, but it wasn't as if Django was going to say anything that could compromise his uncle's safety or betray any sign that he knew of the Resurgence or their mission, because he didn't *know* anything.

In reality, the Resurgence's mission was to bring men like Commander Aries down, which, unquestionably, made Aries his uncle's enemy.

The only question in Django's mind was whether this commander was a small cog in the machine, like Benson, or did he hold more sway?

Everything about the man's office and stature suggested the latter to be true.

"He's my uncle," Django hesitantly replied. Would being related to a wanted man be enough to incriminate him? He swallowed back his doubt and continued. "Or at least, I *thought* he was. He revealed the truth about the FLOW stations to me and led me to the *Redemption*. He helped me escape."

Aries adopted a confused look, as if part of what Django had told him didn't make sense.

"As you've probably guessed—or perhaps, have been told—his real name is Marvin Alejandro," Aries said, regaining his composure. "Did you know that he's a wanted criminal?"

Django paused. With his uncle's involvement in the Resurgence, it made sense that his uncle would be wanted by the organization they opposed. But he hesitated, as it felt like Aries was after something more. Was he being asked to defend his relationship with his uncle? Was *he* really the one under scrutiny?

"I didn't even know there was anything outside of the station. How could I know anyone was looking for him? As far as I knew, Marvin was a shuttle pilot. It was only after I left that I learned he hadn't been born there; that he'd been marooned on the *Eclipse*."

"He wasn't 'marooned,'" there was grit in Aries' voice. "That's an interesting story he's concocted, but the truth is, he's been in hiding."

Django wasn't sure of the path Commander Aries was leading him down, but something didn't feel right. His fingers tingled in anticipation of what was coming next, but he couldn't get a read on Aries. Whichever path he was being led down, he knew that the man was going to attempt to distort how he saw his uncle.

*Question is, why does my uncle matter to this man?*

"What does any of this have to do with *me?*"

"You left a FLOW station. That doesn't happen every day. I have a keen finger on the pulse of the colonies, and I have *never* heard of it happening before."

"We were told nothing exists out here; that we were all that remains of humanity. Nobody tries to leave because, as far as we understood, there's nowhere to go."

"I bet you wish your friends on the stations knew the truth, don't you?"

"Of course."

Aries clicked another key on his console. Marvin's figure disappeared, replaced by the busts of nearly two dozen other men and women, ranging in age from their mid-twenties to much older. None of them looked familiar. Their heads hovered above the console. Many looked to be military, though the rest could have been any random person he had passed by on the docks.

"Investigators have tied Marvin Alejandro to the murders of each of these men and women." Aries crossed the room and lifted the short glass of amber liquid, a fierce intensity in his eyes. "He's never been a 'shuttle pilot'. He has been, in fact, a mercenary, hired by various terrorist groups to kill high-ranking officials and influential figures."

Django studied the faces that hovered above the display and swallowed. He wanted to say it wasn't true, that Commander Aries was fabricating a lie, but he couldn't bring himself to. Not because he didn't think Aries was lying, but because he didn't *truly* know anything about his uncle. Before today, Django would never have imagined him leading a group of rebels toward a coup d'état against an empire that controlled an unknown number of colonies throughout the solar system. What other secrets did the man hold?

But he didn't put it past this Commander Aries to lie through his teeth, either.

He let his gaze rest on the images. Most of them were no

older than he was. How many had people who loved them? How many had families?

Was it possible his uncle could have killed these people?

Leading a rogue band of rebels is one thing, but killing men and women? *That* didn't add up.

"Who are they? Why *these* people?"

Aries took a sip from his glass. "Some of them deserved it. Military captains who let their credentials go to their heads. Some of them raped and tormented prisoners under their charge."

That explained why Marvin would seek them out: to protect the greater good.

"But not *all* of them," Aries continued. "Some of them were good people who happened to be funding the wrong causes. Heading the wrong projects. The day before he landed on the *Eclipse,* Alejandro had been contracted to kill a councillor who was on board the FLOW station *Infinity.*"

"I heard what happened to the *Infinity.* The Syndicate destroyed it because the people learned the truth."

Aries raised a placating hand. "I'm not here to defend what the former Prefect and Council did to that station. In fact, my plan is to overthrow the current Council and replace their political system with one that is more . . . *equitable.* I'm only mentioning it to let you know the true reason Alejandro was aboard that station."

That gave Django pause. Why was this man, this *stranger*, telling him anything of his plans? His head was spinning at all the talk of uprisings, rebellions, and coups. Why was he being pulled into this alien political landscape?

"Why does this matter?" he asked. "I never asked to be involved."

"I need your help, Django," Aries said with a smile. His face relaxed, adopting the appearance of a friend reaching out rather than a leader commanding an action. "And for me to ask for it, I need you to know the truth about Alejandro. That's what you want after all, isn't it? The truth?"

Django nodded. "Yes, of course. No more lies."

"I can see that you're thinking Alejandro likely targeted these individuals for a reason. He did, but there was no honor in it. Marvin didn't *choose* who he was killing; he was hired. He took on private contracts, sought his targets, and killed them in cold blood."

Django's spine grew cold. He didn't want to believe it, but something in his gut told him Aries wasn't lying. As the commander's hands moved over the console controls, a blip on a holo-feed next to him caught his attention.

It took Django a moment to interpret what he was seeing. It looked to be a security feed. The quality wasn't as crisp as some of the other images in the room, but it was of a high enough resolution that there was no mistaking any of the detail. A dark-haired woman with light brown skin lounged on a white couch, her legs bent under her, stretching the black and white dress she wore. She draped one arm over the back of the chair, the other holding a stemmed glass that contained a bright red liquid. Black, high-heeled shoes she had kicked off lay loose on the floor beneath her. She was smiling, looking at someone off camera. There was no audio, but she was visibly enjoying the company of whoever she was with.

Then, in an instant, her amusement turned to horror. She stood in a panic, and her glass shattered as it fell to the floor. Defensively, she stretched her arms out in front of her.

Django jumped as the woman flew backward onto the couch. And there she stayed, motionless, folded over like a pile of laundry. The feed wasn't fast enough to catch the motion, but it was clear a bullet had caused her fall. Dark red stained the white of her dress as blood flowed from the wound. Red liquid spilled from her glass and splashed over a thick white rug that lay on the floor beneath her.

A man entered the frame, still holding the weapon that had ended her life.

Uncle Marvin tucked the gun into his belt and hovered over the woman, putting two fingers on her neck to check her pulse. Satisfied she was dead, he turned and left the room.

Django did his best to maintain his composure. Never in a million years had Django expected to see what he had just witnessed. His uncle, killing someone. The smile on her face had radiated trust—until the moment his uncle had pulled on a gun on her.

Everything Aries had told him was true. The evidence was right in front of him.

How many others had Marvin killed? At least as many people as were on the display above Aries's holo-projector.

"Why are you telling me this?" Django repeated.

"I want you to have all the information about who you align yourself with before I make you my offer."

Django eyed the man suspiciously. "What kind of offer?"

"Do you think the people who have pulled the wool over your eyes for so long should be brought to justice?"

Django felt like he was being baited. "You're asking me if I think Marvin should pay for his crimes?"

"Potentially, but I think someone else's crimes have been eating away at you. Someone whose secrets affect you more . . . *directly.*"

There was only one person Aries could have meant.

"Commander Benson?"

A smile curved across Aries's face. It was a peculiar look, like the man didn't smile often and was out of practice.

"Precisely. In fact, how would you like to help take Benson down?"

# CHAPTER THIRTY-ONE

Django
Shackleton City


DJANGO'S HEART LEAPT, but he tried to rein in his enthusiasm. Was Aries serious?

Bringing Benson down would be a dream come true. There was only one thing he wanted more, and that was to have Eventide returned safely.

*But why should I trust this guy?* There had to be a catch, something criminal Aries wanted from him.

Django held himself back from diving in headfirst, resisting throwing up his hands and accepting whatever mission this man offered him. With Benson out of the picture, it meant his sister, Nova, would be safe. It meant that maybe one day, Django could return home.

But he needed to learn more. Instead, he asked, "What is it you want from me?"

Aries smiled. This man was not the old-school operator Benson was. They both might have held the title of commander, but Aries was younger—perhaps in his late thirties or early forties—and handsome. And while Benson had an air of pomp and self-indulgence, Aries seemed to have more drive behind him, like a man who was eager to achieve goals rather than trying to maintain a stranglehold on his own power.

"Your connections make you valuable to me, Django, and I enjoy making deals. I enjoy helping people, but it's only fair for me to ask for a favor in return. It's a win-win for both parties. Benson's days are numbered, and I know there's no love lost between the two of you. I am offering you the privilege of being a part of his downfall; to expunge him. Plus, if there's anything else you desire, I'll see if it's within my power to grant it. Once I know your price, I'll let you know what I'd like in return, and perhaps we can make a deal that will benefit both of us. Don't hold back; what I will ask of you is of great value to me, and I have significant influence."

Django lifted an eyebrow. What could this man want from *him* so badly? A farmer from a space station, with no knowledge of this world? If this man was also after Benson, perhaps he wanted intel on the station? If that was the case, Django would disappoint Aries with the little information he could provide.

His forearm itched at the spot Marvin had run a finger over, and Django resisted the urge to move his hand to his arm for a second time. Perhaps Aries wanted the same thing—to chip Django and use him for his own purposes.

But if this man was serious and would offer Django *anything*, there really was only one other thing he needed.

"My friend, Eventide—she was arrested at the same time

as me. Authority officers sold her to a ship called the *Inanna*. I want her set free . . ."

Django's mind drifted back to the people lying on the floor of the transition house, desperate for food and drink, and the stories Rowyn had told him of people living in the Tubes. For the second time, he thought of Rowyn's dirtbag brother, willing to sell his own flesh and blood for a few lousy credits.

He had quickly learned that it wasn't enough to be free in this world.

"And I want her to be looked after. I don't want her worrying about food, water, or a place to live."

Aries tilted his head, amused. His eyes met Django's, as though he was waiting for Django to say more.

"That's it? No riches for yourself? No luxury accommodation, or a fleet of ships? I don't know if you grasp the prestige of my position, lad, but I can offer you much more than a house for your girlfriend."

Django swallowed at the word 'girlfriend'. Some things were unattainable, even for a Syndicate commander.

But this man was pressing him to ask for something more, which meant that whatever he was about to ask of Django was either treacherous or invaluable—and Django got the distinct impression it wasn't truly a choice. He suspected Commander Aries wasn't someone people said no to.

And if it meant a chance of freeing Eventide, there was almost nothing he wouldn't agree to.

Django knew enough to know that he was too naïve to barter a fair deal. He also didn't know what was of worth in this empire. Should he ask for land? Would land be of value?

Should he ask for a home? Food? Livestock? He felt put on the spot, and he didn't want to look back at this decision and feel foolish for selling himself short.

Finally, he said, "I have lived on a space station my entire life. I don't know enough of this world to even know what to ask for. So, what I would ask is for one favor, to be called on by me at a future date. Something that is within your power to grant, of any value."

A spark lit behind Aries's eyes. Something about the request had piqued his interest.

At first, when he'd voiced it, Django thought it was a ridiculous idea; something that nobody would ever agree to. But with that one simple request, he'd learned something about Commander Aries.

The man was both curious and arrogant.

Django was going to be extremely careful with whatever request he eventually made; Aries seemed the type that would try to get out of his promise on a technicality. But if he played his cards right, he could use the situation to his advantage.

"Agreed," Aries said. "With one caveat. We are about to enter a period of civil war. You cannot ask me to change military tactics, or go back on any order you may disagree with. It must also be a single request. You cannot ask for multiple favors or a position of rank you have not earned."

Django nodded. "That sounds fair."

"And if you get yourself into trouble, you cannot use it to free yourself or grant yourself, or anyone you know, immunity from the law. I won't have you using this favor to promote treason against me."

Django hesitated. He'd been arrested once already, simply for being in the wrong place.

"Am I being sent back to the cell, then?" he asked.

Aries displayed his crooked smile and chuckled softly. "No, Django. You have committed no crimes—not yet. And you won't be of much use to me if you're detained."

Django swallowed. "Well, I don't plan on committing any crimes, so I'm guess I'm okay with the terms."

"Excellent. Then we are in agreement," Aries said swiftly. "Now, here is what I'll ask of you. The Resurgence has been a thorn in my side for years, but their activities have escalated over the past few months. I have no doubt that Alejandro's return is only going to amplify their bravado. You already have Marvin's trust. I'd like you to go back to them, find out what you can of their plans, and report back to me."

"You want me to spy on my uncle?"

Django should have seen the request coming, but he hadn't. It was the one thing he could offer the commander, but the one thing he had no desire to do.

Regardless of Uncle Marvin's past.

The holo-projections of murdered men and women still floated above Aries's terminal. Who was his uncle, really?

A leader? A revolutionary?

A murderer?

"Why should I do this for you?" he asked. "You're a leader in an empire of killers."

"Killing has been part of the Syndicate's playbook," Aries admitted. "It has probably taken more lives than you or I will ever know. That is why I have chosen to act. I'm working to remove those who currently exploit the Syndicate's resources, but I cannot say much more than that. I will not send you into the heart of a rebellion with knowledge its people could torture out of you. Once I am through, the current Prefect will no longer be in power, and I will implement a system that benefits all our people on the Moon, Mars, and other colonies as much as those on the planet's surface. And for the first time in generations, we'll all be able to return home."

*That sounds familiar.* "The Resurgence talks of the same thing," Django said, puzzled.

"The Resurgence seeks lawlessness," Aries snapped, his voice filled with agitation. "Anarchy. They want to overthrow the system that has been the key to humanity's survival for hundreds of years. And then what? The Syndicate is brutal, but they have proper processes in place. Infrastructure for getting materials from one world to another. Rules to promote order. You can't just rip that all away in an instant. If you tear out the foundations of a building, it crumbles. Processes need time to evolve, or they fall apart.

"The Resurgence doesn't have the structure to rule a moonbase, never mind an entire solar system. Do you think they have the utility to control the masses? Lunar alone has thirty cities, plus surrounding territories, mines, and farms. That doesn't even begin to account for the colonies on Mars and Ceres. Do you think a small band of rebels has the resources to transport tonnes of helium-3 to Ganymede? Water to Io? Uranium to the Belt? Not to mention overseeing space docks and ports or maintaining communications networks and transportation systems. Even if the Resurgence were to succeed, what will happen when the vacuum opens where the Syndicate once was?"

Django's mind scrambled for an answer. He had barely learned that there were people on the Earth's moon, never mind pondering how it might all be governed.

"The complete breakdown of humanity." Aries answered his own question before Django had even wrapped his head around it. "I won't allow that. There must still be order. Fighting the Syndicate Council and Prefect will be difficult enough as it is. Our systems run like a poorly maintained spacecraft; if one piece falls out of place, it could bring everything down with it. Humanity could cease to exist. No, the Syndicate has worked too hard to build an empire that runs; there's just a better way of administrating it. The system has outgrown its humble Earth origins. There is a better way—but it is not theirs.

"I know the Resurgence are planning something, but I need to know details. If it's a terrorist attack, I need to know where and when. If Alejandro's going after a high-profile target, I need to know who. We can't be caught off guard, and my people haven't been able to get close enough to secure any reliable intel."

Spy on his uncle and reveal his plans to a Syndicate commander? Django bit the inside of his cheek. It was an impossible decision. Either he betrayed his uncle or he'd be sent back to the prison cell, or sent out an airlock. He'd be of no use to Eventide then.

Maybe there was a third way. Maybe he could let the man think he was going to co-operate and decide later which move to make.

At least if he went back to his uncle, Django could try to gain more information about who he truly was. If he *was* a cold-blooded killer, perhaps the commander was providing a better way forward.

Both men had promised to help Eventide. He needed any advantage he could get.

"If I am to help you," he said, "I want to ensure Eventide is okay. I won't betray my uncle until I know she's safe."

"That could take some time." Aries's expression remained unchanged. "But I'll agree. If you'll go back to the Resurgence and gain their trust, I'll secure this woman's safety before I request any information from you."

Django nodded.

"How do you know I won't betray you? How do you know I won't warn Marvin, or run?"

Aries smiled. "Because the Resurgence *will* disappoint you. It may take some time, but you will eventually learn they aren't as noble as you'd like to believe, nor are they as powerful as they say. They'll come up against a wall where they will be unable to deliver on something they've promised you, or they'll fail in executing a plan that was crucial to their rebellion. When that happens, I know you will return to me. Why? Because I don't have the same restrictions as they do. I have near unlimited funds and resources at my disposal, and I don't need to skirt the law to get things done—because on this rock, I am the law."

That hardly seemed like an assurance, but Django was in no position to argue.

Aries stuck out a hand. "We have a deal?"

Django hesitated. The frozen image of the woman Marvin had murdered was still aglow on the holo-screen.

Marvin had promised to rescue Eventide, but how could

Django trust the man knowing what he was capable of? Would he go back on his word, as Aries predicted?

And if Aries stayed true to his word, it would mean his sister—and the other residents aboard the *Eclipse*—would be protected from Commander Benson. The station would be safe. Marvin wasn't offering that.

Aries was offering both Eventide and, potentially, a way for them to return home.

Django grabbed Aries's hand. He had to at least entertain the possibility.

"Deal."

# AFTERWORD

Thank you for reading Chimera and joining Django, Mikka and Eventide on their journey.

As an independent author, reviews are really important. They help other readers—like you—discover my work.

If you liked the book, and have a couple of minutes to spare, it would be great if you could leave a short, honest review on Amazon, Goodreads, your bookish blog, social media or of course, on the book's retail page.

Thank you!

Watch for the third instalment, *Resurgence*, of *The Fractured Orbit*, available in November, 2023.

# ACKNOWLEDGMENTS

When I started writing Eclipse, I knew I had stumbled into a special story. Django and Mikka were characters that came to life so quickly; it was as if they had always been there.

In this book, I also introduced Eventide's point of view. That's because she refused to be pushed to the sidelines like a damsel in distress.

She's also the reason why this book ended up taking longer to publish than I had anticipated when I finished Eclipse. Her story extended the plot line I had initially envisioned for this book, carrying on into Resurgence. However, in doing so, it meant I have been able to explore this universe more in-depth than I thought I was going to get a chance to, and for that, I am grateful.

I'd like to thank each and every one of you who have been part of this journey. I am sure to miss somebody, but please know you are appreciated.

Shane Millar gave this book an initial beta read and pointed out where some of the flaws in the story were. You were a cheerleader for Eventide throughout, and you helped me to realize that I had to give her even more page time to do justice to her story.

I'd like to thank Pete Smith from Novel Approach

Manuscript Services for providing a copy edit, and assisting with details and phrasings that I was at a loss for.

Covers by Christian continues to blow me away with his cover design, and I thank him for making these books look amazing.

I want to thank all of my author friends from my various writing circles who have provided feedback and encouragement. To the Rebel Author Slack group, thank you for your encouragement and motivation to set goals and stick to them. To my friends in the Dystopian Author League who are always willing to promote and lift each other up. The Write Better Fiction Discord group for letting me agonize about each step of the process of editing and completing this manuscript. And to all of the others who have offered words of support and encouragement along the way.

To my wife Nettie, who always supports of me when I need to head to a coffee shop on the weekends to write. Who encourages me when things don't go as planned, and who won't let me quit. This wouldn't have been possible without your unwavering belief in me.

# ABOUT THE AUTHOR

Herman Steuernagel is a science fiction and fantasy author. His internationally best-selling debut Lies the Guardians Tell reached the top of the science fiction charts in multiple countries.

Herman grew up with a love of story and science fiction, watching Star Trek, The Next Generation with his father. As a teenager he fell in love with The Sword of Shannara by Terry Brooks, and The Wheel of Time series by Robert Jordan.

His currently published works are dystopian science fiction that highlight the struggle between humanity and the technology we keep, as well as the motivations that keep us fighting with each other.

Herman currently lives in British Columbia, Canada, While he's not working on a new book he can be found cycling, running and dreaming up new worlds.

9 781990 505119